EVERY RAKE HAS A SILVER LINING

A Regency Era Romance

LONDON LADIES' LEAGUE

TRISHA MESSMER

DEDICATION

I am going to take a heroine whom no one but myself will much like.
~ JANE AUSTEN (on Emma)

I feel you, Jane. To strong women everywhere. You are lovable.

CONTENTS

ACKNOWLEDGMENTS

I am so grateful to so many people who have helped this book come into being. First and foremost, to my family for always supporting and encouraging me. There are times when I question why I bother, and they remind me it's because I love sharing the stories and the characters who live inside me.

To my critique partners at Critique Circle. You guys always tell it to me straight and don't let me get away with any crap. So thanks to Brad, Ellie, Izzy, Jess, and Lisa for helping me make each story the best it can be.

To Lisa Messegee at the Write Designer for the gorgeous cover. Thank you for capturing Charlotte and Rosehaven Park so well.

To my editor, Peter Senftleben at PES Editorial. You helped me take a good book and make it so much better. I'm so glad you loved Simon and Charlotte as much as I did.

To my eagle-eyed proofreader, Jess Kelly, at Gray Cat Publishing and Designs. Any errors remaining in the manuscript are all mine. (I promise I will try not to tinker after you send it back to me, Jess).

And last but certainly not least, to you, dear reader. Thank you from the bottom of my heart for continuing to read my stories and allowing me to do the thing I love.

And Tori, my three-legged cat, thanks you, too, for helping me buy her kibble.

CHAPTER 1

LONDON—LATE MARCH 1830

S imon's day could have been worse. Or so he told himself.
The waves of fatigue and sudden chills creeping in might be
his imagination instead of another malaria attack.

Or so he told himself.

He squeezed against the wall of the hallway as servants
bustled past, carrying the Duke and Duchess of Burwood's
trunks.

"Excuse us, Mr. Beckham," one of the footmen said as Simon
tried in vain to stay out of their way.

The atmosphere at Pendrake House—situated in the most
elite part of London—had been nothing short of funereal.

Simon grunted at the thought. *Poor choice of words.*

Indeed, Honoria's sister-in-law, Margery, had expired from
consumption two days prior, word having just reached them in
London that very morning. Naturally, Honoria was distraught,
and Drake had insisted they pack up and head to Somerset
posthaste.

Drake's voice boomed with ducal authority from the gallery below. "Simon! A word, if you please."

Simon couldn't help but smile. Drake had taken to his role as duke so quickly, one would never imagine how reluctant he'd been to assume the responsibility of his ancestors. In fact, less than a year prior, Simon and Drake had perpetrated a deception at a house party wherein they had switched roles, with Drake pretending to be Simon's man-of-business. Thank goodness the scheme didn't backfire and lose Drake the woman of his dreams.

Drake peered up from where he had his arm wrapped around his wife's waist, his brow furrowed and eyes tense. He had every reason to be tense. In addition to the death of his brother-in-law's wife, Honoria expected their first child in less than a month. Both the Duke of Ashton, functioning as Honoria's physician, and Drake had urged her not to chance the journey so late in her confinement. But even two dukes could not dissuade her. Honoria would hear none of it.

"I need to be there for Colin," she'd said.

So like Honoria to put others' needs before her own. And as much as Simon admired her, like her husband and physician, he worried for both her and her child's safety.

No doubt Drake—who ran worst case scenarios in his mind constantly—had planned for every possibility.

Simon managed to skirt past the footmen once again as they returned upstairs to retrieve—no doubt—another trunk, finally making it down the long staircase.

Honoria sent him a tremulous smile. Dark shadows under her eyes, red from weeping, marred her fair complexion.

Unable to bear her pain, Simon jerked his gaze away and faced Drake. "Write as soon as you make it to Somerset safely."

Drake gave a curt nod, his drawn face mirroring the woman he loved. "The journey will take longer than usual. We'll have to make more frequent stops, so don't worry."

Impossible. And also excruciatingly painful. And Simon tried to avoid pain at all costs. A wave of heat hit him, reminiscent of the blasted Indian desert, and he swayed.

Luckily, Drake's attention remained on Honoria. The last thing he wanted was to add to Drake's list of concerns. By the time Drake turned back toward him, Simon had recovered.

Drake tugged on his gloves. "With both Stratford and myself away, Ashton promised to take the helm with our argument in Parliament for reform. Harcourt will fill in when Ashton has to be at his clinic. I've asked them to relay any information directly to you. If you would compile it and write to me with any news, I would appreciate it."

"Of course. I still can't believe you've managed to get Stratford on your side." Simon sent an apologetic glance toward Honoria. "I beg your pardon, Your Grace. I didn't mean to disparage your father."

"No offense taken, Simon. And please cease with the 'Your Grace' when we're alone. There is nothing graceful about the way I feel." She placed a hand on her back, stretched forward, and gave a very delicate groan.

Drake straightened to attention, reminding Simon of their days in the military. "We need to get you settled in the carriage, my darling."

Simon would never understand the quiet communication his friends had with each other. It was as if they could read each other's thoughts. The idea was both appealing and disconcerting.

And nothing he would ever experience with a woman if he had any say in the matter.

Footmen maneuvered around them with yet another trunk, and Frampton appeared. The butler's usual stoic expression softened as he waited to be acknowledged.

"Is all readied?" Drake asked.

"Yes, Your Grace. That"—he tipped his head in the direction the footmen had gone—"was the last trunk. Brown and Miss

Price are aboard the second carriage. Are you certain I can't accompany you?"

Drake shook his head. "No offense, Frampton. My brother-in-law's home is fully staffed. Besides, someone needs to look after Simon, especially since I'm taking Brown while Dawson is away."

Frampton's lips twitched slightly.

Simon rolled his eyes. "I've managed without a valet before, and Dawson will return from Lincolnshire after his sister's wedding. If you don't trust me to not run off with the silver, fine. But at least allow the other servants to take an extended holiday while you're away."

Frampton turned toward Drake, awaiting approval. Simon prayed he would give it. The fewer witnesses the better if he wound up having another episode. Less chance to have it wind up in the scandal sheet for his mother to see.

"What about your meals, Simon?"

Simon forced a smile. "Frampton and I will manage, won't we?"

Drake lifted his eyebrows, then, ignoring Simon completely, turned toward Frampton. "Have Cook stay as well. But you may relieve the rest of the staff. Tell them they will be paid fully for their time away. If Simon insists, he can make his own bed, draw his own bath water, and shave himself." Drake gave a soft chuckle. "I give him three days before he's begging you to call them back. I'll write advising when we expect to return."

"Please don't give *The Muckraker* any fodder while we're away, Simon." Her hand moving to support her large stomach, Honoria leaned in and kissed him on the cheek.

"Who? Me?" Simon did his damnedest to appear affronted.

Honoria only laughed and headed out the door.

With a quick peek over his shoulder at his wife, Drake said, "Are you certain you're well? You look a little pale."

Before Simon could make up a lie and answer, Honoria gave

another delicate groan, and Drake rushed over to help her into the carriage.

Simon lifted a hand, waving goodbye as his friends drove off for Somerset.

When Frampton finally closed the door, Simon collapsed into a nearby chair. "If you would, Frampton, be a good chap and help me to my room. Then dismiss the servants and send for Dr. Somersby."

⚜

CHARLOTTE'S HANDS CURLED INTO FISTS IN HER LAP. HER LIPS pressed together so tightly that, if possible, they would fuse together. Inside, the rage seethed. Surely, she'd misheard her brother's words.

Roland, the Marquess of Edgerton, sat before her, pompous on his throne of a chair. It had become increasingly more difficult to tolerate her eldest brother since her more amiable brother, Nash, had left for America. At least with Nash, she could commiserate in private about Roland's brutish nature.

One of Roland's dark eyebrows hitched. "Well? Have you nothing to say?"

She uttered the only words she dared. "I refuse to marry him."

Roland gave a nasty laugh. "I've signed the marriage contract. Of course, legally you can refuse, but I would caution you, Lady Charlotte. Doing so will result in unfortunate consequences."

Her fists tightened. Addressing her formally indicated Roland meant business. No brotherly warmth or affection shone in his voice or eyes. Still, she challenged him. "Such as?"

He leaned forward, his already cold eyes frosting her through. "How does losing your home sound? It's well past the time you marry and become some other man's liability. I grow tired of supporting you. Both you and Nash apparently believed you would live off my generosity in perpetuity."

Charlotte snorted a derisive laugh. Generous was a word never used in conjunction with the Marquess of Edgerton—past or present. "Nash *never* wanted your money."

"Yet he was quick enough to take and spend it." Roland's upper lip curled, and his eyes narrowed.

It was enough to send a chill racing down her spine.

"Perhaps I should ship you off to America to be with him."

The prospect wasn't necessarily unappealing. Still . . .

Roland leaned back in his chair and steepled his fingers. "But no. You're a better bargaining tool here. Ashton, Harcourt, and that new upstart Burwood"—Roland scrunched his face as if just speaking the man's name sickened him—"have joined forces with Commons, supporting parliamentary reform. Even Stratford has changed sides. I need an ally to oppose them."

Charlotte found her voice. "Lord Felix Davies can hardly assist in your efforts. He's not in line to inherit." *Unless both his elder brother and his brother's young son die.* Honoria's husband, Drake, was proof how happenstance could bring a man to the forefront of the aristocracy. But Felix was no Drake. The man was a worm.

"Oh, I beg to differ, dear sister." Where Roland was concerned, the term was not one of endearment. "It would seem Lord Scarborough is tiring of his son's rakish reputation and wishes him to marry well. Naturally, he came to me suggesting an *alliance.* Unlike our brother's, your reputation is spotless"— Roland tugged on his ruffled shirt sleeves, then satisfied they measured exactly one-half inch from his coat sleeve, met her gaze, the sinister glee dancing in their dark depths chilling her— "so far."

She swallowed, her jaw as tense as her tight fists. "What do you mean, so far?"

With an insouciant shrug, he diverted his attention to the papers before him. The marriage contract? "Only that Felix was heard bragging that he'd despoiled you, thus sullying your pristine reputation. That alone is grounds for a forced marriage in my opinion. But Scarborough and I can cover that up easily enough with a little coin."

A knot formed in Charlotte's stomach. How could he be so nonchalant about the matter? "Lord Felix is a liar."

Roland's dark eyebrow quirked. "Is he?"

"How dare you!"

Her *brother* simply stared. The man was infuriating. "Whether he is or is not is pointless. His words alone can damage you—unless we do something about it immediately." He flicked a hand toward the door. "He's waiting in the yellow parlor for you. Now, go and let him make his proposal. It's simply a formality at this point, but perhaps he'll manage a few pretty words to win you over."

With enough force to knock the chair over, Charlotte pushed back from Roland's desk and rose. There were not enough words, nor none pretty enough to ever get her to accept Lord Felix Davies. Not after what he'd tried to do to her. "You can't do this."

Roland slammed his hand on the desk, the vibration ruffling the papers. "I can, and I will. Not only will you cease living under my protection, but you will face the consequences of a ruined reputation on your own."

Charlotte straightened her back and—head held high—strode from the room. She would have to learn to live with a ruined reputation. It was better than a miserable life married to a worm like Felix.

Or so she hoped.

CHAPTER 2

Simon felt like bloody hell. How had it only been two hours since Drake and Honoria had left for Somerset? Hopefully, the quinine would start working its magic.

Dr. Somersby snapped his medical bag shut. "Let me know if you need more. The willow bark tea should also relieve the fever. I'll check on you tomorrow."

Simon shook his head. "No need. I'll send word if I need you. I don't want to take you from the clinic more than necessary."

Simon had come to respect both Oliver Somersby and Ashton—or as the duke insisted he be called—Harry.

"Harry would have come himself, but there was an important meeting in Parliament he didn't want to miss, especially with Burwood gone."

His head weary, Simon did his best to nod. "So Drake said. I appreciate it. But that's even more reason not to keep you from the people who really need your care."

Oliver patted his arm. "Dr. Marbry is there, and if any patients complain, his wife will keep them in line."

Simon had no doubt about that. Word had it that Priscilla Marbry ran the clinic like a general. The more Simon had become acquainted with Honoria's circle of friends, the more he'd come to appreciate them for the oddities they were. Good people among the snobbish aristocracy.

All except the ice queen, Lady Charlotte Talbot, that was. Lord, why did he have to make himself feel worse by thinking of her? Her pugnacious demeanor could sour even his best of days.

"Be a good fellow and give the bell pull a tug. I don't think I have the strength." God, how he hated admitting that to anyone. "Frampton will show you out."

"Formalities aren't necessary with me," Oliver said. "I'm a big lad and am capable of finding the door myself."

Simon summoned the strength to grunt. Then he rolled over, hoping to find some respite in sleep. Thoughts of cool, calming water and the fresh scent of nature helped him slowly drift off to fitful slumber.

CHARLOTTE PAUSED AT THE ENTRANCE TO THE YELLOW PARLOR. Felix faced the window, his hands clasped behind his back as if it were any ordinary day and he was simply admiring the views of the gardens. If outward appearances were all that made up a man, Lord Felix Davies would have been considered an excellent catch. He could be charming when it suited him. She had thought so herself at one time—until he revealed the darkness lurking beneath his handsome exterior. She vowed never to allow any man's quick smile and pretty words cloud her judgment again.

Summoning the glower simmering beneath the surface, she strode forward. "Lord Felix."

He turned, his face breaking into a wide grin. Lord, she hated that about him. "Lady Charlotte. You're looking as *agreeable* as ever. I trust Edgerton has spoken with you."

"He has. And if you think for one moment I will agree to this atrocity of an arrangement, you're an even bigger imbecile than I took you for."

The grin remained, and he stepped closer. "Now, now, Charlotte. No need to be so testy. Although I admit it's part of your charm. I like a woman with a bit of fight in her." He stretched out a finger and trailed it up her arm.

She shuddered, his touch resurrecting the horrible memory. "Remove your hand, *sir*."

The grin vanished, and his eyes grew sinister. "No." He wrapped his hand around her arm—tight, his fingers pressing into her flesh. There would be a bruise. "Get used to that word if you dare try to give me orders."

"It is you who should get used to the word." She struggled to pull away. But as before, he was too strong.

His cold, hollow laugh chilled her. "You can't say no to a husband." He grabbed her around the neck with his other hand and hauled her against his body. Then he forced his mouth on hers.

She bit him on the lip.

"You little . . ." He wiped at his lip, then gawked at the blood on his fingers. With a speed she didn't think him capable of, he reared back and struck her across the face. "You had better learn to mind, or you shall become intimately acquainted with the back of my hand."

Tears stung Charlotte's eyes, but she willed them back. She refused to show any weakness to the worm in front of her. Instead, she delivered a sound slap of her own. "I will . . . and do . . . say *no* to you. And you will never be my husband."

With narrowed eyes, he rubbed his cheek. "Perhaps Edgerton didn't make it clear. If you value your reputation—which knowing you, you do—you'll think long and hard about refusing me."

"Do your worst, sir. If you besmirch my innocence, you do damage to your own reputation as well. No man of honor would admit to taking a woman's virtue without marrying her."

He doubled over, laughing so hard the air around her seemed to vibrate. Tears of mirth formed in his eyes, and he wiped them away. "You fool. Even if I were a man of honor—which you know very well I'm not—both my father and your brother will attest to the fact that I *have* offered for you, and you turned me down." He tugged on the sleeves of his coat, reminding her of Roland. "And there *might* be a bit more gossip leaked about how I wasn't the first to experience your *carnal pleasures.*"

Every muscle in Charlotte's body tensed tighter than a bowstring. Blood pounded in her head. "You are lower than a worm. You are a . . . a . . . ." What was a lower lifeform? At the moment, Charlotte would have gladly traded places with Beatrix Townsend. Bluestocking that she was, she would know.

Felix hitched a well-trimmed sandy eyebrow. "Yes?"

"I don't know. But it's an insult to worms to make a comparison to you." She trounced to the door and tugged the bell pull.

When a footman appeared, she said, "Show Lord Felix out. And make certain you slam the door after him, preferably before he's fully exited."

Felix had the audacity to laugh. "You'll change your mind soon enough." The slimy worm slithered forward. He leaned in and Charlotte felt his hot breath. "But bear in mind, I won't be as forgiving."

The footman motioned for Felix to precede him, then gave her a nervous nod.

She had no doubt Roland would be informed she had refused Felix's proposal—had he even proposed?—either by the footman or by Felix himself.

She needed a plan of action—somewhere to go. A haven. A sanctuary.

Honoria!

⊙⌘⊙

SIMON WAS DROWNING IN A FOUL-SMELLING SWAMP. FLAILING HIS arms, he startled awake and clutched the sweat-soaked bed linens.

God. What was that stench? He took a tentative sniff of his armpit, discovering it was *him*.

Cursing the fact he'd had Frampton send all the servants away, he swung his legs off the bed and tried to rise. *You can do this.*

As he tried to stand, Simon's legs jiggled just about as much as the delicious jellied concoction Drake's cook had prepared for supper a week ago. He grabbed the bedside table, steadying himself.

His gaze drifted to a note lying on top.

Mr. Beckham,

Dr. Somersby said he expected you to sleep for hours. Cook left for the market, and I've taken the liberty of using the time for a personal errand. I will return shortly.

~ Frampton

"Damnation," Simon muttered. A little voice in the back of his fevered mind whispered he should wait for Frampton to return. He brushed the niggling aside. *Simon Beckham waits for no one.* And he could damn well take care of himself. Slowly releasing his grip on the bedside table, he pulled in a deep breath. *You can do this.*

Once he assured himself he wouldn't fall over, he pulled the soaked nightshirt off and tossed it aside. He'd only worn the bloody thing for Dr. Somersby's visit because Frampton insisted upon it.

Although he still smelled like a sewer, the cool air on his skin was a welcome relief. He needed to bathe and change the bed linens.

With tentative steps, he shuffled to the washstand, only to find the water remaining in the bowl had grown colder than the room itself. Nevertheless, he splashed some on his face, generating a series of intense shivers.

He stared down at the discarded nightshirt, quickly dismissing the idea of throwing it back on. He wasn't fully recovered yet, but he would feel somewhat human again if he could only get a bath and some clean linens.

The door seemed impossibly far away, and the kitchen on the ground floor where he could boil some water might as well be heaven for him to reach it. Managing both would be a herculean task in his condition.

One step at a time.

Thank goodness Drake had chairs placed strategically along the hallway and at the top and foot of the stairway. As Honoria increased, Drake worried about her walking too far, even though she assured him he was being ridiculous. Simon only recalled seeing her use the chair at the top of the stairs once, but at the moment, he was extremely grateful for Drake's overprotective nature.

Still foregoing the nightshirt, he tugged on a pair of trousers in case Cook was present in the kitchen. Admittedly, he might have missed a button or two as his trembling hands fastened the fall, but he was relatively decent.

You can do this.

You can do this.

You can do this.

He blew out a heavy breath and told himself to quit saying it and just do it! With each step, his legs wobbled like a newborn colt's, and more sweat beaded his brow. Finally out of his room, he made it to the first chair in the hallway in the nick of time.

Plop.

Gauging the distance to the next chair, which mercifully was the one near the top of the staircase, he calculated perhaps thirty steps. Once there, going down the stairs would be easier. Gravity would be on his side.

He refused to think about climbing them on his return—especially carrying a pot of hot water.

You can do this.

Convinced he had regained his strength, he forged forward, pleased he closed the distance with less difficulty. After a brief debate about foregoing another rest, he sat, but only for a few moments before he proceeded on his never-ending trek. The stairs did indeed prove easier, and he managed them quite well.

Perhaps he was improving already. The thought cheered him, which in turn cheered him more. He hated being sullen or dwelling on the negative.

Or stagnating in the damn bed. As difficult as his odyssey to the kitchen was, simply moving about improved his mood.

He'd just passed the front door, deciding to sit for a moment before heading toward the back stairs that led to the ground floor, when several knocks sounded.

If he was lucky, they would go away.

Knock.

Knock.

Knock, knock, knock.

"Bloody hell." Unsure why he murmured since he was the only one to hear himself curse, he rose from the chair and prepared to shoo off the impatient visitor.

He plastered on his most charming smile and threw open the door.

His nightmare waited on the other side.

CHAPTER 3

Charlotte reeled back at the sight of a half-naked Simon Beckham, his body filling the open doorway. Her gaze locked on the smattering of dark hair on his bare—and annoyingly muscular—chest. "How dare you answer the door in that state of dishabille?! Where is the butler?"

The man flashed that ridiculous grin at her, reminding her of Felix and what she had just escaped. "Good afternoon to you, too, Lady Charlotte. Frampton is out on some errands. To what do I owe the *pleasure*?"

She tried to peer around him and not stare at his chest—which admittedly was a difficult feat. "Where is Honoria?" Her grip tightened on the handle of her bulging portmanteau.

"She and Drake are on their way to Somerset. The viscountess died."

At that bit of news, Charlotte's gaze snapped back to Mr. Beckham.

Sweat dotted his forehead, and his skin appeared flushed. She darted a quick—very well, it most likely wasn't quick—glance at his lower half. Two buttons on his fall appeared undone, and one was most definitely in the wrong opening. *What is going—oh!*

Heat flooded her cheeks—not something that happened to her often. She attributed it to being taken completely off guard. She summoned her most caustic tone. "I beg your pardon. I didn't mean to interrupt your liaison. Although, I shouldn't be surprised. While the cat's away and all that. But you should be ashamed, sir, taking advantage of Honoria's time of grief for your own pleasure."

She turned away from him. Where in the world could she go next? Miranda still lived with her parents. Anne was out of the question, regardless of where she lived. Admittedly, Charlotte had few female friends she could trust. In truth, she had few female friends in general. Oh, very well, she had very few friends at all, female or male.

"There's no one here with me," Mr. Beckham said. "I wish there were." His mumbled addition caught her attention.

She spun around to face him again. "What do you mean?" On closer inspection, he looked—ghastly. Odd, it was not a word she would have used in conjunction with the rake, no matter how much she disliked him.

He grabbed the edge of the door as if he needed it for support.

"You're ill," she said as matter-of-fact as if she'd said the grass was green.

"How very astute of you, my lady." He pressed his lips together, the grim expression once again so unlike his usual unwavering and unrealistic optimism that drove her mad. The man lived in a make-believe world of rainbows and puppies. "I hate to ask, but since you're here . . . ."

"Where are the servants?"

"What about 'no one's here' don't you understand? Not simply a paramour, although I hate to admit I'm in no shape to be entertaining with any degree of satisfaction for my partner."

Her cheeks flamed again. *Damnation.*

He had the audacity to grin. "But the servants are gone. Except for Cook and Frampton, and Frampton, as I said, is not here at the moment."

His gaze jerked to the overstuffed bag in her hand. Then his eyes returned to her face, his eyes narrowing. "What in the devil happened to your cheek?"

Unbidden, her free hand flew to her face, the area tender from where Felix had backhanded her. "It's nothing."

"The hell it's nothing." He released his grip on the door and hauled her inside the doorway, then proceeded to slam the door. "What happened? Did someone strike you?"

Oh, no. She refused to admit what Felix did. Not to another rake just like him. "It's none of your concern."

"It is most definitely my concern. You have a bag with you and a bruise upon your cheek. Are you seeking shelter from someone, Lady Charlotte?"

She jerked back—his words buffeting her almost like the blow from Felix. He actually sounded sincere—and kind. "I . . . only for a few days. But Honoria isn't here. I should leave." She reached for the doorknob, fully intending to go. Where, she still didn't know.

Until he fell into the chair by the door. He really did look ghastly.

Halting, she recalled his unfinished request. "You were going to ask me something."

Slumped in the chair, he peered up, his striking blue eyes pleading. "Would you see if Cook is in the kitchen?"

For a man of business, Mr. Beckham was clearly dense. "Why didn't you simply ring for her?"

"She may not be there. Frampton left a note saying she went to the market."

"And you didn't check first?" With no need for propriety around the dolt of a man, Charlotte rolled her eyes, then trudged to the nearest room and searched for a bell pull. "Men and their stupid pride," she muttered and pulled the cord.

"It's not pride."

Charlotte spun to find Mr. Beckham leaning against the doorframe. However, his posture indicated he did so to support himself rather than appear rakish. *Hmm.* "No? You're clearly in no condition to be doing whatever it was you planned to do." She motioned back to the chair in the entrance. "Now, sit before you fall over."

Delivering a scowl, he lumbered back to the entry and plopped back in the chair. "Bossy," he muttered.

"So, let me understand. You were going to the kitchen?"

"Give the woman an award."

Insufferable. The man couldn't be serious if he tried, which irked her to distraction. And the fact that everyone seemed to like him for his buffoonery galled her even more. "I'm trying to help you."

"Ha!" He scowled again.

People often assumed because Charlotte didn't wear her heart on her sleeve, she didn't have one. However, her forthright demeanor served as a suit of armor, encasing the extremely tender heart she held within. One must protect what is most vulnerable, especially from rakes such as Mr. Beckham.

"What were you going to do if your cook wasn't there?"

"Heat some water."

She laughed. "For tea?"

"Yes and no."

"Stop being obtuse." Goodness, why was she still standing there discussing this nonsense with this ridiculous man? Oh, right. She had nowhere else to go.

The cad had the nerve to grin at her. He motioned her forward.

Unsure what he was about, she took one tentative step toward him.

He motioned again. "Closer."

With each step, he motioned to her again until she was standing less than a foot in front of him. "Goodness, what *is* that stench?"

His grin widened. "Me."

She held her free hand to her nose and mouth. "It's revolting." She grinned back at him. "You're revolting."

"For once, I agree with you. Or maybe that's twice. We did seem to be in agreement about Drake and Honoria. So you see, I need some hot water for a bath as well as some to brew some medicinal tea."

Minutes later, as Charlotte waited, quietly tapping her foot in agitation, neither the cook nor the butler appeared. "It doesn't appear anyone is here."

He quirked a dark eyebrow. "Really? Isn't that what I said in the first place?" He rose, holding onto the chair for support. "Now, if you'll excuse me, I'll be off to the kitchen."

Oh, he truly was insufferable. "Wait. You'll no doubt fall down the stairs and break your neck, and I have no desire to be accused of your murder."

"Ha! It would almost be worth it."

She should leave and let him wait until the butler returned. But with his unfailing optimism, the fool would no doubt attempt to navigate the steps on his own. Exhaling an audible sigh, she placed her bag on the floor. "Very well. I'll help you. First, let's get you in bed."

He chuckled, the sound doing odd things to her stomach.

Argh. She shouldn't have said that.

"I thought you'd never ask. Now, if you could allow me to lean on you a bit." He lifted his arm. "Around your shoulders would work best."

Good grief!

She made no further comments lest he twist them into something inappropriate. Goodness, but he stank. After much struggling, she managed to get him up the stairs, and he directed her toward his bedchamber.

"Now I shall need a bath of my own," she said, dumping him onto his mattress.

"You could join me."

Gah!

Ignoring that ridiculous but oddly enticing comment, she said, "Now, where is the kitchen?"

"Down the hall to the right of the entrance. At the back, there is a flight of stairs to the ground floor. You can't miss it."

At least he didn't pursue his obscene suggestion about them bathing together. She nodded. "I'll be back."

As she walked toward the door, he chuckled. "Do you even know how to boil water?"

"How hard can it be?" With that, she slammed the door behind her.

⚜

Simon fell against the foul-smelling sheets. Hopefully, Frampton would arrive to change them before Simon finished his bath. He couldn't imagine Lady Charlotte performing the task. Hell, even Frampton might object.

Lady Charlotte Talbot. He chuckled to himself. Oh, the irony of it all. Seeing her at the front door made him think he was still dreaming—or whatever the appropriate verb form was regarding nightmares. Nightmaring? As irritatingly attractive as she was, Lady Charlotte was no one's dream, but she was certainly his nightmare.

He'd almost considered asking her to pinch him to ensure he was awake but thought better of it. No doubt she would pinch him so hard she'd leave a bruise.

And speaking of bruises. Who had left that mark on her cheek? And why did she need to seek shelter for a few days?

Granted, he knew little about her other than she lived with her brother, the Marquess of Edgerton—who had declined to attend the house party Drake had given the previous summer. Not that the marquess's subtle cut had surprised Simon. He'd never dealt with the younger marquess, but he knew the callous reputation of his father well.

The smaller estate the marquess held in Chippenham bordered the Beckham's property near Swindon. And people talked. From all accounts, the son followed in his father's cruel footsteps.

Honoria called the man most disagreeable—harsh indeed coming from Honoria, who liked everyone. Drake was less generous, calling the man uncharitable with a malevolent disposition. Simon expected no less of the sister.

When Simon first met Lady Charlotte, her relationship to Edgerton had been enough to set his teeth on edge. However, Honoria liked her, so Simon had made an effort—a half-hearted effort, to be honest. He wanted nothing to do with any of the Talbots.

Which made the powerful pull of attraction he felt whenever Lady Charlotte was near even more irksome than her icy demeanor. Those dark eyes promised mysteries and pleasures he could only imagine—although his imagination was quite vivid.

Lady Charlotte Talbot was not the kind of woman he should be attracted to—regardless of the undeniable spark between them. Cold and opinionated with a tongue as sharp as his valet's razor, she was the embodiment of a termagant. And—as much as he hated to admit it—a challenge. Yet, try as he might, Lady Charlotte resisted his flirtatious advances. Not only resisted but grew even more prickly. It was enough to boil a man's blood.

He paused, reflecting on her bruised cheek. Perhaps the ice queen's sullen nature was defensive rather than offensive.

Hmm. The only times he'd given Lady Charlotte much thought were late at night when—

The door burst open. "I have water."

She carried in a large bowl of water. How in the world had she heated it so quickly?

"I'll need more than that for a bath."

She looked around the room. "Where is your tub?"

Damn. He hadn't thought about that. "The footmen usually bring it in. I'll just have to have a sponge bath."

"Can you manage?" Was there a nervous tremor in her voice?

Even so, he couldn't resist goading her. "Are you offering to assist me?"

Those rich, dark eyes of hers widened.

Why did she have to be so damn beautiful? And why, oh why, did he have to think about that while he was half-naked? "If you could please pour the water in the washbasin and place some towels on the floor by the dressing table, that will be sufficient."

An audible *huff* came from her delectable lips—damnation, why did he have to think about her lips—and she stomped to the dressing table.

"Towels are on the shelf below," he said.

Muttered words, which he suspected were curses, drifted his way. When she bent over to lay the towels on the floor, his gaze drifted to her backside.

"Thank you." His gratitude was for more than her help in laying the towels, but he kept that to himself. When he rose from the bed, another wave of heat assaulted him. Stumbling, he grabbed onto the side table. As before, the temporary respite of symptoms was far too brief, and he knew he was in for another round of fever, headache, fatigue—and God help him —vomiting.

Charlotte took a step toward him, but he held up his hand, signaling he was fine. Humiliating enough she witnessed as much as she did. He would not admit how sick he really was— especially to her. "If you would be so kind as to wait out in the hall. As you no doubt noticed, there are chairs stationed there at regular intervals. Leave the door ajar, and I will call if I need you."

She nodded. "Very well."

As she turned to leave, he stopped her. "And Lady Charlotte, I am most sincere when I say, 'Thank you.'"

His ears may have been deceiving him, but he thought he heard a soft, "You're welcome."

After several deep breaths, he unbuttoned the already lopsided job he'd done on his trousers, slipped out of them, tossed them aside, then shuffled to the dressing table. His stomach roiled. *Not now.* The chamber pot was on the other side of the room. *Deep breaths. In. Out. In. Out.*

When he dipped the sponge into the water and squeezed it out, it felt—cold. No wonder Charlotte had returned so quickly. He sighed. Stupid of him to expect more from the ice queen. An inadvertent chuckle rumbled in his chest. Ice queen. Cold water. Fever was making him delirious.

At times in the military, they'd been forced to bathe using cold water. The best approach was to do so as quickly as possible to get it over with. Convincing himself a sudden deluge of cold water would also reduce the inferno growing inside him, he put down the sponge, picked up the basin, and dumped the contents over his head.

A series of colorful—and loud—curses flew from his lips.

CHAPTER 4

W aiting in the hall, Charlotte paced nervously, careful to avoid walking in front of the partially opened door to Mr. Beckham's bed chamber—although her treacherous gaze flitted toward it more than once.

The amber bottle on the bedside table had captured her attention, but not as much as the word on the label. Quinine. She searched her memory, which she was proud to say was excellent. Where had she heard that term?

Before she could puzzle out the answer, footsteps sounded from below, and she peeped over the balustrade. A head of salt-and-pepper hair—attached to the body of Burwood's butler —appeared. When he approached the staircase and his gaze caught hers, his eyes widened.

Charlotte would never be certain of the exact order in the subsequent chain of events—the only certainty being the outcome. But if she had to guess, her logical mind would have explained the sequence thusly.

A thunderous knock sounded at the front door, and the butler jerked his attention away and headed toward the door. Whoever the impatient caller was, must not see her unchaperoned in a house with Mr. Beckham—who, at the very same moment, uttered an exceedingly raucous string of curses, some of which she had to admit she'd never heard before—even from her brother Nash—but were in fact, most creative.

Had he fallen? After a moment's hesitation, she dashed toward Mr. Beckham's door.

She skidded to an abrupt halt at the sight of Mr. Beckham, completely nude and dripping wet. A little *eeek* escaped unbidden.

He turned and faced her, which, in retrospect, had not been the wisest choice.

Voices shouting from below grew louder as did the pounding of footsteps.

Roland and Felix burst into the room with Burwood's butler close on their heels.

"Sirs, I beg of you," the poor butler said, darting a glance between her and Mr. Beckham. To his credit, the man looked more apologetic than shocked.

Roland's face purpled. "What is the meaning of this?" he roared. Roared!

Felix's gaze bounced from Charlotte to Mr. Beckham's . . .

Oh, dear.

"If you're choosing that"—he pointed to Mr. Beckham's . . . well, a genteel woman didn't discuss a man's private parts—"over me. You'll be sorely disappointed." The man smirked.

Charlotte wanted to slap his smug face.

Mr. Beckham took a step forward. "The water was *cold*." He snapped the word, his glare just as glacial.

"Sir." The butler, Frampton, she believed was his name, rushed over, grabbed a towel from the dressing table, and held it in front of Mr. Beckham.

Mr. Beckham snapped the towel out of Frampton's hands, then wrapped it around his torso. He still appeared ghastly, with

25

his hair plastered to his head. Water dripped down his chest—his very muscular chest, Charlotte was loath to note—but his strength seemed to have returned.

Nose-to-nose with Felix, he grabbed Felix by the cravat. "What do you mean 'over me?' Are you the blackguard who did this to her face?" Not looking back, he pointed in her direction.

When he turned toward her brother, Charlotte took a breath.

"Who the bloody hell are you people? And what are you doing here?"

Roland ignored Mr. Beckham, pushing him out of the way. "Lady Charlotte, return home at once."

Anger helped Charlotte find her voice amid her mortification. "How did you find me?"

"When I discovered you had left—unchaperoned, no less—I made enquiries. The coachman was most forthcoming."

Charlotte should have known the precious five shillings she gave the driver wouldn't maintain his silence. Not when Roland most likely threatened his position.

"However, I had no idea this"—Roland pointed at Mr. Beckham—"is *how* I would find you. You have no choice now but to marry Lord Felix."

Mr. Beckham's head snapped around toward her. "Is this why you came here? To escape from marrying this—"

Charlotte squared her shoulders. "Worm. Yes, I did. And yes, he struck me."

The worm—err, Felix—studied his well-manicured nails, then lifted his icy gaze to hers. "Unless you would like to see the details of this"—he waved a hand between her and Mr. Beckham —"discussed in *The Muckraker*, I suggest you change your mind."

"She's not going to marry you," Mr. Beckham said. He swayed a little on his feet. Goodness, but he looked almost green.

Something in her memory snapped into place. Quinine treated malaria. Mr. Beckham had been in the military in India. Mr. Beckham had malaria!

"Because she's going to marry me."

Then he promptly cast up his accounts on the front of Roland's brocade waistcoat.

If Charlotte hadn't been in shock over Mr. Beckham's declaration, she would have cheered.

◈

SIMON'S BIT OF LUNCH COVERED THE ONE CHAP'S GOLD waistcoat. He should have aimed for the blackguard, Felix.

Giving a shout of disgust, both men jumped back out of range of any further projectiles.

Frampton ran over with a towel and, like the exceptional butler he was, tried to dab Simon's stomach contents off the man.

"Get your hands off me!" The churlish lout snatched the towel, pushed Frampton out of the way, then proceeded to brush off his waistcoat.

Served him right for bursting into his room unannounced. However, at the moment, vomiting on the man wasn't Simon's greatest concern.

This infernal illness is affecting my brain. Simon shook himself. There could be no other explanation for his rash, and admittedly stupid, declaration. Marry the ice queen? Really. What was he thinking?

Mad. The illness was driving him mad.

And yet . . .

He stared at the bruise darkening Charlotte's cheek. The situation—*her* situation, in all honesty—was untenable. Personally, he'd survived worse. But here she was, caught alone in a room with a naked man.

"She will *not* marry you," the vomit-covered dandy said. "My sister is a well-bred, aristocratic lady, and I won't even utter the word *sir* in relation to you."

Ah, her brother. The infamous Marquess of Edgerton. The insult bounced off Simon like a pesky mosquito.

Considering his current condition, perhaps that was a poor analogy. However, he pressed forward. "Isn't that up to the lady? She's well past the age of majority." He slid a glance toward Lady Charlotte.

She winced.

He *should* apologize for the slight, but he felt like bloody hell and only wanted everyone out of his bedchamber so he could climb back into his foul-smelling bed and let sleep ease his pain.

Before he could open his mouth, Charlotte stepped forward. Fierce determination shone in her dark eyes—like a warrior ready to charge into battle.

He braced himself for a slap across his face and an exhortation to take his insincere offer and go to the devil.

She squared her shoulders and met her brother's contemptuous glare. "I *will* marry Mr. Beckham, and there isn't anything you can do to stop me."

If it were possible, his whole body blinked. Well, that was a surprise.

"We'll see about that." Edgerton flung the towel on the floor. "You'll both be sorry for this. Come, Davies."

Simon couldn't resist goading the man further. "Frampton, when you see the *gentlemen* out, please bring Lady Charlotte's bag upstairs. Settle her in the room next to mine. I would like easy access so we can continue cavorting."

"Barbarians!" Edgerton stomped from the room.

Lord Felix gaped like the nodcock he was, then scurried away on Edgerton's heels.

Charlotte's dark brows formed a pronounced V over her seductive eyes. "Did you mean it?"

"What? The cavorting?" He snorted a laugh. "Setting your brother's teeth on edge was too good to resist. I hate to admit this

—to you especially—but I'm in no condition for cavorting." He managed a wink. "As tempting as you are."

"No, you buffoon." She rolled those dark eyes. "That you would marry me."

"Ah. That." He rubbed a hand at the back of his neck, the heat from his skin scorching. His gaze flicked to the quinine on his bedside table. "Well, the situation seemed to demand a proposal. At least to appease your brother and make your refusal clear to Davies."

"You're not answering my question. Was your offer genuine?"

The cold-water bath had done nothing to ease his elevated temperature but everything to place both him and Charlotte in this horrible situation. He needed to sit down—he needed his quinine.

With a brief wave of his hand, he motioned Charlotte to the chair by the window, then sat on the bed.

Her back ramrod straight, Charlotte perched herself on the edge of the chair. She flitted her gaze toward him, her cheeks blooming with color, then turned her attention toward the door.

Simon followed her line of sight and saw—nothing. "What are you looking at?"

"It's not what I'm looking at, but what I'm trying *not* to look at. Please, close your legs."

Oh. He chuckled softly and moved his legs and the gaping towel closer together. "I'm decent now."

She kept her attention on the door. "I doubt that's possible for you."

Even though she didn't look at him, he shrugged. "Very well. You asked if my offer to marry you was genuine. Do you want it to be?"

"You are insufferable!"

Great satisfaction filled him when she jerked her attention from the door and dropped her gaze to his towel-covered groin. A smile tugged at his lips.

"Stop smirking! This is not in any way humorous. For once, would you be a gentleman and answer my question directly?"

It was so easy to bait her, but she was right. They needed to clear up this mess. "Yes. My offer was sincere. You are in a rather sticky pickle. I'm offering you a way out."

"I hardly think being bound to you for life is a preferable solution."

Interesting choice of words, and one reason why this mad idea might work. But he would have to confide in her. "That may not be as long as you imagine."

Her head swiveled to the quinine bottle. "You're sick."

"Yes."

"Is it . . ." Movement, subtle and barely noticeable, in the long column of her neck caught his eye. "Malaria?"

"Yes." All the joy of teasing her seeped out of him. She actually appeared concerned.

"And fatal?"

"I don't know. It's the most truthful answer I can give you."

After what seemed like a few hours of staring at each other, that in truth were probably only a few seconds, he said, "Since it's only the two of us, let's be honest. You want to be married to me about as much as I want to be married to you. But your reputation is at risk. You may not think much of me, but my mother raised me to be a gentleman. And I'll be damned if I'll stand by and allow you to get leg-shackled to Lord Worm, who would beat his wife."

A tiny smile ghosted her lips but disappeared so quickly, he might have imagined it. "What would this . . . arrangement entail?"

He hitched a brow at her. "What would you like it to entail?"

"Please spare us these games. Would you expect a marriage in the truest sense?"

She asked for direct, so he delivered. "Do you mean, would I expect sex?"

"If you wish to phrase it so crudely."

He laughed. "If you think that's crude . . . I have never forced a woman, nor do I intend to start now. I won't ask for anything you're not willing to give."

"So, a business arrangement? You will be expecting a dowry, I presume?"

"Again. To be clear. I don't expect anything from you, other than your promise to keep my illness from the scandal sheets."

"Why? It's nothing to be ashamed of."

"No. But my mother doesn't know, and I want to spare her the worry. Reading those rags is her one weakness."

"And who precisely is your mother? Some tenant farmer's wife?"

Another type of heat rushed through his body, not one caused by the fever ravaging him. He rose from the bed. "Now see here. You can insult me all you wish. But never—I mean *never* — disparage my mother! A kinder soul does not exist. The only women I've met who even come close are both duchesses."

Charlotte's chin jerked back, and she paled.

Good. She should be sorry.

"However, since you asked. My mother and father live in Wiltshire, where my father owns a prosperous estate."

"Although my brother's seat is in Shropshire, he also owns property in Wiltshire." Several moments later, her eyes widened. "Not Mr. Theodore Beckham of Swindon?"

"The very one. The property is entailed, and I'm the only son. So you see, if my mother learns of my illness, she will hound me even more to marry and produce an heir."

"Why on earth are you working as a man of business?"

Growing tired of the interrogation, he yawned. "Can we discuss this later? I promise I will give you all the details your heart desires. But right now, I need more quinine and sleep."

Frampton knocked on the open door. "Sir, I've placed Lady Charlotte's bag in the next room."

"I was bamming you, Frampton. Please show Lady Charlotte to the last room down the hall where she'll have privacy."

"Very good, sir. Might I suggest recalling one of the maids to attend to Lady Charlotte?"

"Could you send for my maid, Frampton?" Charlotte turned toward Simon. "Is that agreeable with you as my future husband?"

"If she can be discreet."

Charlotte nodded and addressed Frampton. "Tell her we'll double her wages."

Simon took a step forward, swayed on his feet, and stopped. "Now, wait just a moment. You're free with my money."

"I would presume Burwood would pay her wages for the time being, and he is not a stingy man."

Ouch. The barb stung just enough.

"And if you wish to pay for her silence . . ."

"Very well." Simon waved a hand. He needed to lie down.

Frampton bowed and exited.

"Cook should return for supper, if she hasn't already. We can speak more then about the details of our arrangement." The towel slipped from his waist, and his initial reaction was to grasp it. Instead, he allowed it to drop to the floor.

Warm satisfaction filled him—or was that still the fever?—when Charlotte's jaw dropped.

"Just in case you want to see what you would be missing without the effects of cold water."

"Your mother would be ashamed," she said, then hurried from the room to follow Frampton.

Simon laughed and fell on the bed. "True," he said to himself. But Lady Charlotte Talbot brought out the worst in him.

CHAPTER 5

Oh, that man! Charlotte's cheeks burned. And speaking of fire, had she jumped from one impossible situation to another? Had she lost her mind? How could a man who only saw the sunny side ever understand her? He probably never faced a hardship in his life. She had no desire to marry and be controlled by any man, especially an insufferable buffoon like Simon Beckham.

Why, he would probably gallivant off to a bawdy house before their signatures on the register had even dried.

Argh!

Once in her room—which was indeed some distance from that rake—she wrote a letter and gave it to Frampton to deliver. "Make certain it goes into my maid's hands directly, Frampton."

"I shall deliver it myself, my lady."

Of course he would. He was the only servant, save for possibly the cook, in the house. "Frampton." She stopped him before he left. "Why are the other servants gone?"

"Mr. Beckham requested it."

"To keep his illness secret?" Was his situation really so dire?

If she married him, might she truly become a widow in short order? As heartless as he believed she was, the thought didn't comfort her.

Frampton hesitated. "I'm not at liberty to say, my lady. Will there be anything else?"

She shook her head and waved the butler off, admiring his loyalty and ability to be discreet, something she sorely required.

Two hours later, she grew restless and decided to go to the library and retrieve a book. Knowing both Honoria and Drake as she did, there would be an abundance of reading material available. As she walked toward the staircase and past Mr. Beckham's door, loud snores sounded from within.

She sighed. Of course, he would snore—loudly. She brightened, remembering she wouldn't have to share a bedroom with him, and proceeded downstairs.

Although not as grand as the library at Hartridge House, Burwood's seat in Dorset, the selection of books was extensive. She browsed the shelves, looking for something more entertaining than cerebral. Honoria always praised Jane Austen, although Charlotte found romances to be overly sentimental and unrealistic. However, she supposed that was the point of them. She plucked *Pride and Prejudice* from the shelf.

Opening the book, she read the first line.

"It is a truth universally acknowledged, that a single man in possession of a good fortune, must be in want of a wife."

She barely resisted the chuckle. Perhaps Miss Austen did have her thumb on the pulse of society after all. Before long, she had settled into a comfortable chair and fully immersed herself in the story. Although, truth be told, she understood the austere Mr. Darcy much more than the gregarious and sometimes impertinent Elizabeth. One could hardly blame a refined gentleman such as Mr. Darcy to take affront to her family's lack of decorum. However, Charlotte did admire Miss Bennet's wit.

Elizabeth Bennet, in Charlotte's estimation, had much in common with the insufferable Mr. Beckham.

Argh! When would she stop thinking about *that man?!*

"My lady," a male voice called from the doorway.

Charlotte peered up from the book, pleased to see Frampton had retrieved her maid. "Rose." Charlotte made note of the page number, then closed the book. "Thank heavens you've arrived." She turned toward Frampton. "Did my brother ask any questions?"

"No, my lady. His valet said his lordship would be at Parliament for some time."

Rose shook her head. "He was not pleased with your decision to leave his household."

"Well, he will continue to be disappointed, because I'm not returning. Now, were you able to retrieve any of my belongings?"

"Yes, my lady. A few."

Frampton said, "Miss Rose and I carried the trunk up to your room."

A hand on her back, Rose frowned. "It was heavy. Why are there no footmen here?"

Charlotte exchanged a look with Frampton. "About that. Allow me to speak with Mr. Beckham. Perhaps I can convince him to send for at least a few of the servants to alleviate your burden, Frampton."

"Very good, my lady." He sketched an elegant bow. "Unless you need anything else, I shall show Miss Rose to her quarters."

"Shall I arrive to dress you for supper at six as usual, my lady?"

Charlotte nodded out of habit. Her thoughts were elsewhere.

Rose curtsied again and followed Frampton.

With a glance at the grandfather clock nestled in the far corner, Charlotte sighed. Nearly quarter past five. Not much time to plan a stratagem necessary to convince Mr. Beckham they needed more servants at hand. But if Charlotte was good at anything, she excelled at making a sound argument and winning a debate.

However, persuading Mr. Beckham to recall a few servants was only one item on her list of things to discuss, and to be honest, not the most important one at that.

No. His impetuous statement that he would marry her superseded any discussion of returning servants. The book still clutched in her hand, she paced the floor of the library.

Think. Think.

Marriage to Mr. Beckham would free her from Roland's scheme to shackle her to The Worm. Icy shivers ran down her spine at the thought of having to endure Felix's demands as a husband. But would Mr. Beckham have similar demands?

Simply because a man *said* he wouldn't force a woman didn't necessarily mean he was truthful. And Charlotte had many, many doubts about Mr. Beckham's veracity. Men often said things to get what they wanted, and then as soon as they had it in their grasp, they forgot their promise.

Odd, though, that the thought of his touch didn't sicken her like the idea of Felix's hands on her.

However, he *did* snore. If—and that was a decided if—she accepted his proposal, she should request certain things in writing, such as not sharing a bedroom.

She considered her other options. She had no skills other than knowing how to run a household, embroidery, and making shirts. *Ha!* Roland would have to rely on his wife Hortense's abominable skill with a needle. The only thing her sister-in-law seemed adept at was producing sons.

Charlotte had no patience to be a governess, even if she could swallow her pride and stoop to such a position. Governesses were ghosts, living in a limbo. Not quite family nor servant—meant to be seen, not heard, and as little of the former as possible. As a realist, Charlotte conceded her vocal opinions would most likely have her employer turning her out on the streets before a week was out.

If she could raise enough money, she could travel to America and live with her brother Nash and his wife. But as she did when Roland made the threat, she dismissed the idea as quickly as it came. Not only were Nash and Adalyn struggling themselves while Nash waited for his investment to produce fruit, but Adalyn was expecting their first child, and the idea of being around a squalling infant in a tiny house set Charlotte's teeth on edge almost as much as the thought of Felix's touch.

Facing the facts, she admitted she'd been reared for one thing: to become a wife. Never one to delude herself that some great love waited for her, she only hoped to find a man attractive enough to not make her want to cast up her accounts when he demanded his husbandly rights—which she prayed would end when she produced a son. A man who would give her at least a semblance of being in charge of her own life, who wouldn't bore her to tears, and who wouldn't beat her.

Contrary to her marquess brother's opinion, she wasn't captious.

When Lord Felix Davies first began courting her, she held hope that she'd found such a man. Until he quickly showed his true colors when he tried to force himself on her and told her she needed to stop thinking!

Admittedly, she wasn't the easiest person to get along with. Nothing like Honoria, whom everyone loved, or Miranda, who was cheerful and quick-witted, or even flighty Anne, the consummate flirt.

No. Charlotte fully accepted that her outspoken nature and icy demeanor sent many a man scurrying away in search of a more affable and biddable bride.

And yet, Mr. Beckham had thrown himself on his sword for her. Regarding her *requirements*, his attractiveness was unquestionable—

perhaps he was *too* attractive. He himself said he couldn't abide a man who would beat his wife. Life with him might be a constant annoyance with his ridiculous buffoonery, but it wouldn't be boring. He promised he would never force himself on her, but his family situation indicated he would no doubt expect an heir.

She'd never experienced the attraction of motherhood as most women did. The risks of delivering in itself made her nervous, but children required nurturing, and Charlotte was not the nurturing type. Small children made her uneasy. Granted, other than her nephews, she had little exposure to them, but they seemed so—breakable. Hopefully, like Mr. Darcy, Mr. Beckham possessed enough wealth to hire a nanny.

By all accounts, at least as she considered them, he met all conditions. If she could learn to tolerate his flippant manner, his irritating cheerfulness, and his mission to have everyone like him, perhaps marriage to Mr. Simon Beckham could indeed be her salvation.

Or her hell.

⚜

SIMON SLEPT LIKE THE DEAD. AT LEAST HE FELT DEAD WHEN HE finally stirred awake. His head still pounded like the devil, and his already soaked sheets were even wetter. Lord, he needed a bath —with *warm* water.

He stumbled from his bed and tugged the bell pull.

Frampton took longer than usual to appear. "Sir?"

"Please ask cook to heat some water for a bath."

Frampton's wiry brows rose. "There are no footmen to bring in the tub, sir."

Right. But he promised Lady Charlotte they would discuss their possible marriage at supper, and even if he didn't want to impress her—or so he told himself—he had to smell himself. A sponge bath would have to suffice. "Could you at least bring several bowls of water, then?"

Frampton gave an abbreviated bow. "Very good, sir."

"Make sure it's warm," he shouted at Frampton's retreating back.

By the time Simon had finished washing and dressing, the clock struck quarter past seven. He didn't bother with a neckcloth, waistcoat, or coat, which would only exacerbate the heat flowing through him. The ice queen would just have to excuse his state of dishabille.

Thankfully, some of his strength had returned, and he managed the distance from his room to the dining hall with little difficulty, pausing to rest once along the way. However, by the time he entered the room, the chair beckoned him in the most welcoming way.

Lady Charlotte peered up from her consommé, disapproval clearly written on her face. She arched a haughty brow. "Is this your idea of dressing for supper, Mr. Beckham?"

He sketched a deep bow before collapsing into the chair. "Forgive me for offending your *delicate sensibilities*, my lady. I'd hoped to forgo the formalities."

Even from his distance at the opposite end of the table, he heard her huff. He waited until her spoon was a breath from her lips before saying, "Especially considering you've seen me with decidedly fewer garments earlier today."

Liquid sputtered from her mouth. But drat it all, she made even that look elegant as if she'd intended it. She wiped her lips with the serviette.

The fever raging in him all day either had decreased or had turned his brain to a crisp because all he could think about was that—as her husband—he would be allowed to kiss those lips.

If she let him.

Frampton approached, placing a bowl of the consommé before him.

He studied it. "I'm not sure my stomach can handle eating anything."

Lady Charlotte's rich alto traveled down the table and skimmed along his skin like a siren. "You need to eat to regain your strength, and broth will be the easiest to keep down. I asked your cook to prepare it especially for you."

Well, that was a surprise. "Yes, Mother." He spooned some up, finding the temperature perfect, swallowed, and waited. His stomach did not revolt. The broth was surprisingly delicious, considering he had little appetite earlier. "How do you know so much about what foods are easy on the digestion?"

"I have three young nephews who eat the most horrendous things that upset their stomachs. Consommé is the one thing they manage to keep down when they're indisposed."

He finished every drop, but when Frampton removed the bowl, he held up a hand. "That's all for me. Just serve Lady Charlotte."

As she waited for Frampton to place the next course before her, her long, graceful fingers toyed with the rim of her wine glass.

Fascinating.

That answered it. His brain was surely crisped.

She cleared her throat, drawing his attention back to those lips.

Dammit.

"I understand your desire for privacy, sir. But I implore you to call at least several footmen and maids back into service."

Simon swore Frampton's lips twitched as he laid the entrée before the demanding woman.

"Oh, you do, do you?"

Those delicate shoulders straightened. Had they always been so white and creamy?

"Yes. I do. It's unfair of you to lay the burden of everything on Frampton's shoulders."

Shoulders. Had she read his mind?

Perhaps not, as she continued speaking. "Surely there are a few in Burwood's service who are trustworthy?"

"Very well." He turned toward Frampton. "Two footmen and two maids. I trust your judgment whom to choose."

A tight-lipped smile stretched Charlotte's lips.

"You don't have to look so smug, my lady." He grinned at her. "It's simply that I need a proper bath and some fresh bed linens."

"I won't argue with the first item. You reek, sir."

Oh, that did it. He pulled himself from the chair, walked down the length of the long table, sat down next to her, and placed a hand to his ear. "What's that? I couldn't hear you from way down there."

She refused to meet his gaze, but her muttered words were as crystal clear as the fine goblet holding her wine. "You are incorrigible."

"So you've told me. On multiple occasions. Now, I believe we have something serious to discuss. So, if you could refrain from your pointed barbs—at least for a few moments—I would appreciate it. I want to get back to my bed."

He waited, gauging her reaction. Unfortunately, she remained stone-faced. "Have you considered my proposal?"

"I've thought of little else. But before I answer, I have a few questions." Her gaze flicked toward Frampton, then back to him. "May we speak in private?"

Simon waved a hand at Frampton. "It's fine. The lady's reputation is already in tatters. Hence the need for this discussion. Besides, I'm in no condition for ravishing at the moment."

Once Frampton had left them alone, she said, "Ribald comments such as that are precisely why I must know what your expectations are. You said you wouldn't force me."

He sucked in a breath. "And I meant that. Forcing a woman is beyond the pale. However . . ."

Her eyes widened, and her breath hitched. "What?"

"As I said, my father's estate is entailed, and I'm his only son. It would bring my mother comfort knowing she had a grandson to inherit when I die."

"So you *do* expect to bed me?"

"I hope to, which is different from expecting. You can refuse me until my dying day. There are couples who—for whatever reason—can't have children. My mother need never be the wiser. She would simply chalk it up to bad luck. However . . ."

"You keep saying that."

"Because it's necessary." He leaned in, hoping to make his point. "I promise I would make it pleasant for you. I'm told I'm quite skilled in bedsport."

She snorted a derisive laugh. "Perhaps in your estimation."

He shook his head. "In my partners' estimations. I've never had complaints."

Pink bloomed on her cheeks, giving him satisfaction.

"And would such . . . associations continue after we're married?"

Ah, there was the rub. "No. As difficult as it would be—and make no mistake, it would be difficult for me—I would be faithful to you. You have my word."

"Ha! The word of a self-proclaimed rake!"

"I've never claimed to be perfect—unlike you. Believe what you will. But I hope with time, you will at least tolerate me enough to share my bed enough to produce a child"—he grinned —"or two."

"So I'm only a brood mare."

Lord, the woman was exasperating. She was sucking all the joy out of him. "No. You are in a sticky situation. And the more I thought about it, the more a marriage between us made sense. I was planning on marrying anyway—someday. If this infernal illness would ever leave me for good. I can't bear the thought of leaving my mother and sisters homeless should both my father and I die without someone directly in line to inherit."

"You have sisters?" She appeared surprised, as if having grown up with other women didn't suit him.

"Five. All younger than I."

"And the next in line?"

"A cousin thrice removed. An oily sort of man, quite like your Lord Felix." His stomach turned at the thought of Cousin Horace, and he worried the consommé, which had tasted so delicious minutes before, would make a reappearance.

She bristled at that. "He's not mine. Nor do I intend to make him such."

He nodded. "Be that as it may, my cousin is not the sort to welcome my mother and sisters with open arms. He's more the sort to show them the door with only the clothes on their backs."

"Surely Burwood would help."

"I would expect no less. Drake is like the brother I never had, and I suspect he feels the same about me." He managed a grin. "It's one area where his typically perfect judgment is lacking."

She scoffed.

"But my mother is a proud woman. Perhaps in my weakened state earlier, I was mistaken, and it is a second flaw."

"In addition to the love of scandal sheets?"

Ah, but she had an excellent memory. "Yes. I don't want my mother to have to beg for a roof over her head or bread for her belly. She deserves better than that." He studied her, probing the depth of those dark, seductive eyes, fully aware her own situation was quite similar.

She shifted in her chair, the movement so slight and natural, had he not been watching for her reaction, he would have missed it.

"Why would you wait until you were certain the malaria wouldn't return before marrying, then? Why not take a wife, produce an heir, and secure your family's legacy?"

Her question brought him into painful territory, and he had no desire to subject himself to it.

"I have my reasons."

"Hmph. Such as wishing to cavort as long as possible."

Oh, she pushed him right in the middle of it—as if she literally placed her hands on his back. It might have been his weakened condition. It might have been because he knew she wouldn't let it go. But he knew she would see through a lie. So he risked telling her a partial truth, even if it exposed his soft underbelly. "If you must know, it's because I hate the idea of a woman falling in love with me. Perhaps it was all those years listening to Drake moan about losing Honoria. And I couldn't bear the thought of leaving a grieving widow behind if this wretched malaria takes me to my grave before my time."

Her jaw dropped.

He prepared himself for a scathing insult about his gigantic ego.

When she remained silent, he continued, "I suppose that's why this arrangement, should we wish to pursue it, is so perfect. For I have no fear you would grieve my death, and you could easily find yourself a young widow with a substantial living. I would say that's a winning hand for both of us, wouldn't you?"

CHAPTER 6

Charlotte admitted, the man had a point even if she didn't agree that his death would be a winning hand—at least for him. "And what if you survive and live a long life? If you find a woman who captures *your* heart?"

He shifted in his chair, and his face clouded as if he were in pain. "When and if that happens, you and I will discuss it at that time."

"I want some of this in writing."

His dark brows hitched. "What in particular?"

Heat raced up her neck to her cheeks. She blamed those sapphire eyes of his. They held her captive and pulled her in until she couldn't think straight. Such a color should be illegal.

Or immoral. They made her imagine . . . things. Like being pulled into his arms and kissed until her head spun.

Gah! Stop! Stop, stop, stop.

"That you won't require me to share a bed."

Surprisingly, he nodded. "Fine. But I'll draw up a second document for your eyes only with that stipulation. It would be best not to present anything like that to your brother. Anything else? Your widow's portion?"

Goodness. He was serious about predeceasing her. How could he be so calm? And why did she care? She returned to the practical—something she could control. "Precisely how much does Burwood pay you?"

"Ha! Afraid you won't get your tenth?" He shook his head. "I promise you will be well provided for. Drake is a very generous employer, but the bulk of my wealth comes from other sources. I only ask that, should I not have an heir, you look after my mother and sisters after my father's death. Help the girls find suitable husbands if they've not already married."

How could she refuse such a request? Wasn't she in a similar position? Her mind reeled back to the word *heir*. With his family's welfare at stake, would he truly respect her wishes if she refused to allow him into her bed? Or did he have so much confidence in his ability to seduce her he believed it was a moot point?

People could say she was unfeeling, but queasy guilt soured her stomach at the possibility of not upholding her end of their devil's bargain. The least she could do was take care of his family. "You have my word."

"Good." He nodded. "I won't ask for that in writing. I trust you." He rose, somewhat shakily, and she had the urge to reach out and steady him. "I'll draw up the marriage contract in addition to the one with your stipulations when I'm feeling a little better and present the contract to your brother."

"Roland won't release my dowry. And he may not accept the contract at all."

"It's only formality. I won't have him accusing me of not doing things properly. As I said to him earlier today, you're of age. You don't need his permission. And I don't want your dowry. If he does release it, it's yours to keep. Now, if that concludes our business, I'll leave you to the rest of your meal."

As he lumbered from the room, his voice echoed back. "Frampton, be a good fellow and help me upstairs."

She stared at the roast chicken growing cold on her plate, her appetite vanishing.

How in the world had all of this happened?

Business. Is that how he truly saw their arrangement? A worrisome bit of disappointment skittered across her heart but made a quick exit. Chiding herself for the brief moment of weakness, she accepted that, before long, she would be Lady Charlotte Beckham.

Even if it was in name only.

⚜

When Rose arrived to dress her the next morning, Charlotte learned that several footmen and maids had returned per Mr. Beckham's agreement.

Rose chattered in her usual nonsensical way about their faults and failings as she fashioned Charlotte's hair into an intricate design. "I'm afraid I didn't have time to retrieve your jewelry from the safe, my lady. Perhaps you can send for it."

Charlotte internally rolled her eyes. No doubt Roland would find great pleasure withholding her finer pieces as punishment. At the moment, Charlotte was more concerned about the miserable number of gowns Rose brought with her. If Roland was so petty as to refuse to release her clothing, she would need new ones, but she had no money.

She would have to ask her future husband.

Gah! She hated being dependent on anyone, much less a man who could lord it over her every chance he got, but between Mr. Beckham and Roland, her future husband was more approachable.

Mr. Beckham—Simon. She would have to get used to calling him that, she supposed.

Did he really expect she would succumb to his *charms* and give him an heir? Still, an odd yearning had tightened low in her belly when he spoke of his prowess in the bedroom.

Braggart.

And—yet, she wondered . . .

Gah! Stop thinking of that man!

She needed a distraction. The duke's mansion was one of the finest in London, and Honoria had taken great pride in the gardens of both their country seat in Dorset and their city home. Charlotte rose, resolved that a walk in the garden would rid her mind from thoughts of Mr. Beckham

Male voices drifted from inside Simon's bedchamber, and she hurried past. No doubt either Frampton or a footman attended to him, and she didn't want him to accuse her of eavesdropping should the door open suddenly.

A maid paused her dusting and curtsied as Charlotte passed on her way to the ballroom. Charlotte gave her a curt nod before proceeding on her way to the doors leading to the terrace and gardens.

Cool air brushed her skin, and she shivered as she stepped outside. When she'd arrived at the duke's mansion the day before, the afternoon sun had shone full and bright, warming the normally brisk and damp March air. In such a rush to leave, she had not thought to wear a pelisse or a spencer.

Unlike the day before, gray clouds—thick and heavy with their accumulated contents—gathered in the sky. Dashes of color on the ground shook a fist of protest against the sky's gloomy canopy. Bright shoots of hyacinths lined a footpath leading to the rose beds. Tight buds of peonies waited on green foliage, ready to burst into luscious blooms of pink. Several remaining daffodils fought the good fight, holding onto their sunny, yellow petals and refusing to go the way of their companions who slumbered until the next spring.

Strange, but the trumpet-like flower made her think of Simon with his cheerful disposition and carefree attitude. Of course, it may have been that the flower was also called a narcissus. She chuckled softly at the idea.

"Something funny?"

She spun at the male voice, her hand inadvertently flying to her throat. "Mr. Beckham! Must you sneak up on people?"

He lifted a coat. "I came to bring you this. It's rather chilly out here. One of us ill at a time is sufficient, wouldn't you agree?"

"People don't become ill from being cold."

His lips tilted rakishly on one side. "They don't? Are you a physician?"

She jerked her chin at him. "No. But my sister-in-law is. She says such things are silly superstitions."

Those dark-blue eyes widened. "The marquess's wife is a physician?"

"No. My other sister-in-law. In America."

He snorted a laugh. "Leave it to Americans to blaze the trail. You must tell me about her. But first . . ." He held the coat out, shaking it a little. "It's mine, so it will probably be too big. But it's warm. When I enquired about a pelisse, your maid admitted she didn't bring one."

With her back to him, she slipped her arms through the sleeves.

Heat pressed into her shoulders as he smoothed the material over her. He turned her around, buttoned it, then stood back and assessed her. "There." Fingering the lapels, he ran his large hands down the length, their backs brushing lightly against her breasts as he skimmed the surface of the coat.

Instinctively, she stepped back. "We are not married yet, so I would kindly ask you to keep your hands to yourself."

Those large hands lifted in a defensive stance. "Forgive me. I meant no offense. Now, tell me why you were laughing. I need something to cheer me."

Unbidden, she chortled again. No doubt her musings would do little to lift his spirits. "The daffodils remind me of you."

His brow furrowed as he jerked back, his head tilting at a rather roguish angle. "And that's . . . funny?"

An unexpected moment of compassion flitted through her. The man had been ill, and quite frankly, he didn't appear much improved. "They're cheerful."

The familiar grin stretched across his lips, and her gaze immediately homed in on them.

Gah!

"Why—thank you. Although I still don't see the humor, it's possibly the first compliment I've ever received from you." He leaned in but didn't touch her. "The first of many, I hope." The rake had the audacity to wiggle his eyebrows and wink.

"It was a moment of weakness. I promise to be stronger in the future." She fought the smile tugging her lips.

She only hoped she could.

◈

Simon recognized the tiniest chink in Charlotte's armor, but he decided to play along and let her think she'd won. It was merely one battle, and he would win the war. "Ah, so it was a derisive laugh at your rare moment of weakness."

"Should you even be out of bed?"

Another chink?

"Are you concerned for my health?"

"Only that I don't want you to expire before you marry me and secure my reputation and financial situation."

"Cold, my lady, cold. It would seem I wasn't quick enough with my coat. But since you asked, the footman had just finished shaving me, and I happened to look out my window and noticed you without a coat."

Her gaze raked over him, assessing.

"You needed a shave. I'm surprised you trust a footman to perform a valet's job."

"I would have done it myself. I know how. Had to do it in the military. But my hands are still a little shaky. And as you said, I don't want to leave you before we've had a chance to really get to know each other."

"You are——"

"Incorrigible. So you've said. On multiple occasions. Perhaps a new adjective? Dashing? Charming?" He wiggled his eyebrows. "Irresistible?"

"Hmph."

When her lips twitched, he pressed on.

"In truth, after an actual bath and fresh clothing, I feel almost like a new man." He stepped closer, even though it would goad her. "Care to take a sniff? I would love your opinion, since you found me so foul-smelling before."

Arms folded over her enticing bosom answered his question.

"No? Pity. I think the sandalwood is quite nice." He sniffed under his arm. "Ah."

She huffed, the ghost of a smile vanishing. "I'm going back inside since I can't even have a moment's peace by myself out here."

Regret pricked at his conscience that he had pushed her a bit too far. "No. Stay out here and enjoy the daffodils. I'll leave you now that I'm assured you won't catch a chill." He didn't wait for her response, but turned and headed back inside the house, deciding to use the small bit of resumed strength to begin drafting the marriage contract.

In his study adjacent to Drake's, Simon settled at his desk and dipped his pen into the inkpot. He remembered the last marriage contract he'd drawn up. A much happier occasion, for certain. Drake and Honoria's marriage was like a fairy tale, although Drake's deception had nearly cost him the woman of his dreams.

But Drake's unwavering love for Honoria made Simon wonder if he could experience such a love himself.

Damnation.

He'd never hoped for love, marriage, and a family before. Oh, he realized he would have to marry someday, if nothing else, to ensure his mother and sisters were provided for, as he told Charlotte.

And although his parents had a happy marriage, personal experience taught him that even a perceived betrayal of one party could destroy the other. Grief was the price of loving someone. And that was too much pain for Simon to contemplate.

Pain—of any kind—was the one thing he wanted to avoid at any cost. It didn't mean he was a coward. He'd charged into the fray of battle as determined as any other soldier. The difference being, he simply refused to think about the possibility of being injured and the subsequent pain.

And then malaria had struck, swift and hard.

Free from attacks since he'd returned home to England, hope dangled before him like a string before a cat. But the moment he reached for it, another attack snatched it away.

With pain being something he didn't dwell on, he couldn't remember if this last attack was better or worse than the ones before. The only clear thing was the cursed illness still had its hooks in him.

And that meant one thing. He needed a wife and a son, and although he hadn't given much thought as to whom the *lucky* woman would be, the moment Lady Charlotte Talbot appeared on his doorstep seeking refuge from an untenable position, fate had chosen for him.

Tap, tap.

He wrenched his attention from the still blank parchment to the open door of the study.

His coat dangled from Charlotte's fingers. "I'm sorry to

intrude. Frampton told me you were in here. I thought you would like this back."

Wonder of wonders.

She seemed . . . apologetic.

Pointing to the chair on the opposite side of the desk, he said, "You can lay it there. I'll take it up with me later."

He watched as she folded it neatly and draped it across the back of the chair. Entranced as her long, elegant fingers caressed the material, lingering a moment longer than necessary.

"You could have given it to Frampton."

She didn't meet his gaze. "I wanted to thank you. It was gallant—and unexpected."

His mouth flew open, and for a moment, no longer than a blink, he considered delivering a snappy retort. But for the first time in his memory, she actually appeared vulnerable. "You're welcome."

Still not meeting his eyes, she nodded. "I should leave you to your work."

In a breath, she was gone.

An uncomfortable thought flashed through his mind. Charlotte Talbot was a woman he could love whether he wanted to or not.

The blob of ink on the tip of his pen dropped like a fat mosquito onto the white paper.

CHAPTER 7

During the next two days, Charlotte saw little of Simon. According to Frampton, Mr. Beckham had suffered another relapse and had sequestered himself to his room. With the return of the two footmen and two maids, Charlotte felt no compulsion to enquire if he had need of her. Surely, the staff would take care of anything he should require.

Yet, each time she passed his door, she would pause, her fist raised to knock and enquire as to his recovery before she thought better of it.

Worried that the worm Felix had spread word about discovering her with Mr. Beckham, she remained in the confines of the house. And as much as she enjoyed the quiet solitude, part of her yearned to do something.

She'd been trying to read more of the book she pulled from the shelves the day of her arrival and had only managed as far as the arrival of the odious Mr. Collins, heir to Longbourn and the Bennet estate—such as it was.

Her thoughts traveled to Simon and the situation with his own family's estate.

"Good book?" The arousing scent of sandalwood enveloped her.

She practically jumped from her seat. "Goodness, must you always be sneaking up on people?"

He laughed, bright and full of life. "Other than your hair color and furrowed brow, I might have mistaken you for Her Grace. She often has her nose buried in a book."

"Reading is an admirable pastime."

"So I'm told." He strode to the sideboard and poured himself a finger of brandy.

"Isn't it a little early for that? It's barely eleven o'clock."

In answer, he hitched a dark brow and poured another finger's worth. After taking a seat opposite her, he perched an ankle on the opposing knee with a casual male elegance, then tipped his glass toward her. "What are you reading?"

"*Pride and Prejudice.*"

"What's it about?"

"Two people who detest each other."

He sipped, his dark-blue eyes watching her over the rim of his glass. "So. Like us."

"I see you're feeling like yourself again."

"Indeed. In fact, that's why I needed a drink. I plan to go see your brother with the marriage contract."

Frampton knocked. "Lady Charlotte. Mr. Beckham. Lady Miranda Townsend here to see Lady Charlotte."

Charlotte cast a glance toward Simon. "Which room would you like me to use?"

"This is fine, if it suits you." He rose. "I shall leave after greeting her."

Moments later, Frampton escorted Miranda to the library. She stopped short, her head swiveling between Charlotte and Simon. "So, it is true?"

"Yes," Simon answered with alacrity.

"Is what true?" Charlotte asked, considerably more cautious

and—in her opinion—more prudent with her response to a question of unknown content. She glared at Simon. "You don't even know what she's asking about."

He flashed that audacious grin at her. "It pleases women when I agree with them. And as I told you the other day, my goal in life is to please women."

Heat seared Charlotte's face at his subtle reference to his prowess in the bedroom. When she returned her attention to Miranda, a similar grin split her friend's face. Charlotte huffed in frustration. "You, too?"

"Don't mind me. Pray continue." Miranda waved a hand.

Charlotte ignored her as well as Simon—who continued to grin like the buffoon he was. "You asked if something was true." Charlotte's gaze drifted to the sheet of parchment Miranda held, and her stomach cinched tighter than a corset. "Does it regard something in that scandal sheet?"

Simon moved toward the door. "I'll just take my leave and allow you ladies to discuss the latest gossip."

Miranda stopped him. "No. Wait. You should hear this, since it involves you."

"Oh?" Simon said, as if his name appeared in the gossip rags on a daily basis.

Once seated, Miranda cleared her throat. "This"—she held up the spurious paper as if Charlotte didn't already know what it was—"is the latest copy of *The Muckraker*. When I received it this morning, I went straight to Edgerton's home, Charlotte, only to learn you had left. That disagreeable butler of your brother's wouldn't tell me where you were, but for a shilling, a groom was most forthcoming with information. This, of course, only made me worry more, since Honoria had written about her sister-in-law's death, stating they would be away from London for an indeterminate amount of time."

Charlotte's typically sharp mind jolted, trying to make a connection. And why didn't she receive something from

Honoria? She would puzzle that out later. First . . . "Why did Honoria's letter cause you more concern?"

Miranda rolled her eyes. "Because the groom said you were staying at Burwood's."

Simon, who had remained blessedly silent up until that point, raised a hand. "If I may suggest. Why don't you read us what has you so concerned?"

Charlotte blinked at his sensible request. "I was going to suggest that."

He chuffed a laugh. "Of course you were."

A tiny smile flitted across Miranda's lips. "Yes. Well." She cleared her throat again and held up the horrible paper. "'Some falls from grace are sharper than others. Just ask Lady Charlotte Talbot. This reporter has it on good authority that she refused Lord Felix Davies's honorable proposal—'"

"Honorable, my foot!" Charlotte wanted to tear the paper in half. But first she needed to hear everything it said.

"Shall I continue?" Miranda lifted her dark brows. "'Refused Lord Felix Davies's honorable proposal to fall into a bed of iniquity with Mr. Simon Beckham. Or should that be inequity, as said Mr. Beckham is not of the peerage and clearly beneath her.'"

Charlotte studied Simon, who appeared unfazed by the insult. No, not exactly unfazed—amused. Not sure she heard him correctly, he appeared to mutter, "Beneath her" before snorting a little laugh.

Gah! That man!

Thankfully, Miranda's attention remained on the atrocious accusations. "'Furthermore, Mr. Beckham serves as man of business to the upstart new Duke of Burwood, who perpetuated the despicable ruse upon society last summer—a ruse that Mr. Beckham took full part in. Should society expect anything less from such uncivilized and uncouth *gentlemen*?'"

Simon straightened in his chair. "Now they've gone too far insulting Drake."

Miranda nodded. "I'm afraid it gets worse. 'Sources confirm Lord Felix is heartbroken over the incident and, while assuaging his sorrow with a fine whisky, let slip that Lady Charlotte was caught in Mr. Beckham's bedchamber while the man was in a complete state of undress. No doubt the duke has fully sanctioned and encouraged such behavior, allowing them full access to his home.'"

Miranda lowered the paper and waited.

"Is that all?" Simon asked.

"All? Is that all?" Charlotte hated how her voice escalated to a soprano pitch.

"Only that it fails to report several crucial elements."

Miranda leaned forward. "Such as?"

"That Lady Charlotte and I are to be married. I'm taking the marriage contract to her brother today. And Lord Felix Davies is a blackguard who doesn't deserve her. To quote the lady, 'Honorable, my foot.' And I would add my skepticism to the heartbroken assertion as well. Clearly, that report is skewed with the intent to damage."

"Well, yes," Miranda said. "It's what *The Muckraker* does."

Charlotte's mind had stuttered on *who doesn't deserve her*. She gaped at Simon, who remained oblivious and continued to prattle on to Miranda.

"—on my doorstep with a bruise upon her cheek. That cad struck her! And I couldn't . . ." His gaze snagged hers. "What is it?"

"You're defending me?"

"Of course I'm defending you. That's what a future husband should do, isn't it?"

Something odd squeezed her chest, but before she could examine it further, Miranda began her line of questioning.

୬ℬ

Simon's conscience insisted he remove himself so the women could speak freely, but before he could rise and take his leave, Lady Miranda fired forth a barrage of questions at Charlotte.

"So you really are going to marry Mr. Beckham? Was the . . . other part true?" Miranda's gaze darted toward him. "And did you truly turn down Lord Felix? Although that shouldn't surprise me, the man is vile. But why did you come here of all places? And—"

"Miranda!" Charlotte said, her dark eyes fiery. "You sound like Anne."

As much as Simon enjoyed Charlotte's passionate arguments, as a gentleman, he felt compelled to say something in Lady Miranda's defense. "Really, Lady Charlotte, was that necessary? Not that I don't think Miss Weatherby is a delightful distraction."

Charlotte glowered at him. Glowered! "She stopped talking, didn't she?"

"You could have asked her nicely to keep her questions to one at a time."

Lady Miranda cleared her throat. Was the woman coming down with something? "Thank you, Mr. Beckham, for coming to my aid. But I assure you, I'm quite accustomed to Charlotte's bluntness. She's right, of course. I got carried away."

In truth, at least it gave him the opportunity for an escape—err, exit—and he rose. "Then, if you can assure me things won't devolve into a wrestling match, I'll take my leave and let you discuss things privately. Although if a wrestling match does ensue, I would love to watch." He flashed a grin at Charlotte and hoped to see the blush of pink form on her cheeks. He was not disappointed.

Standing before Charlotte, he lifted her hand and placed a kiss on her knuckles. "Darling."

Lady Miranda's jaw dropped a fraction. Charlotte, on the other hand, continued to glower.

He bowed to Lady Miranda and turned to leave. For effect, he paused and faced Charlotte once again. "Oh. In addition to the marriage contract, I've drawn up the stipulations we discussed. However, I wish to amend it slightly. In light of the spurious accusations against Drake, I want you to promise me you will do whatever is in your power to take down the culprit responsible for that gossip sheet."

As he exited the room, he chuckled softly when Miranda's voice echoed behind him.

"He *knows?!* What stipulations? And he called you darling!"

True, it wasn't very gentlemanly of him to leave Charlotte to explain those comments herself, but no one would accuse Simon of playing fair, least of all him.

Charlotte wasn't wrong when she remarked on his return to his usual demeanor. And it felt damn good. He whistled, bounding up the stairs two at a time to retrieve the marriage contract from his desk. He refused to dwell on the more than likely unpleasant outcome of the meeting with Edgerton. Instead, the prospect of getting out of the house filled him with restless energy.

Which he needed. In addition to confronting the high-and-mighty marquess, Simon had written to the vicar of St. James's and made an appointment to discuss the wedding. Both undertakings were necessary, but he relished neither.

After informing Frampton of his destination, he exited the back of the house to the mews. He would take his phaeton, which would provide a bit of cheer as he performed his less than enjoyable tasks.

A groom rose to attention from where he was slumped in a chair. "Sir."

Surprised, Simon jerked back. "Didn't Frampton inform you that you could go home to your family for a few weeks?"

The groom pulled off his cap and nodded. "Yes, sir. But I don't really have no family close by. And the horses"—he motioned to the few remaining horses—"need feeding and caring for. I don't mind, sir."

"Have you been getting something to eat for yourself?"

"Oh, yes, sir. Cook's had lots of extra food these past few days." He patted his stomach. "And that's another reason I don't mind staying around."

Simon chuckled. The lad was young, probably no older than nineteen or twenty, and he thought of Drake. "Well, I'll make sure the duke knows of your loyalty and dedication to your position. Now, if you would be a good fellow, I was going to take the phaeton out." Simon motioned with his hat to the sleek racing carriage.

The groom hopped right to work, asking Simon if he had a preference of horses. Simon chose two dappled grays. The boy nodded his approval. "They be fast 'uns for sure, sir."

Before long, the phaeton was hitched and ready, and Simon made his way across Grosvenor Square the short distance to Edgerton's mansion. He'd only been by the formidable palace-like structure twice, and Honoria had mentioned in passing it's where Charlotte resided with her brother.

Funny how Simon remembered that tiny detail.

He pulled the grays to a halt in front of the imposing rose-colored stone building, and a groom jumped to attention from his station by the wall. The lad didn't look nearly as amiable as the groom he'd just left. "Will you be staying long, sir?"

"I'm not certain." He hoped not. "Best keep them ready." *For a quick escape.* As Simon strode up the steps, he patted the papers in his coat pocket, assuring himself they were still there.

A dour-looking gentleman opened the door a crack before Simon reached the top step. "May I help you?"

"Simon Beckham to see the marquess."

The man sniffed, peering down his long-pointy nose as if

Simon were horse manure to be scraped from his shoe. His eyes were sunken so deep in his skeletal face, Simon swore he could pour a finger of brandy in the sockets. "I'll see if the master is at home. A card?" He held out a white-gloved hand.

Lord, didn't Edgerton feed his staff? Simon pulled out his card and placed it on the man's extended palm. "Tell him it's about his sister."

Rather than usher him inside, the man closed the door in Simon's face with a curt, "Wait here."

Simon's joyful mood was slipping from his grasp faster than sand through his fingers. He turned his face up to the sky, where the sun shone brightly, the warmth and light rejuvenating him.

Glancing back at the groom holding his horses, Simon called, "Perhaps take them around back. It might be longer than anticipated."

The groom nodded, gleeful as he jumped onto the seat of the phaeton and gave the ribbons a snap.

His lips pressed together, Simon muffled a laugh, imagining the lad taking off with his prized carriage for a ride in the park.

Which sounded like a marvelous idea once he'd finished his business with the marquess. Perhaps he could even find some young buck who wished to race. Even better if a wager was involved.

The door creaked open again, this time wider, as the butler motioned him inside.

All the brightness and warmth outside disappeared behind him as Simon stepped through the door into the dreary entrance hall. Shadowy and foreboding, dark colors dominated the wall coverings, draperies, and tapestries. Expensive, Simon had no doubt, they exuded a *don't touch* undercurrent of negative ambiance, making Simon feel like a small boy told to behave by Nanny.

As the butler led Simon up the staircase, he resisted the urge to bolt for the door and call back the groom. Among the portraits of sour looking patriarchs lining the walls, a flower bloomed. A woman with dark, serious eyes seemed to plead with him. *Help me* she called out. Charlotte's mother? The similarity was striking, but she lacked the hard shell enveloping her daughter.

The woman in the portrait appeared vulnerable, and she called him to task. He needed to do this for Charlotte.

The Marquess of Edgerton sat behind a tall desk, his fingers steepled in front of him and a sneer on his smug face. "Sit," he commanded, as if Simon were a dog. The vacant chair appeared low to the ground until Simon realized elongated legs elevated the desk itself.

He tried to peer over to the marquess's chair, wondering if it had been perched on a platform. It reminded him of a king's throne.

Edgerton craned his neck around toward the butler. "Clayton, remain here. I don't trust this man." The butler closed the door and stood ramrod straight against the wall.

Simon took the seat, then pulled out the contract and dispensed with formalities. "For your information. We don't need your signature, permission, or even your approval. But I wanted to do you the courtesy of showing you I plan to do what is right for Charlotte."

"Lady Charlotte." Edgerton snapped the words. "Don't forget that. She will remain so even after her unfortunate union with you." Edgerton picked up the paper with a thumb and forefinger as if it contained some vile disease, then he picked up his lorgnette and read.

"Hmph," he muttered once. Then, for the briefest moment, his eyes widened, and he gazed up at Simon. "Not Theodore Beckham's son?"

Ah, he must have reached the part about my own inheritance.

Simon splayed his hands in front of him. "The one and only.

So, you see, I have no need for Charlotte's dowry," he said, leaving off her honorific simply to vex the man. "As you can see, she will be well-provided for. Even more so if she bears a son to inherit after me."

Edgerton leaned forward. "You can't provide the connections marriage to a peer can."

Simon tamped down the desire to gloat. "Ah, but you forget my connection to the Duke of Burwood. He includes me in everything. Charlotte will continue to be among society."

Edgerton slammed his hand on the desk. "*Lady* Charlotte. And that upstart duke has offended a good portion of the *ton* with his duplicity." The man sneered again. "Which you took part in."

Odd. Those words were extremely close to what Lady Miranda read from *The Muckraker.* "Will you sign, sir?"

"My *Lord.* One would think Theodore Beckham would have taught his son some manners and respect for his superiors. As to the signature . . ." Edgerton picked up the contract and ripped it in half.

"Then our business is concluded." Simon rose, eager to remove himself from the depressing house and ill-tempered marquess. No wonder Charlotte had bolted. "One thing, Edgerton. If you would *kindly* send *Lady* Charlotte's clothing to Pendrake House, it would be most appreciated. She hasn't needed any for the moment." He let that sink in, and Edgerton's face reddened. "But I suppose I'll have to get her out of bed and take her outside for the wedding."

"Escort him out, Clayton. Make sure he doesn't lift anything."

Head held high, Simon hurried from the room, down the stairs, and out into the sunlight. He flipped the groom a shilling. "Retrieve my carriage as fast as you can, lad."

More than anything, Simon needed to cleanse his mind of the unpleasantness, and he sorely needed to laugh.

A brisk ride in his phaeton would do the trick. He checked his pocket watch. *Damn.* Somehow, appealing as it was, the appointment with the vicar awaited, and he needed to fetch Charlotte.

His spirits lifted. No one said he couldn't have both a brisk ride and go to the church.

Charlotte would love it!

CHAPTER 8

"No! He didn't?!" Miranda dropped the teacup on the saucer with a *clink*.

"Oh, he did. Vomited all over Roland's favorite waistcoat with the diamond buttons." Charlotte had been careful not to reveal the nature of Mr. Beckham's illness when she recounted the events that led to her current predicament.

"And he was really completely"—Miranda looked over her shoulder to confirm they were still alone—"nude?"

"As the day he was born." Charlotte restrained her smile. Mr. Beckham looked nothing like a newborn babe.

"And you're really going to marry him?"

Just hearing Miranda say the words made them all too real.

Every muscle in her body felt heavy and numb. "Yes. I suppose I am. What choice do I have, Miranda? Roland won't take me back. Not that I want to return if it means marrying Felix. At least Mr. Beckham has promised . . ."

"Promised what?"

Before she could answer, Simon burst through the door. "It's done. Now, hurry and grab a pelisse, there's much to do." His gaze jerked to Miranda. "Oh, beg pardon, I didn't know you would still be here."

She and Miranda exchanged a look, Miranda's undoubtedly more amused than her own.

Miranda placed her teacup on the table. "I should go."

"Don't go," Charlotte said in unison with Miranda.

Miranda rose and brushed off her skirts. "No. I really must. I promised Bea and Laurence I would stop by and watch the girls. They're concocting some new invention, and the poor darlings will be left to their own devices."

"Their children are inventors?" Simon asked.

Charlotte rolled her eyes, making sure he noticed. "No. Lord and Lady Montgomery, you buffoon." She redirected her attention to the more reasonable person in the room. "Don't they employ a nanny?"

"Yes. But Bea insists on having a family member available at all times."

"No offense, Miranda, but your sister-in-law has the most outrageous beliefs."

"I think it's delightful," Simon said.

Charlotte glared. "No one asked you."

Miranda laughed. "I'll go and allow you to attend to your business. But I expect to resume this conversation at a later time."

She left in a swish of lilac, Simon's head swiveling around to watch her leave.

"If you ever rush my guests off again, I'll . . ."

As he turned back toward her, he grinned like the fool he was. "You'll what?"

Perhaps she hadn't used a harsh enough tone. "I will . . . I will . . . smash your toes each time we dance."

He grew serious—a strange sight, she had to admit—and threw a hand to his heart. "A most grievous punishment, and one I have fond memories of. Then I must simply not ask you to dance."

Argh!

"Now, find your pelisse. I have my phaeton ready and waiting in front."

"Have you forgotten? I didn't bring a pelisse."

He snapped his fingers. "Right-O. I wasn't at my best when you first arrived. Surely, Her Grace hasn't taken all her pelisses with her?"

Men. "Honoria is several inches shorter than I."

Ignoring her, he rang the bell pull. "Would you rather be warm or fashionable?"

Before she could formulate a suitable setdown—because truly his common sense on the matter stunned her—Frampton appeared.

"Have one of the maids go through Her Grace's clothing and see if she's left a pelisse Lady Charlotte can borrow."

As Frampton turned, Simon called, "And hurry!"

Uncomfortable silence stretched between them as they waited, Charlotte with her arms crossed and glaring, and Simon with the perpetual and ingratiating grin plastered on his face.

She jumped when he severed the stillness. "Come now, Charlotte. We both need a bit of fun outside."

Rose appeared at the doorway, holding out a pelisse of robin's-egg blue and a cream poke bonnet. "I thought this would go best with your bonnet, my lady."

It wasn't the best color on her, favoring more Honoria's fair complexion, but it would have to do. No doubt Honoria left the brightly colored garment behind because it wasn't fitting for a house in mourning. At least the bonnet would shield her face from curious onlookers.

Simon watched as Rose slipped the coat over Charlotte's shoulders.

The hem ended several inches above the bottom of Charlotte's skirts, clashing with the green sprigged muslin. She plucked the bonnet from Rose's fingers and shoved it on her head. Even the open body of the phaeton wouldn't hide the offending mishmash of materials and colors when she sat.

Simon held out his arm. "Shall we?"

Although she strode toward him, she refused to take his arm. *Have him interpret that as he will.*

Without a word, he followed her, grabbed his hat from Frampton, and escorted her to the carriage.

"Is this thing safe?" she asked as she climbed aboard, this time accepting his offered hand. Heat traveled through the fine kid leather of his gloves to hers.

He climbed in next to her and lifted the ribbons. "It depends on who's driving." He winked and snapped the ribbons. The horses darted forward with such force it jolted her into him.

This was a very bad idea.

AH, THE WIND AND SUN ON HIS FACE WAS PURE HEAVEN AS SIMON raced the phaeton up the street. He felt alive again and ready to tackle whatever came next.

Charlotte, on the other hand, latched onto his arm, gripping it until he feared it would grow numb. "Where are we going?"

"First, to our appointment with the vicar to make arrangements at church. I doubt I'll be able to convince him to forego reading the banns, but we can try. I have a weapon." He released the ribbons with one hand and patted his pocket.

Her brown eyes widened, horror written all over her face. "You're going to threaten him with a gun?"

"Worse. A copy of that scandal sheet. A boy on the street by your brother's was handing them out. Charged me three pennies, the rascal."

"Speaking of my brother, if you try to get a special license from the archbishop, Edgerton will surely stop it. Just to punish me more."

Sharp pain poked his chest at the word *punish*. He placed his free hand on hers and, much more gently than the vise-like grip she had on his arm, squeezed.

She jerked away as if he'd burned her. "Please use both hands. The horses are getting out of control."

He laughed until he looked at her face. Lord, she was serious! Some of the joy he'd felt moments before seeped out of him at her distress. Why couldn't she relax and simply enjoy the ride? He returned his attention to the road ahead of him, deftly maneuvering the carriage between two vegetable carts and pedestrians crossing in front of them.

"The people!" She grasped at the ribbons. "You almost ran them over!"

"Nonsense," he said, but he pulled back on the ribbons and slowed the horses a bit.

Tension pulsed the muscles in her jaw when he slid a glance toward her, and she visibly relaxed when he brought them to a halt in front of the church. After throwing the ribbons to a boy waiting in front, he flipped him a shilling, then held out his hand and helped Charlotte down.

"You are mad!" she hissed through her teeth. "And I am mad to agree to this marriage."

He held out his hands in supplication. "Yet, here we are."

"Unfortunately."

Clicking his tongue, he shook his head. "Now, now, Lady Charlotte. We must give the appearance of being in love and desiring to marry as soon as possible." He swept one arm in front of him. "After you."

She trounced inside the church, making no attempt to follow his suggestion. "I'm surprised the ceiling didn't fall on us the moment you stepped through the doors," she whispered.

"Me?" He adopted his most innocent expression. "I'm a paragon of virtue"—he winked—"when I need to be."

"Ha!" Her exclamation drew the attention of a man standing at the transept.

"I say, good man." Simon took off his hat and waved it at the man. "Are you the vicar?"

"I'm the curate, sir. Are you Mr. Beckham and his betrothed?"

After Simon answered him, the curate led them back to a small space next to the sacristy. "The vicar, Mr. Trembly, is at prayer, preparing for your meeting." The curate knocked twice, and they received permission to enter.

As they took their seats, Mr. Trembly studied them. "I'm puzzled and even a little concerned by the request in your letter, Mr. Beckham. Why the great urgency to wed without the customary reading of banns?"

Simon slid a glance toward Charlotte, who raised her brows at him in question. Good, he'd hoped she would allow him to take the lead.

"Good vicar, Mr. Trembly. Our reason is as old as time immemorial. We are so desperately in love, waiting is torturous."

Charlotte snorted, admittedly a rather dainty snort, but it didn't go unnoticed by the vicar.

"Miss? Do you disagree with Mr. Beckham's assessment of your reason?"

"It's Lady Charlotte Talbot, sir. And I just found it rather humorous that my *intended* used such an unimaginative reason. He's usually quite creative."

Well, well. Was there a compliment hidden in that scathing insult?

"Allow me to be more blunt, Lady Charlotte. Do you wish to marry Mr. Beckham? The Church has no desire to force people into a union they do not want."

Simon held his breath and watched Charlotte's face, mentally pleading with her to lie for once in her life and save her reputation.

Mr. Trembly waited, his face a mask of patience.

Simon could almost hear the cogs clicking as Charlotte's sharp mind worked out the simple question.

"I have agreed to marry Mr. Beckham of my own free will, sir."

Clever girl. Not quite a straightforward answer, but truthful.

Mr. Trembly hesitated but a moment. "Very well. But I see no reason to omit the reading of banns. We shall start this Sunday and plan for the wedding three weeks hence." He pulled out a book and dipped his pen into an inkpot. "Which day of the week would you prefer?"

Simon pulled out his trump card. "Sir, may we speak in private?"

The vicar raised his brows. "We are in private, sir."

"What I mean is, may you and I speak in private—without my beloved?"

"That is most irregular."

"Irregularity is a constant state with my *beloved*," Charlotte quipped.

"Well, then. If the lady has no objection."

Both Simon and the vicar stood as Charlotte exited the room.

Simon patted the copy of *The Muckraker* in his pocket and said, "Mr. Trembly, allow me to tell you about my future wife."

⁂

Saints and angels looked down on Charlotte from their lofty places high above in the stained-glass windows of the church. Judging? Advising? Consoling? Pitying? She wasn't certain. She'd never had much faith in help from above.

At least she'd made it to the church alive. For several long moments, she'd had her doubts. Shivers traveled up her spine, expecting the journey back to Pendrake House would be just as harrowing. Although, rather exciting as well. Of course, she would never admit that to Simon. Any encouragement and he'd probably be even more reckless.

The curate had vanished, no doubt leaving once he'd completed his task of showing them to the vicar's study, and she was alone in the large church. She pleaded with the somber faces. "Can you tell him to hurry?"

The door to the vicar's study creaked open, and she looked back up at the window. She could swear one of the saints was smirking.

As was Simon. Mr. Trembly, however, avoided her gaze. He shook Simon's hand. "I can't promise anything, but I'll try to speak with the bishop as soon as I'm able."

With a promise from the vicar to keep them informed, they said their goodbyes.

As they waited for the boy to retrieve Simon's carriage, Charlotte asked, "What did you tell him to change his mind?"

"That you were unable to contain your carnal desires, and I worried that you would wear down my defenses and I would take your innocence before the vows were exchanged. So, to save you from yourself, we should marry as soon as possible."

She gawked at him in disbelief. "Surely, you did not?"

He only smiled, his lips pressed together as if he were containing his laughter.

Oh, she wanted to strangle him! "You cad!"

"Would you feel better if I told him we needed to hurry due to your advanced age? It is a usual condition to obtain a license."

"You are——"

"Incorrigible? Insufferable?" He wiggled his eyebrows. "Irresistible?"

"Argh!"

The carriage pulled up before she could question him further. Once she'd settled in the seat, which suddenly seemed impossibly small, she inched away from him only to have him move closer. "Do you mind?" she huffed.

"Not at all. I like closeness."

Argh!

He snapped the ribbons. "Where to, my lady? The park? A ride along Rotten Row?"

"Home."

He turned a sour look her way. "Stop being such a stick in the mud. Where's your sense of adventure? You'd think you'd be happy to get out of the house and get some air."

"Very well, then. Take me to the modiste. I need some more gowns. Rose didn't bring many with her."

"I asked your brother to send your clothing."

Oh, but he had so much to learn. "And you expect him to respect your request?"

He arched that devilish dark brow at her again. "To the modiste then. Just don't bankrupt me."

When he guided the carriage to the left at the end of the street, she frowned. "You're going the wrong way. Madame Treadwell's shop is to the right."

"We're taking the scenic route through the park." He snapped the ribbons again, and the horses picked up speed.

Her body was thrust back into the squab of the carriage, and she clutched her bonnet to her head lest it fly off.

The man was mad. Reckless. Irresponsible.

And she had never felt more exhilarated.

CHAPTER 9

T he days following Simon's meeting with Edgerton flew by.
He'd written to his family with the news of his upcoming
nuptials. Word arrived from the bishop on a Monday that, after
carefully considering the information Simon presented to the
vicar, he would issue a license for Simon and Charlotte to marry
at the time of their choosing.

Charlotte insisted on wearing a new gown for the wedding.
And when Madame Treadwell assured them the gown would be
ready the following Wednesday, Simon called on the vicar and set
the wedding for Thursday morning next.

Lady Miranda agreed to be Charlotte's witness for the
ceremony. And although Simon had written to Drake to inform
him of the startling development, he held little hope his friend
would be at his side to support him in his moment of . . . *joy.*
Lady Miranda suggested her brother, the Viscount Montgomery,
would be happy to act as a proxy.

Charlotte refused to contact her brother, so Simon wrote on
her behalf, appealing with the man to put aside his personal

feelings and, as her closest living male relative, give her away. The marquess's answer came in the form of several large trunks containing all of Charlotte's clothes.

Ripped to shreds.

Thank goodness Simon had taken her to the modiste after they had met with the vicar—which resulted in a rather large bill. Simon's sympathy for his father increased. How could women's clothing cost so much? As he'd rather not be bothered with bills for fripperies, he'd have to increase Charlotte's pin money allotment. Let her manage her own purchases.

On Frampton's suggestion—perhaps instigated with encouragement from Charlotte—the remaining staff was called back into duty. The house bustled with activity as if the wedding were a cause for celebration. Flowers arrived, filling the house with fragrant scents of hyacinth, peonies, and lilac.

As Simon turned sideways, narrowly missing a footman carrying a vase with an enormous arrangement of pink and white peonies into the large parlor, Frampton announced, "Your family has arrived, sir."

With the words barely out of Frampton's mouth, Simon braced himself as his sisters launched themselves at him.

"When can we meet her?" Frannie asked.

Kate swatted his arm. "Why didn't you tell us you were courting?"

Georgie bounced on her toes as she clasped his arm. "What's she like? Is she pretty?"

"Of course, she's pretty, Georgie! Simon wouldn't marry someone who was plain."

Beth frowned. "You're being shallow, Rebecca."

"Girls, girls," his mother intervened. "Let Simon catch his breath." She kissed him on the cheek and whispered, "But I want to know all of those things as well. I read the scandal sheet but didn't tell your father."

His father stood silently by, grinning at the scene. The knave!

"Father, come get these females off of me," Simon said, still hugging three of his sisters close to him. He needed either more arms or longer arms to wrap around them all.

"You're on your own, son. That will teach you to find a sweetheart without so much as a by-your-leave to your family."

Simon extracted himself from all the feminine hands and strode to his father. "It's good to see you're in fine health, Father."

His father's blue eyes widened. "Why wouldn't I be? Fit as a fiddle." He patted his midsection. "Although a little wider in the middle."

"Still speaking in rhymes, I see."

With a hard swat on Simon's back, his father let out a huge guffaw.

Lord, how he loved his gregarious family.

Frampton remained in the doorway, his typically stoic expression one of a man who had been run over by a coach and four. When the Beckhams gathered in toto, they had that effect on people. "Shall I bring tea, sir?"

"And sandwiches. Georgie has the appetite of a horse." He slid a glance at his youngest sister.

She pouted, much like twelve-year-old children do. "I do not!"

"Very well. Frampton, no sandwiches, then."

"Wait!" Georgie called. "I didn't say I didn't want them."

After Frampton bowed and left them, Simon's mother pulled him toward the sofa. "You said so little in your letter. Tell us about Charlotte." Her eyes told him she would have more questions when they could speak privately.

"First, it's Lady Charlotte, and I would advise you all to be respectful."

His father settled into a wingback, away from all the women.

"Her family is of the peerage? Judith, you failed to mention that." His father sent his mother a chastising glance.

"Oooh, Simon." His eldest sister, Rebecca, turned toward him from where she had been admiring a portrait. His own situation made him wonder why, at three and twenty, she still hadn't married. She was pretty enough. Of course, he found all women were pretty, and being his sister, he may have been a trifle biased.

"Yes," Simon answered, reluctant to put forth too many details at the moment. He'd prefer they not make any judgments before meeting his intended. "Her brother is a marquess. And to answer Georgie's question, yes, she's very pretty with her dark hair and eyes. Fair warning, she's a bit prickly. Outspoken, too."

Frannie, his third eldest sister, straightened. "Did the duke introduce you?"

"In a manner of speaking. She attended Drake's house party last summer."

Smoothing her skirts, his mother gave him *the look*. "I'm still disappointed in both you and His Grace for that act of duplicity. But I suppose since it worked out well . . ."

Like a naughty schoolboy, he grinned at her. "It was all Drake's idea."

"Really, Simon. You should show more respect. He's a duke." Always the odd woman out, Beth's serious nature brought him to task.

"He doesn't mind. Truly. I think if he'd had his way, he would have allowed me to continue acting as duke in his stead."

"Thank heavens he didn't."

His head swung toward the door at the seductive alto. A teasing smile tilted her lips, and color rose to her cheeks. "Charlotte! You're back." Both he and his father bolted from their seats.

Charlotte's gaze flitted to each of his sisters, finally piercing him with her dark eyes. Lord, those eyes pulled him in and dragged him under until he struggled to breathe.

Georgie let out a little, "Oooh. You're in trouble."

More trouble than his adorable, rambunctious sister realized.

A SEA OF DARK HEADS AND LAUGHING VOICES SWELLED BEFORE Charlotte. Panic knotted in her throat as seven smiling faces turned toward her. Were they all like her future husband? How would she endure so much ebullience all at once? All the happiness—the *joy* would suffocate her. How could she trust so many *nice* people?

When Frampton had told her Simon was in the large parlor, she'd only wanted to tell him she had returned from the modiste. Even though Simon offered to take her in his phaeton, she insisted on going by herself, having barely survived Simon's reckless driving previously. But at that moment, she'd wished she had simply gone straight to her room.

The older woman among the tide of females rose and approached, her hands outstretched in greeting. "My dear Lady Charlotte. Simon's description of you pales in comparison to reality." As the woman clasped Charlotte's hands in her own, she turned toward the older gentleman. "She's lovely, Teddy, isn't she?"

"Indeed," the man, who could only be Simon's father, answered. Although older, he had the same merry blue eyes and handsome face. "Our son has acquired himself a diamond, Judith."

Charlotte's gaze snapped toward Simon. What in the world had he told them?

The man himself slithered up to her. "Lady Charlotte, may I present my mother, Mrs. Judith Beckham and my father, Mr. Theodore Beckham."

A girl about ten or twelve—Charlotte was terrible with the ages of children—rushed up, grabbing Simon's arm. "Me next, me next."

"Georgie hates that as the youngest, she's always introduced last." He gazed down at the girl, his eyes filled with such affection it squeezed what Charlotte imagined was her heart. "This bit of fluff is my sister Georgina. But even at the ripe age of twelve, she prefers to be called Georgie. I think she was Father's last attempt at another son, and she's trying to accommodate him."

The elder Mr. Beckham chuffed a laugh.

Charlotte thought Georgie was rather like a young Anne Weatherby. If so, Mr. Beckham had his hands full, poor man. "I'm pleased to meet you, Georgie."

Simon continued the introductions.

Rebecca, the eldest, executed a perfect curtsy. Simon teased her that he would have to find her a husband because she was growing dangerously close to being on the shelf. "Why soon, you'll be Charlotte's age. How old are you again, *darling*?"

Charlotte glowered daggers at him, hoping one would land directly in his chest.

Beth, the second eldest, announced she was very pleased to meet a woman who could tolerate her brother enough to marry him.

"Whether I can tolerate him is yet to be determined, Miss Beth." Charlotte stole a peek toward her intended, dismayed when he had no reaction.

"Oh, don't change your mind," fifteen-year-old Kate said, a genuine pleading in her voice. "Mama has been so worried he would never marry. Papa can't live forever, you know."

Mr. Beckham coughed. "Don't bring out the shovel yet, Katie girl."

Frannie, the middle sister, stood off to the side. Simon pulled her forward. "Don't be shy, Frannie. Charlotte doesn't bite." He delivered one of his devilish winks. "Much."

Charlotte decided she liked Frannie, who seemed to be the one calm port in the storm of Beckhams. Quiet and reserved, Frannie seemed to take in everything around her as if she were collecting it for future use. "Simon says your brother is a marquess."

Oh, she really didn't want to talk about Roland, especially after what he did to her gowns. But she also didn't want to be rude to the girl. "Yes. The Marquess of Edgerton."

Mr. Beckham stiffened. His head jerked toward Simon, then to his wife, his eyes questioning.

Simon shifted, his usual carefree demeanor vanishing. He rubbed the back of his neck. "Um. I may have failed to provide that one little detail."

The mood in the room changed in an instant, and the entire Beckham family—moments ago warm and gregarious—appeared uncomfortable.

Guilt by association. Over the years, Charlotte had grown accustomed to the feeling. She turned toward Simon. "Perhaps I should excuse myself and allow you time with your family in private. I didn't mean to intrude." As if she wasn't already aware, Simon's family's reactions confirmed it.

The marriage was destined for disaster.

Silence fell over the group—taut and awkward.

A footman and maid appeared with trays of tea and sandwiches.

Quiet Frannie spoke up. "She can't help who she's related to." She took Charlotte's hand, and although Charlotte's first reaction was to pull away, she resisted. "Stay, Lady Charlotte, and have refreshment with us."

The girl's blue eyes, lined with thick dark lashes, so like her brother's, met Charlotte's with a sharp understanding. Charlotte found such unexpected kindness overwhelming. She really needed to remove herself from the situation.

Before she could open her mouth and make her apologies, a

commotion arose from deep in the house. Voices grew closer, and Burwood barreled into the room. Moments later, Honoria waddled in behind him. Charlotte worried she would have the baby on the spot.

"Drake!" Simon threw his hands out as if he'd expected the duke.

Honoria's gaze slipped between Charlotte, Simon, and his family, her face a mask of concern. She stepped close to Charlotte and whispered, "Has the wedding occurred already?"

Charlotte shook her head. "It's tomorrow. My condolences about Lady Compton. But you shouldn't have left on our account."

"There wasn't anything else I could do. I felt so helpless. Simon's letter gave me purpose."

"It's not your mess to clean up."

Honoria's brows lifted. "A mess? Simon was vague in his letter." Honoria's gaze darted toward Simon, who had pulled Burwood into a fierce hug. "What happened?"

Charlotte nodded toward Simon's family, who had seemed to forget about her and were greeting Burwood. "Not now in front of his family. I was just trying to extricate myself when you arrived."

"Food!" Burwood exclaimed and plucked a sandwich from the tray. "I'm famished. We hurried back as soon as we received your letter, Simon."

Honoria gazed at her husband with so much love, Charlotte had to look away. "You would think he was the one feeding two people."

A sandwich half-shoved in his mouth, the duke turned and hurried to Honoria's side, wrapping an arm around her waist. He swallowed with a gulp. "I'm an insensitive dolt. Do you want a sandwich?"

"No. I want to be introduced to our guests and then go upstairs with Lady Charlotte. My back hurts from our journey."

Charlotte waited while Simon made the introductions, reassured that Honoria had made the perfect excuse for her exit.

"You will stay with us, of course. I'll tell Frampton to prepare rooms. Now, if you would all excuse me." Honoria took Charlotte's arm and led her out of the room.

When they were at the staircase, Honoria leaned in. "Tell me exactly what happened."

"Let's get you upstairs first and settled. This is going to take a while."

❦

As Georgie attacked a cucumber sandwich, and Simon's other sisters and mother prepared tea, Drake pulled him by the elbow. "What the blazes, Simon? I'm barely gone two weeks, and you decide to get married. Did you finally come to your senses and admit your feelings for Lady Charlotte?"

"What feelings? Loathing? Annoyance? The way she drains all the joy from a room?"

"Attraction?"

Simon wanted to wipe the smug look off his friend's face. "Attraction aside—and I admit to nothing—I can't talk about what happened right now with my family present, although my mother has read about it in that scandal sheet."

"*The Muckraker?*"

"Yes. And I'd like to keep it from my father and sisters. As far as they know, this is a love match."

"And just how do you expect to pull that off?"

"I fooled society into thinking I was a duke. How hard can this be?"

"Need I remind you that you're not the only party in this arrangement? What about Lady Charlotte? Does she truly want this?"

"No. But she knows it's the only way."

"Simon!" his mother called. "Quit monopolizing the duke."

"We'll discuss this later. But will you at least stand by my side tomorrow?"

"Yes," his friend said. "But I won't like being part of this deception."

Honestly, neither would he.

CHAPTER 10

The next morning, Charlotte stared out the window of her bedchamber. Dark clouds hovered, reflecting her mood. The gray skies scowled in ominous portent. Her hand trembled as she released the curtain and whispered a prayer it wouldn't thunder and lightning. At least, should it storm, the daylight kept the night's darker terrors at bay.

When Honoria had married the duke last summer, Lady Stratford kissed her daughter and said, "Happy the bride the sun shines upon."

Charlotte cast another glance out the window, and a derisive laugh escaped that the building storm forecasted her fate.

Despite Honoria's insistence that they could find another way to salvage her reputation, Charlotte knew accepting Simon's offer was the only way. And even marriage wouldn't undo the damage *The Muckraker* had already wrought. Lady Cartwright had been in Madame Treadwell's when Charlotte went for her last fitting, and the woman had given Charlotte the cut direct.

Lady Cartwright! The very woman who orchestrated a

compromise between her own daughter and the Duke of Ashton. *The nerve! The audacity!*

Well, Charlotte would show them all. She'd hold her head high and act like nothing had happened.

She sighed. Who was she fooling? They'd laugh behind her back that she had married below her station, that she had been so disgraced she had no other choice than to marry a commoner —and a rake.

"Charlotte?"

She turned at Honoria's soft voice. Goodness, her friend looked exhausted. She held a hand to her back, her slight frame bulging with the weight of the child inside her.

Charlotte worried for her friend. "Are you sure you want to attend this debacle?"

"There is still time to change your mind if you want."

Charlotte shook her head. "No. It isn't like I would make a good match with someone else now. And Mr. Beckham has promised to respect all my wishes. He even put it in writing as I asked." An ironic smile tugged at her lips. "And at least he's not Lord Middlebury. Nash told me about the scheme Beatrix Townsend concocted to get out of that mess. Of course, Nash played a huge part in it. Which he was quite proud of. And that worked out well for her."

"Well, then we best get you to the church. Drake will accompany Simon, but I thought I would ride in the carriage with you. Miranda will meet us there."

As they turned to exit the room, Simon's father appeared. "Pardon, ladies. Lady Charlotte, I wondered if you would do me the honor of escorting you to church and walking you down the aisle. I'm not your father, but"—he splayed his hands out—"I will be your father-in-law."

Something strange lodged in Charlotte's throat. She'd hardly said two words to Simon's family at supper the previous evening. Granted, her lack of participation didn't deter the rest of them from chattering excitedly. Joyous exuberance emanated from them. Even Frannie, the quiet one, cracked a few jokes at Simon's expense, which—to Charlotte's further annoyance—he received in good fun. Such family love and acceptance was foreign to Charlotte, and although they tried to pull her into the conversation, she felt like an orphaned child outside in the cold, peeking in through a window and gazing upon a warm hearth and full table.

No one brought up Roland again, but Charlotte felt him lurking in the shadows. And yet, Mr. Beckham was offering to act in Roland's stead. Why would he offer such kindness?

Suspicion colored her words. "Did Simon ask you to do this?" And more importantly, if he did, what would he want in return?

"Don't be angry with him on your wedding day, my lady. He only mentioned that your brother was unable to attend, and you had no other male relative available."

Unable. Simon had tempered the truth, but in Mr. Beckham's eyes she could see he knew. The mass in her throat grew, and she pushed it down so she could speak. "That would be lovely, Mr. Beckham."

"Oh, and before I forget." Mr. Beckham reached into his pocket and pulled out a strand of pearls. "From your future husband—a wedding gift. He mentioned you have been unable to locate your jewels."

Unable again. She had no jewels, not any longer.

He held them out. "May I?"

It was a generous and thoughtful gesture. Certainly not one she expected for a marriage of convenience. She nodded and turned her back to him, allowing him to slip the necklace around her and fasten it.

Charlotte traced her fingers over the lustrous pearls, noting their fine quality. Simple and elegant, something she would have chosen for herself. How did he know they would be so perfect?

"Oh, Charlotte, they're lovely," Honoria said.

"Almost as lovely as the bride." Mr. Beckham smiled and held out his arm. "Now, shall we proceed? You have an anxious bridegroom awaiting you."

As she slipped her hand over his arm, her gaze flitted to Honoria, who appeared to be on the verge of tears. "None of that, Your Grace. Weddings are supposed to be joyous occasions."

If only it truly was.

"And no *Your Grace*, today, Charlotte. At least not when we're alone. Today we are simply friends and equals."

As they settled in the carriage, Mr. Beckham regaled them with stories of Simon as a boy. Mischief followed him everywhere, and with five younger sisters, he directed the majority of his pranks toward them. And none of it surprised Charlotte.

"Once," Mr. Beckham said, wiping tears from his eyes from the last account of ridiculous behavior, "Simon snuck into Rebecca's room at night and tied her braids to the bedpost."

"Oh, my goodness!" Honoria said, her hand held over her mouth to hold in her laughter.

"Did you beat him?" Charlotte asked.

The man laughed. *Laughed.*

Then his eyes widened. "Good gracious. You're serious."

"Well, yes. Didn't you punish him?" Punishment was Charlotte's close companion as a child—regardless if she deserved it. She could recall times when she'd received a beating simply for good measure after one of her brothers had done something naughty.

"Punish?" Mr. Beckham seemed to consider the word. "In a matter of speaking. Disciplined, for certain. For Simon, staying still was torture. As you no doubt have noticed about your future husband, he is a whirling dervish. The worst sentence for him was to be kept in his room for a day with nothing to do except read."

Honoria seemed to take it all in. "That might explain his disdain for books."

"Oh, he doesn't hate them," Mr. Beckham continued. "He just prefers doing rather than reading about it. There was nothing worse for him than to read about the adventures of knights and not be able to run outside and pretend he was the one fighting dragons and winning the fair maiden."

"And racing chariots, no doubt," Charlotte said, remembering how he drove the phaeton like a demon.

Mr. Beckham reached across the seat and patted Charlotte's hand. "You do understand him! And now he has won his fair maiden and is off to start a new adventure."

Before Charlotte could respond, the carriage slowed, coming to a halt before the church. Fat drops of rain plopped against the pavement and church steps in greeting. She felt numb, empty inside, as her gaze locked on the church doors where her future awaited.

Rather than an adventure, Charlotte envisioned her upcoming marriage as another punishment for something she hadn't done. And like Simon, sitting in his room relegated to reading rather than doing, she felt trapped in a prison of someone else's making.

❦

SIMON PACED THE AREA NEXT TO THE TRANSEPT. RAIN BATTERED against the church windows with angry fists. A warning? His skin felt tight and his hands clammy.

Drake huffed. "Will you stand still for one moment? You've pulled your cravat loose from tugging at it."

As Drake repaired the damage, Simon's fingers tapped restlessly against his leg. "Do you think she's here?"

Drake gave a curt nod. Whether it was from satisfaction that he'd fixed the neckcloth or in answer to Simon's question, Simon wasn't sure, until he said, "Honoria will see to it."

When Simon had explained everything that had transpired, Drake didn't even question Simon's plan to marry Charlotte. "You must, Simon. It's the right thing to do. I'm proud of you. I know how hard that was for you."

Simon forced a smile. "It's not so bad. She hates me. I hate her. I'll probably be dead in a year or so and leave her a wealthy widow. She wins."

"Don't say that! And why didn't you tell me you were on the verge of another attack when we left for Somerset?"

Simon arched a brow at his friend. "Because Honoria needed you more than I did."

Ignoring his own admonition not to fidget, Drake ran a hand around his neck. "But if I'd been there, this wouldn't have happened."

Simon refused to think about what ifs. Looking back accomplished nothing. Fortunately or unfortunately, depending on how one viewed it, the vicar appeared and motioned Simon and Drake to take their places.

Drake's besotted gaze followed Honoria as she took her seat in the front next to Anne Weatherby, and a bittersweet longing washed over Simon. He never considered himself a romantic, but at that moment, he wished more than anything that his marriage would be one like his friends'—happy and filled with love.

His mother and sisters beamed at him from the other side of the church.

Inside, he felt hollow, as if someone had reached inside and scooped out his intestines.

Until the doors of the nave opened and Lady Miranda made her way to the front of the church. Simon held his breath, waiting for Charlotte to appear. A long moment followed before she entered the church.

Air still trapped in his lungs, he could only stare. Dazzling in her new gown, she strode forward on his father's arm. The cream-colored fabric complemented her dark coloring to perfection. And she wore the pearls he gave her.

Surely, that was a good sign.

She didn't smile when he caught her eye, but she didn't glare at him either. She simply appeared—resigned. He finally let the air out of his lungs. When his father placed Charlotte's hand in his, the only one to express any emotion was his father, who appeared on the verge of tears. The man no doubt expected a grandson within a year.

Each recited their vows without stumbling. Although Simon's *I will* rang louder than Charlotte's, neither hesitated, and Simon reluctantly admired her strength to face the situation head-on. It was as if he were concluding one of the complicated business arrangements he'd negotiated for Drake.

Her eyes widened for a second when he slipped the ring on her finger. He'd chosen a perfect opal set in a simple gold band flanked by two sapphires. The opal reminded him of Charlotte, multicolored, unpredictable and changing, but breathtakingly beautiful.

The hollow sensation returned, this time located in his chest, but he brushed it aside as soon as the ceremony ended and friends and family descended upon them, huddled under umbrellas outside the church.

Among them, Drake's Aunt Kitty, the Countess of Gryffin, who had received wind of it from Drake, leaned upon her cane some distance from his family.

"Kiss her, Simon!" Georgie said, while his mother dabbed at her eyes with a handkerchief.

"Now, Georgie. Such things are private." Simon peeked toward Charlotte, expecting to see a look of horror on her face.

She shrugged. "It's fine. They expect it."

He leaned in and whispered, "A chaste peck then." Such was his intention, but when he brushed his lips lightly against hers, tingles shot through him. Suddenly, he wanted more. He threaded his umbrella-free arm around her waist and deepened the kiss. Fevered visions of getting her out of that lovely dress raced through his mind.

Perhaps he was having another malaria attack? He pulled back, surprised she hadn't pushed him away first. "My apologies."

Her dark eyes widened and appeared almost black as she stared at him. She lifted a hand to her lips—which had captured his attention to the omission of all else. Pink bloomed on her cheeks. "It's fine. Just don't let it happen again."

The slow smile that had sent many ladies into a swoon crept across his face. Oh, she very much wanted it to happen again.

As did he.

⚜

WHAT IN THE WORLD WAS THAT? CHARLOTTE RESISTED BRUSHING at her tingling lips again. Everyone watched them with interest. The Countess of Gryffin's gray brows rose. Mrs. Beckham and several of Simon's sisters—she couldn't tell which—sighed.

And Simon, the rake, grinned like the buffoon he was.

"Don't look so pleased with yourself," she whispered. "If that was a chaste kiss, I shudder at what you think of as carnal."

He laughed, the cad. "I might enjoy making you shudder."

Oh. Oh! "You, sir, are incorrigible."

He placed his hat on his head and gave it a little tap at the top. "So you've said. Repeatedly. Might I suggest you expand your vocabulary? I understand the duke has a magnificent dictionary in his library."

The countess hobbled toward them. "Should I wish you joy or condolences? I believe I've never witnessed a more somber bride. And you, sir!" She smacked Simon on the arm and lowered her voice. "I read that gossip rag. If even half of it is true, I'm ashamed of you. But at least you're doing the right thing by the girl."

"Thank you?" Simon said, more question than statement.

The countess's gaze softened as she raked it over Charlotte. "If anyone can get this rascal to toe the line, I believe it's you. He needs a firm hand."

Simon chortled a laugh, and Charlotte suspected he'd imagined something inappropriate. She had grown accustomed to such reactions from her brother, Nash.

Holding out his arm, Simon led her to—of all things—the phaeton.

"Oh, no. No, no, no. It's raining. Don't you have another conveyance? Or perhaps I can ride back to Pendrake House with Honoria."

He adopted the most innocent of expressions, belying the rake within. "I have the top up."

"It's still open in front. We'll get soaked."

"Not the way I drive. We'll race right through the raindrops."

She snorted her disbelief. "That's what I'm afraid of." She folded her arms over her chest. "No."

"I promise. I'll behave." He waggled his dark brows. "It will be my wedding gift to you."

"What? To frighten me into an early grave? A wet grave, I might add."

His only answer was to laugh and hand her into the carriage of death.

Settling next to her, he picked up the ribbons and gave them a snap. "Now that we're alone, are we going to talk about that kiss?"

It was precisely what she didn't want to talk about. But the memory of the kiss burned her lips.

CHAPTER 11

Wonder of wonders, to Charlotte's surprise, they made it back to Pendrake House relatively dry and without further discussion of that kiss. Only the hem of her lovely gown where it peeped out from beneath her pelisse was damp, and that had more than likely occurred when they stood outside the church.

Luckily, Simon didn't comment as he pulled the phaeton up to the house and threw the ribbons to the groom. He opened the umbrella and held out a hand to help her down. "Ready to face our adoring family, Mrs. Beckham?"

"It's still Lady Charlotte, regardless."

Had she imagined the flicker of disappointment that passed over his face?

Frampton opened the door for them, ushering them inside and taking Charlotte's pelisse and Simon's hat. "Felicitations, Lady Charlotte. Mr. Beckham."

Charlotte darted a smug glance toward her husband. "You see?"

"Very well. Lady Charlotte Beckham. But I presume I'm

allowed to call you Charlotte?" He paused, studying her. "Or do you have a pet name you prefer? Something for when we're in private?" The rogue waggled those dark brows at her again.

"Will you cease that ridiculous movement? And to remind you, there will be no *private* moments. You agreed."

"Not even after that kiss?"

She adopted her most innocent expression. Which, in truth, was probably as unnatural for her as it was for him. "What kiss?"

He leaned in, his incredible blue eyes growing hooded. His voice slid over her, caressing her skin as sultry and soft as velvet. "You know very well what kiss."

Even with the damp, cold early April day, heat raced up her neck to her cheeks.

The cad had the audacity to grin.

Thankfully, before the rogue could say something else and embarrass her further, Frampton opened the door again, and Simon's family poured into the entryway. Charlotte imagined a rapid, rushing stream, unfettered and wild.

What had she got herself into?

His father shook rain from his hat and handed it to Frampton. "A devil of a day to be married, but rain does make young things grow."

Simon laughed, loud and hearty. "Father, I think that's only for plants."

"Nonsense. Why, Rebecca was conceived in the worst possible storm imaginable."

Mrs. Beckham's face whitened. "Teddy! You're embarrassing our new daughter."

Charlotte blinked, the description of *daughter* catching her off-guard.

Once Honoria and Drake arrived, they all gathered for a sumptuous wedding breakfast. Charlotte, however, had little appetite, and she pushed her eggs around her plate with her fork.

Keeping her responses succinct, she answered everyone's questions as truthfully and carefully as possible.

Kate lifted a scone from her plate. "When did you know you loved my brother?"

Well aware Simon studied her, Charlotte smiled. "Who says I love him? Perhaps he simply wore down my defenses?"

Mr. Beckham barked a laugh. "That does sound like Simon. Never one to give up on a challenge."

Burwood nodded. "I believe I said the very thing to Miss Weatherby last year when she indicated interest in him. Of course, that's when she thought he was the duke."

Simon's eyes widened. "You did? Was that before she latched herself onto you?"

"Yes. During the fox hunt."

Like Charlotte, Honoria pushed her food around aimlessly. "Let's not rehash that debacle." She moaned a little as she shifted in her seat.

Burwood placed a hand on Honoria's arm, his brow furrowed. "Darling, are you feeling unwell?"

"Simply tired."

Mrs. Beckham exchanged a look with her husband. "Your Grace, forgive me. But when is your confinement expected?"

"Not for another few weeks. However, I wish it were sooner. If I grow any larger, I won't be able to reach anything."

True, Honoria's girth prevented her from sitting closer to the table.

And although the food was perfectly prepared and delicious, guilt soured Charlotte's stomach like bad fish. Honoria would still be with her family in Somerset, the Beckhams would be attending to their lives in Wiltshire, and she would be . . . She pushed that thought from her mind. Even if Roland hadn't arranged the horrendous match with Felix, since Nash had left for America, her life under Roland's critical eye had grown unbearable.

At least marriage to Simon would provide some freedom—and hopefully not imprisonment of a different variety.

"Lady Charlotte." The Countess Gryffin pulled Charlotte from her depressing musings. The old woman had been unusually silent throughout the day's events. "Is this rascal going to take you anywhere exciting for your wedding trip?"

Charlotte's fork clattered to her plate. Alone with Simon. She hadn't thought about that. "Are you?"

A chagrined grimace passed over Simon's face. "Well, everything was so rushed, I hadn't actually thought about it."

"And why was it rushed, brother?" Beth asked.

Mrs. Beckham sent her daughter a castigatory glance. "Beth! Forgive her, Lady Charlotte. Beth tends to speak her mind."

A trait Charlotte admired, for the most part. Except at that moment.

"Um." Simon swallowed an overly large bite of toast and wiped his mouth with the serviette.

Perhaps he would choke. Charlotte smiled at the thought.

"I worried she would change her mind," Simon continued, completely ignoring her. "You women are so mercurial, especially my lovely wife."

"Come to my senses, you mean," she muttered.

Turning toward her, he grew serious. "Would you like to go somewhere? There is a very nice cottage on my father's estate. Fully equipped, and the hunting and fishing are marvelous."

Surely, he wasn't serious?

Lady Gryffin gawked in disbelief. "Good grief, man!" She turned toward her great-nephew. "Talk some sense into him, Drake." She speared a kipper and shook her head. "Fishing and hunting. On a wedding trip. Take her somewhere romantic. To Florence. Venice."

"What about Scotland?" Kate asked.

Lady Gryffin shook her head. "Don't go to Scotland this time of year, much too cold."

Location wasn't Charlotte's concern as much as the fact that she would be alone with Simon for an extended period. "Perhaps we can discuss it later?"

Simon patted her hand. "As you wish, dumpling."

Dumpling!!

"Thank you, pudding face."

Georgie spit out her milk.

Burwood chuckled into his serviette. "If you would all excuse us. I think I will get my wife upstairs to rest for a while. Please make yourselves at home."

An awkward silence filled the space Honoria and Burwood left with their departure.

"Would you like to rest as well, dearest?" Simon said, with only the slightest trace of acid in the endearment.

Beth giggled.

"What's so funny?" Georgie asked.

Charlotte darted a glance at Simon, who grinned like the cat who got the cream. "You are incorrigible," she whispered.

Simon rose and pulled out her chair. He leaned down, his warm breath tickling the nape of her neck. "So you've told me. Now, shall we go up and allow my family to imagine all sorts of things?"

Only married to the man for a few hours, Charlotte already regretted it.

As Simon led Charlotte upstairs, he formulated a plan. His father's words rang true. He never gave up on a challenge.

And wooing Lady Charlotte Talbot—err, Beckham—would be a monumental challenge. Determined to crack her hard outer shell and reveal the heart that he knew resided within, he would persevere until he prevailed. Not that he wanted her to fall in love with him.

Heaven forbid! The wistful romantic thoughts he'd had earlier must have been because the wedding ceremony addled his brain. But if the marriage had any chance of providing an heir, she'd have to allow him to touch her.

Oh, how he wanted to touch her—and more.

He slid a gaze over at her.

Passive? No. Not in the least. Determined was more like it. Determined to resist his charms.

A slow smile tugged at his lips.

We'll see about that, my lady.

When he paused and opened the door of the room next to his, she sent him a quizzical look. "My room is at the end of the hall."

"It was. Yes. I instructed Frampton and Rose to move your belongings to the room next to mine. For appearances, you understand."

Those seductive brown eyes narrowed. "But it is *my* room?"

"As opposed to ours? Yes."

"And Honoria and Burwood?"

"Ah, if you're worried about that, they're in the other wing." He inclined his head to the left. "After they were married, I insisted on a room farther from theirs." He grinned. "To help with the noise."

"Noi—" Her cheeks reddened. Just as he hoped.

"Now, shall we have our discussion out in the hallway, or go inside where it's private?" Without waiting for her answer, he gave her a gentle push into the room.

The sweet scent of peonies filled the room, placed there by his request. Unbidden, his gaze drifted to the bed where a maid had already turned down the counterpane.

If only.

Charlotte glared at him, popping that dream like a fragile soap bubble on a strong breeze. "What is it you wish to *discuss*?"

"Well, our wedding trip, for one."

She sat in a chair by the window—far away from the tempting bed. "Can't we stay here in London?"

His new wife might think him simple-minded, but he'd already developed a strong argument to convince her. "If we remain here, it will be harder to keep up appearances. Especially if my family extends their stay. They will expect us to be, shall we say, privately occupied most of the time. Do you want to be cooped up in your room for days on end? Or would you rather go somewhere away from watchful eyes where you can spend your days coming and going as you wish?"

As she sucked in half of her bottom lip and worried it with her teeth, his blood stirred, remembering their kiss at the church.

"What if I don't mind staying in my room for days?"

Fine for her. But he would surely go mad if he had to stare at the four walls of his bedchamber for days. However, if he could get her into bed, that was another matter entirely.

Her brows drew down into a sharp V. "What are you thinking about? You've gone from looking horrified to enormously pleased."

He took a seat on the bed, hoping to nudge her mind toward more passionate pursuits. "I was thinking about being alone with you."

"Hmph. And get off my bed." The determination in her voice faltered—or was that his imagination? "Your father said you hate to be confined to your room. He said it was your punishment as a child."

Surprised both that his father would share this information and she remembered it, he nodded. "Yes, that's true."

Unreflected in her eyes, the smile spreading across her face was positively malicious. "Then perhaps a week isn't long enough? Don't wedding trips typically last months?"

Dear God! She'd kill him within the first year. Chills ran up his spine, his limbs grew numb, and he wanted to sprint from the room—and from her. To find his phaeton, the fastest horse, the riskiest dare—anything to save him from staying in one place and drowning of boredom. He forced down the mass in his throat. "You're serious?"

"Quite. But please tell me this *cottage* you mentioned is larger than a tenant's hovel. I require servants and some comforts."

What? He blinked, trying to clear his head. "I don't understand."

Her dry laugh brought him up short. "You wouldn't. You expect the worst from me, it's clear. But I yield to your argument. Reluctantly. Besides, Honoria's time of confinement grows near, and she and Burwood need time alone rather than worrying about us. And as much as I love to read, unlike my dear friend, I can only do it for so long before I need other diversions. So tell me about this cottage."

He wanted to kiss her. To jump up, grab her by the shoulders, and kiss her so hard it made her head spin. But he promised himself he would go slowly. To ease into things with her. And she had just given him an enormous gift. The last thing he wanted to do was frighten her and have her rescind her agreement.

"It's a dower house, actually. It was my grandmother's before she died. It's very cozy, and yes, large enough for a few servants, but still providing privacy for us."

"And you would spend the time hunting and fishing? Leaving me alone?"

He studied her, unsure how he should answer. Did she truly want him to leave her alone, or was she casting a line of her own, hoping he would bite? "I will yield to your will. If you want me with you, I will be with you. If you want me away, I will find something with which to occupy myself."

"And how will being confined to a cottage differ from remaining in my room here?"

"No one will question us. Swindon is but a half-hour away. Or, should you wish to spend time with my family, they are nearby but will not bother us unless invited. If you like to ride, we have a fine stable of horses. If you want a fête, my family would be happy to host one and introduce you to neighbors and friends."

"Very well. If you promise I shall have my own room there as well."

He placed his hand on his heart and adopted the most solemn expression he could muster. "I promise. It will take time to prepare. I'll advise my parents this evening when we reemerge for supper. We can leave in a few days."

"Not tomorrow?"

He shook his head. "Allow my parents to return before us and have servants sent to ready the house. But having them out from underfoot will help here as well. Drake and Honoria are aware of our situation."

"Speaking of, how long do you intend to remain here in my room?"

"At least a few hours. I wouldn't want to chance anyone seeing me slip into my room alone." Oh, it was an excuse, for certain, and it pleased him that it vexed her—just a little.

She exhaled a sigh. "Well, then. What shall we do to pass the time?"

He grinned. "I have some ideas."

CHAPTER 12

C ards. Charlotte sighed, half in relief, half in exasperation.
Simon wanted to play cards. After checking to confirm no
servants roamed the hallway, Simon sneaked into his room for a
deck of cards and some markers, telling her he'd anticipated
things in advance and had pilfered some from the duke's billiard
room.

Thirteen hands later, why he had chosen such a pastime
became clear.

He turned over a six of spades, a five of diamonds, a seven of
spades, and lastly a three of hearts. "Vingt-et-un. My goodness, I
win again."

"You're cheating!" Charlotte threw her cards at Simon. The
king of hearts and a ten of clubs fluttered against his waistcoat.

He grinned and scooped up the markers in front of him.

She rewarded him with a scowl.

In mock horror, he slapped a hand to his cheek. "Oh dear, it
would appear you're out of betting chips."

"You cheat."

"I assure you, my dear wife, I do not need to cheat. I'm simply that lucky."

"Does this mean you'll finally leave me alone?"

He pulled out his pocket watch. "Only quarter past three. I suppose I could emerge requesting sustenance. A new husband must keep up his strength."

Rising, he stretched, emitted a languorous yawn, and tugged off his coat.

Pressure squeezed her chest, and she gasped. "What are you doing?"

"We've been in here alone nigh on two hours. They won't expect me to come out as I went in." With that, he yanked at the knot in his neckcloth and tossed it aside by his coat. He locked his gaze with hers as, one by one, he unfastened each button on his waistcoat.

Warmth raced up her neck to her face, and she swallowed. "How far are you going to take this—deception?"

He laughed, his blue eyes still tangled with hers. "Only this far." Unfastened, the waistcoat hung loosely but remained on his body. "But why so shy? You've seen me in nothing."

"It's not me I'm concerned about." A lie, but she wouldn't give him the satisfaction of knowing how he affected her.

Of course, one glance at his face told her that her deception failed.

He leaned down and touched her chin with his fingertip. "And it is precisely the others this act is for." Stooping in front of her dressing table, he looked in the mirror and mussed his hair.

She imagined he appeared exactly like a man who had been recently bedded. A different tightness attacked her stomach, knowing that, unlike her, he was intimately familiar with the look.

Perhaps intimately was a poor choice of words. The heat that had confined itself to her neck and face traveled to the rest of her body.

However, he wasn't finished with his illusion. He pulled the counterpane from the bed, and rumpled the sheets, tossing the pillows at odd angles. Hands on his hips, he studied the tableau, then nodded.

At the door, he turned. "I shall return with some refreshment shortly. Is there anything you . . . desire?"

"No." She choked on the word.

With a soft chuckle, he exited, closing the door with a much too loud *click*.

Charlotte stared at the twisted linens far too long. How long could she put him off? Or perhaps the real question was: How long did she *wish* to put him off? If the kiss at the church was any indication, Simon's boasts about his bedroom skills were not exaggerated, and to be honest, she found the prospect of experiencing them rather tempting. Her mind wandered, wondering what sort of naughty things Simon might do on the bed. Before her imagination could take her much farther than a few sensual kisses, the door opened.

"I brought a few things for you anyway." He placed a tray holding tea, some sandwiches, and a glass of wine on a nearby table.

"Why didn't you have a servant bring that up?" If he expected her to serve him, he was sadly mistaken.

"Ah, they would expect you to be naked and purring like a kitten in bed. And being a gentleman—"

Purring like a kitten?! The man had an ego the size of—well, she couldn't think of anything large enough at the moment. "You flatter yourself," she said, unwilling to admit her own thoughts moments before had been similar.

He frowned, something she admitted he did rarely. "Being a gentleman, I offered to bring it myself." He poured some tea, forgoing the sugar but adding a dash of milk, then handed it to her.

She blinked. "How did you . . . ?"

He shrugged, the careless lift of his shoulder natural and so like him. "I observe and learn. Besides, it's tea. How many ways can one take it?"

She sipped the perfectly prepared beverage, studying him over the rim. "It's early in the afternoon for wine, wouldn't you say?" With her luck, he was a drunk who hid it well.

"No. I wouldn't say. But it's not to drink. At least not all of it." With calculated precision, he peeled aside the rumpled sheets and dripped wine onto the middle of the bed.

"You fool! Wine is difficult to get out!"

A smirk covered his face as he peered over his shoulder. "So is blood. Oh, it's not a perfect match, but it will discourage any questions."

Oooh. That pesky heat made a reappearance, but mercifully, Simon either didn't notice or had the decency not to comment. She suspected the former, for surely, given the opportunity to chide her, he would leap upon it like a lion on its prey.

"So a tiny splash of wine is to indicate my deflowering?"

He frowned again at the splotch on the bed linens. "Yes."

"And how many women have you deflowered?" she asked, not certain she really wanted to know.

He met her gaze. "Doesn't it look realistic enough?"

"How would I know?"

"Right." He rubbed a hand across the back of his cravat-less neck. "I don't suppose you have a razor?"

"Whatever fo—" She recoiled. "To cut me?"

Eyes widened, he stared. "Of course not. Myself."

"You didn't answer my question."

He blinked. "I promise you; I didn't mean to cut you."

"Not that. About the women? How many have you deflowered?

Simon's face contorted, the rakish grin typically spreading across his face—gone. He appeared, in a word, pained. "Only one. It was a long time ago. I don't want to discuss it. It's not important."

Oh, but from his reaction, it clearly was.

And Charlotte was determined to find out.

CURSED MEMORY. SIMON PUSHED IT BACK INTO THE DARK recesses where it belonged. How dare Charlotte dredge it up! He should have known better. And how the hell had that Pandora's box been pried open?

Oh, yes. The wine on the sheet.

Charlotte pointed at the rumpled bed. "If you think that's going to fool anyone, you're a bigger nodcock than I presumed you were."

"Would you rather I slit my throat and make you a widow right away?" He hated the mocking tone in his voice, but he had to deflect her questioning.

She grinned at him, the harpy. "If you're offering."

How could she make his blood boil so much? And not just with anger. He hated how much he wanted her.

Pursing his lips, he tilted his head to the ceiling. "Um. I think not. It would make you too happy, and I relish spending more of my time on earth to vex you as much as possible." He picked up the deck of cards and shuffled them. "Which speaking of. Shall we?"

"As you rightly noted, I'm out of markers."

"Ah, yes. So you are. Perhaps we could wager for something else?"

"Such as?"

Oh, it was too tempting, especially given her challenging tone. He set the cards down and placed his hands on the arms of her chair, leaning toward her and boxing her in. "What about a kiss?"

"Ha! Not interested. That's not prize enough for me."

"I didn't say it was if you won. That's if I win—which I will, of course. But"—he pulled away—"In the spirit of fairness. Name your price."

"If I win, you must answer any question I ask honestly."

The determination in her luscious dark eyes gave him pause. She could call him a dolt, a rake, a scapegrace, and he would answer to them all. But in all things, he was an honest man.

The prospect was not appealing.

However, honest didn't necessarily mean truthful. Although he hadn't yet, he *could* cheat. "Very well. But one question, one answer at a time."

"And only one kiss at a time. On the hand."

"No specifying the body part. That is up to the winner's discretion." And he thought of many parts of her body he'd like to kiss.

As she mulled over the stakes, he stalked to the bed, sat down and patted the mattress next to him. "We could find other ways to pass the time."

Ah, there was the bloom of pink on her cheeks, softening her usual austere expression.

"You are—"

"Incorrigible?"

Rather than freeze him, her scowl heated his blood.

Narrowed, her dark eyes challenged him. "Deal the cards."

Outside, the rain continued its patter against the windows, and occasionally, Charlotte glanced toward them, a flash of concern in her eyes at a distant sound of thunder.

"You think you'd be used to the rain, living in England." He meant nothing nefarious in his idle comment, but her attention jerked back to him as if he'd struck her.

"Of course I'm used to it. What type of ridiculous statement is that?" She studied her cards, her lips twitching.

"Do you want another card?" he asked, even though he knew her answer.

"No." She grinned.

"You have a horrible tell. If you expect to play cards well, you must control your emotions."

She stiffened at his words.

What had he said? He studied his cards, restraining his sigh of disappointment at the ten of clubs and six of diamonds. Too soon to cheat, he resigned himself to answering one question. How bad could it be? He laid down his hand. "Sixteen."

With a whoop of triumph, she laid down her ace of diamonds and queen of hearts. "Vingt-et-un!"

"You don't have to gloat. It's hardly a satisfying win against such a poor hand."

"You're a poor loser. Now, for my question." She rubbed her hands together. "Hmm. What shall I ask?"

Although he suspected the type of question she would ask, he hoped he could circumvent it with a vague answer. Much would depend on her phrasing.

Tapping her forefinger against her lips—why did it have to be her lips?—she spent a great deal of time considering her question. Or perhaps giving the appearance of considering it in order to vex him.

Yes, it had to be the latter.

"Well?" If he had to sit still waiting for her to ask her infernal question one moment longer, he would start drifting downward into that abyss of inactivity.

"Don't rush me. I must phrase it perfectly to avoid any chance of you skirting it."

Drat. His wife was a formidable opponent.

At long last, she said, "Tell me the name of the woman you deflowered."

Ah-ha! "That's a statement, not a question."

"Semantics, but very well. What is the name of the woman you deflowered?"

Is. Not was. Oh, he had an out in her phrasing, but if he used it, it would only lead to more questioning. He weighed his choices.

She held up a hand. "And before you answer, remember, you must be honest."

Decision made, he hoped her admittedly sharp mind would gloss over his meaning. "Her name was Joy."

She snorted her disbelief. "Joy? Likely story."

He shrugged. "It is your choice to believe or not believe. But it is the truth." Thank goodness she chose to focus on Joy's name instead of her state of being. However, a warning rang in his mind that more questions in the same vein would follow.

If necessary, he would have to cheat. He dealt the next hand. Eighteen. *Damn.* Good, but would it be good enough? He considered her upturned ten of hearts. At least his visible card was the eight of clubs.

Eyes trained on her face, he watched for her tell.

There. A slight flinch. Surely she didn't have a hidden ten or ace.

"Another card, my lady?" he asked, keeping his voice innocent.

She waved him off, and he held his breath, taking a gamble he had her beat and refraining from risking going over hoping for a two or three.

As she turned over a seven of diamonds, he withheld the excitement brewing in his veins.

Instead, he pouted, lifting the corner of his king of spades.

"Well, are you going to stare at that card all day or play it?" she snapped.

He met her gaze, drilling into the depths of her dark brown eyes. His only decision was where to kiss her.

Her gaze dipped to his card, and he took great care to turn it over as slowly as possible.

Her little rosebud mouth opened the tiniest bit, and he imagined probing inside with his tongue for a deep kiss.

"Now, that, my lady, is a satisfying win." Before claiming his prize, he leaned back in his chair, enjoying his moment of victory.

"You don't have to look so smug."

"Do you mean as you did with your win? My, my, how the tables have turned."

She crossed her arms over her chest, drawing his gaze to her breasts.

And lovely breasts they were. Full and round, the tops pushed up over her bodice.

"Are you going to take all day? Please get this over with," she snarled.

"Now, now. A kiss is nothing to rush or endure. It is to be savored, like an expensive brandy, or fine chocolate. My only dilemma is where to kiss you."

After rising from his seat, he moved over to her and touched her temple. "Here, perhaps?" His finger trailed a line to her jaw. "Or here? Maybe here?"

As his fingertip brushed the hollow of her throat, she shuddered.

Oh, he would definitely come back to that spot later. But first . . .

"I think I shall start here."

When he lifted her hand, he kept his eyes trained on her face.

The trepidation in her eyes vanished, and her shoulders relaxed.

Until he turned her hand over and pressed his lips to her palm.

She drew in an audible breath.

He lingered for a moment, his tongue sliding over her soft skin that tasted sweet and a little salty. His kiss sketched a line to the pulse point on her wrist, which quickened beneath his touch, the scent of lilac filling his nostrils and arousing his desire.

Yet, he wasn't the only one affected. The ice queen trembled. Perhaps she had a heart after all.

She jerked her hand away. "Enough! One kiss. You are taking liberties which I have not granted."

"Then I shall have to win another hand . . . and another . . . and another. For there are many places I wish to kiss you." If his face in any way evidenced the fire burning inside him, he would surely melt her icy heart with his gaze.

"I don't want to play any longer."

"You're just afraid to lose."

Oh, there was the glare he'd come to know and love. "I am *not* afraid. Deal the damn cards and prepare to answer the most outrageous of questions."

Hurried footsteps sounded out in the hall, followed by raised voices. Mid-deal, he stopped and, striding to the door, threw it open. A maid rushed past, carrying a large stack of towels.

He stepped into the hall. "What's going on?"

"Her Grace is having her baby!" the maid called over her shoulder as she rushed down the hall.

Simon spun toward Charlotte, only to find her right behind him. Panic slid up his spine and grabbed onto his mind with sharp claws.

CHAPTER 13

W hat was wrong with the man? Charlotte stared at Simon's absolute expression of terror. One would think he was the one about to become a father—or even the one to give birth.

Ha! She couldn't restrain the smile demanding to make an entrance.

"This is *not* funny!" he said through gritted teeth.

He was right, of course. "Come! We must see if we can be of use."

As she edged past him, he grasped her wrist. "Wait. You're much too put together. Take your hair down."

"What? This is not the time to think of ourselves."

"Do you want my parents to believe this sham or not? Do you even care? They are good people. Whatever your feelings for me, I'm asking you to consider them."

She wrenched her arm from his grasp. After marching back into the room, she quickly pulled the pins from her hair, letting it fall in messy waves against her back and shoulders.

"There," she said. "For your family." Still, when his gaze

raked over her, her mind drifted back to the feel of his lips on her wrist, and her heart raced.

Unfettered, she strode past him and followed the sounds of excited voices. A cluster of people—footmen, maids, and Simon's father—gathered outside the ducal bedchamber in the far wing.

Memories of her mother came flooding back. The difficult birth and the death of both mother and child. "Isn't it too soon?" Charlotte asked, a wave of fear tightening her lungs. She shouldn't have been so quick to judge Simon.

Mr. Beckham took her hands in his. "Babies come when they wish. My wife said it may be due to all the excitement Her Grace has gone through these past days." His eyes held a note of apology that Charlotte's rushed wedding played a part in Honoria's distress.

Simon appeared at her side. "Did someone send for a doctor?"

Mr. Beckham nodded. "His Grace sent word for someone named Ashton. I presume he's a physician."

Simon's eyes glazed over. He swayed, and if Charlotte hadn't spent the last four hours in his presence, she would swear he was foxed. "Where's Drake?"

Inclining his head toward the closed door, Mr. Beckham said, "Inside. Although I expect your mother will throw him out at any moment."

A moan, starting low and growing in intensity, reverberated through the walls into the hallway. The door opened, and as if fulfilling Mr. Beckham's prediction, Mrs. Beckham pushed Burwood from the room.

"I'm sorry, Your Grace, but you should wait outside. You're upsetting Her Grace." She closed the door with a firm *click*.

Poor Drake. At the moment, she couldn't think of him as the duke. Only a man who dearly loved his wife and worried for her safety and that of his child. His eyes were haunted, like a cornered animal, wanting to fight but not knowing exactly how.

Charlotte understood that feeling. "Your Grace. Drake." She touched him on the sleeve, and his gaze lifted to hers, pleading and frantic. "May I see her?"

The weak smile he offered didn't meet his eyes. "I think she'd like that. She didn't want to bother you, all things considered." His gaze shot to Simon, and like Mr. Beckham's, it held an apology.

"Simon," she said to her husband. "Take care of him."

The dolt gave a wooden nod.

Men!

When Charlotte stepped into the room, Mrs. Beckman gazed up from where she was wiping Honoria's brow and motioned her over. "Look who's here, Your Grace."

Unlike Honoria, Charlotte wasn't adept at providing soothing and reassuring words. Losing her mother at a young age had deprived Charlotte of a nurturing example, and she had no natural instinct for mothering. Oh, she would fight to the death to defend those she loved, but offering comfort was a foreign task. She thought back to when Anne's recklessness had resulted in a horrible fall the previous year. Honoria had held the ninnyhammer's hand and stroked her forehead.

So she took Honoria's outstretched hand. "How are you feeling?" *Drat.* What a stupid question!

However, Honoria either didn't notice or didn't care. Which didn't surprise Charlotte. "It's not so terribly bad. There is rest in between the spasms. I'm sorry to interrupt your wedding day."

"Nonsense," Charlotte said and meant it. "I'm grateful the attention is on someone else instead of me."

Honoria gave a weak laugh. "That sounds like something I would say."

"I learned from the best." Charlotte stroked Honoria's hair. "The duke will be here soon."

Mrs. Beckham's gaze shot to Charlotte. "I just shooed him out."

"The other duke. Ashton is a physician, but he's also a duke."

With a chuckle, Mrs. Beckham said, "The best for the best. You are all the oddest group of nobles I've ever met." As if realizing how her statement might appear, the woman's face whitened, and her eyes locked on Charlotte's. "I didn't mean any disrespect."

Charlotte shook her head. "None taken, Mrs. Beckham."

"Perhaps you might call me Judith, or someday, Mother."

Aware how Honoria watched her with Mrs. Beckham—Judith—her green eyes shining with interest, Charlotte forced a smile. "Of course, Judith. I should be honored. Although I pray you will give me time to call you Mother."

Beatific peacefulness shone on Honoria's face. She actually radiated beauty. "I'm so glad you have a loving family now."

A strand of Charlotte's hair swung loose, and Honoria grasped the end with her fingers. "Your hair looks lovely like this. Now I understand why Drake likes mine down." She smiled shyly. "Is all going well with Simon?"

Charlotte grappled for an answer—especially with her mother-in-law present.

Unexpectedly, Honoria's grip on Charlotte's hand became crushing. Pain contorted her face as she lifted her head and cried out. "Oh, here's another one!"

"Breathe through it, Your Grace. Deep breath in and blow out."

"Honoria," Honoria said through her moans of pain. "Not. A time. For. Formalities."

Something tight and uncomfortable rose in Charlotte's throat. Is this why Simon appeared so terrified? Having five younger sisters, he had probably heard his own mother's cries from the pain of childbirth. But panic and terror wouldn't help Honoria.

"You can do this, Honoria. You're one of the strongest people I know." Charlotte bit her lip as Honoria continued her vise-like grip on her hand. At last the episode seemed to pass, and Honoria released the pressure on Charlotte's fingers.

Mrs. Beckham wiped Honoria's forehead with a wet cloth. "That was a strong one. You're getting close."

Charlotte knew little about giving birth, but she'd heard it could take many hours, sometimes a whole day. "Is that normal? She was fine this morning at the wedding."

Honoria's chagrined expression said otherwise. "I didn't want to upset anyone."

If they had been alone, Charlotte might have told her that it would have been a blessing to have her wedding interrupted and postponed. Instead she remained silent and sent her friend a censorious, but gentle shake of her head.

After a sharp knock, the door opened, and Ashton poked his head inside. "May I come in?"

"Ashton," Charlotte said and silently added, *Thank God.*

"Your Grace." Mrs. Beckham curtsied.

"No offense, madam, but we don't have time for frivolous courtesies. If you would both excuse me while I examine my patient."

As he ushered them from the room, Charlotte grabbed his arm. "I know you and my brother Nash had your difficulties, but I'm begging you as Honoria's friend, please make sure she survives."

He patted her hand. "Nash and I have mended things. And rest assured, Lady Charlotte. Women have given birth for eons. I will give her the best care possible."

In the hall, she locked eyes with Simon, somehow now sharing his fear.

Because Honoria wasn't simply any woman.

SIMON HAD PRACTICALLY WORN A PATH IN THE CARPET, WALKING in circles outside Honoria's room.

"Will you stop. You're making me more nervous." Drake ran a hand through his hair. "Thank God, Ashton is here."

"Get used to it, son." His father chuckled.

Simon wasn't sure if he addressed him or Drake. Perhaps both of them. But unlike Drake—who most certainly would have a houseful of children—at the rate Simon was progressing with Charlotte, he would be lucky to produce one.

But he had made a little leeway before the commotion began, hadn't he? Charlotte certainly responded to the kiss on her wrist.

The door opened, and his mother and Charlotte emerged, then closed the door behind them. His gaze snagged with Charlotte's, and the panic taking hold of him expanded in his chest.

Drake spun around. "Why can't I go in?" He took three steps toward the door, and Simon grabbed his arm, holding him back.

"Ashton will let us know how she is." At least Simon hoped so. His mother always had midwives, who had been less than forthcoming, always complaining men had no place in the birthing room. His mother seemed to agree.

And as much as Simon would be paralyzed to be in a room with a woman giving birth, he understood Drake's frustration, wanting to be with his wife.

Because Drake loved her.

The door opened, and Ashton stepped through, closing the door behind him.

Drake shook himself from Simon's grasp. "How is she?" The terror in his friend's voice cut through Simon like a blade.

"She's doing remarkably well. She's been having pains since last night. At first she didn't understand what they were."

"She stood up to use the necessary and, well—" Drake blushed. "She didn't make it."

"That was her waters, Drake. All quite normal. It won't be

too long now. Would you like to come in and watch your child be born?"

Simon imagined his shocked expression mirrored everyone's around him.

His mother said, "Begging your pardon, Your Grace, but is that wise?"

Ashton chuckled. Actually chuckled. At such a time? "I have delivered my own children. If Drake can remain calm and supportive, Honoria has asked that he be by her side so they can share this together."

Drake didn't hesitate and stepped toward the door.

Simon's world started crumbling around him. He'd expected to keep Drake occupied while they waited. Selfish though it was, at least it would give him something to do. But without a task, an objective, he felt rudderless, sinking into a mire of inactivity. He would drown.

Hand on the doorknob, Drake turned toward him. "Go. You don't have to wait. I'll be all right. Occupy yourself. Otherwise you'll go mad."

Oh, how his friend knew him, and he vowed he would repay him in full measure someday.

Until that moment, no one had commented on his or Charlotte's disheveled appearances. But as Ashton paused before following Drake into the chamber of horrors, his gaze bounced between the newly married couple. "I understand felicitations are in order. If nothing else, Mr. Beckham, you will have another reminder of your wedding date." With that, he stepped inside and closed the door, shutting out a renewed cry from Honoria.

Simon wanted to jump out of his skin. Every inch prickled at the sounds of pain. "Can we at least go somewhere else?"

Charlotte motioned with her arms as if gathering a group of lost ducklings. "Why don't we all go to the drawing room? I'll tell Frampton to prepare some refreshment. Mr. Beckham, you drink coffee, is that correct?"

Simon's head jerked toward her. She'd noticed his father's preference?

"I do, my dear."

"And the girls," Charlotte continued. "Where are they?"

"In the music room," his mother said, admiration shining in her eyes.

Simon concurred. His wife had taken charge of the situation.

"Even better than the drawing room," Charlotte said. "We shall bring the young heir into the world to some lovely music. Do the girls play?"

At that point, the conversation became a buzz around him, indistinct, but calming words, and he followed his family to the music room.

He lasted all of forty minutes. Each time there was a lull in the music—which varied from exquisite when Charlotte played to clumsy and headache-inducing when Georgie pounded at the piano's keys—Honoria's screams broke through the silence.

How could Drake stand it? Torture. Unmitigated on-the-rack torture. Tightness clamped his chest. He had to get out of there. Rain pounded against the pavement and lawn outside, and he wanted nothing more than to be out there, soaked to the skin and washed clean of the helplessness gripping him.

Someone touched his arm—gently, but he still jumped.

Charlotte's dark eyes met his. He expected derision, contempt, or, at the very least, castigation. He blinked, trying to clear his vision. Could it be compassion and understanding shining in those brown depths?

Wonder of wonders.

"Your father shared stories of your boyhood with me this morning. I sense your restlessness and need to be doing something. There's nothing here for you to do. Go. Busy yourself however you choose." Her voice cracked at the last two words.

Or was that his imagination? Open-mouthed, he gaped at the

mere idea she was encouraging him to leave while everyone else waited patiently.

"Even Drake said so. And he knows you better than I do."

He grasped her hands and squeezed. "You're sure?"

She nodded. "Just promise me one thing."

At that moment, he would promise her the moon if it meant he could rid himself of the situation. "What?"

"Be discreet."

Oh. *Oooh.* "I won't do what you're thinking. Especially not on our wedding day. And when I told you I would not seek out other women, I meant it."

"Thank you," she said, but something in her eyes said she didn't quite believe him.

"I'll make it up to you, I promise." He made quick apologies to his family, with his mother sending him the look that made him feel like he was ten years old. Then he bounded up the stairs, two at a time. After buttoning his waistcoat, hastily tying his neckcloth, and slipping on his coat, he raced downstairs and ordered a carriage brought around.

Rain pelted his hat as he climbed inside.

But at least he could breathe again.

CHAPTER 14

Charlotte should have been angry with her husband. And truth be told, at first, she was furious at his cowardly behavior. But her heart softened at the fear and panic in his eyes each time Honoria cried out in the pains of childbirth.

Only a little, mind you. The iron wall she'd built around her heart was practically impenetrable. Or perhaps it wasn't shielded so much as buried. Deep under layers of childhood rejection and disappointment, she'd safeguarded it from attack. Unsure when it happened—it had been quite sudden—but one day she realized her father's constant complaint that she wasn't born a son no longer stung. His grousing over the fact he would have to pay for a dowry and having nothing to show for it when she married no longer mattered.

"The one thing you could do for me is marry well. The king and queen have several unmarried sons, but a duke would do. Even a foreign prince would be acceptable. But if you ever—and I mean ever—wish to marry an untitled man, you will be dead to me. Do you understand? I don't care how rich he is or how much land he owns."

So she did what any self-respecting woman would do; she refused to marry anyone at all. Spiteful? Yes. She prided herself on how clever she had been. Knowing full well if her father made a match for her with an *acceptable* suitor she would have little choice, she made herself as disagreeable as possible. A sharp tongue and acerbic wit had sent many a hopeful man scampering away in search of a more biddable wife. Scowls and disdainful glances replaced the smiles and batting eyelashes of more hopeful debutantes.

When her father died, Roland not only assumed the marquessate, but their father's requirements for a spouse. Oh, how Roland hated when Nash had married Adalyn, whom Roland called "the American woman." One who dared venture into the man's world of medicine, no less!

As much as she silently celebrated and rejoiced in Nash's freedom, she knew it would only exacerbate Roland's efforts to secure an advantageous match for her. Or should she say—for him? The deal he had struck with Lord Felix and his father, Lord Scarborough, had been diabolical, and he cared little how it would harm her.

All she wanted was to live her life in peace, unencumbered by another man who would control her. She had no illusions of love like her friends did. And with her rejection of The Worm, she fully expected to face a future alone and disgraced. And she had accepted it, embraced it even. It was preferable to the alternative.

And yet, here she was. Married. To an untitled man who vexed her. With a large and boisterous family.

Her father was probably tossing in his grave.

The idea made her smile.

"What is it, my dear?" Mrs. Beckham pulled her from her musings. "You seem wistful. Are you perhaps thinking of the time when you and Simon will be having your own children?"

Goodness, no! Charlotte's stomach knotted with each of Honoria's cries, exacerbating her fear of childbirth. And unlike

Drake, who braved the birthing room to remain by his wife's side, if Simon turned tail and ran when he wasn't even the father, what would he do when his own child was being born? Desert her entirely?

"I was simply wondering if the baby might have Honoria's red hair." A lie, certainly, but if nothing else, Charlotte was adept at prevarication.

Mrs. Beckham pursed her lips and gave her an odd look.

Mr. Beckham chuckled, setting down his coffee on the saucer. "Leave the lady alone, Judith. They've been married less than a day, and already you're expecting grandchildren. Allow them the enjoyment of each other for a while. I dare say things might have been interrupted." The man's gaze traveled to Charlotte's hastily unpinned hair.

Why had she listened to her fool husband simply to give the appearance they'd been . . . ?

Gah!

"Now, *you've* embarrassed her, Teddy." Mrs. Beckham playfully slapped her husband on the arm. She turned toward Charlotte. "Forgive my husband. Your hair looks lovely down, just as Her Grace said. And you are among family here."

Family?

The word had never struck a harmonious chord in Charlotte before, only one of dissonance.

Frannie tugged on Charlotte's arm. "Don't mind my parents. Come sit by me. We can commiserate as Georgie massacres poor Amadeus."

Charlotte couldn't help but smile at Frannie's matter-of-fact assessment of her youngest sister's talents. An unexpected spark of generosity ignited in Charlotte's chest. "Ah, but she plays with such verve."

Settled next to her, Frannie leaned in. "How is it you know my brother so well already? You met him less than a year ago. Is that not correct?"

"It is. In what respect are you referring?"

"That you understood Simon would go mad if he had to remain here and listen to Her Grace's cries." She nodded toward Georgie as she finished the piece with a flourish and bang. "Georgie is the most like him. A constant whirlwind of action, and no matter what they do, they do it with unbridled enthusiasm. Except stand still and wait. Simon told me once when he was stationed in the Indian desert, they had to wait in silence, simply watching a group of suspected marauders. He said it felt as if he was sinking into the sand and it would swallow him whole, choking the life out of him."

Did that explain the terror and panic in his eyes? Charlotte had her doubts. "You give me more credit than I am due, I'm afraid. I simply believed him to be like most men. Unwilling or unable to deal with a woman's pain."

Frannie shook her head. "I don't think it's that. I think it's because he fears for those in pain, especially those he cares for deeply."

Charlotte rather thought Frannie also gave her brother too much credit. However, she admitted the girl knew her brother better than she did. "One must confront one's fears in order to conquer them."

Tense silence settled in the room, punctuated with scrambling footsteps and a few more feminine cries as time dragged on.

Shadows stretched across the room as the sun lowered in the sky. The clock chimed quarter past seven, and Charlotte frowned. The last cries had been almost thirty minutes ago. The knot tightened in her stomach.

Was something wrong?

She exchanged a questioning glance with Mrs. Beckham.

No doubt her mother-in-law's smile was meant to be reassuring, but something in the woman's eyes bothered Charlotte. "We should hear something soon."

Whether she meant another cry or news, Charlotte wasn't entirely sure.

Long minutes later, with shirtsleeves rolled to his elbows, Ashton appeared at the music room's entrance. "All is well. His and Her Grace have a beautiful and healthy baby girl."

A collective sigh of relief rose from the group.

"And Honoria?" Charlotte asked.

Ashton motioned her forward. "Come see for yourself. She's asking for you."

Me? Frannie's comment about sinking and drowning in sand took on new meaning. Charlotte rose, but unlike Simon, who feared standing still, the thought of moving paralyzed Charlotte. Her legs were numb, her feet uncooperative.

Ashton motioned for her again. "Lady Charlotte?"

From behind, Frannie's voice, soft and non-accusatory, released her. "One must face one's fear."

One step. Then two, and Ashton was escorting her from the room.

Once out of earshot of the others, Charlotte asked, "Is something wrong?"

"Not at all. I believe she has something to ask you." Upstairs, he paused at the door. "Do be prepared, my lady. Honoria has had a trying day." Smiling, he opened the door and ushered Charlotte inside.

A wrinkled, pink, and squalling bundle lay in Honoria's arms. Drake—Charlotte couldn't think of him as Burwood any longer —towered over them, his little finger prodding at the bundle's fist, his expression pure adoration.

Ashton's warning was hardly necessary. Charlotte had never seen Honoria look more beautiful, even on her wedding day. Beatific would be a suitable descriptor as she gazed up from her daughter, her eyes brightening upon seeing Charlotte. "Come, meet Katherine Abigail Constance Pendrake."

Without removing his attention from the baby, Drake said, "We're going to call her Kitty. Like Aunt Kitty."

The child screamed.

"It does seem to fit," Charlotte said.

Drake nodded, finally looking away from the baby's face. "The moment she displayed her temperament, the matter was settled."

Charlotte stepped closer. "And the Abigail Constance?" The baby stopped screaming, but her tiny bottom lip quivered.

"Abigail after Drake's mother, and Constance after mine," Honoria said, then cooed to little Kitty.

"Ashton said you had something to ask me." She took another tentative step closer, fear still gripping her feet to the floor.

Honoria exchanged a glance with Drake. The love the two shared tugged at Charlotte's cold heart. "As Drake's best friend, we already decided to ask Simon to be Kitty's godfather, and it seemed fitting to ask you to be her godmother. Especially now."

The trepidation rooting Charlotte to the floor twined up her legs like vines, wrapping around her and squeezing her chest. "Why now?"

"Well, of course, with your marriage to Simon. But more because we decided Kitty might need a strong woman in her life." The love for her infant daughter lit Honoria's entire face.

Drake nodded. "Especially since I expect Simon will spoil her by catering to her every whim. She'll need a clear head to counter his flattery. If her few moments in this world are any indication, she will be strong willed like my aunt, and who better to guide her than you?"

Oh. Something wet pricked the corners of Charlotte's eyes. "I'm honored."

"Besides," Drake said, lifting Kitty in his arms, "she'll get the perfect balance of frivolity and seriousness, making for a perfect whole. Just like you and Simon."

As Drake cradled his infant daughter, Charlotte didn't have the heart to tell him there was nothing perfect about her union with Simon Beckham.

SIMON BANGED ON THE CARRIAGE ROOF, BRINGING IT TO A HALT IN front of the new gaming hell, *The Knave of Hearts*. Since it had opened a year ago, he'd wanted to see for himself what all the chatter was about. Unable to attend White's, which in all honesty was fine with him, Simon longed for a place a little more genteel than the dingy backrooms of public houses where a man could lose more than just his money. Even he had his standards. He was the man of business for a duke, after all.

"Don't wait for me. I'll hire a hackney when I return," he called to the driver. Even the location was strategically placed— far enough from the East End, but also not close enough to St. James Street to not create a stir of competition with the more elite clubs. Whoever owned the club was clearly a man with vision.

A burly man stood at the entrance, his hands crossed and clasped in front of him. He eyed Simon from head to toe and back up again. "Ain't seen you here before, gov'nur."

"First time, my good man. I've heard many good things." Simon flashed his signature smile, hoping his teeth caught the glint of the moon. It *might* have been a *slight* prevarication.

"Such as?"

Uh-oh. Perhaps the man had more between his ears than Simon had given him credit for. "Well, that the owner is a gentleman, and he tolerates no riff-raff in his club."

The giant barked a laugh. "Wait till the Cap'n gets wind of that one!" He eyed Simon again. "Very well. You look like you have some blunt to lose." With an arm the size of a tree trunk, the man pushed the door open, then gave a bow, his lips curling in irony as he motioned Simon forward with his other massive limb. "Your lordship."

Simon stepped through, vowing to be on his very best behavior lest the man break him in half like a twig.

Although White's wouldn't welcome Simon on his own, he had been there once as Drake's guest. He'd never been so anxious to leave an establishment—except perhaps Pendrake House a short half hour before. Fear of reprisal for laughing a bit too loudly or failing to follow *the rules* had made him jittery and longing for the door.

But as he took in the scene before him at *The Knave*, the dreaded pressure around his chest failed to manifest. Voices weren't hushed into submission. Raucous laughter and shouts of disappointment as men won and lost at the tables drowned out the same *clinks* of glasses that broke through the oppressive silence at White's.

The unrestrained vocalizations contrasted with the elegant decor in a strange juxtaposition that somehow seemed *right*. Appointed well, with fine furnishings and wall coverings, the gaming hell was unlike any other he'd been in. Simon scanned the room, taking in the patrons.

Well-dressed, all of them, Simon was unable to discern who was a lord and who was a Cit.

Ah! Lord Montgomery occupied one of the tables. When Simon had met the man at Drake's house party the previous summer, he'd immediately liked him. Quiet and serious, he reminded Simon of Drake. Especially considering how besotted he was with his red-headed wife. Next to him sat Andrew Weatherby, also a guest at Drake's party and brother of the impossible flirt, Miss Anne Weatherby. Simon shuddered at how close poor Drake had come to being leg-shackled to the wrong redhead.

Simon strode toward them. "Gentlemen."

They glanced up, and Weatherby's eyes widened. "Beckham. Fancy meeting you here. Didn't you get married this morning?"

Simon hadn't thought about that. "Um. Yes?"

Montgomery laughed. "You're not sure?"

"Don't laugh, Montgomery," Weatherby said. "I found you at White's the day after your wedding."

Red colored the tips of Montgomery's ears.

Interesting.

Montgomery straightened. "That was different."

"And how would you know? Beckham could be having the same trouble with women you did."

Very interesting. Although . . . he had to defend himself. "I don't have any trouble with women."

Both men stared at him, apparently forgetting Simon was the reason they'd begun arguing in the first place.

A hand clapped Simon on the shoulder—hard. "Well, well. Trouble in paradise already, Beckham?"

Turning, Simon was confronted with none other than The Worm himself, Lord Felix Davies. Had the entire *ton* decided to descend upon the new gaming hell? The torture of the music room at Pendrake House suddenly seemed preferable.

"His and Her Grace are expecting their first child," Simon said, hoping the explanation would appease them and stop their probing questions.

Montgomery and Weatherby exchanged a look, and Davies simply chortled.

"So?" The snide question had come from Davies.

"It's coming. Now," Simon clarified.

Davies gave an insouciant shrug. "I suppose it doesn't matter that tonight is your wedding night, considering you've already had Lady Charlotte. But I didn't quite expect you to be bored with her so soon." He studied his well-manicured nails. "Or maybe I did. I've had a taste myself and found it quite lacking."

Simon lunged at him. If he could just get his hands around the man's neck, he'd . . .

Hands gripped Simon's arms, restraining him. Expecting to see either Montgomery or Weatherby, Simon prepared to tell them to go to the devil and let him tear The Worm limb from limb.

A tower of a man with serious amber eyes met his gaze. Not as large as the giant at the front door, the man still had Simon by a good four inches. "Easy, friend. He's not worth it." He peered over Simon's head. "Hartley Two!" he yelled over the din of the room.

The giant appeared from the side of the room.

"Weren't you just at the door?" Simon pointed toward the entrance.

"That was my brother," the man answered.

"They're twins. Identical," the man with the amber eyes said. He was well-dressed like everyone else, but he had an air of command about him. "Hartley, show Lord Felix the door. I warned you, Davies. If you continue to make trouble in here, I will ban you for good."

Grumbling and throwing the giant's hands off him, Davies strode to the door, leaving a trail of obscenities in his wake.

"Shame," the amber-eyed man said. "His money is good." A dimple broke through his cheek when he grinned. "And he tends to leave a lot of it when he comes here." He cocked his head. "Don't think I've seen you in here before. Am I going to have trouble with you, too?"

Simon stuck out his hand. "Simon Beckham. And no, I try to avoid trouble as much as possible. However, he disparaged my wife."

The man's large hand engulfed Simon's in a hearty shake. "Everyone calls me Captain. And unfortunately, that doesn't surprise me about Davies. The man is trouble on two legs."

"Are you the owner of this fine establishment?"

"I am. And if your money is good and you don't cause trouble, I'm happy to make your acquaintance."

"He's the Duke of Burwood's man of business," Weatherby said.

A sandy eyebrow hitched. "Is that so?"

Something about the way the man's interest seemed to pique tickled Simon's own intuition. And something in his features seemed familiar. Around Simon's age, he looked to be in his early or mid-thirties. Women would call him handsome, no doubt, but with a hint of danger flashing in those eyes. A pale scar stretching from his cheek to his jaw added to the intimidating picture.

"So, were you a military man?" Simon asked. Perhaps they had something in common.

"Navy. Like my father." A look of discomfort crossed his face. "Well, I need to get back to my office." Without another word, he turned and strode away.

"Imposing fellow," Simon said to no one in particular.

"He terrifies me." Weatherby gave a little shudder.

Montgomery laughed.

But Simon had a strange sense that he'd met the man before. Shaking it off, he took the unoccupied seat at the table with Montgomery and Weatherby. "What's the game?" He rubbed his hands together, eager for a distraction from arriving babies, loathsome aristocrats, and one all-too-tempting bride.

Montgomery shuffled the cards. "Speculation."

At least it wasn't vingt-et-un.

Yet with each hand he won, even as he pulled the markers toward him, kisses seemed far more valuable and satisfying. He thought about where he might be kissing Charlotte. The sensitive spot on her throat? The inner part of her elbow? Her lips?

"Beckham, are you quite all right?"

Blink. Unsure who had asked, Simon cleared his throat. "Pardon?"

"You . . . ahem . . . sighed. Exhausted from the day's events, perhaps?" Montgomery asked, color rising to the tips of his ears.

Sighed? Surely, not. Although Charlotte's lips stirred his blood and incited wicked ideas.

Montgomery laid down the winning card. "Word of friendly advice from someone who's been where you are."

The balding gentleman next to Simon groaned. "What's that? To quit now?"

Montgomery ignored the man, and a slow smile stretched his lips. "Go home. Be with your wife. I've read the scandal sheets—well, Bea has read them to me. She detests that rag and says she only reads it to seek clues as to the author's identity. And although I've not had many dealings with Lady Charlotte, neither Bea nor I have any admiration for Edgerton or Davies. I don't know the true circumstances leading to your marriage, nor am I asking. But whatever they were, you did what any gentleman should. Now you should make the best of it. It might surprise you how good that best can be."

Guilt slithered in his stomach. He'd deserted his own wife on their wedding day. "How long does it take for a child to be born?" It had always seemed an eternity with his mother, and he pushed back the memory of Alexander.

All three other men at the table laughed, but it was Weatherby who answered. "As long as it takes. There is no set time. My twin girls came quickly."

Montgomery nodded. "True. My eldest took her time, almost as if she needed to have everything just so. Then the second came out so quickly we feared she would arrive before the doctor."

What a horrible friend he was, leaving Drake alone when he should be by his side, supporting him. And Charlotte. Did she deserve a husband who would run away at the slightest sign of difficulty? Simon swallowed and rose. "It was a pleasure, gentlemen."

He gazed around the establishment and gave an approving nod. "But I shall return, so save your blunt."

As he stepped out into the night air, he tapped his hat, securing it on his head.

"Hartley. Would you be a good fellow and hail me a carriage? I'm going home."

The question remained: Would his bride be happy to see him?

CHAPTER 15

After everyone had a glimpse of little Kitty, Drake ushered them all out with instruction to Frampton to provide whatever was necessary for his guests, but stating he would remain by Honoria's side and take supper with her in her bedchamber.

Charlotte took it upon herself to act as hostess in Honoria's absence. Grudgingly, she admitted she enjoyed Simon's lively family. The younger girls filled any lulls in the conversation, chattering excitedly about the baby, the latest fashions, asking if they would have a Season since Simon resided in London with the duke and was married to a real Lady.

Still, Charlotte couldn't help but compare Drake's devotion to Honoria and even Mr. Beckham's attentiveness to his wife and daughters to her own situation. She'd had Frampton lay a place at supper for Simon, should he return.

His seat remained empty, and as she gazed across the expanse of the table at the vacant spot, her thoughts drifted to their game of vingt-et-un.

And to the kiss.

Unbidden, she touched her palm where his lips had lingered.

Ninny! She must desist such foolishness forthwith. It would only lead to heartache.

An incongruous laugh escaped at the thought. Did she even have a heart any longer, or had she buried it so deep as to be irretrievable?

Beth's spoon of syllabub hovered at her lips. "What is it?"

"Pardon?"

"You laughed. What's funny?" Beth's spoon completed the trajectory to her mouth.

"Your brother." A mild untruth. And Simon *had* precipitated the line of thought leading to her ill-timed laugh.

Beth appeared unconvinced. "He does make everyone smile."

Not everyone. His flippant manner and hollow compliments vexed her. Was there a shred of sincerity and genuineness in the man? Or was it all one big game? When things grew serious or difficult, he turned tail and ran away. Her attention snagged on the empty plate.

He should be here. With his family. With his friend.

With me.

"Simon suggested we spend some time at your estate, Mr. Beckham. He mentioned a cottage there previously used by your mother."

With a mouthful of dessert, Georgie exclaimed, "Oh, yes. Please come. I can show you my favorite hiding places."

"Georgie." Mrs. Beckham lifted a castigatory brow. "Don't speak with your mouth full."

Charlotte chuckled softly to herself. She might need to hide from Simon.

Before Charlotte could answer the girl, Rebecca sent her sister a chastising glance. "Simon and Lady Charlotte will want to be alone. Not pestered by an obnoxious twelve-year-old."

"I am *not* obnoxious." Georgie sent a pleading look to her mother. "Am I?"

"Only on days ending in y," Beth said.

At first Georgie nodded, her dark curls bobbing, then her eyes widened. "Oh, you!" She glowered at her sister.

"Georgie, I'm certain I will be able to spare time away from Simon long enough for you to show me around." *Especially if Simon deserts me as he did this evening.*

Georgie stuck her tongue out at Rebecca and then Beth, which earned her another reprimand from her mother.

"If you would all excuse me, I'm rather tired. It has been a most eventful day." She placed the serviette next to her plate. "Please, feel free to gather in the drawing room after supper."

When she rose, Mr. Beckham followed suit, approaching and touching her arm. "Don't be too hard on him when he returns, my dear. His actions may seem selfish and uncaring, but Simon never did well when his mother delivered. The cries of pain become too much for him, I'm afraid. Then when Simon was fifteen, Judith lost a baby eighteen months before Georgie was born. The boy came too early and didn't survive." Mr. Beckham's eyes grew misty, and he wiped at them hastily. "Our little Alexander. A difficult time for all of us, Simon most of all. I thought he would lose his mind when Georgie was being born."

Oh, poor Simon. Poor Judith. Poor Mr. Beckham. "I'm so sorry."

Charlotte had her doubts about her husband, but Mr. Beckham's news explained Simon's terrified reaction. Still, she worried about where he had gone. She forced a weak smile. "I shall do my best to be a good wife to him, sir. However, my husband must also keep his own promises."

As she exited the dining room, Georgie's voice rose in the quiet. "Oh, Simon's in trouble now."

Unbidden, a genuine smile tugged at Charlotte's lips.

UPON ARRIVING HOME, SIMON HAD THE CARRIAGE DRIVER LET him off several homes away. Not up for any lectures, he walked around and through the mews, sneaking into the house through the kitchen in the back. The room was empty, clean of all evidence of the evening's supper, and his stomach growled in protest. As quietly as he could, he crept up the hallway and spied around the corner.

When the footman stationed at the front door caught sight of him, Simon put his finger to his lips, and the man nodded. If he could make it to the study undiscovered, he kept some whisky in a drawer there. It wasn't solid, but it might take off the edge gnawing at him.

He discovered Drake, his head back, cravat untied, staring at the ceiling. Simon turned to leave but the creaking floorboard in front of the room betrayed him.

"You're back," Drake called from behind.

"Ah, yes. I didn't want to disturb you." Simon stepped into the room, praying Drake's demeanor was simple exhaustion and not one of sorrow. "Um, how is Honoria?"

The tension in Simon's chest eased at the grin breaking across Drake's face. "She's sleeping. At least for a while. She was magnificent, Simon. How do women do it?"

"So you stayed for the whole—" Simon waved a hand, not willing to utter the word.

"Birth," Drake said for him. "Yes. She's so tiny. Fragile."

"You have a daughter?"

Drake nodded. "I've been sitting here worrying about all the ways I need to protect her." His expression grew solemn, knifing Simon in the heart for having deserted his friend.

Simon retrieved the whisky and poured them both a glass. "You're not in this alone. You have Honoria. And me."

Drake's eyebrow rose as he studied Simon over the rim of his crystal glass. He sipped. "Do I?"

"You told me to go." The metaphorical knife twisted by Simon's own hand as he redirected the accusation.

"True." Drake took another sip, then laid the glass down. "However, I didn't expect you to be gone so long. After all, it is your wedding day, and you have a bride waiting for you."

The knife plunged deep. Simon winced from the pain. "Ah. Have you spoken to Charlotte?"

Drake toyed with the glass of amber liquid. "Not about that. I took supper with Honoria in her room. But Charlotte, bless her, took charge with your family. When I came down a short while ago, your mother said Charlotte had retired for the evening. She had some rather harsh words about you."

Simon snorted a laugh. "Charlotte?" That would be no surprise.

Drake shook his head. "Your mother. In fact, she said Charlotte was most gracious at supper. Are you really going to take her to your family's estate for a wedding trip?"

"If you don't need me here."

"I think I can manage for a while without you. One of the advantages of being a duke is having servants at your bidding. And I know how to review my own books should the need arise." Lifting the whisky, he took a longer sip, closing his eyes. When he opened them, he met Simon's gaze directly. "And I think you have more important business to attend to."

"Such as?"

"Making good on your boast."

Lord, there had been so many boasts. "Which in particular?"

"The one where you claimed you could woo any woman into your bed."

Oh, *that* one. Simon's eyes inadvertently gazed toward the ceiling, much in the same manner he'd found Drake. He tugged on the cuffs of his sleeves. "Well, never let it be said that Simon Beckham backed down from a challenge."

As he headed upstairs to face his dragon—err, his bride—Drake's laugh echoed behind him.

⊷✿⊶

ROSE HAD FIXED CHARLOTTE'S DISHEVELED HAIR BEFORE SUPPER, and Charlotte was glad to have regained that much control over her situation. Seriously, the idea of going around with her hair down for so long in the day made her stomach cramp. But as Rose readied her for bed, removing the pins and brushing the thick dark locks, Charlotte studied herself in the mirror.

With her hair flowing around her shoulders, it softened her face and reminded her of a girl of ten-and-four who couldn't wait to pin her hair up like an adult. She'd been so naïve, eager to be grown up without truly understanding the heavy burden being a woman brought. She instructed Rose to leave her hair loose and unplaited.

After she dismissed Rose, Charlotte tightened the silk dressing gown around her and sat at the small escritoire. The last time she'd written to Nash had been after Honoria's wedding. He'd been delighted, as had his wife Adalyn, to learn of Honoria's love match. Charlotte had grown to admire her brother's wife, who transcribed his personal correspondence for him. Adalyn had a way of sneaking in little tidbits about Nash that made Charlotte smile—especially how he doted on their son, Benjamin. Charlotte suspected Adalyn kept those additions secret from her husband, who never wanted anyone to know he had a soft side.

Charlotte pulled out foolscap, ink, and pen. She'd refrained from writing with her news sooner in the unlikely—but hopeful—event some miracle would intervene and circumvent her marriage.

Dipping her pen in the inkpot, she sighed. The pen hovered over the paper.

My dearest brother,

I hope this letter finds you, Adalyn, and Benjamin well. I write to you with both joyous and disconcerting news.

She paused, her pen poised over the words *and disconcerting*. Should she strike them? No, best to prepare him. She left them for the moment and continued.

Honoria has given birth to a healthy baby girl. They have named the child Katherine and will call her Kitty after the duke's great aunt. The duke shows no distress over the sex of the child. In fact, he is overjoyed, cuddling and cooing at the infant. He is completely besotted. I can no longer think of him as Burwood, which conjures a cold and uncaring image, much like our father and brother, but only as Drake, which he has requested I call him. Honoria, of course, radiates happiness.

She pondered how to deliver her next news. Better to ease into it.

Odd to think there was a time when Honoria could have become my sister, should you have courted her in earnest. I have done my best to fulfill your wish to look after her. And now, by an unforeseen series of events, I find myself as close to her as a sister could be. Not only has she requested I be the godmother of her beautiful little daughter, but

She paused again, pulling in a breath before writing the words of stark reality.

I am married to the duke's man of business, Mr. Simon Beckham. It was quite sudden, and I hope you do not hear of it through other sources. Know that it was completely of my choosing, and I intend to make the best of it.

Please write again when you are able with news of young Benjamin, Adalyn, and your ventures in America.

With affection,

Your sister, Charlotte.

There. Short and to the point. No need to coat it with sweetness. Nash would see past such insincerity in a blink. She would have Frampton frank and post it first thing in the morning.

Even with such forthrightness, Nash would have an ocean of questions. And at that moment, she was grateful he was so far away, giving her time to think and plan appropriate responses.

Tap-tap-tap.

Had the rain increased again? Mercifully, it had eased as night came. She rose and moved toward the window. But when she pulled back the curtain, no streaks of water dripped down the pane of glass.

Tap-tap-tap.

"Charlotte?" the now familiar voice called.

She pulled her wrapper around her more tightly, making certain the tie was secure, then opened the door to her husband.

❧

AFTER MAKING IT UPSTAIRS UNSEEN BY HIS FAMILY, SIMON washed and prepared for bed. With a deep breath, he fortified himself, stepped from his room, and knocked on Charlotte's door.

She didn't answer. Perhaps she had already fallen asleep. He knocked again and called her name.

When she opened the door, Simon literally felt his jaw drop as Charlotte stood before him in her dressing gown.

Lord, she was beautiful with all that glorious dark hair flowing over her shoulders. When she'd taken the pins out earlier, it had been haphazard and messy—fitting for the illusion that they'd been busy in the bedroom.

But with it brushed smooth, he wanted to run his hands through it and muss it in earnest.

She glared at him. "Close your mouth. You'll catch something."

Her words hit him like the douse of cold water that had got them into this mess to begin with. He snapped his mouth shut. "I came to say goodnight and see if there is anything I can do to make you more *comfortable.*" He winked.

She glowered. "I'm fine, no thanks to you." She leaned in, and for a moment, he thought she might kiss him. She sniffed. "At least you don't reek of liquor. Where did you go?"

"Early in our marriage to start nagging me about my whereabouts, don't you think?"

She quirked a dark brow, but all he wanted to do was kiss it. *Damn.*

He needed a different approach. "If you allow me to come in, we can discuss it away from servants' ears."

Craning her neck, which also was quite kissable, she scanned the hallway. "I don't see any servants."

Admittedly, not his most effective approach. "Charlotte, you're being childish. I'm your husband. Let me inside."

"*I'm* being childish?! Ha!" Still, she threw the door open and stood aside, allowing him to enter.

When Simon turned around after closing the door, Drake's words became reality. The challenge seemed insurmountable.

Charlotte crossed her arms over her chest, pushing her breasts up—the tops, round and luscious—peeking over the edge of her nightdress. "Well? I'm waiting."

He summoned his most charming grin, the one where one side of his mouth lifted in careless ease. "Why don't we discuss this on the bed?"

She continued to glare, unmoved.

No—wait. There was something—a shift in her eyes toward the bed, a slight bloom of color on her cheeks.

"No."

"How long are we to dance around this?"

"Considering we've been married less than a day, and under unusual circumstances, no less, I would say as long as it takes. And I'm still waiting to hear where you were."

"Am I to make an account of everywhere I go? Who I see? Speak with? What? For your approval? Like a *real* marriage?"

She huffed and took a seat in a chair by the window. "I don't want to argue with you. Not today."

"Because it's our wedding day?"

"Because it's a day of joy for our dear friends. We should *both* have been by their sides. He didn't say anything, but Drake wanted to show off his daughter to you."

The knife, still lodged in his chest, twisted anew, and as always, he deflected the pain. "I'll see her tomorrow. I spoke to Drake when I came home. He was the one who reminded me I had a bride waiting for me. Shall we keep the discussion centered on us for the time being?" Simply to vex her, he stretched out on the bed and patted the mattress.

"Fine. Where were you?"

"I paid a visit to the new gaming hell. Ran into a few familiar faces, met some new ones."

"Which of your ruffian friends did you see?"

"Lord Montgomery. Mr. Weatherby. Although I don't think they'd take too kindly to being called ruffians." He waited for her reaction, sorely disappointed when she remained stoic. "They weren't the only ones. Lord Felix Davies sullied the place with his presence."

"Ugh. The Worm no doubt seized the opportunity to point out you were catting around instead of being with your new wife."

"He did. And for that, I'm truly sorry, Charlotte. I had no idea he'd be there. If it helps, the owner, a tower of a man called The Captain, had him thrown out. Apparently it wasn't the first time Davies caused a disturbance in the man's club."

With a faraway look in her eyes, Charlotte muttered, "I wonder . . ."

Simon straightened on the bed. "What?"

Her attention jerked back to him. "Nothing. Just something Miranda told us last year during the duke's house party. How long has this new gaming hell been open?"

He shrugged. "About a year, I believe." Something was brewing in that mind of hers. He had to give his wife credit. She wasn't simply a pretty face. "If it makes you feel better, I wanted to strangle the man."

"The owner?"

"No, of course not. Davies. The owner stopped me, said he quite understood." He patted the bed again. "Am I forgiven? Perhaps a little physical demonstration of your understanding for the grievous neglect of my beautiful wife?"

Both of her dark eyebrows rose. "Does that actually work for you?"

He grinned. "Most of the time. Yes."

"Go to bed, Simon."

He made a show of gazing around. "Why, look at that. I'm already there." He scooted toward the middle and stretched out again. "Ah! So comfortable." His arms folded over his chest in a semblance of repose, he closed his eyes.

Rustle of silk and the shuffle of footsteps approached, and Simon smiled inwardly.

Here she comes.

Pressure dipped the mattress.

He cracked open one eyelid.

Kneeling with her dark hair curtaining him, she glared down, her teeth bared like a lioness. "Get. Off. My. Bed."

He turned to prop himself on an elbow, but her hair caught under his arm.

"Ow!" she howled.

Reflexes keen, he slipped an arm around her waist and

flipped her on her back, reversing their positions. He grinned down at her. "Hello."

He expected her to rail at him. To tell him to go to the devil. Or if he were really lucky to kiss him.

He didn't expect the panic in her eyes.

"Get off me!"

He scrambled off both her and the bed.

She swiped at her face, then turned away. "You promised!" Lord, her voice sounded like a wounded animal's.

Nausea churned his stomach. Too bad neither her brother nor Felix Davies was there to receive his accounts. "I'm so, so sorry. I'll leave."

She sat on the bed with her knees drawn to her chest, her hair curtaining and shielding her face from view.

"I didn't mean to scare you, Charlotte. Please forgive me."

"Just go." Her hand slipped up to her face again.

Unable to bear the guilt compressing his chest, he bowed his head and stared at his hand on the door handle. "Goodnight," he whispered as he slipped through the door.

On the other side, he pulled in a breath, releasing it slowly through his mouth.

What in the devil had he got himself into?

CHAPTER 16

Charlotte rose early the next morning. Truth be told, she didn't sleep much. Ashamed not of her outburst, but for her reaction to what she knew in her heart Simon had meant as playful, she played it over and over in her mind.

The desperation in her voice, the fear shaking within her as he grinned down at her, haunted her most of the night. She'd been weak, exposing her vulnerability.

And she cursed herself for her lapse. It would not happen again.

In the breakfast room, Drake rose as she entered. "Lady Charlotte. I didn't expect to see you this early." He glanced behind her, no doubt expecting to see Simon trailing behind.

"I could say the same for you, Your Grace. You had an eventful day yesterday."

Waiting until she served herself some toast and jam and took a seat, he reseated himself. "We both did."

"How is Honoria feeling?"

"She would lie and say she's feeling marvelous, but the pain in her eyes when she moves about gives her away. And she insists on feeding Kitty herself rather than using a wet nurse, so she was up half the night."

Charlotte spread the jam on her toast. "That does sound like Honoria." As nonchalantly as she could, she asked, "Have you seen Simon this morning?"

Cup poised at his lips, Drake's eyes widened. "No. I presumed he would be with you."

"Did I hear someone mention my name?" Simon waltzed in as if he had nary a care in the world. His world, perhaps, especially since he seemed to live in one filled with fantasy.

However, when his eyes met hers, they didn't match the easy smile on his face. "Good morning, darling. Sleep well?"

"Perfectly," she lied. "And you?"

"Like the dead." He jerked his gaze away quickly, as if even that bit of connection was too much for him.

Guilt slithered anew that her reaction had affected him as well, inadvertently accusing him of something he swore he would never do.

He strode to the sideboard. "Ah, breakfast. I'm famished."

Drake's attention bounced between them. He shook his head, then sipped his tea.

After Simon loaded his plate with what Charlotte was certain he couldn't finish, he took a seat next to Drake. "I want to meet that beautiful daughter of yours as soon as she's accepting callers."

Tea sputtered from Drake's lips. "Callers?! Good grief, don't even make me think of that yet. She's not even a day old." He set the cup down and wiped his mouth with the serviette. "However, I do want you to meet her. Honoria and I have something to ask you."

"Oh?"

"If I may," Charlotte interjected, "I'd like to accompany you. I have something I wish to discuss with Honoria." Charlotte avoided Simon's eyes, finding a spot between Drake and her husband to direct her gaze.

The men exchanged a questioning glance, but Drake answered. "If you are asking my permission, you have it. I'm sure Honoria would be glad to see you."

Simon stared at his plate of eggs, toast, and bacon. "Have my mother and sisters been pestering you to no end, wishing to hold the baby?"

Drake laughed, nodding. "And your father. He informed me not to hesitate to seek his counsel about rearing daughters. I may take him up on it, especially since the two oldest are yet unmarried. How has he kept the men at bay? Your sisters are all so lovely."

"A gun. And he's a crack shot," Simon answered, then shoved a piece of bacon in his mouth.

Charlotte's cup dropped on the saucer with a *clink*. "Truly? He shoots them?"

Simon's gaze tangled with hers. The earlier discomfort had disappeared, and his eyes glinted with the merriment she'd grown accustomed to. "Doesn't have to. He invites them into his study displaying his trophies. The gun hangs on the wall next to them, and he stands next to it as he explains in his sternest voice how he will not tolerate any disrespect of his daughters."

"That's bloody brilliant!" Drake shot an apologetic glance toward Charlotte. "I beg your pardon."

She waved it off, more interested in Simon's account of his father. "You're jesting."

"Not at all. You'll see for yourself when we spend time there for our wedding trip."

With Kitty's unexpected birth, Charlotte wondered if leaving was such a good idea. "Can you manage without him, Your Grace?"

"I've already informed Simon that as much as I depend on him—and make no mistake, Lady Charlotte, I do depend on him as flighty as my friend may seem—I can manage my own books, and servants can assume any other duties. Go. Enjoy getting to know each other better." Something unsaid lingered in the duke's statement.

But she didn't dwell on it. Enjoyment itself would be a tall order.

"Very well. I should like to see this so-called suitor detractor. It makes me wonder why your father goes to such lengths. Doesn't he have faith in your sisters making an acceptable match?"

Simon laughed. "You've met my sisters. What do you think?"

"Frannie seems most sensible."

"And Frannie is only ten-and-seven. But no, it's not so much he doesn't trust *their* judgment, but he wants them to make a love match like his own. He's very good at reading others' true feelings."

Not so very good. Hadn't the man rambled on about how happy he was that Simon had found a woman he loved and who loved him in return? The man's ability to read feelings had either deteriorated greatly since Simon had last seen them in action or both men were delusional.

Drake clapped his hands together. "Finish your breakfast, Simon. I want to introduce you to my daughter."

Simon shoveled in the last of his eggs.

Really, the man had shown better manners when he was impersonating the duke.

Bent over his plate, he peered up at her. "You're giving me the look my mother gives me."

"Hmph. Might that be because you are acting like a slovenly pig?"

Wiping his lips, he rose, moved to her side, and held out his hand. "Redundant, don't you think? I don't know of many tidy pigs. They do love their mud."

An unexpected laugh bubbled up. She slipped her hand into

his, and rising, whispered in his ear. "Don't interpret that laugh for more than it was."

His lips quirked, but he kept his gaze straight ahead. "I would never presume something so preposterous as the idea of you having a sense of humor." He cleared his throat. "To the baby!"

Upstairs, Drake knocked on Honoria's door, cracked it, and peeked inside. "Simon and Charlotte are here, my love."

"Well, let them in, Drake." Although Honoria's voice still held a note of exhaustion, it sparkled with cheerfulness.

When they stepped inside, Simon hesitated, his eyes widening at the tiny bundle in Honoria's arms.

Honoria's eyes filled with love as she gazed at her husband. "Have you asked him?"

Drake shook his head. "I wanted us to do it together as we did for Charlotte." He turned toward Simon. "Would you do us the honor of being Kitty's godfather? Charlotte has already agreed to be godmother."

Simon's head jerked toward her as if the announcement was the most absurd thing he'd heard all day. He seemed overtaken with emotion. For what, Charlotte wasn't entirely sure, but she suspected it was the same she felt when presented with the honor.

"Of course," he choked out.

"Good. I'm glad that's settled before you leave for Wiltshire." Drake said.

Honoria stopped cooing to the baby. "You're leaving?"

"Only for a while," Charlotte said.

"My love," Drake said, lifting the baby from Honoria's arms. "They've just been married. We must allow them a wedding trip." He rocked the baby, and a secret smile crossed his lips. "I still remember ours."

Simon coughed, his gaze sliding to Charlotte's. "I'll tell my family this morning and send them ahead, then I'll have our trunks packed. Is tomorrow too soon?"

Charlotte shook her head.

"Then perhaps you might wish to hold Kitty a bit before you leave?" Drake placed the baby in Charlotte's arms.

Kitty scrunched her face and let out an ear-piercing scream. Charlotte tensed. How did one calm a crying child? She jostled the baby, whose face reddened further.

"Here. Allow me." Simon strode over and rescued both her and the baby. He cooed to Kitty much like Honoria had earlier, his dazzling smile directed solely toward her. "There, there. That is no way for a beautiful lady to act. And you are beautiful, little Kitty. Where's a smile for Simon?"

Charlotte rolled her eyes. "Babies don't smile."

And yet, Kitty's cries diminished to little sobs and pulls of breath as she quieted and gazed up in Simon's face with adoration and wonder, as if Simon's world revolved around only her.

Charlotte couldn't help but wonder what that would be like, and a weed of envy poked through her armor.

❧

SIMON GAZED AT THE INFANT IN HIS ARMS, SO TINY AND HELPLESS. Kitty was fortunate to have Drake as a father. Dependable, trustworthy, considering all manner of dangers that might await his charge and doing all that was necessary to protect her.

Simon was none of those things. How could Drake even think of asking him to be Kitty's godfather? He would more likely lead her into the jaws of danger, eager to tackle the next challenge and stare down the next dangerous beast.

But wait. Charlotte was to be the child's godmother. Surely, she would balance him out. He couldn't imagine the woman taking any type of risk. Rather, she would calculate every potential danger and forge a safe and unexciting path.

At least he was good at soothing. Pretty words, and soft smiles, he could give. Stability and safety—not really.

"You have a gift, Simon." Honoria drew his attention from the infant. "I will miss you and Charlotte, but Drake is right. You need the time alone to begin your lives together. If I may, could I speak to Charlotte in private?"

"May I keep holding her for a while?" Simon asked.

Drake placed a hand on Simon's shoulder. "Of course. Your family was in the drawing room earlier. Let's take Kitty down there and let your mother have some time with her before they leave."

"I won't keep her long, Simon," Honoria said as he and Drake slipped out the door.

Unease tightened Simon's chest, and Kitty squirmed in his arms. "What does Honoria want to talk to Charlotte about?"

Drake shrugged. "I don't know. Perhaps she wants to know how things are going between you two." Drake's probing gaze indicated Honoria wasn't the only one to wonder.

"About as well as one would expect for a forced marriage."

The tips of Drake's ears colored. "Um. Did you two . . .?"

"Consummate the marriage? Really, Drake, you've been married for a little over nine months and sex still embarrasses you?"

Simon almost laughed at Drake's affronted expression.

"It's not embarrassment. I'm trying to be delicate."

"And yet, you asked anyway." Simon held the infant closer to his chest as they descended the staircase. "The answer to your question is no. We did not. I promised I wouldn't demand anything from her." His mind jolted back to Charlotte's panicked reaction the night before, and strangely it went to Davies. Had the man done more than strike her? For the moment, he brushed the uncomfortable thought aside and focused on the child in his arms.

"So, the state of Charlotte's and your disheveled hair and clothing was—"

"A ruse for my family's benefit. They think I married for love, although I suspect my mother has read the scandal sheet and has her doubts."

Drake shook his head. "Are you certain staying with your family is the wisest thing? You and Charlotte need time alone."

"And we'll have it. In the cottage my grandmother used. It's far enough away to give us some privacy, but close enough to make an appearance or two to satisfy my family." And he secretly hoped Charlotte would grow to love his family, not only as a support when he died but also to convince her to provide an heir to secure all of their futures.

Of course, he also hoped for some good fishing and hunting, but he kept all that to himself. No need to have Drake chiding him for his lack of romantic feelings.

At the foot of the staircase, Frampton greeted them. "The Countess Gryffin has come to pay her respects and see the baby, Your Grace. She wouldn't allow me to announce her; she's in the drawing room with Mr. Beckham's family."

Boisterous chatter rose from the drawing room, energizing Simon. He thrived on the lively conversation that busied his mind and distracted it from less pleasant things.

Such as how to win over his ice queen of a wife.

CHARLOTTE STRAIGHTENED THE COUNTERPANE AROUND HONORIA, busying herself to avoid her friend's questioning. She had no doubt what Honoria wished to speak to her about. "Would you like some tea? Have you eaten?" She slipped into the role of caretaker with an ease that surprised her.

"Stop fussing and sit." Honoria patted the mattress beside her.

The action pulled Charlotte back to the previous night and Simon on her bed.

"Are you certain it won't disturb you?"

Honoria winced as she pushed against the mattress, pulling herself upright a little more. "No more than Drake did tossing and turning all night."

What in the world had the man been thinking? His wife had just given birth! "Should I speak with him and suggest he stay in his own bed?"

Honoria laughed. "Only you would dare to reprimand a duke. No, he wanted to be close to me and Kitty. And I can't refuse him anything." Color flooded her cheeks. "Truth be told, we never sleep apart."

She patted the mattress again, and Charlotte sat and took Honoria's hand.

Honoria's brow furrowed. "I don't even know quite how to ask this."

"Perhaps you could try my approach and be direct?" Charlotte prepared herself.

"Did things go well last night? Was Simon gentle with you?"

"Didn't Drake tell you? My husband spent most of the evening at a gaming hell. Nothing happened between us." At least not what Honoria was dancing around.

"Oh." Honoria seemed . . . disappointed.

"Remember, ours is not a love match like yours and Drake's. Neither of us wanted this. It's an arrangement, nothing more. There are no tender feelings which need to be acted upon."

Honoria shook her head. "How can you not see it? Simon cares for you. Why else would he offer for you to save your reputation?"

"He has his reasons, which I'm not at liberty to reveal. But Simon Beckham only cares for what folly awaits him."

"Oh, Charlotte, that's not true. Simon is an honorable man. And I'm not the only one to notice there is something between you." Pink bloomed on her cheeks again. "Surely, he would be willing if you gave him the slightest encouragement. And I'm certain he would be gentle and attentive. I've found great pleasure in being married."

"If this is supposed to replace the conversation I would have had with my mother on the eve of my wedding, consider your task complete."

"Promise me you'll give him a chance?"

Pressure tightened around Charlotte's chest. She knew she couldn't put off Simon forever. But promising Honoria made it much too real. She swallowed. "I promise."

"Good." She yawned and stretched. "Now, while I have an opportunity, I think I shall try to sleep."

Charlotte rose and once again straightened the counterpane around her friend.

Then she strode out the door, summoning the strength to see her promise through.

CHAPTER 17

Between his family and Aunt Kitty, Simon hardly had time to think about what had happened—or not happened—between him and Charlotte the night before, and the day sped by faster than a race through Hyde Park in his phaeton.

Aunt Kitty monopolized her namesake much of the time, barely allowing his mother or sisters an opportunity to hold the darling child. Oddly, each time someone offered Charlotte an opportunity to hold the infant, she lifted her hand and waved them off, saying, "I feel a sniffle coming on," or "She looks so peaceful; let's not disturb her."

Yet, when she was preoccupied and unaware of observation, he stole glances at her, catching how her eyes filled with a sad longing. He took a seat next to her on the settee.

"It's an excuse," he whispered.

She stiffened next to him, sending him the all-too-familiar glare. "I beg your pardon!" The exclamation was muffled and overshadowed by Kitty's cries.

"You're nervous about holding her."

She huffed and turned away. "That's ridiculous."

"Practice. That's all you need."

"Hmph!"

"But if you're too afraid of trying . . ."

Aha! That did it.

"I'm not afraid. I simply don't want to disturb her."

He quirked an eyebrow at her. "She's wailing her head off from the way Georgie is jerking her about. Allow me to rescue the child and show you how to quiet her."

After removing Kitty from Georgie's inexperienced arms, he soothed her just enough to quiet her wails to sobs. Then he gave her to Charlotte, positioning her securely. "Cradle her head in the crook of your elbow. There. That's it. Now, place your other hand here." He moved Charlotte's other arm under the baby's back. "Support her and give her back gentle pats. That's it. Now, the most important part. Relax and smile at her. Don't frown at her like she's me."

Charlotte actually laughed, and Kitty ceased mid-sob, gazing up into Charlotte's face with the wonder only a baby can manage.

Or so he thought until Charlotte's face brightened with the same expression. "I did it!"

"You did." Not quite painful, but still disconcerting, the twinge in his chest took him off guard. He did what he always did. He deflected. "Thanks to me."

"Hmph! Your head is already inflated. Isn't it, Kitty?" Kitty stirred, her rosebud mouth puckering and preparing for another onset of objection.

Simon prepared to pluck the child from Charlotte's arms, but Charlotte quickly soothed Kitty back into submission.

Well, I'll be damned.

"Don't mind him, little one. He's very full of himself, and we ladies cannot let him get the best of us."

Seeing Charlotte's confidence with Kitty grow diminished the insult she'd flung his way. But Simon also paid heed to her words.

They were no surprise, but if he could still his mind long enough, he would ponder them later. Perhaps they provided a clue to wooing her.

When the nanny stepped in and removed the baby, she clucked her tongue over the fact that it wasn't good for a newborn to be held so much.

Simon rather thought holding an infant was the best possible thing for them, ensuring they felt loved and secure. However, he conceded that too many hands on the child might not be the best.

With the lure of cuddling an infant gone, and after Aunt Kitty departed, Simon instructed the servants to pack his family's trunks first, then his and Charlotte's.

Three hours later, his mother squished his face in her hands as she bade him a tearful goodbye.

"We should be less than a day behind you. You act like I'm enlisting in the military again."

"You're too old for that," Kate said. "Your decrepit bones couldn't handle it."

Next to him, Charlotte uttered a laugh before his father engulfed her in a hug. "I'm overjoyed you're part of our family, Lady Charlotte. Keep this rapscallion in line!"

"I shall make it my life's mission," his wife answered, no doubt planning multiple ways to vex him.

"Maybe we can hold a ball in Swindon's assembly hall in your honor," Beth said.

Frannie rolled her eyes.

"If they can pull themselves away from each other," Rebecca said.

"Promise you'll let me take you around the estate?" Georgie asked.

"I . . . promise," Charlotte answered.

Curious. Why did she hesitate?

As the carriage drove off, disappearing in the busy streets of

Mayfair, he said, "If you don't want Georgie to show you around, I'll make your excuses."

"It's not that. Exploring your family's estate will occupy my mind while you're out murdering animals and torturing the fish."

He laughed. "You do have a way with words." He studied her. "I'd like for us not to keep secrets from one another. We may not have what Drake and Honoria do, but it could at least be a civil marriage. Why did you hesitate to promise?"

"It made me think of a promise I made to Honoria."

"Oh?" He waited a moment.

"To give you a chance." Without further explanation, she left, leaving him enveloped in lilac and a flicker of hope.

Unlike the day before, Simon stayed at home, spending the time instructing the staff and imploring them to handle as much as possible without bothering Drake. "Don't plague His Grace with questions," he said to the footmen gathered. "Frampton is your first line of defense."

Frampton puffed out his chest. "No need to worry, Mr. Beckham. We will all do our best to ensure His Grace gets rest and is not troubled with unnecessary details in your absence."

With that task complete, he watched the clock in the drawing room for a solid twenty-three minutes while Charlotte read her book. The prospect of being confined in a carriage for long hours pressed down like a great weight. He needed to *do* something. He pulled back the curtain and peeked out the window.

Twilight approached, and the air would soon chill. "Would you care to go for a short stroll?"

"No." She waved a hand at him as if shooing away a pesky insect. "You go."

And she called *him* incorrigible. "And risk your ire if I leave you again? No, thank you." He plopped back down in the chair, exhaling an exaggerated, "Oomph."

She slammed the book on the table next to her. "If you're

going to behave like a spoiled child and make irritating noises, I capitulate."

He wanted to kiss her in gratitude, but he feared a repeat of the night before. He must take things slowly.

AT THE FRONT DOOR, FRAMPTON HELD OUT CHARLOTTE'S pelisse, but Simon snatched it from the butler's hands and held it open to her. "Allow me." He had the audacity to flash that ridiculous grin at her.

Her knees might have weakened—if she believed he could evoke such a response. More likely, it was simply her joints adjusting. She slipped her arms through, and the heat of his hands pressed against her shoulders as he smoothed the material over them.

"Wouldn't want you to catch a chill before our trip." Wisps of his breath, hot and soft, brushed against her cheek as he leaned in.

When he held out his arm to lead her through the door, she ignored him, stepping outside into the dimming light and hoping to complete the walk quickly. Until Honoria's request demanded her attention.

Give him a chance.

Gah!

Simon stepped outside beside her.

"Very well," she said with as much annoyance as she could muster.

He blinked. "Very well, what?"

Damn the man. Did he have to draw her attention to his incredible blue eyes?

"I'll take your stupid arm."

He laughed—the fool. "I'll have you know my arm has been known to make very wise decisions." With the ridiculous smile plastered on his face, he stared straight ahead, yet he held out his arm.

When she slid her gloved hand over it, it felt—right, as if it had been waiting specifically for her.

Absurd. How could an arm be waiting for a hand? The recent weeks spent in his presence had turned her mind into mush. Yet, she couldn't help but notice the firm muscle beneath the material of his superfine coat. Muscle she had observed first-hand. And more than just his arms. Her face burned at the memory of his naked form.

He slid a sideways glance toward her. "Perhaps the pelisse is too much. It is still rather warm for this time of day."

"I'm fine."

They strolled in silence the short distance to the park. Other than the modiste and their meeting with the vicar, Charlotte had not dealt with the aftermath of the scandal in *The Muckraker*. But as people passed, she couldn't help but notice how many gave them the cut—indirect, granted, acting as if they had not seen her, but a cut nonetheless.

Oblivious to the insult, Simon tipped his hat to each one of the judgmental churls, greeting them with a cheery, "Good evening!" Or, "Fine evening for a stroll, wouldn't you say?"

"How can you be so pleasant to these . . . these . . ." Even through gritted teeth, she couldn't say the word.

"Arses? You can say it to me. I won't be offended, especially when it's the truth."

Her mouth fell open.

"Close your mouth, darling, here comes another group of them. As to your question. Let them think their rudeness doesn't bother us in the least. Don't give them the satisfaction. 'Kill them with kindness' has worked well for me." He lay his free hand on top of hers and gave a gentle squeeze. "Go ahead, try it."

As Lord and Lady Cheswick approached, Charlotte forced a smile to her lips.

Simon leaned in, caressing her again with his warm breath. "Try to appear natural, not like you're going to eat them."

Odd, but the idea made her laugh, genuine and full-throated.

Lady Cheswick turned up her nose and tugged on her husband's arm, giving Charlotte and Simon a wide berth as if they had some horrible disease. "Some people have no sense of shame." Although muttered, Lady Cheswick's words were clear enough.

"How good to see you, Lord Cheswick." She nodded at them as they gawked, aghast. "Lady Cheswick, are you quite well? You appear a little green. Or perhaps it is the unfortunate color of your gown." She shook her head, delivering a little *tsk, tsk,* and then forced the smile back, this time hoping it appeared as Simon had described.

Lady Cheswick tugged on her husband's arm, muttering, "The nerve!"

Safely past them, Simon threw his head back and laughed. "Well done! How did it feel?"

"Marvelous. Like I'm myself again."

"I must say, it's good to have your sharp tongue directed at someone other than me." When their gazes tangled, heat burned in his eyes, as if something naughty had crossed his mind. He coughed and turned away.

With her new approach, the stroll became enjoyable as each of them took turns in confronting each challenger with courage and wit.

Puddles remained from the previous day's rain, most easy to avoid. But as they returned home by an alternate route, a muddy patch of water pooled in a dip in the path, obstructing their progress.

Simon removed her hand from his arm. "Wait here a moment." He stepped forward, placing his booted foot into the puddle. Water rose past his ankle. "Damn." He turned toward her. "Don't suppose you have boots on?"

"No." The whole idea had been so impromptu she hadn't even thought to put on her half boots. Even if she lifted her skirts, her slippers would get soaked.

Returning to her, he said, "Put your arms around my neck."

She stepped back as if pushed. "Wh—what?"

He huffed. "Never mind." Instead of turning away, he moved forward, scooping her up and lifting her off the ground.

Instinctively, her arms went around his neck to anchor herself. "You're mad!"

He traversed the puddle in three long strides, splashing water in his wake. "Kept you dry, didn't I? Isn't that a husband's job? To protect his wife."

Charlotte gritted her teeth. "Put me down this instant!"

"Capital idea, Mr. Beckham!" a voice called from behind.

Simon turned, still holding her in his arms.

Laurence and Beatrix Townsend approached, and imitating Simon, Laurence swung his wife up and carried her across the puddle.

"Down!" Charlotte demanded again.

Simon finally lowered her to the ground.

Beatrix, on the other hand, seemed delighted to be manhandled in such a fashion. However, one must consider the source. Beatrix had always been a strange woman. In fact, she rewarded her husband with a kiss on the cheek when he placed her back on her feet on the dry side of the puddle. "Don't we have the most gallant of husbands, Lady Charlotte?"

Gallant? Is that what Simon's action was meant to be? She stole a peek at her husband.

He certainly seemed pleased with himself, as did Lord Montgomery.

Lord Montgomery held out his hand to Simon. "Good to see you again so soon. I trust all is well?" Laurence's eyes shifted toward Charlotte.

"Quite well, sir."

"Good. Smart of you to make a public appearance and silence those wagging tongues. Bea and I have our own experience in that regard."

Beatrix narrowed her sharp eyes on Charlotte. "To be clear, Lady Charlotte, I give little credence to what's published in that rag—and neither should you. Someone should stop that abomination posing as news."

Charlotte reconsidered the bookish redhead. With her intelligence, she might prove to be a valuable ally. When she and Simon returned from their wedding trip, Charlotte would speak to Honoria about inviting Lady Montgomery into the League.

"If you are in contact with your brother Lord Nash, please tell him how much I am enjoying the Broadwood. I hope he was able to purchase another piano in America. I never told him, but he is quite talented."

Charlotte blinked at the kindness. "I will, Lady Montgomery. Nash will be pleased his cherished instrument is in such capable hands."

Laurence tipped his hat. "Well, we should be off. I'm anxious to get Bea home. In fact . . ." He swooped her up again, eliciting a squeal from his wife, and raced off, carrying her.

Charlotte shook her head. "They are a strange couple."

Simon nodded, his eyes growing distant as he watched them. "And in love." He shook his head as if to clear it. "What was that about a Broadwood?"

"When my brother left for America, he sold his piano to Lord Montgomery, who planned to give it to his wife for their anniversary."

"She does play prodigiously well. As I understand from my mother, so do you."

"Not as well as Lady Montgomery or my brother Nash. Both make the keys come to life."

"Unlike Georgie, who makes them cry in pain?"

She laughed again. A momentous day. Reluctantly, she

admitted she could get used to her husband's sense of humor. Goodness, she was growing soft.

When he held out his arm again, she took it immediately. The sun had set fully, and men climbed ladders, lighting the last of the gas lamps along Grosvenor Square.

A sense of peace enveloped her in the quiet stillness of the evening, and Simon's arm, firm and strong beneath her hand, seemed right and true.

"Charlotte," Simon said, shaking her from her sentimental reverie.

She jerked toward him. "Hmm?"

His smile was gentle, void of any teasing at her distractedness. "Do we have a chance?"

Blink.

"What?"

Unusual seriousness painted his face. "You said you promised Honoria to give me a chance. I simply want to know if you believe you can. I'm not asking for love; I'm not that naïve. Can you tolerate me enough to not shrink from my touch?"

She shook her head and huffed a sigh. "I'm touching you now, aren't I?"

"You know what I mean. Are we going to discuss last night?"

No. "You took me by surprise. Give me fair warning if you're going to manhandle me again."

"Are you speaking of last night or the puddle?"

"Both."

A lopsided grin lifted his mouth at one corner. "I did ask you to put your arms around my neck. Not warning enough?"

Pressing her lips together, she almost bit her tongue to keep from railing at him. She *did* promise Honoria. "You promised not to force me. Last night . . ."

"My playfulness frightened you, and I'm sorry."

Playfulness. Is that what he called it?

"But I can't help but wonder." He looked away for a moment,

and when he turned back, he was all seriousness. "Did Davies do more than strike you?"

The words knotted in her throat. "He tried. Once. I would prefer not to speak of it."

Still solemn, he nodded. "I'll keep my hands to myself until you're ready."

Thank goodness they were almost back at the house, and Simon remained quiet the rest of the way. But as she played the scene back in her mind, she understood how she may have misinterpreted his actions.

Simon wasn't Felix. And truth be told, she might actually enjoy her husband's touch.

CHAPTER 18

That evening at supper, the table seemed enormous. With his family gone and Drake and Honoria taking their meals in her bedchamber, Simon did his best to fill the void. Normally, scintillating conversation was his gift, but with Charlotte, he worried over each thing that came from his mouth. Would he offend her with a joke? Insult her when all he'd meant to do was compliment her? Would she storm off in a huff from the most innocuous comment?

She was so damned unpredictable.

Except her revelation that Davies had tried to force himself on her gave Simon a peek inside that lovely head. Not to mention making him want to get his hands on the man's throat even more. Simon latched on to the word *tried*. No wonder Charlotte insisted he put his promise in writing.

He speared a piece of beef. "How are you enjoying your book about people who detest each other?"

She eyed him askance, then returned her attention to her plate. "Very well."

His attempt at civil conversation was like pulling a mature carrot from hard ground. He wanted to shake her.

"Tell me about it."

She eyed him over the rim of her wine goblet. "I thought you didn't like to read."

"That doesn't mean I'm not interested in the story itself. Dazzle me with your storytelling skills."

Her eyes narrowed. "There's an insult hidden in there."

His fork dropped to his plate. "Must you be defensive about everything? I'm simply asking you a question to fill this interminable silence."

When her eyes widened, he cursed his own impatience. He softened his tone. "I apologize. Please, tell me more about the book?"

"You wouldn't enjoy it. It's become an utter fantasy. Even though the two people despise one another, they are also attracted to each other."

He snorted a laugh. "Like us." *Oh.* That shouldn't have slipped out. Holding his breath, he waited for her to rail and say she wasn't attracted to him.

Wine sloshed in her glass as she set it down none too gently. "You're attracted to me?"

"Well, you're a beautiful, intelligent woman, and I'm not blind. And contrary to your belief, I'm not stupid either."

Damn. He did it again. How could he be so careless and open himself up to her barbs?

She blinked—several times, then stared at her plate. "No, you're not. But"—she met his gaze—"I am *not* attracted to you."

Ah. There it is.

"So, these two people who are *not* like us. Tell me about them. Why do they despise each other?"

"She finds him proud and aloof. Frankly, I don't understand why she despises him. He's sensible and careful to avoid scandal."

"Unlike us—at least the scandal part."

She pointed her fork at him. "That was your fault."

"For being naked?"

Her cheeks pinked. "He, on the other hand," she continued, completely ignoring his comment, "has every reason to be concerned about her. Her family is disgraceful. Except for her older sister, whom I find also sensible, if somewhat lacking a backbone. However, Elizabeth has more than enough for the both of them. In fact, I find her rather rude."

He pressed his lips together, holding in the retort.

Charlotte glared. "I know what you want to say. That she's like me."

"Actually, I think you sound more like the man. What's his name?"

"Darcy. And if you think that comparison bothers me, you're wrong."

He chewed his beef, contemplating how best to say the next thing. "So Darcy and Elizabeth are fighting their attraction for one another. What, in your estimation, would encourage him to give in?"

From the expression on her face, she truly appeared confounded.

"Would sending him flowers and little notes do the trick?"

"Don't be ridiculous. Why would a woman send a man flow —" Her fork clattered to her plate. "You're not talking about Darcy and Elizabeth."

He shrugged. "I was thinking in generalities. Just for example, mind you, what gesture could a man make to win you over?"

Her glower was lethal. "Nothing."

"Didn't you promise Honoria to give me a chance? I'm trying here, Charlotte, but I seem to be the only one. If our marriage isn't based on love, could it at least be based on honesty?"

"You won't like what I have to say."

He pulled in a breath. *Probably not.* "Tell me anyway."

"I don't know." She held up her hand when he opened his

mouth. "I honestly don't know. No one has ever considered what I want before. What I needed. I don't think it's things most women want. It's more . . ."

He leaned forward.

Tears glistened in the rims of her eyes, but she blinked them back. Her rich alto voice dropped to a whisper. "I get so tired sometimes. Of being strong, from fighting for control, from protecting myself."

"Protecting yourself from whom? Davies?" He swallowed, dread constricting his throat. "Me?"

As if she'd been shaken from a dream, the faraway look in her eyes vanished. "No one. I don't know why I said that." She wiped her lips and rose. "If you would excuse me."

He bolted from his seat, more from concern than etiquette. "Charlotte, wait."

She turned, and the vulnerable woman seated before him moments ago disappeared. "What I want is to be left alone."

She marched from the room, head held high, shoulders straightened as if she were marching to the front lines of battle.

"But you haven't had dessert," Simon said, his words wasted on the footman, who shifted his eyes toward Simon before returning his attention to the empty space before him.

Charlotte had been on the cusp of sharing something with him. Something painful.

And Simon was unsure he wanted to hear it. He plopped back into his seat and pushed his beef and carrots around the plate, his own appetite diminishing.

Finally giving up, he motioned the footman over. "Put the dessert on a tray—two servings." Tray in hand, Simon checked the drawing room, the library, and the other common rooms, all devoid of Charlotte.

Upstairs, Rose, Charlotte's maid, approached from the servant's staircase. "Is Lady Charlotte in her room?" he asked.

"Yes, sir." She eyed the tray and held out her hands. "If that is for my lady, I can take it to her."

"Thank you, Rose, but I would like to deliver it myself and take care of whatever she needs."

Rose eyed him suspiciously. "I suspect she called me to ready her for bed, sir."

"I'll have her ring again if she needs you. But if you would be so kind as to knock and open the door. As you see, my hands are occupied."

Rose gave two raps on Charlotte's door, and Charlotte answered, "Enter."

When he stepped inside, his breath hitched in his throat.

At the window, Charlotte stood in silhouette from the bright full moon, giving her an unworldly appearance, like a fairy queen. Warm and inviting, the moonlight glowed against her skin.

"I brought dessert." He cringed as his voice cracked like a boy transitioning to manhood.

Charlotte spun toward him. "I thought you were Rose."

After placing the tray on a table, he grinned. "I'm not as pretty as Rose."

A laugh sounded behind him, and the door closed with a *click*.

"Is she gone?" he whispered.

"Yes. And I believe you may have finally won over my maid. Have you actually looked at Rose?"

"To me, all women are pretty. Some"—he stared pointedly at her—"are beautiful."

"Flattery is not on my list of things to win me over."

He pulled out a chair and motioned her over. "It's not flattery if it's true."

Her gaze drifted to the dessert tray. "Is that trifle?"

"Yes. I didn't want you to miss it. Now come."

As she took the offered seat, she studied him from under thick lashes. "Don't you ever give up?"

"Hopeless causes are my favorite." He made himself comfortable in the chair across from her.

"Enjoy disappointment, do you?" She spooned up some of the orange trifle. Those lush lashes drifted down as she closed her eyes, and an expression of bliss slid across her face as she savored the dessert.

Mentally, he patted himself on the back for the idea. "If this is disappointment, I've been avoiding it unnecessarily." He propped his chin on his hand and waited for her to open her eyes.

"What are you staring at?"

"You. The way you licked that spoon . . ."

"Wipe that stupid grin off your face. Don't you tire of looking like a fool?"

"I'm just appreciating how you enjoy your dessert. Last year at the house party, I noticed you favored it. So I asked Cook to make some."

Her mouth formed a little *O* he found rather erotic. "Because I enjoy it?"

He pressed his lips together, fighting what she called the ridiculous grin.

Before he could respond in a manner she would find more dignified, she cocked her head. "Oh. I see. You thought I would be so overwhelmed by your thoughtfulness that I would swoon at your feet." She waved a hand around her. "Conveniently in my bedroom."

She jabbed at the trifle with an aggression that would have had the thing fleeing for its life had it been alive, then spooned it into her mouth. After she swallowed, she said, "But if you had really taken notice of my preferences, you would know I like my orange trifle with chocolate shavings on top."

He tucked that away for a later date. At the moment, he simply enjoyed watching her eat.

Finished, she pushed the dish away. "Aren't you going to eat yours?"

When her gaze slid to his still untouched dessert, he pulled it closer. "Yes, and I would ask you to stop lusting after it. I see the hunger in your eyes."

"You're in——" She snapped her mouth shut and huffed.

Laughing, he spooned up some of his dessert, enjoying it with dramatic flair. "Mmmm. So good." He licked his spoon, his tongue lingering on the back of the bowl and his eyes never leaving hers.

She tore her gaze from his, her cheeks reddened. "When are we leaving for your hovel?"

He practically choked on the trifle. "My *hovel*? What on earth are you expecting, Charlotte? A one-room hut?"

"No." Her dark eyes bored into his with icy seriousness. "No doubt it has two rooms."

He scraped the last of the sweet deliciousness onto his spoon. "You'll just have to wait and see, won't you? But I'd like to leave before ten."

"Then I should prepare for bed." She rose, and he followed suit.

"Before I go, I have a question."

She rolled her eyes. "Another one? Hasn't your brain been overtaxed enough for one day?"

Lord, she tried his patience—which admittedly was poor to begin with. "Well, it's more of a statement, so I think I can manage through it. You promised you would give us a chance."

"We've established that. What is your point?"

"My point is, what in your opinion does that entail? To continue keeping me at arm's length? I promised I wouldn't force you, but I hoped you could rein in your dislike of me long enough to give me an heir before I die."

Her gaze jerked away from him, moving momentarily toward the bed. "And you promised . . ."

He nodded. "I did. But I suggest we start small. Work our way up to *that*."

"How?"

"We never did discuss the kiss after our wedding yesterday. Don't deny you felt something. You may not like it, but I have enough experience to know when a woman responds to me."

She huffed and turned aside. "Arrogant fool."

"Truthful. Not arrogant. If anyone is deceiving themselves, it's you."

"What do you propose?"

"Why don't we start with a goodnight kiss?"

Like a marble statue, her whole body stiffened. "Fine. Make it quick." She closed her eyes, her brow scrunched up and her lips puckered as if she were going to kiss the devil himself.

He withheld his laugh, but he stepped closer, stopping within a hair's breadth from her. "Open your eyes, Charlotte. If we're going to do this—and really have a chance—we're going to do this my way."

Perhaps he should have allowed her to keep her eyes shut. The contempt within them chilled him. "You can close them in a moment but look at me first. I'm going to slip my arm around your waist."

"You didn't say anything about touching."

"Kissing requires touching, but I promise I won't do anything *extra*." He slid his arm around her, remembering how much he loved the new gowns with their lower, trim waistlines. "For support when your knees buckle."

"Ha!"

He silenced her first by cupping her cheek with his free hand. Then, when her lips parted the tiniest amount from surprise, he lowered his head, capturing them with his own. Gently at first, a slight brush of flesh upon flesh, he teased her into submission.

Her eyelids fluttered shut, those long lashes creating little half-moons upon her cheeks. *Lovely*. When she exhaled a soft sigh into his mouth, his own eyes closed. Tense muscles under his hand at her waist softened, and her shoulders relaxed as he deepened the kiss.

And oh, what a glorious kiss it was. Better than the one at the church. And although he had prepared himself, his quickening pulse and the hitch of his breath still took him by surprise.

With difficulty, he refrained from delving his tongue inside her mouth. That would wait for another day—another kiss. But he increased the pressure gradually, a little more each time she responded.

Slowly counting to ten, he tore himself away, satisfaction blooming in his chest when her lips chased his. "That's enough for one evening. Wouldn't want to spoil you." A half-truth, he admitted. He needed to go slow—to make her want to want him.

The glazed look in her eyes told him he'd accomplished his task. He turned quickly, preventing her from seeing his *ridiculous* grin and the similar look in his own eyes, and strode toward the door. "Goodnight, Charlotte. May you have beautiful dreams."

Outside in the hallway, he congratulated himself for his hard-won battle.

What he didn't want to admit was how much the kiss had affected him as well.

"Incorrigible!" Charlotte yelled from the other side. Something crashed against the door with a mighty *thud*.

He smiled to himself. Not only the battle, but he was inching closer to winning the war. He only hoped he wouldn't become a casualty in the victory.

※

Fists balled at her side, Charlotte muttered to herself. "Arrogant buffoon. Nodcock. Dolt." And because she was alone, she added a few less ladylike insults she'd picked up from Nash to her list. Simon Beckham deserved every last one.

Pieces of porcelain that had once been a vase littered the floor. She tromped to the bell pull, tugging it so hard, she thought it might come off in her hand.

How could one kiss affect her so much? She'd wanted to run her hands through the hair on his empty head. Pull him closer to her as the heat of his body burned through her gown.

Gah!

And he knew! The sparkle in his eyes when he'd released her belied his restrained demeanor as he ended the kiss—too soon.

She'd wanted it to go on, and on, and on.

How would she suffer him on the long journey to Wiltshire? He'd no doubt bring it up countless times.

And what would he *suggest* next?

Knock, knock.

"Enter!" The single word came out of her like a strong wind.

"My lady—" Rose's gaze dropped to the shattered vase. "What happened? Are you injured? Cut?" She stepped around the mess, then pulled Charlotte's hands into her own. Her brow furrowed upon seeing Charlotte's unblemished skin.

"I'm fine," Charlotte lied. She was anything but fine. She most certainly was losing her mind.

Once Rose swept away the remains of the poor vase, she readied Charlotte for bed, *tsk, tsking* at Charlotte's misfortune to have married a man who was all charm and no substance. "He vexes you, my lady. Anyone can see it."

Charlotte kept her opinions about her husband to herself. Because something had shifted—only a fraction, mind you. But it disconcerted her nonetheless.

And as she lay in bed, trying to sleep, she wondered how she could rid herself of the troublesome feelings creeping up from her long-buried heart.

Because she wanted Simon Beckham.

And that would spell her ruin.

CHAPTER 19

At the sideboard the next morning, Simon whistled as he piled food on his plate. He'd slept soundly. Why did the expression say *like a baby*? He peeked over his shoulder at his best friend. From the looks of him, Drake appeared not to have slept well at all. "Rough night?" Simon asked, adding one more piece of bacon before turning around.

Drake peered up over his cup. Wisps of steam wafted from the dark beverage.

"Is that coffee?"

Drake nodded. Half-moon shadows darkened the skin under his eyes.

"But you hate coffee."

"It keeps me awake. I don't know if it's the coffee itself or the taste." Drake scrunched up his face as he took another sip.

Unfamiliar guilt snaked through Simon's chest. "Are you certain you'll manage without me? Charlotte and I can change our plans." A small voice inside him pleaded, *say you don't need me.* He pulled in a breath and waited.

Drake shook his head. "Go. I wrote to Mother and Juliana,

and Honoria managed a letter to her parents. We expect they will descend upon us any day. Of course, she doesn't expect Colin. Margery's death devastated him. Between my mother and Lady Stratford, they'll have everything running smoothly."

Simon took his seat, breathing a sigh of relief. *Thank you, God.* He sent an encouraging smile toward his friend, hoping his next words would cheer him. "And no doubt Juliana will keep them busy with the 'smoothing' as she leaves chaos in her wake."

Drake chuckled and sipped more of his coffee, the distaste on his face not as exaggerated. "Hopefully enough to give Honoria and me some peace. I welcome their help, but . . ."

"Say no more. Family is wonderful—in small amounts. They won't all be staying with you, will they?"

"No. Mother and Juliana will, but I expect Lord and Lady Stratford will be more comfortable in their own home here in London. Even so, they will probably be underfoot most of the day—no doubt asking a multitude of questions about your marriage if you were here." He yawned, then sipped again. "This stuff isn't so bad once you get used to it."

"You are looking more alive than dead, so perhaps it's working, too."

Drake's famous one-sided smile tipped his lips. "You wait. When you and Charlotte have your first child, I'll be first in line to note your deathly appearance."

The mention of having children twisted the earlier guilt into something worse—deprivation. "Unless things have changed, children don't magically appear," he muttered, more to himself than Drake. Chances of him getting Charlotte with child were bleak. But the kiss had been promising . . .

"You mean you still haven't . . ."

"Haven't what?" Charlotte breezed into the room in a cloud of—wait. She'd changed her perfume. Notes of vanilla tickled his nose, lighter and fresher than her usual lilac.

Simon exchanged a glance with Drake, pleading with Drake to remain silent.

"Paid the staff's wages for the month," Simon lied. He met Drake's amused expression. "No, we haven't. But I expect we will shortly."

In the process of pouring herself some tea, Charlotte halted and spun toward him, her brow furrowing in that too familiar manner. "We? Is someone else responsible for paying the staff's salaries besides you?"

"No. I'm responsible."

"You said, 'We haven't.'"

Leave it to the woman to pick up on the nuance he'd meant only for Drake. She was too intelligent for her own good—or rather, for Simon's.

Drake chuckled, lifting his coffee once more. "You were speaking metaphorically, were you not, Simon? Since, in reality, I pay the staff's wages, but you disburse them." Amusement danced in his friend's amber eyes.

Simon wanted to punch him—as a friend, of course. In his own estimation, he was the least aggressive man he knew, with Drake coming in a close second. Why fight when you could have fun?

Charlotte took a seat several places away from him, one slice of toast and a blob of jam on her plate.

"It's a long journey. Perhaps you should eat a little mo—" His mouth snapped shut at the icy glare Charlotte delivered. "Or perhaps not."

Drake chuckled. "You're learning," he whispered.

After delicately chewing one tiny bite of toast, Charlotte asked, "How is Honoria this morning?"

"Eager to get out of bed. Ashton promised to come by today to see how she is faring," Drake said.

"I'm glad I'm not a woman," Simon quipped.

Charlotte ignored him. "And Lady Kitty?"

"Making her presence known every few hours. Frampton said we could set our clocks by her cries."

"I'd love to see her and say goodbye to Honoria before we leave," Charlotte said.

"Honoria asked for the very thing when she shooed me out of the room earlier this morning." Drake rose. "But now, I should get back to her."

Simon thought he would never leave.

Once Drake disappeared, Charlotte said, "I wouldn't say this to his face, but he looks dreadful."

Simon pulled back in surprise. "When have you failed to deliver an insult—especially if it's the truth?"

"I don't insult people I like." A ghost of a smile crossed her lips, hidden quickly by her teacup.

"Ouch." Simon threw a hand to his forehead. He cracked one eye, catching the twinkle in hers. "You should smile more often, especially when it reaches your eyes."

The twinkle vanished. "I don't have to do anything you tell me to." In a huff, she rose. "I'll be ready at ten, after I say goodbye to Honoria and Kitty."

He dropped his head in his hands. It was going to be a long journey to Wiltshire.

⚜

CHARLOTTE DID INDEED SAY GOODBYE TO HONORIA AND LITTLE Kitty, holding the infant in her arms again as Simon taught her. She'd never imagined herself one to become all soft over babies, but when Kitty grasped her finger with her tiny fist, a strange—not uncomfortable—twinge squeezed in her chest.

"Remember your promise." Honoria's gaze flitted to Simon, who stood nearby.

The cad's lips pressed together as if holding back a smile.

Lips.

Kisses—one in particular came to mind.

Alone in a carriage with Simon for hours on end? It was going to be a long journey to Wiltshire.

Drake reassured them both again, and veritably pushed them out the door. "Go. Get to know each other better. Come back happy."

A tall order indeed. Charlotte never regarded Drake as an optimist.

As the carriage bounced along the Bath Road, Charlotte tried to read her book—tried being the operative word.

She huffed in disbelief at the part where Elizabeth first sees Pemberley—and by association, falls in love with Mr. Darcy. Shallow girl.

Simon moved from his seat across from her to sit next to her, peering over her shoulder at her book. A few moments later, he moved back to the opposite seat, only to repeat the process multiple times.

"Would you please sit still?"

His knee bounced endlessly even when he stared out the window of the carriage.

"And cease that knee jiggling." She gave a *harrumph* and turned back to Elizabeth's tour of Pemberley.

Simon banged on the carriage roof, and it slowed to a halt.

Charlotte peeked out the window, expecting to have arrived at a posting inn. Country road stretched as far as she could see. "What are you doing? Why are we stopping?"

Without answering her, Simon bounded from the carriage, leaving the door swinging back and forth.

The footman riding on the back descended and held out his hand. "Do you wish to exit, my lady?"

She most certainly did. If nothing else, to see what her buffoon of a husband was up to.

She expected to see him off in the tree line, using the greenery as a necessary. Instead, he was running down the road.

"What's happening, my lady?" Rose called from her seat atop the carriage.

That was precisely what Charlotte wanted to know. "What on earth is he doing?"

The footman shook his head. "Not quite sure, my lady."

Seated next to Rose, Simon's valet, Mr. Brown, said, "He's done it a few times before when we've traveled to and from Hartridge House and London. He runs for a while, then turns and runs back."

That settled it. She had officially married a madman.

"How far are we from a posting inn?"

The footman asked the driver, who stated it was approximately another two miles to Maidenhead. Thank goodness it was still daylight, and they would be traveling farther before spending the night. No doubt Simon would make some obscene joke about staying overnight in the unfortunately named town.

"Will we spend the night at Reading?" she asked the footman, who relayed the question to the driver, who in turn confirmed, barring any unforeseen circumstances, that was their destination for the day's journey.

Almost a speck on the horizon, Simon finally turned and headed back.

Wind blew at Charlotte's bonnet, catching underneath the brim and tugging it backward. She studied the sky, grateful the clouds were white and puffy rather than dark and foreboding.

Simon slowed his pace as he approached, then bent over, his hands on his knees, panting heavily. "That felt wonderful."

Charlotte shook her head, hoping the bonnet was still firmly seated. "You are—"

"Incorrigible. Really, Charlotte, you need to expand your vocabulary."

She huffed. "I was going to say out of your mind." Then she

grasped the footman's offered hand and climbed back into the carriage.

The stretch between the impromptu stop and Maidenhead proceeded without incident—and without Simon's constant restlessness. Once they'd changed horses at the posting inn and had some refreshment, they continued their journey in relative peace.

Indeed, once he settled himself back in the carriage next to her, he leaned his head against the squabs and fell asleep, snoring softly.

Oddly, the sound didn't annoy her as she expected, but rather lulled her into a state of drowsiness herself. Even as she tried to read how Mr. Darcy explained Mr. Wickham's dastardly plans for Georgiana, Charlotte's eyelids grew heavy, and the print on the pages fuzzy.

Before she knew it, the carriage had come to a halt again, and she opened her eyes to find Simon grinning down at her like a fool, her head resting on his—ahem, broad—shoulder.

"Sleep well?"

She jerked upright. "I was simply resting."

He laughed. "You were snoring." He held up a hand. "A most delightful little snore, mind you." He tilted his head and pointed a finger at her lips. "Although you do have a little drool right there."

She slapped his finger away and quickly swiped at her mouth, then peeked down at her white gloves for a telltale sign of moisture—and found none.

"You, sir, are a liar." She scooted away from him, only to have him follow her. His thigh brushed against her, but already pressed against the side of the carriage, she could go no farther.

"Not about the snoring." He bumped his shoulder against hers. "Relax, Charlotte. Lots of women snore. It's not something unique to men."

"And how would you kno—?" *Oh.*

He gave an insouciant shrug but said nothing.

Curse the rogue. How could she forget about his dalliances? Did he think knowledge of his experience would win her over? Inwardly, she grinned, anticipating his disappointment.

Light within the carriage dimmed as dusk descended, making it impossible for her to continue reading. Even staring out the window was pointless when only blackness remained.

Pulling out his pocket watch, Simon said, "We should be reaching Reading soon. If we rise early tomorrow, we will make it to Swindon by late afternoon." He stretched and yawned. "If memory serves, the inn has soft beds."

"Separate rooms," she said through gritted teeth.

A flash of disappointment flickered across his face, so brief she wondered if she had imagined it. "And here, I believed we were making progress after our kiss last night."

Why did he have to bring up the kiss? Her lips tingled with the memory of his pressed against hers. Yet, she refused to give him the satisfaction of knowing how he affected her, and she balled her hands into fists. "You flatter yourself—as usual."

"And you delude yourself." He shrugged again. "So be it. You can only lie to yourself for so long."

The carriage slowed, and the urge to jump out and race away as he did earlier gripped her with such ferocity, she grabbed at the cushioned seat instead, holding herself in place.

He exited first and held out his hand to assist her descent, but she refused. Unfortunately, when she stepped down, she stumbled on the uneven ground and tilted precariously.

With unmatched speed, his arm wrapped around her waist, righting and stabilizing her. "You're safe. I won't let you fall." His whispered breath tickled her neck.

Safe? She hadn't felt safe for the last twenty-three years of her life, which, considering she was nine-and-twenty, was an exceedingly long time. Long enough to sense warning signs and slip into her armor of self-protection at the first hint of danger.

In truth, she wore it almost constantly. Yet, something not only in Simon's words, but his tone led her to believe—oddly—it was true.

It was a foreign feeling, like being in a strange country and not knowing the customs and rules of behavior.

Simon, on the other hand, seemed to have no qualms about forging into the heart of the unknown, dangerous or not.

Pushing the uncomfortable thoughts from her mind, she followed him into the inn.

"Good evening, my good man!" Simon greeted the innkeeper with a dazzling smile. Did candlelight actually glint off the man's teeth? "My wife, my servants, and I require your best rooms for the night."

Simon signed the register while the innkeeper retrieved the keys.

"Our best is number three, sir. For you and your good lady." The innkeeper laid down three keys on the counter.

"We shall require one more room," Charlotte said.

The man frowned. "Beg pardon, my lady?" He pointed at each key as if she were an imbecile. "One for your man servants, one for your lady's maid, and one for you and your husband."

"That is unacceptable. My husband and I require separate rooms."

When the man shook his head, Charlotte's stomach dipped. "I have no more rooms."

Simon continued to grin like a dolt. "It's fine, my good fellow. We will make do." After handing Mr. Brown and Rose the keys for rooms four and five, he took Charlotte by the elbow. "Upstairs, now," he whispered. "Don't make a scene."

Charlotte jerked out of Simon's grasp. "Perhaps you can stay with the other men." However, when Mr. Brown opened number four and Charlotte peeked inside, the bed only appeared large enough for two people, and neither Simon, Mr. Brown, nor the footman were small men.

"I will not ask one of these fine men to sleep on the floor. Not when a perfectly good bed that will hold two *married* people awaits in the other room. Unless you would rather share it with Rose and allow me to take number five?"

Share a room with a servant! Who did Simon think she was? Honoria?! Charlotte darted a glance at Rose, who seemed no more eager to share a room with her employer than Charlotte did with her.

To assist in her decision, Simon opened number three. Lushly appointed for a posting inn, it boasted a large canopied bed, a small settee, and even a writing desk. A cozy fire burned in the hearth as if waiting only for her. She exhaled a sigh.

"Very well." She chewed her bottom lip—a nasty habit she'd been punished for as a child. But the settee gave her an idea.

Simon dropped his valise on the bed. "I'll go request some food for all of us while Rose makes you comfortable."

He stepped out, closing the door behind him with a sound *click*.

All Charlotte could concentrate on was the bed.

Rose cast her gaze down to the floor, her mouth curving suspiciously.

"I can see you thinking, Rose. But you would be advised to keep whatever it is to yourself. Now ready me for bed."

"Yes, my lady." And although Rose turned around to unpack Charlotte's nightrail from her traveling bag, the smile in her voice was unmistakable.

Yes. The settee would be a perfect solution.

CHAPTER 20

After Simon ordered plates of food brought to each of the three rooms, he pulled out his pocket watch. Only fifteen minutes had passed since he'd left Charlotte. He spent a few more minutes chatting with the innkeeper, assuring him all was well and the rooms were more than adequate.

In fact, the room he and Charlotte shared was more than adequate, and his mind wandered to the comfortable poster bed filling half the room. So many pleasant things awaited on that bed.

Back upstairs, he raised his fist to knock, paused but a moment, and decided to make a small change to his announced return.

Knock, knock. "Charlotte, it's Simon. Are you indecent?" He chuckled to himself and pressed an ear to the door, waiting for her vexed reply.

"I'm—what?!"

The door swung open, and he stumbled forward into her. "Hello."

Using both hands, she pushed him away. "Ugh! Have you been drinking? You can't even remain upright."

"Of course not. It's only been twenty minutes. I'm as sober as —well, I would say Aunt Kitty, but she's been known to enjoy her sherry. I simply pressed my ear to the door to listen for your dulcet tones of joy upon my return. I didn't expect you to be so eager to see me that you would fling the door open quite so forcefully."

She rewarded him with a bone-chilling glower.

"The food has arrived." She pointed to plates of steaming food on the table.

"Excellent. I'm starving."

He held out a chair, and she took a seat, giving him the side-eye. He leaned down, keeping his lips a hair's breadth from her neck. "Worried I'll yank the chair out from under you?"

She grunted. "I wouldn't put it past you."

They ate in relative silence—well, other than Charlotte complaining the chicken was overcooked and the vegetables were dry.

He swallowed a bite of crusty bread, which, in his opinion, was delicious. "Are you always so critical? I thought you reserved your umbrage for me alone."

"No. For you especially."

He chuckled. "Ah. That makes me feel so much better."

With vigor, she tore off a chunk of bread, then waved it at him. "Do you find everything amusing? It's most annoying."

"What would you have me do? This is our meal. Complaining about it won't make me enjoy it more." He laid his fork down. "Try to find one thing about it that you like. One thing, Charlotte."

She stared at her plate, her mouth pursed in thought.

He liked her lips. Very much.

"Well," she said. "This bread is tolerable. And the butter is creamy."

Creamy. Like a magnet, his gaze pulled to the exposed skin above her nightrail. Her hair had been brushed and braided for bed, draped lazily over her shoulder, the dark end resting on her left breast. He'd like to be the end of that braid.

"What are you staring at?"

His mind jerked back to reality. "Was I staring?"

She adjusted her nightrail, checking the little ribbon that tied it together at the neck.

He wanted to tug on it and let it fall loose, then he would . . .

"You're staring again."

"Can I help it if I have such a desirable wife?" Used on any other woman, his words might have paved a swift path to the bed. But Charlotte? He braced himself for a scathing retort.

She blinked, appearing nonplussed, but quickly recovered. "Empty words." She poked at the tiny remaining piece of chicken, her gaze fastened to it as if it might regrow its feathers and flap away. "Have they proved effective in the past?" Had she developed the ability to read minds?

Best to keep that bit of information to himself. He wasn't as daft as she believed. "At the moment, I'm only concerned about their effect on you."

"None." She pushed the plate away and rose. "I'm going to retire."

Energy pulsed through him as she strolled toward the bed.

Her hips swayed, the nightrail swishing against her legs.

He pushed away from the table with such force the chair screeched in protest. With speed he didn't know he possessed, he set the plates outside the door, then locked it, double-checking the bolt. "I'll join you."

As she perched on the edge of the bed, he couldn't take his eyes off her. Was that a coquettish, come-hither smile?

He shook his head to clear it.

The smile remained.

He shucked off his coat, tossing it onto the settee behind him. His neckcloth followed.

Her smile widened, displaying—?

What was that in her cheek? He sucked in a breath. Oh, dear God. She had a dimple. He was a fool for dimples. His fingers fumbled with the buttons on his waistcoat, shouldered off the garment, and threw it behind him.

His boots and stockings were next, and as he yanked each one off, Charlotte's eyes followed his every movement. He slipped the braces from his shoulders, letting them fall loosely against his hips and thighs, and when he pulled the shirt over his head, those dark eyes of hers widened.

Satisfaction—or perhaps pride—swelled in his chest at the way her gaze locked on his bare chest, and he withheld the grin threatening to break free. She might deny it with words, but she was attracted to him, perhaps even as much as he was to her.

But when his hands moved to the buttons on his trousers, her demeanor shifted from interested to alarmed.

"What are you doing?"

"Getting undressed for bed. I thought that was clear."

"At least have the courtesy of putting on a nightshirt before you remove your trousers."

"Nightshirts confine my movement. I'm told I'm a restless sleeper." At that, he released the grin. Let her make of that what she will.

"Which is yet another reason you will be spending the night on the settee."

Another reason? He spun around to the clothes-cluttered, and much-too-small-to-sleep-on settee. "Do you mean you had been planning on relegating me to sleep on this"—he pointed to the offending piece of furniture—"all along?"

She made a show of studying her nails. "Of course."

"But you . . . that smile . . ." He squinted at her. The termagant had teased him into believing she wanted him. No!

She *did* want him. He hadn't lost his instinct for sensing that in a few short days of being married.

"That settee isn't made for a man of six-feet-two. Why, even Boney wouldn't fit on that thing—though it would be fun to watch him try."

"You're not suggesting *I* sleep on it?" The harpy had the gall to appear affronted.

"No. Even you're too tall for it."

As tall as he was, her forehead topped his shoulder. Exceptionally tall for a woman, she had to be at least five-feet-eight. Why, he didn't even have to stoop much to kiss her, and in bed they would fit perfectly. Which, speaking of . . .

"Besides, contrary to what you believe, I would never be so ungentlemanly to force you to sleep on a hard piece of furniture when there is such a soft—*big*—bed at our disposal. Big enough to share, Charlotte."

Her shoulders squared, becoming so perpendicular to her body, he could have balanced one of their supper plates upon it and not spilled a bit of food. "You promised."

He arched a brow at her. "If memory serves, you also made a promise. I will abide by mine. As I said, the bed has plenty of room for both of us, and I will not do anything you don't want me to. But our marriage doesn't stand a chance if you keep me at arm's length." He allowed her some time to let that sink in.

Seconds stretched into minutes, and he silently screamed for his mind to still. His fingers had already mutinied, drumming against his thigh.

After an excruciatingly long time—at least for him, although in truth, only about a minute had passed—she nodded. "Very well. But keep your trousers on."

"No." He had to draw the line somewhere. "And you've seen me without them before. It shouldn't be some great shock. We're married, Charlotte."

Her bottom lip protruded enough to make him want to take it between his teeth and—

"Fine. If you must be that way." She stood and strolled toward the settee. Surely, she didn't prefer trying to sleep there. Did she really detest him that much? Instead, she removed a blanket thrown over the back.

"This should work." Back at the bed, she studied the canopy. "If I can hang this up there, it could drape down and provide a dividing line."

He laughed. "You can't be serious?"

Her icy glare told him otherwise, and to prove her point, she climbed up on the mattress. With wobbly steps, she reached up to tuck the blanket into one end in canopy's frame.

Tilting precariously, she stretched, perhaps a little too far, and he raced up, catching her before she stumbled and fell to the floor. Her back pressed into his chest, and in his haste to right her, although his right arm looped around her waist, his left hand latched onto something soft and very familiar.

She froze against him. He could almost feel the chill coming from her body.

"Unhand me." Imbued with more than anger, she croaked the words as if she were in pain.

Releasing her breast, he spun her around, needing to see into her eyes to be certain. "What is it? More than my misplaced hand."

The trembling in her voice vanished. "Misplaced? You manhandled me!"

"It wasn't intentional. You were going to fall."

"A likely story."

"Is this because of Davies? What you don't want to talk about? Because I am *not* him. Get that through your stubborn head."

She eyed him for a moment, then nodded.

When she started to climb back onto the mattress, he tugged

the blanket from her hands. "Allow me." Although the mattress sagged beneath him, he kept his balance, and his height made it easier to reach the frame. "And don't flatter yourself. It's not like I can't keep my hands off you. You're not *that* tempting."

Liar.

With both of the blanket's ends secured, a curtain formed in the middle of the bed, neatly dividing it in two.

Simon jumped down, placed his hands on his hips, and said, "Now, if you don't wish to view my nakedness, I suggest you move to the other side."

With a sound harrumph, she turned to do just that, but he caught her arm.

"But first, what about your promise to give me a chance?"

Miss Haughtiness jerked her chin at him. "What do you suggest? If it's anything that involves removing clothing, I politely decline."

"Politely! Ha! You wouldn't know politely if it bit you on the —" Speaking of biting, he bit his tongue. She could rile him like no other. He was a congenial fellow, really he was. He blew out an exasperated breath. "At least give me a kiss goodnight. It's no more than we did last night."

Why he bothered to ask would forever remain a mystery. The hostility on her face would mean it would be like kissing a marble statue.

"I have an idea," she said.

His normally eager-for-adventure mind screeched to a halt. This was Charlotte, after all. He canted his body away from her. "What kind of idea?"

"We never finished our card game. You win, you get a kiss. I win, I ask a question."

The glint in her eyes should have made him nervous. But he had a secret weapon.

If necessary, he would cheat.

CHARLOTTE STUDIED HER ATROCIOUS HAND OF CARDS. FIFTEEN! Could it be any worse? Possibly, but not much. Should she ask for another card? Simon had appeared pleased when viewing his hand, giving the slightest upward twitch of his lips. When Nash taught her to play, he called them tells. To Charlotte's knowledge, the only woman who was a more proficient card player was Lady Miranda. Charlotte had always requested Miranda as a partner for whist, and they rarely lost.

What would Miranda do in this situation?

"Well?" Simon said, perhaps a little too impatiently. "Do you want another card?"

"I'm thinking." A difficult task considering the man sat half-naked before her. The hard planes of his chest, covered with a curious smattering of dark hair, constantly drew her attention.

"You can count, can't you? It's rather simple. If need be, remove your slippers and use your toes."

"You are insufferable." Her muttered complaint elicited a chuckle from her husband. *Buffoon.*

The nasty habit resurfaced twice in one night, and her bottom lip found its way between her teeth again. With Simon's reaction to his cards, he must believe he had a winning hand. Without an additional card, she would surely lose anyway. Simon had already won one hand, kissing her wrist as he had done on their wedding day. And as before, her blood raced through her veins like a thoroughbred at the Epsom Derby. He promised a more intimate kiss when he won again.

Losing was not an option.

She met his gaze—realizing her mistake too late and falling captive to his wickedly blue eyes. "I believe I will have a card. Thank you." She added an extra dose of vitriol to the last.

Simon's hand hovered over the top card of the deck. "What

was that? Did someone knock?" His gaze swiveled toward the door.

She turned, following suit, frowning at the closed—and locked—door. "What? I didn't hear anything."

When she turned back, Simon lifted his shoulder in that careless and irritatingly attractive manner. "Must have been the wind. Now, you were saying?"

"A card."

"What's that?" He cupped a hand around his ear. "I must have missed the *please.*"

"Please," she said through gritted teeth.

Before looking at her card, she pulled in a breath and held it. *A ten! Gah!* She flung the cards at him, wishing they had more weight as they flew against his chest.

"My. My. No need to be such a sore loser." He rose, his movements slow and measured, like a cat stalking its prey. That exasperating grin spread across his lips. "Especially since your loss is actually a win." He moved behind her.

"A win! I hardly think—" She pulled in a gasp as his fingertips brushed the back of her neck. Then his lips pressed against a spot under her right earlobe. "Oooh." Unbidden, the sound of pleasure rose from deep within her.

He chuckled, his mouth still so close his breath brushed against her already sensitive skin. "Told you."

"Ugh!" *Stupid traitorous body!* She pushed her chair back, hoping he would topple to the floor from the force of it. "I'm going to bed."

"This was your idea. I never imagined you as a quitter, Charlotte. And I still haven't received my proper kiss goodnight. That was going to be when I won next."

"Fine! Take your infernal kiss and let me go to sleep." She braced herself, closing her eyes, lifting her chin, and pursing her lips, determined not to succumb to his talented mouth.

Some battles are lost before they've begun.

She didn't have to open her eyes to sense he was near. Every nerve in her body tingled at his nearness. Faint scents of sandalwood and leather teased her nose, the heat of him radiating through her clothes as he stood in front of her. Sounds of his breathing, at first slow and even, grew more rapid.

The weight of his arm slipping around her secured her to him, and he tugged her closer, her breasts pressing against his bare chest. Heat from his skin traveled through the thin cotton of her nightdress.

His other hand, large and warm, cupped her cheek. "Open your eyes, Charlotte. I want to look into them before I kiss you. You have the most beautiful eyes. Dark and mysterious, as if you're holding secrets."

She opened her eyes. Not because he had asked her, but to see his amusement from his lies and manipulation. Confusion— no, fear—tripped up her spine at the sincerity shining in them. Her lips parted as she drew in a shocked breath.

"Better," he said, then lowered his head.

The soft press of his lips first caressed then captured hers more fully, and her eyelids drifted shut of their own accord as she surrendered herself to the kiss. Barely discernable, a hint of wetness traced along the seam of her lips.

In truth, her mind was so muddled she wasn't sure what she was feeling, except for the riotous fluttering in her stomach.

Something rigid pressed into her abdomen. No, not *something*. She knew what that was, and her mind shook itself from its dangerous stupor as she pushed against his chest. "You promised!"

"What?" He honestly appeared confused.

"That!" She pointed at the bulge in his trousers.

He rolled his eyes. "I can't help what my body does. It has a mind of its own." He laughed at the last, muttering something about head and mind. However, he held out his hands. "But as you wish."

"I'm going to sleep. Stay on your side of the blanket."

"You stay on yours." He started unbuttoning his trousers.

She raced to the other side, shielding herself from his nakedness, and climbed into the bed, lying as close to the edge as possible.

Rustle of clothes sounded from the other side, then the bed sagged a little as Simon climbed in, releasing an exaggerated sigh.

Charlotte stared up at the canopy and prayed the blanket would hold during the night. Before long, snoring drifted across from the other side. Grumbling to herself, she scooted a little closer to the middle, careful not to disturb the barrier, and tried to sleep.

CHAPTER 21

Restrained. Suffocating. Charlotte struggled to free herself and breathe. Heavy bonds wrapped around her shoulders and hips. A dark figure loomed over her. "Let me go!" the voice of a child cried, echoing as if it were in a long tunnel. Charlotte realized it was her own. *Not real. It's not real.* She clawed her way to consciousness and safety.

Her heart still racing, and her breathing labored, she opened her eyes.

A bare arm wrapped around her upper body, the hand cupping her breast, and a muscled thigh draped across her hip, the blanket that had once been their barrier tangled in his feet.

Pressed up against her, Simon nuzzled against her neck, his unshaven face now scratchy from a day's growth. "Mmm."

She turned and shoved him away. "Get off me, you oaf!"

"Ough," he groaned, rolling over on his back.

"Eeek!" She hated that her cry sounded like the childish persona from her dream. Why wasn't he under the counterpane? She grabbed the blanket and tossed it over him.

Simon stretched his arms over his head and yawned. "Is it

morning?" He smacked his lips and stared at her through heavily lidded, groggy eyes.

She hated the fluttering in her stomach at his dopey grin.

"Put some clothes on!" she said, her words snapping like a bowstring pulled too taut. "And when did you pull down our barrier?"

As if finally gaining consciousness, he looked upward at the canopy, then down at the blanket covering his nakedness. "Oh. Sorry. I assure you, it was quite by accident, and I *did* mention I was a restless sleeper."

Carelessly ignoring her presence, he pushed the blanket off of him, swung his legs over the edge, and stood.

Unbidden, Charlotte's traitorous gaze followed, fascinated with the way his muscles bunched in his rounded derrière. A sigh slipped from her lips as he stooped to retrieve his trousers from the floor.

Casting her a look over his shoulder, he said, "What did you say?"

Quickly, she jerked her gaze away. "Nothing. You're hearing things."

As he tugged on his shirt and boots, she eased from the bed and threw a dressing gown over her nightrail.

"I'll request some warm water for washing and shaving. Would you like me to fetch Rose for you?"

She blinked at his consideration, then nodded.

Simon gave her privacy as she washed and dressed, returning only when Rose left. "You're welcome to remain here while I bathe and dress, or you can go downstairs with Rose for breakfast, and I'll join you shortly."

"Rose has already eaten."

"Well, have her accompany you anyway. Don't go down alone."

Although his tone was not demanding, she bristled nonetheless. "If I want to go to breakfast alone, I will do so."

He hung his head, shaking it and sighing. "Charlotte. Charlotte. Charlotte. I'm trying to look out for you. There were a few unsavory characters downstairs earlier. But if you feel the need to face them rather than stay here with me . . ." He waved a hand toward the door. "Be my guest."

Torn, she debated which of his dictates to defy. Her need to control the situation waged war with her instinct to protect herself. "I think I shall stay."

When Mr. Brown knocked, Simon admitted him, explaining to his valet that his wife would remain during his ablutions. Like most well-trained servants, Mr. Brown made no comment other than, "Very good, sir," and proceeded to lay out Simon's clothes while Simon stripped down and washed himself.

Charlotte pretended to read her book, sneaking glances over the edge when Simon wasn't looking. Once or twice, he caught her, and although he grinned, he remained blessedly silent.

As Mr. Brown sharpened the razor, Charlotte addressed Simon, "Would you like me to shave you?"

Mr. Brown's eyes widened, his jaw dropping as his gaze darted between her and Simon. "Sir?"

"Don't let her anywhere near that razor. She'd as soon cut my throat as scrape my whiskers."

"And here I thought you liked adventure," she muttered and returned to her book.

Once Simon finished, they both went downstairs for breakfast. When an unkempt man made a lewd comment upon seeing her, she knew she'd made the right decision to wait for Simon.

Simon shot the man a glare—a rare expression for him, except when it came to her. "If you wish to keep the remaining two teeth in your ugly head, keep your mouth shut about my wife."

"Oooh," the man said, lifting his hands in mock horror. "Like this dandy has it in him to take me down."

His equally filthy friend threw back his head and laughed as he pounded the table.

"Oh, you don't have to worry about me," Simon said. "It's my wife who will gut you like a fish." He leaned in, scrunching his nose at the stench, and whispered. "She's already killed three men in the last week just for failing to tip their hats. Slit them from throat to tip with a shaving razor."

"You lie!"

Simon gave his signature shrug, then eyed the man up and down. "On second thought, she'd probably just cut it off and stuff it down your throat. She's especially good at emasculation." With that, he gently tapped Charlotte's arm, guiding her to a vacant table.

"What on earth were you thinking?" she hissed at her husband.

"Shut him up, didn't it? Did you see how wary he became when he looked at you? Excellent work sending him your iciest glower. I think it topped the one you reserve for me."

"I—" Her mouth snapped shut. Had she glowered? "You buffoon. Why did you antagonize him? He could have killed you."

He lurched back. "Careful, Charlotte. I might think you cared."

"I . . . you . . . don't be ridiculous," she stammered.

"Honestly, I know men like him. All bluster and nothing to back it up. And don't worry about me, I can take care of myself." He delivered a pointed look. "And you, if the need arises."

Out of sheer instinct, Charlotte prepared to deliver her setdown, telling Simon she could take care of herself, thank you very much. But the softness in his eyes, the way he caressed the word *you*, halted the words on her tongue. Discomfort from the unexpected and unfamiliar—yet not unwelcome—concern tightened her around her chest, squeezing and rousing her dead and buried heart back to life.

If Simon wasn't careful, she might think *he* cared.

As they ate their breakfast, she paused, considering her husband. Did he care? Had what she believed to be manipulative tactics to take advantage of her been gestures of genuine concern for her well-being? Care for her as a person?

Preposterous! The idea unnerved her. So much so she pushed it aside, promising to examine it later.

Safely aboard the coach, they continued their journey to Swindon. Mercifully, Simon seemed more content to sit still, only changing his seat and position seven or eight times and only tapping on the carriage roof to stop and perform his ridiculous running ritual once.

Most of the time, Charlotte caught him looking at her intensely. Then he would wink and turn toward the window.

Having slept fitfully, she found her eyelids drooping, the rocking motion of the carriage like a mother's lullaby.

Next to her, Simon said, "Put your head on my shoulder."

"And have you toss me to the floor when you decide to jump up and move across to the other seat?" She laughed. "No, thank you."

"Think of it as punishment for whatever offense I've committed. For I promise, I won't move."

The thought had a certain appeal. Settled against him, she drifted off to a dreamless slumber.

"Charlotte. Charlotte."

Confused and disoriented, she bolted awake. She rubbed her eyes and gazed around her. *Oh, the carriage.* Simon as her pillow. "Have you reached your breaking point of sitting still?"

"No. Well, not exactly. We're here!"

As the last dregs of slumber left her cobwebbed mind, comprehension dawned that the carriage had stopped.

The door opened, and rather than allow her to exit first, Simon hurried out and stood before the door. "Close your eyes, Charlotte."

"Don't be ridiculous. I will not close my eyes!"

"Please? Humor me. I won't allow you to fall."

She shouldn't trust him. He hadn't earned that, which to be honest was a difficult feat for anyone. Yet, Honoria's words took that very moment to seep through Charlotte's stubbornness. *Give him a chance.*

"Very well. But I warn you." Closing her eyes, she fumbled for the frame of the carriage, rose, then stretched out her hand.

"Trust me." Simon grasped her hand. "One step ahead. Move your foot a little more forward. That's it. Now, one more and you'll be on the ground."

Annoyed, she huffed. "How long must I keep my eyes closed?"

Gently grasping her shoulders, he turned her a quarter revolution. "You may open them now. Welcome to Rosehaven Park."

Prepared for a dingy little house, possibly surrounded by pig styes or cows chewing their cud, she opened her eyes.

Not to be left out, her mouth joined in, dropping in awe. Charlotte wanted to laugh, to cheer, to spin around like a child. Like a flash of understanding, she knew how Elizabeth Bennet felt upon seeing Pemberley.

❦

SIMON PLACED HIS HANDS ON HIS HIPS, HOLDING IN THE GRIN HE wanted to release. He gazed out at the expanse of a well-manicured lawn, neat groupings of spring flowers, and best of all, the magnificent house that rivaled the finest in the county.

"This is the main house. What do you think?" He really didn't have to ask. Her expression spoke for her. She was impressed. But would she admit it? Why did he desperately need her to?

When her hand slid around his forearm, he darted a glance,

first to her hand—not quite believing she had touched him voluntarily—then to her face. She lifted her other hand to her mouth.

Oh, she loves it. Pride swelled in his chest.

"Well? I'm waiting for your discerning assessment." He tempered his impatience with a soft chuckle.

"It's . . . adequate." Yet, even with her lips pressed together so tightly they became a sliver of pink, he could make out the slight depression of her dimple as she fought the smile.

"Adequate?!" Before he could question her further, Georgie practically spilled from the front door.

"They're here! Hurry up!" She raced toward them, her skirts flapping around her legs so wildly, Simon worried she would trip and fall.

Arms outstretched then wrapping around his waist, Georgie connected with him so forcefully they both almost tumbled backward.

"Oomph! You've gained weight," he teased, patting her back.

Georgie raised a dark brow, reminding him of Charlotte. "In two days?" Not that Georgie needed any tutelage exhibiting offense.

"Simon, it's rude to comment on a lady's size." Charlotte turned her attention to his sister. "Hello, Georgie."

Like a row of ducklings, the rest of his family filed from the house, led by his mother.

"Darlings!" his mother said, rushing forward with less exuberance than her youngest child, thank goodness. And unlike Georgie, she greeted Charlotte first, pulling her against her well-endowed bosom. "Did he drive you mad on the journey, my dear? How many times did you have to stop for him to stretch his legs?"

Charlotte sent him a smug look. "I lost count. But suffice it to say, I'm glad we have arrived and he can run willy-nilly without disturbing me."

Frannie cracked a burst of a laugh. "I knew I liked her. Simon, you best treat her well so she doesn't leave your sorry a——"

"Frannie!" Amusement in his father's eyes softened his admonishment. After giving instructions to the carriage driver to proceed to the cottage with their trunks, Brown, and Rose, his father waved them toward the house. "Let's get you two inside for some refreshment."

Gently taking Charlotte's arm, Simon leaned down and whispered, "After my parents coddle you, would you like a tour of the estate before I take you to the cottage?"

Eagerness shone in her dark eyes. "That would be lovely. Just to acquaint myself with it, of course."

He bit back the smile. "Of course. Wouldn't want you to get lost. Frannie would have my head."

So quick, had he not been looking, he would have missed it, but the dimple dented her cheek in full measure as she laughed. He promised himself that dimple would be next on his list of places to kiss.

He only glanced at the clock on the mantle seventeen times as his parents and sisters enquired about their journey and asked Charlotte what they could do to make her more comfortable during their stay.

"I've had the servants air out the cottage," his mother said. "You're welcome to say here with us in the main house, but newly wed couples need their privacy."

Georgie made a gagging sound, and Charlotte's dimple popped again.

He would really have to kiss it soon, and as he envisioned the tour of the property, he knew the perfect place to accomplish his mission.

"Simon. Simon?" his mother's voice jolted him from the enticing daydream.

"I promise I will, Mother."

Georgie giggled, Rebecca's eyes widened, Beth cast a glance toward Charlotte, Frannie groaned, and Kate rolled her eyes.

"What?" he asked.

The gleam in Charlotte's eyes indicated whatever had been said, she was about to make good use of it at Simon's expense. "Your mother was saying you become so distracted at times, racing from one thing to the next, she hopes you won't abandon me in the hedge maze."

"Oh. Um." An unexpected burst of heat crept up his neck to his ears. He was thinking about the hedge maze, but abandoning Charlotte was the last thing he'd imagined.

"Which is why you should take me along," Georgie said. "When I was five, Simon left me in there. It took me hours to find my way out. After that, Papa went with me, and I learned every exit possible."

"It's true," his father said. "If there were a race to find a way out, Georgie would win every time."

Everyone laughed at the memory—except Charlotte. Knives shot from her murderous glare, aimed straight for his heart. But when she turned toward Georgie, an unfamiliar expression crossed her face. Compassion. Concern. The urge to defend and protect.

"I didn't do it on purpose!" It was wrong of him, of course, but explaining his reason to Charlotte was out of the question.

"You left a child alone!" The ire in Charlotte's voice made the hair on his arms stand at attention.

Sitting next to Charlotte, Georgie placed a hand on Charlotte's arm. "Don't be angry with him. He didn't mean to. I've forgiven him, and it helped me overcome my fear of being alone."

"Georgie gets that ability to view things from the bright side from Simon," Rebecca said.

"Hmm." Charlotte clearly still had reservations. The prospect of stealing that kiss became a little more challenging. But that wouldn't stop him.

He waited precisely seven more minutes to allow Charlotte's anger to cool. "Shall we take that tour? We can end at the cottage and get settled."

Georgie popped up from the sofa. "Let me come along!"

"Georgie, your brother and Charlotte prefer to be alone." The gleam in his mother's eyes spoke of something entirely different from what he'd seen in Charlotte's—no doubt visions of grandchildren took center stage.

"We would love to have you with us, Georgie," Charlotte said.

"Charlotte's being polite." Simon rose and met his wife's gaze, knowing full well she was being nothing of the sort. "We absolutely would *not* love to have you with us. You can show Charlotte your favorite haunts later." He held out his arm to his wife. "Shall we?"

As he led Charlotte from the drawing room, a feminine sigh rose from behind. Either his mother, or possibly one of his older sisters, expected the tour to culminate into something amorous.

Simon merely hoped to keep his head on his shoulders.

At least long enough to get that kiss.

CHAPTER 22

Charlotte tried to restrain her enthusiasm as Simon escorted her through the house. True, it wasn't as grand as Edgerton's seat in Shropshire, but to call it a *house* seemed woefully inadequate. Yet, the word mansion was much too cold for the warmth exuded within the walls.

It was a home. Filled with people who loved each other—who loved it. Even the pieces of artwork gracing the various rooms had special meaning.

Simon pointed at a sculpted crystal vase. Stems of tulips formed the walls, their leaves linking each flower to the other and the blooms forming the top ridge. "My father gave my mother this for their fifteenth wedding anniversary." Inside, a spring arrangement of yellow tulips brightened the room, their sunny faces smiling at her.

She touched a fingertip to a yellow bloom. "Everything is so cheerful here." Her voice sounded wistful to her ears.

"Not him." Simon pointed to a portrait of a gruff-looking man. His dark hair—or more likely a wig—hung in waves over the shoulders of his elaborate coat. "Mother keeps threatening to hide him away."

"Who was he?"

"My great-great-grandfather. This was his estate. George the First rewarded him for his service in the Jacobite rebellion. No title, but money and land. He invested it well and ruled the tenants with an iron-fist from what I hear. A most disagreeable fellow. Not much to admire about him."

"Except that because of him, you have all this." She swung her arm in an arc about the room.

"Fair enough. Not sure if it's something to admire or, as my father has done, use it to better others and not just ourselves."

She pondered his statement. Would Simon and Mr. Beckham hold to such altruistic beliefs if King George had bestowed a title to their ancestor as well as the land and wealth? The power afforded to those in the peerage had ill effects on many. She'd witnessed that firsthand.

But as Simon led her through the rest of the common rooms of the home, his face brightening as he greeted each servant by name, she thought they would. Perhaps there really were good, incorruptible people in the world. Weren't Honoria and Burwood proof of that?

As much as she hated to admit it, Simon had been reared to be a gentleman of a grand estate. Which begged the question. "Simon, why are you working as Burwood's man of business? Surely not for the money?"

"Hmm?" Simon pulled his attention away from a footman who paused in his duties to welcome Simon home.

"Your duties with Burwood? Why not spend the time here when it will all be yours someday?"

He blinked as if he'd never considered the question. "As his firstborn son, Father began instructing me at his knee. Of course, I could barely sit still long enough to learn anything. All I wanted to do was run around, climb trees, and shuck off my clothing to dive in the pond during the hot summers. But when it became clear I would most likely be his only son, he stressed the importance of being responsible for my mother and sisters should he . . ." Simon's voice cracked as if he couldn't manage the last word.

So unlike Roland, who veritably anticipated their sire's passing with glee. Nash had often remarked that perhaps their father's sudden death wasn't entirely from natural causes. But neither she nor her brothers mourned his loss overmuch.

"Then why not remain here? Why did you join the military?"

A shadow of darkness clouded his face, and he jerked his gaze away. "That's another story for another day. Suffice it to say, I took my father's words to heart, and although you might find it hard to believe, I took my responsibility seriously, learning as much as I could. When Drake discovered his true lineage, he panicked. He knew nothing about running an estate—especially a ducal one with multiple holdings. He needed someone he could trust to teach him and work with him so he could learn the right things to ask—to watch for. As my friend, how could I deny him? And Father encouraged the position, not only to assist Drake, but for what I could learn in managing such enormous properties. But my position with Drake as his man of business is temporary."

"Because you will one day return here when your father dies?"

He nodded. "Or my position will end upon my own death."

As much as she had led him to believe differently, in truth, she had never wished for his death. And with the events of the past few days, as she grew to know her husband, she not only didn't long for his demise, but she dreaded it.

The revelation astonished her. Had she grown to care for the man?

The flicker of darkness disappeared, as if he mentally

brushed it away. "But either way, Drake has taken to his role as if he were born to it." Simon paused, slapping his knee. "Ha! I suppose he was. And he has Honoria, and even Stratford should he need counsel."

"What you did was . . ."

A dark brow hitched up. "Incorrigible? It seems to be your favorite descriptor of me."

"No. I was going to say kind. But that seems inadequate. It was selfless."

He threw a hand to his heart. "Is it still beating? A compliment from my fair wife?"

"Don't let that go to your head. It's large enough already." She couldn't help but laugh at him, but more than that, she was grateful he didn't become all sentimental over her unfortunate slip.

"Ah, there she is. The Charlotte I know. You frightened me for a moment." He peeked out one of the front windows. "Drat. It's too dark to explore the hedge maze. We'll save that for another time. Let's make our quick goodbyes while a footman fetches a carriage."

"Is the cottage so far we can't walk?"

"No. It's only about a quarter mile." His gaze drifted to her feet. "But your slippers aren't meant for walking."

Blast the man. Why did he have to be so thoughtful? Still, she refused to have him think her weak. "I'm perfectly capable of walking a short distance."

That arrogant smirk appeared. "Never said you weren't."

After saying goodbye to everyone and promising they would come tomorrow for tea at two, they set off for the cottage.

Heat from the day had vanished, leaving the country air cool and crisp. She pulled in a great lungful. "I always forget how much cleaner it smells in the country."

"Didn't you return to your brother's estate after the Season?"

"Not often. It was a blessed respite to remain in London with only Rose and a few servants."

"Away from Edgerton's judgmental eye, eh?"

She gave a soft chuckle, surprised at how wonderful it felt to laugh. She must have broken a record for the day. "Perceptive of you."

"Oooh. Selfless and perceptive. Might I coax a third compliment from you today?" He patted her hand lying on his arm. "I will file them away and take them out to look at when you're angry with me."

"They shall become dog-eared and cracked from handling." A smile tugged at her lips.

He chuckled in return.

She stole a peek at his profile as he focused on the path before them. He was handsome. She could admit that—at least to herself. And those kisses! Her face warmed. Thank goodness he couldn't see the blush on her cheeks in the growing darkness.

"Charlotte." Gone was any trace of amusement as he spoke her name. "I want to make this work between us."

A voice inside urged her to respond that she did as well, but old fears held her back. Could she trust him? Or if she allowed him in, would he use that to control and harm her? She remained silent.

"I see." Muscles in his arm tensed beneath her hand. "Well, take heart. You may not have to suffer with me for long."

The bite of his flippant remark cut through her. An apology crowded on her tongue, but before she could release it, the shadow of a building loomed before them.

Although not nearly as magnificent as the main house, the *cottage* was impressive in size and, from what Charlotte could see, elegant in design.

"We're home, Mrs. Beckham."

SIMON TRIED TO HOLD BACK HIS DISAPPOINTMENT AT Charlotte's silence. Was he really asking that much? He didn't ask her to love him. God, he didn't want that anyway, not with the possibility of death looming over him. But they'd spent such a pleasant evening together going through the main house. He had hoped they'd moved from outright hate to tolerating each other.

She'd complimented him twice. Perhaps unintentionally, but she had laughed and smiled more than he ever remembered. She seemed to enjoy his family.

And he still wanted to kiss that dimple in her cheek.

Damnation!

He opened the door to the cottage, but as she moved to enter, he stopped her.

"Tradition." He scooped her up into his arms and carried her into the house. Pleased when she didn't protest, he wondered if they had indeed made progress.

Soft candlelight and lamps cast a golden glow over Charlotte's face, and his breath hitched in his throat. "Alone at last." He gave her his signature wink.

Charlotte pushed against his chest with her fists. "Put me down, you oaf!"

How easily she could break the spell, yet he obeyed her command.

Stationed at the front door, John, one of his father's footmen, took their coats and hats.

"Don't mind my wife, John. It's her way of saying she's mad about me."

John's lips twitched, but like any good servant, he remained silent.

She straightened her skirts, brushing vigorously at them as if the mere act of holding her had wrinkled them. "I'm sure John is brighter than you are and sees the truth in the matter."

He ignored her and took her hand. "Come, I want to show you around."

The servants had not only aired out the cottage, they had fully prepared it for a newly wed couple, no doubt all under the instruction of his mother. Hyacinths, peonies, and yes, tulips—his mother's favorite—brightened the rooms with splashes of color and filled each with the sweet scent of spring. Floorboards shined and crystal sparkled. Rugs were freshly beaten to remove offending dust.

In every room, Simon cast a quick glance to gauge Charlotte's reaction, pleased with her nod of approval. "Disappointed? Perhaps you expected a hovel surrounded by pig styes?"

Her mouth dropped open.

"Oh, dear God. You did, didn't you?" He shook his head, amused at catching her false assumptions.

"I admit to nothing." Her lips tightened, but her eyes glinted with the truth.

Tugging her hand, he pulled her toward the stairs to show her the bedchambers, choosing the largest one first.

When he flung open the door, he kept his eyes on Charlotte's face. Candlelight lit the cheerful room which reflected his grandmother's outlook on life. Given Charlotte's comments about the main house, he knew she would love it.

However, he wasn't prepared for her reaction.

The tiniest gasp escaped her lips before she threw a hand to her mouth.

"What?" he asked, then turned his attention to the room. "Oh."

Someone—presumably one of his sisters—had destroyed numerous flowers by plucking off the petals and depositing them on the bed. He strode to the bell pull by the bed and gave it a sound tug. "I promise you, I had nothing to do with this."

She snorted a laugh. "Of course not. It's too romantic."

Puzzled, Simon blinked and gaped slack-jawed at her. "You . . . *like* it?

John rushed in. "Sir?"

Simon waved a hand toward the bed. "Tell whoever did this——"

"Tell them, 'Thank you,'" Charlotte finished.

"Will there be anything else?" John's gaze flicked between Simon and Charlotte.

Clearly not understanding that John had directed the question toward Simon, Charlotte took charge. "Please have a tub and hot water brought up for a bath."

John cast a quizzical glance toward him. "A tub, sir? But——"

"I'll explain to Lady Charlotte. But do bring some hot water."

John scurried off.

Hands on her—ahem, provocative—hips, Charlotte pounced on him. An adorable frown dented her brow. "Don't tell me you don't have a tub available for a proper bath?"

Rather than answer, he tugged her hand again and led her to the adjoining room. "Grandmother insisted on this addition. She adored her baths and believed in cleanliness."

Charlotte's gaze swept the rather large room. "I never expected this in a cottage." Elevated on a platform, the tub's outer shell was copper, but delicately painted flowers adorned the porcelain lining. Charlotte ran her fingertips along the rim. "It's so beautiful."

"And this." Simon opened the door to the water closet. "Private as well."

She continued to stare at the tub, her face pensive. "If such a convenience had been at Pendrake House, we wouldn't be in this predicament."

"There is in the ducal bedchambers, but Old Burwood had never added them to the guest bedchambers. From what we've heard, he rarely entertained in his later years. Drake plans to make those changes, but with the baby . . ." He shrugged.

She frowned. "And you didn't think to use the available one?"

"I don't invade others' privacy, even when they're not present." Blood thrummed against his temples. How easily she could exasperate him. "And if you recall, I wasn't at my most clear-headed." Yet, even as his temper rose, the lure of her made his pounding blood sing.

He softened his tone. "Let's not argue over what can't be undone. As I said, I want to make this work, but to do so means we must be honest with each other."

Like a soldier in line for inspection, she straightened before him. "Are you accusing me of something?"

He flicked a glance toward the tub. "Let's not discuss this in a room where all I can do is picture you naked—or worse, both of us."

Her cheeks flushed pink, and she flounced from the room.

Following her, he closed the door to the bathing room behind him, shutting out the vision. "Aha! See. How long are we going to dance around the fact that we're attracted to each other?"

"You're mad!"

He grinned. "Not incorrigible?"

Arrows formed in her narrowed eyes, aimed directly for his heart.

"Be honest, Charlotte. I'm not talking about love or tender feelings. I'm talking about physical attraction."

"I'm not attracted to you." She snapped the words a little too forcefully.

With lazy indifference, he plopped into the chair by the window, receiving yet another angry glare.

"A gentleman remains standing until the lady is seated."

He motioned to the chair opposite him. "Then, by all means. Sit."

Huffing, she took the seat, arms folded over her stomach.

He raised a brow at her. "How long are we going to do this, Charlotte? Because frankly, I grow tired of it."

She glowered, her face a mask of stubbornness and pride.

"Deny it to yourself all you wish, but I know when a woman is attracted to me."

"Hmph!" She mumbled something that sounded like *inflated head.*

He continued on. "There are signs. The way you respond to my touch. My kiss."

With agonizing slowness, she turned toward him. "You vex me!" The vitriol in her voice surpassed the words.

"Ah. But do *I* vex you, or is it the fact that you want me that vexes you?"

"I . . ." Her mouth snapped shut.

"I say that because we are of like minds in that regard. You are everything I shouldn't want. Stubborn. Opinionated. Aloof. Controlling. Rigid."

"Because I know how to conduct myself with decorum? Unlike you, who acts like a buffoon. You think because you are handsome and charming people will fall at your feet?! That you can wiggle out of any difficult situation with a smile and joke? There is not one serious bone in your body!"

"You are wound so tight, the slightest breeze might snap you in half. Sadness and pain emanate from you. And I detest pain."

Barely noticeable, she flinched, as if the mere mention of it reflected it back on her. Her chin trembled slightly.

"And yet, you haunt my thoughts day and night. The silky softness of your skin. The sweetness of your lips. How your pulse raced when I kissed the inside of your wrist. That dimple in your cheek when you allow yourself a genuine smile."

Unable to help himself, he rose from his seat, then dropped to his knees before her. His hands pressed on the seat of the chair, framing her hips. "And I want to kiss that dimple so damn badly, I can't think of anything else."

Her lips parted slightly, and she blinked. "You . . . what?"

"I want to kiss that dimple. Let me kiss it, Charlotte. Just once."

Before she could answer, John arrived at the open door, buckets of steaming water in his hands. "Sir?"

Damn.

CHAPTER 23

Charlotte fought to pull air into her lungs.

Simon stared up at her, his blue eyes sincere. Dark stubble of his evening whiskers peppered his cheeks and jaw. She hated how quickly the word *attractive* popped into her mind. Would his beard scratch her skin if she allowed him to kiss her cheek?

How could she be so angry with him and at the same time want to run her fingers through his dark hair, pulling his lips closer for a kiss?

"Sir?" John, the footman, stood at attention in the open doorway. The man's gaze darted away, focusing instead on the ceiling.

"Should I send him away?" Lowered to a whisper, the plea in Simon's voice matched the entreaty in his eyes.

Yes. The word clung to the tip of her tongue. Years of self-preservation, the armor fastened tightly, kept it in place. "Y—y—you should go. I want my bath."

Simon gave a curt nod, then rose, his mouth tightening in a thin, straight line. When he reached the door, he didn't turn back, instead calling over his shoulder. "I'll return to say goodnight. John, bring some water to the guest room when you have a chance. I think I'll have a bath as well."

"The guest room, sir?" John's gaze flitted between her and Simon.

An aching emptiness assaulted her stomach. *Call him back. Tell him to stay.*

But when Simon turned, painful sadness replaced the typical playful mischief on his face. "Yes. Have my belongings moved there after Lady Charlotte has finished her bath."

The words froze on her tongue, then he was gone.

Once the tub was filled and Rose had helped her undress, Charlotte lowered herself into the water. Warmth eased her muscles, stiff from sitting in the coach for days. Rose had scooped up some of the flower petals strewn on the bed and placed them in the water.

As she washed Charlotte's hair, she chattered away. "I didn't expect such a fine house and grounds, did you, my lady? Everyone is so pleasant, and they all seem happy to be of service to Mr. and Mrs. Beckham."

Charlotte barely restrained the snort. "Unlike my brother, you mean."

"Oh. Please, my lady, I didn't mean any disrespect. The marquess has high standards, is all."

"Hmm." Charlotte closed her eyes, drifting into a sated sense of peace as Rose massaged her scalp. And yet, the house and grounds were as impeccably maintained as her brother's—without the iron-fisted rule and acid-laced orders. Mr. Beckham governed with kindness.

The tiny voice that had kept her safe for years whispered in her ear. *Appearances can deceive. Remain on guard.*

Wanting to trust Simon, she'd almost forgotten the sage advice of her inner protector. And still . . . another voice, so quiet she could barely hear it, whispered back. *Let him in.*

Coupled with Honoria's request, the opposing voice grew stronger.

As the water splashed over her, Charlotte couldn't help but imagine Simon's fingers brushing against the sensitive areas of her body. He accused her of being attracted to him, and although she was loath to admit it, truth rang in his words.

She hated the way her stomach flipped when he'd kissed the inside of her wrist. How her fingers itched to test the silkiness of his hair. Hated how she wanted to see if she could make him moan when he kissed her. How that silly grin of his could turn her mind to mush.

Even more, she hated how his family adored him. Teased him. Accepted him for who he was. Hated the love he shared with his family—not because of what *he* had, but because it shone a bright light on what she lacked. Hated it because of the envy that grew like a weed in her heart.

Like a dark void, she felt the lack of such love so greatly, tears welled in her eyes. What would it have been like to be a cherished daughter instead of a millstone around her father's and brother's necks? To be protected by someone other than herself?

"Did I splash water in your eyes, my lady?" Rose's voice startled Charlotte from her self-pity.

She brushed the tears away. "It's fine, Rose."

And Charlotte knew it was a lie.

Simon dried himself with a soft towel and handed it to Brown.

"I've laid out your banyan should you venture to the next room. Will there be anything else?"

Simon chuckled at his valet's veiled suggestion that he take the bull by the horns, so to speak, and enter Charlotte's room. "No. Thank you, Brown." Charlotte was right about one thing; a bath had helped ease his tense muscles and calm his racing mind. However, it didn't help his growing desire for Charlotte.

Damnation!

Alone, he might need to take care of himself.

Brown exited, closing the door with a soft *click*.

Simon sighed and glanced toward the bed.

Knock, knock.

His head jerked toward the door. If Brown had forgotten anything so soon, he would have knocked once and then reentered. After snatching the dressing gown from the bed, he slipped it on. Not bothering to tie it, he held it together with one hand, then pulled the door open with the other.

Charlotte stood before him, looking fresh and pink from her bath. Her dark, thick locks flowed over her shoulders, unbraided and free. Luminous in the golden lamplight coming from his room, her deep brown eyes met his, vulnerability in their depths.

Mmm. So lovely.

"Did you need something?" he asked, immediately kicking himself for the idiotic question. Why else would she come to his room? Why hadn't he thought of something charming to lure her into his bed?

The softness he'd seen in her vanished, replaced with her usual iron resolve.

Maybe he'd imagined it.

"I've given what you said some thought."

Or maybe she was trying to hide it? Holding the door open wider, he motioned her inside.

As she stepped past him, the scent of lemon flooded his senses.

Clean and fresh, it made his mouth water with the urge to taste her. "You've changed your fragrance again. It used to be lilac, then vanilla."

Startled, she pivoted toward him. "You noticed my change in fragrance?"

"I notice a lot of things. Like how the lace on your dressing gown skims your collarbone, drawing my eyes to the soft dent in your throat." He lifted his gaze from said indentation to her face. "Which I want to kiss almost as much as that dimple."

She huffed. "I was hoping you would be serious for once."

"There is nothing I'm more serious about than kissing." Cautiously, he took a step forward, his gaze locked with hers. Pride expanded his ribcage when her lips parted. He schooled his features into his most serious expression. "But forgive me for interrupting. Please have a seat and tell me your thoughts."

This time, he waited until she had seated herself in the room's single chair, then he sat on the bed. The dressing gown gaped, and her eyes flicked down to his exposed chest. "Forgive me. I've just finished bathing as well and thought you had settled in for the night." He tugged the garment closer and tied it.

Ramrod straight, she sat on the chair as if it were a torture device. Although the epitome of control, her hands twisted in her lap. Was she nervous? "I do see some validity in your words."

"Any in particular?"

"That there might be some slight attraction between us."

He felt the twitch of his lips.

Which apparently her keen perception had caught, for she rushed to clarify. "More so on your part, of course." She waved a dismissive hand. "But it would be unfair if I didn't admit the obvious."

"Which is?" It was like pulling teeth. Not that he'd know. Thank goodness, he still had all of his own.

"That you are, by most women's estimations, handsome. So there is a sort of animal appeal."

Oh, he shouldn't bait her. Not with her inching toward the inevitable. However, he simply couldn't resist. "So, I appeal to your baser instincts, eh? Might I hope this means you are becoming amenable to consummating our marriage?" He patted the mattress beside him to emphasize his point.

Infinitesimal at most, the flicker of her eyes toward the bed spoke volumes. "I am considering it. You did mention you wished to have a son to inherit, and consummation is the task to accomplish that goal."

"Task? You make it sound like a chore, sterile and something to endure rather than enjoy."

She gave one of those snorts he found adorable. "Men find it enjoyable."

"For someone without experience in the matter, you seem to have some rather strong opinions on the subject. Wouldn't you rather make your pronouncement based on facts?"

She arched a dark brown at him. "How do you propose I do that?"

"Why don't we start slowly? Experiment a little with what you will enjoy. For example, let's return to the topic we started with —kissing."

Again, only a fraction, and if he'd not been paying attention, he would have missed it, but her shoulders relaxed. Lucky for him, he was a very observant man.

She gave a curt nod. "Very well."

Instinct told him the whole endeavor—good Lord, now even *he* was thinking of it as a duty—would progress better if she maintained control.

"Would you like to come sit by me here, or would you prefer to stand?"

She barely hesitated. "Stand."

He rose first, and in long easy strides so as not to appear too eager—although in truth he was—he stood before her, holding out his hand. "Allow me to help you up."

"Kissing only. You promise?"

"Promise. On my honor."

She slipped her hand into his, the electric charge of contact sparking through his veins. Her lips parted slightly as her gaze darted to his.

"That's called attraction, Charlotte. Do you find it pleasant?"

"I find it disconcerting."

He laughed. "I'll accept that. For now. But first, I want to kiss that dimple. Smile for me and remind me exactly where it is. Think of the look on your brother's face when I cast up my accounts all over him."

Her dark eyes sparkling with mischief, Charlotte graced him with a glorious smile.

Ah, there's that dimple.

Charlotte fought a laugh at Simon's absurd suggestion. However, the expression on Roland's face had been the one bright spot in the day which had tied her to the man in front of her for life.

And now Simon was her husband—wanting husbandly things.

What was she doing? Still, she promised herself she would try. And he promised he wouldn't force her.

Simon's blue eyes grew dusky and hooded as he lowered his head. The kiss against her cheek was soft . . . and nice. The skin on her arms pebbled, and feathery wings battered her stomach. Nothing like the sloppy kiss Felix had forced on her less than a month ago.

Too soon for her liking, he pulled back. "Well? Did you enjoy that? Because I certainly did." He definitely looked like the cat that got into the cream.

"It was not—unpleasant."

He laughed. The buffoon saw right through her. Perhaps he wasn't such a fool after all. "Then might I interest you in another? That hollow in your throat has my name on it."

Unbidden, her hand flew to the soft indentation, already anticipating the press of his lips against her skin.

"Yes. That one." Grasping her hand, he moved it out of his way before lowering his head.

As he pressed his lips against her throat, his fingers traced a featherlight touch over the side of her neck.

Sparks ignited under the skin. "Oh," she moaned, her head lolling back and eyes shuttering in sheer pleasure.

He chuckled, the gravelly sound vibrating against the sensitive area, shooting more sparks across her shoulders and chest, and settling low in her belly.

Damn the man. His boasts about his prowess were not exaggerations.

He lingered as if he had nothing better to do, finally ending with a quick flick of his tongue. "You, Wife, are delicious."

The absurdity of his comment was lost on her muddled brain. Truly, the man had turned it to mush. All she could think about was she wanted him to kiss her lips.

She turned her face up to his, her mouth puckered in what she presumed was the correct arrangement to express her desire.

"More?" The arrogant, self-assured tone of his voice indicated he already knew her answer.

Unwilling or unable—she wasn't certain—to answer him with words, she nodded. A curt down and up motion was all she could manage.

The ridiculous grin broke widely across his face, the rake! "Very well. Hmm, where should I kiss now?" He made a great show of stepping back, his gaze raking her from foot to head.

Tired of waiting, she pulled him toward her, grabbing a fistful of his dark hair, and lowered his mouth to hers.

Strong arms banded her around the waist, tugging her close to his body. Heat from his bare chest peeking through his gaping banyan seared through her nightrail.

She was ablaze. Tempestuous sensations bombarded her. The scent of masculine sandalwood mixed with something uniquely him. The sweet taste of chocolate as he dipped his tongue tentatively between her lips. Silky soft strands of dark hair beneath her fingers. His evening whiskers did indeed scratch, but in the most enjoyable way, causing a tightening in her breasts. Moans of pleasure—from him, from her? Both of them?

She cracked open one eye. The abandon sketching Simon's face surely matched her own. Peering down, she marveled at the wisps of hair covering the expanse of his bare chest. When she slid her other hand up to test the texture, the muscle in his pectoral twitched under her fingers, and power surged through her.

At the juncture of his shoulder and neck, a ropy sinew tightened, and he pulled his mouth from hers. "Careful, Charlotte. If it's only kissing you want, you're treading into dangerous waters."

Somewhere in the recesses of her jumbled mind, she wondered if she cared or if she'd just as soon drown in the waters of desire.

CHAPTER 24

How much was one man supposed to withstand? Charlotte was his wife! But even if he hadn't promised her, he would never force himself on a woman. It was unthinkable. "You should go back to your room." Like his unending impetuosity, the words flew from his lips.

Lips.

He glanced again at Charlotte's, the sweet taste of them still lingering on his own. The touch of her fingertips on his bare chest scorched his skin. How could a person dislike another with such a blazing intensity, and yet have that same fire ignite an inferno of desire in their blood?

And when they finally gave in to their undeniable attraction, would they go up in flames like a phoenix?

He was more than willing to find out. "Unless you want to stay?" He toyed with the shoulder of her nightrail. "Perhaps more kissing in less exposed places?" Hooking a finger in the edge of the material, he tugged it down an inch. "Here, perhaps?"

She hesitated, and his heart stuttered with hope. Would she stay? Welcome the continuation of his seduction?

Blinking as if realizing where they were headed, she stepped back and yanked her nightdress back into place. "I should slap you."

"Ha! So it's perfectly fine for you to run your hands all over my chest, but I can't even touch your shoulder?" He stared her down. "You are such a hypocrite, Charlotte Beckham. Deny it all you wish, but you want me as much as I want you!"

She answered him by storming from the room and slamming the door behind her.

"I hope you're up all night thinking of me," he muttered. Climbing into the cold bed, he knew he'd just sentenced himself to the same fate.

"What a nightmare." He ran a hand down his face, wondering how the hell he was ever going to make this sham of a marriage work.

Lord knows when he finally fell asleep. He'd tossed and turned all night dreaming of Charlotte. When he finally woke, he cracked an eye open, cursing the beam of light coming in through the slit in the curtain. Leave it to the sun to shine directly in his eyes.

After dragging himself from bed, Simon rang for Brown, his usually sunny mood foul. Married four days and he still hadn't bedded his own wife. He began to lose hope that Charlotte would capitulate to his—questionable—seduction tactics.

When Brown arrived, he assembled everything for Simon's morning shave. "Sleep well, sir?" he asked as he finished lathering Simon's face.

"Not especially," Simon said.

His valet wisely remained silent.

The woman would be the death of him. The irony of the idea and his precarious future slammed Simon in the chest like a hammer.

"Ha!"

Brown drew back, the razor—the edge lined with soap and dark beard stubble—poised above Simon's chin. "Sir?" The valet gazed down to where he'd just scraped Simon's face. "I don't see a cut."

"It's my wife, Brown. I've never known a woman so . . . so . . . difficult."

Brown chuckled, lowering the razor to continue his task. "I like her. She seems like a no-nonsense type of woman." He flicked the soapy film off the razor into a bowl of warm water. "Just what you need. Now, lift your chin while I get your neck."

"She'd sooner slit my throat with that razor than let me touch her. How the hell am I supposed to produce an heir with a wife who won't let me bed her?" Simon hated admitting that—especially to his valet. But with Drake unavailable, he had little choice in male confidants. He certainly wouldn't confess to his father the reason he married Charlotte.

"Hold still, sir, or you'll be in no condition to bed anyone."

"Ha. Ha." Yet Simon remained frozen while Brown scraped soap from his throat.

However, talking and wielding a razor wasn't a problem for Brown. "From what I hear from Miss Rose, Lady Charlotte has had little reason to be happy. Rose said Lord Edgerton's cruelty extended to his own family."

"You don't have to tell me about the blackguard Edgerton." Still, what type of cruelty did Charlotte endure under her brother's roof? More than an attempt to marry her to another blackguard and shredding her clothing in spite? Had Edgerton laid hands on his own sister? Simon shuddered at the thought.

"Sir!" Brown shot him a warning, then scraped the last bit of soap from Simon's face.

"Have the cook prepare some coffee, if she has it on hand," Simon said as Brown finished tying his neckcloth.

His valet cocked an eyebrow, but nodded, taking the bowl of —now soapy and whisker-dotted—water away and left.

Dressed and shaved, Simon made his way to the dining room, grateful to find it empty. He wasn't quite ready to face his wife.

The hearty breakfast of sausage, toast, and—yes—coffee revived his spirits. When Charlotte entered, looking almost as haggard as he felt, an unhealthy satisfaction warmed his chest. Well, that might have been the coffee, but Simon wasn't going to split hairs.

"Good morning, Wife. Sleep well?" He added an extra dose of sarcasm to the same question his valet had asked him.

She grunted a response. *Grunted! Excellent.* Simon mentally rubbed his hands together in glee.

She darted a glance toward his cup. "Is that coffee?"

"Yes." He lifted his chin toward the elegant silver container on the sideboard.

She poured herself a cup, then took a seat several places from his.

Yet, even at that distance, the dark smudges under her eyes were visible. Suddenly, the idea of her tossing and turning the majority of the night didn't please him as much as it had moments before.

You're growing soft.

Regrouping, he marshaled a comment sure to vex her. "I know something guaranteed to help you sleep." He took a sip of his own bitter beverage. "If you're interested."

"Hmph. What might that be? Hit me over the head and render me unconscious?"

"Heavens, no. Violence is the opposite of what I have in mind. Although it can be . . . vigorous." Not quite a leer, he flashed her a sultry look that sent most women swooning.

"What is it?" she asked, staring into her coffee.

When he didn't answer, she lifted her gaze to his and her cheeks darkened. "Oh."

"It's quite effective in relaxing the mind and body." He sipped his coffee for another pregnant pause. "If done properly."

"Then I'm sure I have missed nothing."

Oh. That did it! She could insult his intelligence, but attacking his skills in the bedroom was beyond the pale.

Pushing his plate aside, he rose and strode toward the window. Overcast skies replaced the sun that had awoken him. No doubt the one dastardly beam had broken through simply to nettle him. He needed a diversion, something pleasant to get his mind off his wife. He knew just the thing, and it lifted his spirits. "Since you find my company so distasteful, I shall give you a wedding gift and make myself scarce. It's a perfect day for fishing. Please make yourself at home while I'm gone."

"I thought this *was* my home now," she grumbled.

Right.

He turned, only to have his breath hitch.

Bent over her coffee, she offered him a view of her long, graceful—and very kissable—neck.

His lips tingled just looking at it. With quiet steps, he moved behind her, bending over to whisper in her ear. "Unless you want me to stay, and we could continue where we left off last night." He traced a fingertip from the sensitive spot under her ear to the juncture of that kissable neck and her shoulder.

She stiffened, her answer clear before she spoke it. "No."

"Very well." Anxious to remove himself from further temptation, he left her without a word of goodbye.

After grabbing an old battered hat and shoving it on his head, he gathered his tackle and strode from the house.

The fish would be better company. At least they might take his bait.

WITH SIMON OFF FISHING—IF INDEED THAT'S WHAT HE WAS doing—Charlotte grew restless sitting in the cottage alone. When she tried to read, Elizabeth Bennet's growing ardor for Mr. Darcy made Charlotte's mind reel back to the delicious kisses Simon had lavished on her the previous evening, not to mention those she herself had initiated.

Had she truly been so bold as to tug the man's mouth to hers? Why, yes. Yes, she had, and the feeling of being in control sent a surge of power through her. Not to mention Simon's reaction. For a man so experienced—at least to hear him tell it—she seemed to affect him as much as he did her.

She had tossed and turned all night, wondering if she should have allowed him to take things further.

Gah! She would grow mad dwelling on it. She needed something else to occupy her thoughts. She tossed the book aside, rose and looked out the window, pleased earlier clouds had dissipated and the sun dappled the ground outside.

A walk would clear her head and push thoughts of Simon Beckham's roguish grin and talented lips from her mind.

After grabbing her bonnet and a pelisse, she slipped out the front door without a word to any of the servants.

Fragrant lilac floated on the gentle breeze, the grounds between the cottage and the main house immaculately maintained. Away from Simon's watchful eyes, she dropped her armor and freely appreciated the beauty around her, stooping to pick a few flowers, lifting them to her nose, and inhaling deeply.

Birds chirped in the trees, and she spied a nest of robins, the mother bird feeding her young. The sight reminded her Simon would need an heir. Which, in turn, reminded her of the kisses they shared and the passion sparking between them.

It would seem nothing could distract her from thinking about the irritating man.

Even with the abundance of fragrant flowers filling the cottage—the vision of the petals on the bed rising—she couldn't resist picking a few more wildflowers. She thought of the forget-me-nots adorning Honoria's hair at her wedding to the duke. Such a simple flower, but the meaning it held for her dear friends was unmistakable.

One lone daffodil clung to life under the shade of an enormous oak. She laughed, thinking of Simon once again, and how she had compared him to the sunny flower. Pausing, she considered picking it. It would wither and drop its petals soon anyway, returning to slumber and resting until the next spring.

Perhaps she would place it on Simon's pillow, and she could already hear his laugh, wild and free. Decision made, she apologized to the flower before pinching the stem close to the ground.

She ambled along, breathing in the fresh country air, basking in the warm sun upon her cheeks, the rays striping the ground and dancing amid the swaying leaves on the trees.

Peaceful, idyllic. That she would someday be the mistress of the entire estate gave her pause. She would easily grow to love her new home. Not because of the size, beauty, or wealth of the estate itself, but because of the contentment being there generated in her parched soul. And she had Simon Beckham to thank for it.

In the past, when Charlotte had envisioned marriage—and admittedly it had not been often— it had always been to a well-titled man with vast holdings. Both her father and her brother had expected her to marry well and extend their connections within society and their power in the government.

Charlotte had not expected contentment from those imagined unions, and certainly not happiness. But at that moment, she glimpsed the possibility for both. She might even begin to feel safe.

A laugh flew from her lips at the ludicrous idea.

"Charlotte?" a feminine voice called. Frannie stood before her, a basket of flowers clutched in her hands. "It appears we had the same idea. Although I like your choices more than my own. Where in the world did you find a remaining daffodil? I thought they had all died off."

Charlotte's gaze darted to the yellow bloom clutched in her hand, ready to make an apology that wasn't quite an apology. "Hiding among some tall grass over by that oak." She pointed in the direction she had come. "It reminded me of Simon, so I couldn't resist."

Frannie's eyebrow hitched. "Oh? Because of the Greek myth?"

No wonder Charlotte liked the girl. "Precisely. I hope you don't mind that I plucked it."

"Pfft." Frannie waved the apology away. "You may as well take it and enjoy it while you can. I'm surprised it survived this long." She held out an arm. "Why don't you come inside, and we'll put your selections in some water to keep them fresh. Mama is teaching Georgie to embroider, and I'm sure Mama could use some intelligent conversation, and Georgie would love the distraction."

Ah, things Charlotte excelled at—both intelligent conversation and embroidery. "I don't want to intrude."

"Nonsense. And considering you're out here by yourself, I suspect Simon is off doing goodness knows what. It's rude of him to leave you alone on your honeymoon. Mama will have his head."

"Well, in that case." Charlotte drew an unhealthy satisfaction from the thought of Mrs. Beckham giving Simon a dressing down for neglecting his new wife. Not that Charlotte minded. She followed Frannie back to the main house, surprised how closely she had wandered to it on her own.

As Frannie predicted, Mrs. Beckham raged in indignation on Charlotte's behalf as she rang for tea and water for Charlotte's bouquet. "That boy! He's usually so considerate, my dear. I reared him to be better than that. But I will have a firm word with him. Have no fear."

Frannie shot Charlotte an *I told you* look, then excused herself, saying she had some writing to attend to.

Odd, but Charlotte found herself defending her husband. "He did mention something about a favorite fishing spot. And with the favorable weather . . ."

"He's probably still trying to catch Big Gus," Georgie said, poking a needle through a tortured piece of fabric.

"Big Gus? Who, or should I say what, is Big Gus?"

"He's a brown trout. About as big as me," Georgie said, not looking up from her tangle of thread.

Charlotte huffed a laugh. "I'm sure you exaggerate."

"She does," Mrs. Beckham said. "But only because she's grown since the last time Gus got away from Mr. Beckham and Simon. It was right before Simon left for the military. Not one to give up on things, Simon is obsessed with catching that fish. So there's no telling how big Gus is now."

"If the fish is still alive. Didn't Simon meet the Duke of Burwood in the military? Honoria said His Grace had been in India for eight years. That is an extraordinarily long life for a fish."

A maid arrived with a tea tray. Mrs. Beckham poured a cup for Charlotte. "Indeed. Simon enlisted seven years ago." Mrs. Beckham cast a glance toward Georgie. But Georgie's attention remained glued to her embroidery. "He met Drake—I mean His Grace—later."

Curiosity niggled at Charlotte's mind. Was there something about Simon's military service she wished to hide from Georgie?

Charlotte sipped the tea, mulling over the possibilities.

"But"—Mrs. Beckham's attention returned to Charlotte, her smile open and genuine—"I'm sure you are correct, and Gus has gone to the great river beyond."

Georgie snorted. "Simon says Gus is too mean to die."

Such ridiculous conversation normally annoyed Charlotte. But at the moment, she found herself enjoying it immensely.

Beth rushed into the room. "Mama! Frannie has taken all my ink and paper. She says her silly novel is more important than my letter to Mr. Thorpe."

Mrs. Beckham uttered a long-suffering sigh. "Can't the two of you work something out? I'm trying to help Georgie with her embroidery."

Beth shook her head. "She's locked herself in her room and won't answer me."

Exhaling another sigh, Mrs. Beckham gave Charlotte an apologetic smile. "These girls will be the death of me. If you will excuse me, Lady Charlotte."

"If you wish, I can assist Georgie. I'm skilled at embroidery." Anger flashed through her remembering her father's overheard words. *All women are good for are bedding and embroidery.*

"Thank you, my dear." Mrs. Beckham flashed an appreciative smile, then rushed from the room.

Alone with Georgie, Charlotte studied the child. So like Simon with her dark hair, clear-blue eyes, and exuberant spirit. Surprisingly, Charlotte found she rather liked children—at least older ones and, of course, Honoria's adorable daughter Kitty.

Could motherhood be less foreboding than she'd imagined? Contrary to her statement, Mrs. Beckham certainly seemed to enjoy it. Did her own mother enjoy her children? Charlotte always remembered her as gentle but with an aching sadness about her—little wonder considering her tyrant of a husband. When she died so young, Charlotte became like a rudderless ship upon the sea. But perhaps she could learn from Judith.

"Charlotte, may I ask you something?"

"Of course. But depending on your question, I might decline to answer."

Georgie laughed. "I like you. Why do women have to learn to embroider? I'm no good at it. Mama says the back of the fabric should appear much like the front." She turned the hoop over, exposing a tangled mess of thread.

"Embroidery is considered a genteel activity. It keeps a woman's hands and mind busy and away from other things." At least that's what Charlotte's mother had told her.

"Such as?"

Charlotte blinked. "Well . . . I'm not quite sure." However, memories of Simon's kisses made an appearance. "I suppose it's one of the things that mothers pass down to daughter and are never quite sure who started the tradition or why."

"It's silly. Why should someone be forced to do something they don't like or aren't good at?"

The girl had a point. "Given a choice, what would you like to learn?

"Fencing," the child said without hesitation. "I've seen Simon fence, and it looks like such fun. Being able to poke someone with a rapier!" She frowned at her embroidery, stabbing the cloth with gusto.

Charlotte laughed, something she was doing with unexpected regularity, the sensation wonderful. "I have a suspicion you would be quite good at it."

Georgie beamed, and something in Charlotte's heart cracked. Not precisely painful, but unnerving nonetheless.

She must remain on guard. Her heart was at risk.

CHAPTER 25

Simon flicked the line in the water, jerking his rod aggressively and hoping to catch at least one fish. He turned as footsteps squelched against the rain-soaked ground behind him. Had Charlotte sought him out? He pushed down the disappointment at his father's welcoming wave.

"Are you trying to entice the fish with your lure or beat them over the head and knock them out?" His father stepped into the calf-deep water beside him and began expertly flitting his line, the rhythmic snap of his wrist causing the lure to dance across the surface of the river.

Simon had tried to emulate his father's technique for years, the movement so graceful it appeared effortless. Perhaps he *had* been a bit too vigorous in his technique. He blamed it on Charlotte.

Staring ahead at the rushing water, his father said, "Surprised to see you here. Thought you and your new wife would be holed up in the cottage for days on end. Is everything well?"

Simon grunted, the sound reminding him of Charlotte's response earlier that morning.

"Hmph," his father grunted back. "Your mother thinks I don't know."

Warning rang in Simon's head, and he snapped to attention. "Know what?"

"I saw that scandal sheet she tried to hide from me, detailing the reason you married Lady Charlotte." Attention still on the river, he added, "Is it true?"

"Partially, although that rag twisted it into something sordid."

His father shook his head. "Gossip can ruin lives. And regardless of the circumstances, you did the right thing by your wife. I'm proud of you." His line reeled out, and the rod bowed. "Got one!"

How could the man be there less than five minutes and catch something when Simon had worked his line for nearly an hour without a nibble? "Don't lose him."

"Ha!" His father shot him an exasperated look. "Who taught whom? Grab the net."

"It's a big one! Reel him in, Pa! Don't let the line snap!" Excited as he was when he was a boy, Simon watched his father's expertise, giving the fish enough line to run and exhaust itself, and then gradually reeling it in. Simon scooped him up in the net. "He's a beauty. But it's not Gus."

"No. Close though, maybe his brother."

"Is the rascal still alive?"

His father shrugged as he removed the fish from the hook. "Dinner or set the poor bastard free? What do you think your wife would want?"

Simon froze at the last question. What was his father getting at? "Why do I have the feeling you're not talking about the fish?"

His father chuckled. "Because you've always been a smart lad."

The steady fall of raindrops creating concentric circles on the river's surface slowed. Bright sunlight broke through the clouds, sparkling like diamonds on the water.

Peering up, Simon shielded his eyes. "Looks like you made the only possible catch today. Set him free before he dies. Let's see if he can grow as big as Gus."

With a *plop*, Simon's father released the big fish back into the river, and he swam off as fast as he could.

Simon trudged out of the river and sank onto the bank, mulling over his father's words. "Charlotte didn't want to get married. Truth be told, she doesn't like me much, but I was the lesser of two evils, so to speak."

His father joined him, stretching out his legs. "Between you and . . . ?"

"Another man her brother wanted her to marry—Lord Felix Davies. Davies and her brother discovered us together." Simon shook his head. "And for once in my life, I was completely innocent, as was she. But the bruise on her cheek spoke of how Davies would have treated her, and I couldn't allow that."

His father grasped his shoulder, the grip not as strong as Simon remembered. "As I said, I'm proud of you for that. But you're wrong. I think she likes you just fine."

Simon snorted, the sound oddly reminding him of Charlotte. "Then you're not paying attention."

"Your mother couldn't stand me at first."

Simon's head jerked toward his father. "I don't believe it. She adores you."

"Now. But then . . ." He shook his head. "In truth, I didn't care much for her either. But we discovered we had made false assumptions, and when we grew to know each other better, we found not only a common bond, but a deep respect and love. Hate isn't the opposite of love, indifference is. Love and hate are very similar, both deep emotions. There can be a push-pull between them. Perhaps it's not that Charlotte hates you, but that her feelings frighten her, so she pushes you away."

Although his father was known for being loquacious, Simon

had never heard him wax so philosophically. It rendered him speechless.

Which was good because his father continued. "I will admit, learning your wife was Edgerton's sister took me aback. But the sister isn't the brother, and it's unfair to judge her by someone else's actions or reputation."

Finally finding his voice, Simon shook his head. "She's disagreeable in her own right." And truthfully, he couldn't imagine Charlotte being frightened of anything.

"Then it's up to you to find out why. If it's truly who she is, then you will have to choose to accept it or not. But, I suspect buried underneath her prickliness lies a kind, loving woman." He rose and stretched. "Now, I'm going to keep fishing before the sun drives them all deeper."

Simon gathered his rod and tackle and bade his father farewell. As he strode back to the cottage, he pondered his father's words. Was there a reason for Charlotte's abrasiveness? If so, what could it be? Granted, living with Edgerton couldn't have been pleasant. But Simon had known men who had harsh upbringings and grew to be perfectly congenial fellows.

Had he been quick to judge her the moment he learned of her familial connections at Drake's house party the previous summer? Did those judgments color his actions and, in turn, affect hers?

Questions bouncing in his mind made him uncomfortable. He pushed them aside, vowing to ponder them later. More a man of action than thought, perhaps he would discover the answer to those questions by engaging Charlotte in different activities— hopefully leading to one activity in particular.

If he were honest with himself—which he truly tried to be— he wanted to bed Charlotte more than he had any woman since Joy. The similarity ended there. Apart from his desire for them, the two women were nothing alike.

He took a circuitous route back home, stopping at the stables.

Why, he had no idea. But a preternatural tugging pulled him as if someone or something awaited him.

Joseph, the groom, looked up from where he was brushing out one of the horses. "Mr. Simon. I understand felicitations are in order. I wish you joy upon your marriage. Is your lady wife with you?" The man craned his neck to peer around Simon.

"Thank you. No. She's back at the cottage."

Joseph cocked his head. "Will you be wanting a horse saddled?"

Did he? With the sun coming out, a ride would be nice. Then he remembered Charlotte and his father's words. "No. I have no idea why I'm here. Just an impulse."

Soft mewing came from the corner, catching Simon's attention. Cuddled together in a bed of hay, a mother cat lovingly cleaned her kittens, the little fur balls climbing over her, vying for her affection.

"Ah. You've seen Daisy and her new litter. Miss Georgie has laid claim to the black one. Now that they're eight weeks old, I was going to bring him to the house later today when the rain let up."

"I can take him." Simon squatted down by the little family. He held his hand out for the mother cat to sniff, then scratched behind her ears. A calico kitten attacked his finger with its little teeth. He chuckled. "The fierce warrior defends his family."

Joseph came beside him. "That one's a female. Calicoes usually are. Full of spirit, she is."

Like Charlotte.

"Anyone claim her?"

Joseph shook his head. "She's yours if you want her. I expect you'll have your hands full."

"Perfect," he said, gathering the kitten and her little black brother in his arms. "I'll come back for my tackle if that's agreeable. I wouldn't want to drop one of these precious bundles."

Kittens squirming and meowing in protest, he strode first to the cottage to surprise Charlotte, but none of the servants knew where she had gone.

"Well, let's at least please one female, shall we?" The kittens meowed in agreement, and they all set off for the main house.

The footman took Simon's rain-soggy hat, his gaze flickering down to the tiny balls of fur in Simon's grasp. "Your wife, mother, and Miss Georgie are in the large drawing room, sir."

Excellent.

Blissful domesticity slammed Simon in the chest at the scene, and he paused in the open doorway. His mother wasn't present as the footman had stated. But sitting next to Georgie, Charlotte smiled at his sister with a warmth he'd only witnessed in relation to her closest friends—Honoria in particular. It was a surprising tableau.

He leaned against the door frame, gazing at her with wonder.

Georgie exhaled a sigh. "I hate embroidery. I'd rather be fishing with Simon."

Charlotte laughed, the rich alto of her voice washing over him like warm sunlight. "He didn't ask us."

"Ow!" Georgie stuck her thumb in her mouth. "Baiting a hook is no more dangerous than this needle."

"Let me see that." Charlotte took Georgie's finger and examined it, then placed a kiss on the tip. "Better?"

Georgie nodded, then threw her arms around Charlotte's neck.

The warmth he experienced from Charlotte's voice settled into his chest, heating him from the inside out as she fussed over Georgie's hurt thumb. He'd never seen this side of his wife before. Kind. Compassionate. Open. And his father's words echoed in his mind. Perhaps he should look past her prickliness to the woman beneath.

One of the kittens meowed, and both ladies turned their heads.

"Simon!" Georgie sprang from her seat and rushed over. "You brought him!" She plucked the kitten from his arms. As she raced over to show Charlotte, Simon followed her.

"And one for you." When he held out the little calico to his wife, her gaze shot to his, and her eyes widened. The surprise and affection in them nearly undoing him.

Wonder of wonders. He'd actually pleased her.

❧

"For me?" Charlotte's heart squeezed at the little ball of fluff. No one had ever given her a pet. She'd always wanted one, but other than his hunting dogs, her father had forbidden animals in the house. Roland had followed his example.

Yet, her husband, who expressed his dislike for her, had brought her an adorable kitten for her very own. With a tentative hand, she accepted the gift.

So tiny, it meowed vocally. "Oh, it's all right, little one. I won't hurt you." She brought the kitten to her face, the fur soft against her cheek.

"Careful, she might scratch you," Simon said, his hand reaching out, ready to pluck the kitten away should it misbehave.

"You would never hurt me either, would you?" She kissed the kitten's nose, and it meowed again. "She's so soft."

Georgie took a seat next to her, cradling her own little black kitten against her chest. "Haven't you ever had a kitten, Charlotte?"

Charlotte shook her head, her gaze glued to her new love. "Once I found one in the stables and brought it inside our home. My father tore it from my hands and threw it outside, stating cats were only good for mousing."

Simon scratched her kitten behind its ears. "Well, they are good for that, but like people, there can be many sides to them. Even a predator wants love, too."

Charlotte lifted her gaze to her husband, warmth expanding her chest. Was there hidden meaning in his words? An uncomfortable knot formed in her throat. "Thank you."

"You're welcome. What will you name her?"

Charlotte held the kitten at arm's length, studying her tricolored coat. Remembering the dessert she and Simon shared several evenings after their marriage, she pronounced, "Trifle."

Simon's dark brow hitched. "Like the dessert?"

"Yes. And also because she is so tiny."

A deep chuckle rumbled from Simon, one Charlotte was loath to admit she found alluring. "She won't always be so little. They do grow, you know."

"Of course," Charlotte answered, a setdown in her tone. "But that's the beauty of it. She will prove the opposite of what people expect. Won't you, Trifle?" She kissed the kitten on the nose again, eliciting another meow.

"I like the name," Georgie said. "And she does look like the dessert."

Simon balanced a well-muscled thigh on the arm of the sofa next to Charlotte, giving the kitten another scratch. "She even has a little brown patch of fur on the top of her head like chocolate shavings."

Charlotte jerked her gaze toward him. "You remember that?"

"Contrary to belief, I have a splendid memory of things important to me."

Oh. The budding warmth in Charlotte's chest burst into a full-blown fire. Quickly, she schooled her features and turned toward Georgie. "What will you name yours?"

"Sir Nightclaws of the Meow Table."

Simon guffawed. "Georgie, have you been reading the tales of King Arthur?"

"It's an excellent name, Georgie. But it is rather lengthy."

Georgie pouted, then her face brightened. "I'll call him Nightly for short."

As Simon reached across Charlotte to pet Nightly, the scent of rain mixed with sandalwood and shaving soap tickled her nose. Pleasant scents all of them. She expected him to smell of fish. Perhaps he was occupied elsewhere. With another woman? Tension coiled in her stomach like a nest of vipers. However, naming the cause would force her to admit her feelings.

"Didn't you catch anything on your *fishing* excursion?"

Both eyebrows slid high on Simon's forehead, and he locked eyes with her, the implication of her statement clearly understood. "No." He turned his attention toward Georgie. "But Father did. Caught a big one."

Shame burned her cheeks.

Simon glanced toward her, a faint smile touching his lips.

"Was it Gus?" Charlotte asked, burying her hot face into Trifle's soft fur.

His gaze bouncing between Charlotte and Georgie, Simon blinked. "You know about Gus?"

Charlotte waved it away, eager to hear if Mr. Beckham had landed the legendary fish. "Georgie told me."

"No. It wasn't Gus, but it was nearly as big."

"Will we have trout for supper?" Georgie asked, then placed a kiss on Nightly's head. "Maybe Nightly and Trifle can have some."

"I'm afraid not, Poppet. Father released him back to the river. But take heart. Father didn't give up as easily as I did. Perhaps he'll still bring home something for the table. And honestly, I didn't know about the kittens until I had finished my fruitless effort."

Georgie popped up from the sofa. "I'm going to show Nightly to Mama!" She raced out of the room without a goodbye.

Simon's gaze followed his sister, and he laughed again, the sound vibrating on Charlotte's skin and raising gooseflesh. She began to see her husband with new eyes.

Thoughtful.

Caring.

Gentle.

"So. You like her?" Simon gave Trifle another scratch and was rewarded with a meow.

"I do."

"You say that with more conviction than you did at our wedding." For a moment, something flickered in his blue eyes. Pain? Disappointment? Regret?

The emotion vanished so quickly, perhaps she had imagined it.

"Since the sun decided to come out and ruin my fishing, what do you say we take a trip into Swindon? I can show you around. Introduce you to some of the locals."

"What of Trifle? It seems unfair to leave her so soon."

"She'll be fine. We'll let Georgie watch her, and she can play with her brother. It will be good for them both."

"And there are shops?"

"Now that you know I'm not destitute, is the plan to bleed me dry with shopping trips?"

A smile tugged her lips. "I will do my best."

CHAPTER 26

J oyous thoughts of shopping dashed from Charlotte's mind the moment a groom pulled up the curricle. Although not a phaeton, the sleek gig was nearly as bad—made for speed. "What about the carriage we journeyed in from London?"

Simon slid an incredulous glance at her. "I would think you'd know a carriage such as that one is meant for long journeys, not for short jaunts on a sunny day. Swindon is but a half-hour's drive." He held out his hand, motioning her forward. "Now, come."

When she hesitated, he exhaled a heavy sigh. "Very well." Placing his hand on his heart, he adopted a serious affect most unlike him. "I vow to drive so slowly, even the snails shall pass us by."

Reluctantly, she grasped his hand, energy passing through his gloved hand to hers. After assisting her into the seat, he climbed next to her and flicked the ribbons. At first, he kept the horses to a slow walk, but even Charlotte found the pace excruciatingly slow.

"At this rate, we won't arrive until nightfall and the shops will be closed," she mumbled.

"Only trying to please my wife." However, his expression was anything but pleased. A muscle in his jaw pulsed and his knuckles stretched the kid leather of his riding gloves.

"Please increase the speed before you have an attack of apoplexy. I'm not ready to become a widow quite yet." The moment the words flew carelessly from her lips, she regretted them. "Forgive me. I didn't mean to broach the subject of early death."

"Your apology makes it worthwhile. That and—this." He snapped the ribbons with more vigor and the horses broke into a trot, the jolting change of pace flinging Charlotte back in the seat.

She grasped the top of her bonnet, keeping it in place. "Perhaps it's *my* early demise I should be concerned about."

He flashed his signature grin. "Nonsense. You're tough as nails."

Pride expanded her chest at his offhanded compliment.

As they rounded a bend in the road, buildings emerged, and Simon slowed the curricle. Quaint little shops with colorful displays of their wares tempted Charlotte. "Oh, a milliner." She grasped Simon's arm, tugging it. "With the way you drive, I shall need to purchase more bonnets lest one fly off my head."

After pulling the curricle to a stop, he jumped down and offered his hand. "Then that shall be our first stop."

The moment they entered the shop, heads turned. A woman Mrs. Beckham's age glanced up from where she was showing a younger woman a lovely creation with an enormous feather. "Simon! Oh, dear boy, you've returned to us." She shoved the bonnet into the other woman's hands and raced forward.

Close on her heels, the younger woman followed. Blond and rather pretty, her face split into an enormous smile.

"Mrs. Westly." Simon bowed over each lady's hand, brushing

a quick kiss across their knuckles. "Miss Throckmorton. Or is it missus something or other? Has some lucky man snatched you away from the rest of us?"

Dash it all. The man couldn't stop himself from flirting even when married. Of course, Charlotte wasn't so naïve as to think he would stop admiring other women. Theirs was far from a love match.

The younger woman, Miss Throckmorton apparently, blushed, casting a cursory glance Charlotte's way and, as quickly, dismissing her as inconsequential.

"Oh, Mr. Beckham, how you do go on!"

Charlotte refrained from rolling her eyes. She truly did want to make a good impression on these people. Instead, she forced a smile, one she hoped appeared more genuine than what she felt at that moment, and held her tongue.

Miss Throckmorton donned the bonnet and preened before Simon. "What do you think, Mr. Beckham?"

Simon leaned back and tilted his head, a finger pressed to his lips. Lips she had recently kissed. "Hmm. I'm not sure if that color does justice to your engaging blue eyes, Miss Throckmorton."

Charlotte forced back the gag and gave Simon's ribs a subtle jab with her elbow.

"Ough. Forgive my manners, ladies. Charlotte, allow me to introduce Mrs. Westley, the owner of this fine establishment, and Miss Throckmorton. Ladies, Lady Charlotte Beckham, my wife."

Miss Throckmorton's sunny, bright smile devolved into a stormy frown, her former dismissive glance growing devious and predatory.

"*Lady* Charlotte?" Mrs. Westley's brows lifted so briefly Charlotte might have imagined it. "Well, Simon, you have done well, it seems. It's a pleasure to meet you, Lady Charlotte."

Miss Throckmorton didn't seem to agree as she continued to

shoot icy daggers in Charlotte's direction. She pulled the bonnet off her head and pushed it toward Mrs. Westley.

"You have a lovely shop, Mrs. Westley. The way my *husband* drives"—Charlotte darted a glance to the pouting girl—"I shall be a frequent customer."

Simon chuckled, then pointed toward the discarded bonnet. "May I?" After taking it from Mrs. Westley's outstretched hands, he held it in front of Charlotte. "But I think this cream color goes perfectly with your eyes, my dear." He placed the bonnet on Charlotte's head, then criss-crossed the ribbons under her chin.

Charlotte wondered if he planned to choke her with them.

He leaned back to assess the effect. "What do you think, Mrs. Westley? Miss Throckmorton? Doesn't my wife look lovely in this?"

What game was Simon playing at? Mischief danced in his blue eyes. He had something up his sleeve, for certain.

Although Mrs. Westley gave a resounding *yes*, Miss Throckmorton only grunted.

When all was said and done, Simon balanced three stacked hat boxes in his arms—including one containing the bonnet Miss Throckmorton cast aside—as they bade farewell to Mrs. Westley and Miss Throckmorton. He placed them on the floorboard of the curricle, then paid a young boy a half-penny to keep watch while they continued to shop.

"Does everyone fawn over you or just the women?" Charlotte grumbled as they strolled past the other shops, exchanging greetings and introductions with people passing by.

Truly, the face of everyone they met lit up when they caught sight of her husband, but especially the women. Young or old, it didn't matter.

"Can I help it if I'm an overall likable person? You act as if it's a crime to have people like me."

Not a crime. Just something Charlotte was not familiar with

in the least. "And must you flirt so openly? It's a wonder a jealous husband hasn't shot you dead."

He barked a laugh. "Perhaps husbands aren't the only ones jealous. Hmm? Might there be a touch of green-eyed envy in your own heart?"

"Don't be ridiculous." She sniffed and turned her head so as not to expose the truth to him. She *was* jealous. And the thought rankled.

During their evenings together, with the shared kisses and Simon's patient seduction, she'd begun to believe he might truly like her. Want her. *Her.* That perhaps she had become special to him.

And she'd slowly started exposing her buried heart, bit by bit, pushing away the layers of protection she'd carefully constructed over the years. Like the sun peeking through an overcast sky, a shred of hope emerged that finally she could trust someone enough to make herself vulnerable. To risk the hurt. To lay her heart open in someone else's hands.

Foolish. Naïve.

Terrifying.

She cursed the crack in her armor allowing him to sneak in.

He lavished the same attention and affection on everyone he met. He made each woman feel like she was the only thing in his universe when he spoke with her.

Layers of protection slipped back into place.

Just another conquest, she wasn't special to him at all.

As sure as if a cold wind had swept in, Charlotte's mood changed. Simon prided himself on understanding women, but Charlotte was another matter altogether. She'd seemed pleased when he insisted she buy the bonnet with the ridiculous feather Miss Throckmorton had been considering. And there could be no doubt she adored little Trifle. He mentally patted himself on the back for the stroke of genius in giving her the kitten.

But somewhere between the milliner's and the bakery, she'd grown taciturn and sullen.

Not that that was out of the ordinary for his wife. But he'd been encouraged by the few smiles he'd coaxed from her so far that day, only to have his hopes dashed as she grew more distant during each interaction with other people.

But was it *all* people or certain people in particular? When he greeted Mrs. Peabody, a widow near Aunt Kitty's age, Charlotte's hand on his arm remained relaxed. Charlotte even sent the old woman a smile.

Before Simon could puzzle it out further, his stomach tightened when Charlotte said, "Oh, a bakery. I wonder if they have plum tarts."

He tugged on Charlotte's arm to direct her to the other side of the street.

Charlotte scowled. "What are you doing?"

"We have a cook who bakes." True, but not his primary reason for avoiding the shop.

"Simon! Simon!" Simon's stomach clenched at the familiar feminine voice, and he tugged a little more aggressively on Charlotte's arm.

But it was too late. Mixed with the sweet scents of the bakery, Hester's cloying perfume assaulted him from behind.

And the day had been going so well. Simon exhaled a sigh.

He had not ended his brief liaison with the woman on good terms. She had misinterpreted his need for comfort and escape from grief for something more lasting, and when he'd enlisted in the military, she'd cursed him for toying with her feelings.

As Charlotte swiveled toward Hester's voice, her hand on his arm tightened. "Who is *that?*" she whispered.

With his most charming smile plastered on his face, Simon

turned. "Why, hello, Hester." He kept his voice chipper, as if he'd truly been happy to see her.

Time had apparently erased all negative feelings from Hester's mind. Her gray eyes flashed with interest as she seductively ran a hand up his free arm, not once giving Charlotte even a cursory glance.

"Portia Throckmorton told me you were back, and I had to see for myself." Hester batted her eyes at him.

Charlotte cleared her throat, reminding him she was there. As if he could forget.

"Lady Charlotte, may I present Miss Hester Pace." He shifted his attention to Charlotte, but her gaze was locked on Hester. "Hester is a serving maid at the *Hungry Hound*."

Charlotte's hold on his arm became a death grip.

Hester's hand remained on his other arm, the caress much too intimate for encounters in public.

"Lady Charlotte is my wife."

The moment he uttered the additional words, Hester's hand dropped from his arm. "Wife?!" Her brow furrowed, and her mouth dipped as she puffed out her bottom lip. Simon never believed any woman ugly, but the scowl on Hester's face at that moment was decidedly *not* attractive.

Not like Charlotte's, where he itched to kiss between the lines forming between her eyes.

"Darling"—Simon patted Charlotte's hand, at the same time sliding a glance toward Hester from the corner of his eye, certain the endearment landed when she winced—"Why don't you go ahead? Choose any store that pleases you, and I shall join you in a moment." He leaned and whispered, his next words for Charlotte's ears only. "Unless you wish to stay while I tell Miss Pace I am a happily married man. Your reaction might lead her to question my veracity."

"Very well." Charlotte nodded toward Hester. "Miss Pace." Her tone could have frozen the air around them.

Both Simon and Hester remained silent as Charlotte slipped into the bakery. Simon sighed. Why couldn't she have chosen any other shop?

"So it's true?!" Hester's high-pitched voice drew his attention back. "I didn't want to believe that scandal sheet. And why'd you marry such a cold fish?" Hester's eyes widened. "Oh! She's a hoity-toity lady. Did you marry her for her money?"

Sharp words crowded on his tongue. Had he been around Charlotte too long? He reminded himself even a serving wench should be treated like a lady. "You know very well I don't need money."

"Her connections to high society, then?"

"No. I already have connections with a duke." Lord, he hated using Drake as a counterargument.

"Well, it can't be that you love her. What's she do? Lay there while you—"

Even he had a breaking point. "Enough, Hester. She's my wife, and the reasons we married are our own."

Hester's offending hand returned to his arm, stroking it suggestively. "Well, you know where to find me when you're ready for a bit of fun."

With his thumb and forefinger, Simon removed Hester's hand. "I appreciate the offer, but I must decline. Now, if you would excuse me. I need to join my wife."

"You can't be thinking about going in the bakery. Samuel Waters will skin you alive when he sees you again."

"It's been seven years. I'm sure he's calmed down."

Simon didn't want to go into the bakery, but remaining with Hester was just as disagreeable. What was he thinking, suggesting he and Charlotte come to Swindon? Like so many times in his life, his impetuosity led him into another sticky situation.

Although he couldn't avoid it forever. If he lived long enough to inherit Rosehaven Park, he would have to become a staple in the community.

In six long strides, he ate up the pavement leading to the shop. Taking a deep breath, he opened the door and stepped inside.

Aromas of freshly baked bread and sweet biscuits surrounded him, permeating the air stronger than they had outside, making his mouth water. Charlotte stood at the counter, her back to him, but Samuel was nowhere in sight, thank goodness. Perhaps he could whisk Charlotte away before—

Samuel emerged from the back room, carrying a tray of tarts. "Plum tarts fresh out of the oven, miss." His gaze darted toward Simon, his face reddening, his mouth in a grim line. *Bang!* He dropped the metal tray of pastries on the counter. "How dare you come in here!"

Charlotte spun around, and her eyes locked with his, confusion furrowing her brow. With a quick scan of the shop, she no doubt deduced Samuel could be addressing no one but him. "Samuel." He tipped his head toward the man. "I've come to fetch my wife."

"Wife?!"

Must everyone's reaction to his marital status be so incredulous? Although, Samuel had more reason than most to doubt Simon's seriousness when it came to the lifelong commitment.

Wiping his hands on a towel, Samuel gaped at Charlotte. "You're married to this blackguard?" He pointed at Simon. "Nice young miss like you?"

Charlotte? Nice young miss? Simon withheld the laugh. No need to make matters worse.

"I am, unfortunately," Charlotte said, the wry tone twisting the knife in Simon's back a little more. "Now, if I could have a dozen of those plum tarts, we'll be on our way."

Simon wisely remained silent, hoping to deter Samuel from elaborating more fully the reasons for his animosity.

With each tart Samuel removed from the tray, he frosted

Simon with a glare. Finally tying the package with a string, he handed it to Charlotte.

Simon pulled his purse from his pocket. "How much?"

"No charge." Samuel veritably growled the words.

Charlotte's gaze bounced between Simon and Samuel. "That is very kind, sir."

"Hmphf." Samuel glared again.

As Simon lifted the package from Charlotte's hands and opened the door, Samuel muttered, "I just hope you choke to death on one of those tarts, you bastard. It'll be better than you deserve for killing my daughter."

CHAPTER 27

Charlotte stumbled from the bakery, her limbs numb. The baker's words reverberated in her head, wiping away her questions about Miss Pace. Those would wait.

It'll be better than you deserve for killing my daughter.

What in the world? Simon was not the kind of man to physically harm another.

Felix, definitely. Roland, yes. Even when Nash had been accused of Lady Worthington's murder, Charlotte had a brief flash of doubt regarding his innocence. Both of her brothers had terrible tempers. No doubt a result of years of bottled rage from their sire's mistreatment.

As for her, she carried her own scars. One did not survive unscathed when reared by the Marquess of Edgerton. Memories clawed their way up from where she had buried them along with her innocence, and she pushed them back, holding the door tightly shut.

But Simon's parents cherished him. Reared him with love. From what Charlotte had witnessed in their interactions, that much was clear. There were no tense postures or clipped, overly polite words. Genuine laughter and affectionate teasing evidenced the family's love for one another.

In short, the complete opposite of what Charlotte had experienced.

However, appearances could be deceiving. And in truth, did she really know her husband? She struggled to understand. An accident, perhaps?

"Simon." Her whispered voice sounded tentative to her own ears. "Did you kill that man's daughter?"

His body stiffened, and he jerked his head toward her. "Of course not! But Samuel blames me for her death, nonetheless. I'd hoped six years had given him time to cool his head."

"What happened?"

He stared ahead as they approached a cluster of people. "Not now. I'll tell you when we're alone. I promise."

Before she could open her mouth to either protest or acquiesce, angry voices escalated from the group before them.

A man pulled a young boy by the collar of his worn coat. "How many times do I have to tell you, boy?"

About twelve, the boy struggled against the man's grip. His eyes were as wide as saucers, his gaze darting frantically around him, then landing squarely on Charlotte, as if he were screaming, *help me*!

A woman tugged at the man's arm, trying to disengage it from his hold on the child. "Stop, Albie! He didn't mean nothin' by it. The boy's just curious, is all."

Planting his free hand on the woman's face, the man shoved her away, and she stumbled, falling to the ground. Then he proceeded to box the child's ears. When the boy crouched by the woman, hands covering his head, the man kicked him in the ribs.

People hurried by, giving the angry man a wide berth.

Charlotte had had enough. "Someone needs to stop him!"

Drained of color, Simon's face was a mask of horror, but he seemed frozen in place.

"Snap out of it!" She gave his arm a firm shake.

Finally focusing, Simon said, "It's Albert Mooney. Probably drunk again. He'll sleep it off after—"

Charlotte wanted to scream. "After he maims or kills the boy?"

Simon's resigned look broke her heart.

"Coward." She spit the word at her husband, and he flinched as surely as if one of Albert Mooney's blows had struck him squarely in the chest.

"You don't understand."

When Simon grasped her hands in his, she yanked them away. In six determined steps, she stood between Mooney and the boy. "Leave. The. Child. Alone." She punctuated each word with a jab to Mooney's chest.

Mooney leaned forward, inches from her face and bellowed a laugh, his breath sour with whisky and something more foul. "This hellcat belong to you, Beckham?"

"I am no one's property, *sir.*" Charlotte laced as much derision into the address as she could. The man didn't deserve respect. "I am Lady Charlotte, and if you lay one more finger on that boy, you will answer to me."

Mooney's eyes widened, and he threw up his hands, shaking in mock horror. "Oooh. I'm scared." He laughed again, then pranced about like a clumsy dandy, his hand flapping in the air. "Lady Charlotte. Defender of children." He gave the boy another kick, and the child curled into a ball next to the woman.

Anger boiled in Charlotte's stomach, and her hand clenched in a fist. Once again, she placed herself between Mooney and the child. Then, with all her strength, she drew back her arm and punched Mooney in the nose.

"You bloody well better believe it."

Mooney doubled over, blood dripping from his nose. "You little . . ." He straightened and hate spewed from his dark, beady eyes.

Charlotte's hand hurt like the devil, but she didn't care. She braced herself to fend off an attack when Mooney reached out, but his hands dropped to his sides as his gaze darted around her.

Turning, she found Simon behind her.

"You need to control your woman, Beckham." Mooney spit on the ground at Charlotte's feet.

Simon laughed and stepped between them. "She doesn't need controlling."

"Ha!" Mooney barked another laugh. "Saving then? Come to rescue her powdered and pampered arse?"

"Wrong again. She's doing fine by herself. You, on the other hand." Simon shook his head and *tsked*. "I expect the constable will arrive any moment and lock you up until you sleep it off."

Nose-to-nose with Mooney, Simon's face scrunched in distaste, no doubt from the stench emanating off the man. "But, a word of caution. I would take my wife's words to heart. She is true to her word. Now, allow me to rescue *your* sorry arse and escort my wife away." He turned toward her. "Come, Charlotte. I better take you home before you cause any more excitement."

Charlotte hesitated. "We can't leave the boy alone with the brute."

Simon tipped his head, his eyes directed forward, and she followed his motion.

A man wearing an apron rushed up, and several other burly men raced behind.

"That's Mr. Cooper, the constable. The others assist him when Mooney needs to be restrained."

"You mean this is a common occurrence?" She gawked at Simon as he guided her away from Mooney's shouts of anger toward her.

"Unfortunately, yes. However, your interference today may have changed Mooney's course."

Pride swelled in her chest. "I stopped him?"

He held out his hand to assist her into the carriage. "Either that or added your name to his list of vendettas." Simon's usually congenial expression appeared grave and concerned. He flipped the boy watching their carriage a few extra coins, then climbed in beside her.

Questions tangled in her mind from the excursion to Swindon, but she started with the most pressing. "Why didn't you stop that horrible man?"

Simon gave a shrug. "I saw the Andersons rush by and knew they would alert the constable. Confronting Mooney only makes him angrier, and the boy suffers for it."

"Oh." The word slipped out on an exhale. Had she made matters worse? "I didn't realize."

"It's all right, Charlotte. You gave Mooney something to chew on while he's locked up." He handed her the bakery package. "Besides, I had to protect your plum tarts. And I did enjoy watching you plant him a facer. He had it coming. Remind me to never get on your bad side." He snapped the ribbons and urged the horses forward.

She huffed a laugh. "Isn't that our normal state of being?"

His ridiculous grin crept across his lips, and realization dawned that she found it attractive.

"I'd hoped we'd progressed a little." Peering over, he gave her a weak smile.

"Perhaps a little. Much depends on your answers to my questions." She unknotted the cluster of thoughts in her mind and reached for the most pressing ones.

"About?"

"What happened to the baker's daughter?"

As if she'd magically wiped it away, his smile vanished in an instant. "Might we talk about something else?"

"You promised you'd tell me later. I'm asking now. Then I want to know about Miss Pace."

But from the expression on Simon's face, she wasn't sure she wanted to know.

Damn it all! Why did he have to mention the plum tarts and remind her what Samuel had said? Simon pulled in a breath, unsure where to start.

"The two are related," he said, easing into the conversation.

"That doesn't surprise me. Which woman came first?"

"Joy, Samuel's daughter." He focused on the road ahead of him, avoiding her eyes. "You asked how many women I have deflowered. Joy was the only one. Most of the time, she embodied her name, practically bubbling with happiness. But other times . . ." He paused, remembering the sudden bouts of deep sadness during which she seemed unreachable.

"Other times?" Charlotte prodded.

"She was like a different person. Little things would upset her, and sometimes, from what I could tell, nothing at all. She would become so sullen, as if she were trapped in a dark place with no escape. Or at times, she would become angry, lashing out at me." He studied Charlotte, gauging her reaction. Did she consider both the juxtaposition and similarity with herself?

She remained stone-faced. "Did you love her?"

Was there a hint of jealousy in her words?

Truth. Charlotte deserved the truth. "Yes. I think so."

"You *think*? You don't know?" Charlotte's brow furrowed, her tone confused.

"I was barely twenty when she first caught my eye. She had just reached her eighteenth year and had begun helping in her father's bakery. No more than a flirtation at first—children playing at love—our feelings grew into something more. She said she loved me, so I said it back."

"But did you mean it?"

An annoying knot of tension formed in his throat, and he forced it down. "I wanted to. At her sunniest, we had so much in common. Almost as if we were the same person. But when you look in a mirror too long, sometimes all you see are flaws."

He gave himself a mental shake, remembering the uncomfortable arguments he and Joy would have. "Then she would change, and I didn't know what to do. How to act around her. During those times, she wanted me to be more serious, to plan for a future—our future. All I wanted to do was think of the next adventure. I wasn't ready to settle down."

"You were young. From my experience, most men aren't ready to settle down until they're much older."

Blink. "Did you just defend me?

Her lips tipped up, and regardless of the uncomfortable conversation, he still wanted to kiss them. "If the idea makes you happy. Consider it reciprocity for defending me with Mr. Mooney."

"But I didn't really do anything." Did he?

"You didn't fly in to rescue me, flaunting your masculine bravado as if I couldn't take care of myself."

"Oh." He remembered Mooney's expression when Charlotte planted a facer on the man. "You pack a good punch."

She waved off his compliment. So like her. "But back to Joy. How did she die?"

The uncomfortable knot returned. "She wanted to prove her love—her commitment to me. So we . . ." He slid another glance toward Charlotte.

"You deflowered her. Did you promise to marry her?"

Odd how Charlotte placed the blame directly on his shoulders where it belonged. Heat and shame crept up his neck, burning the tips of his ears. "Not in so many words, but she presumed it. Then I—" He shook his head, the memory of the horrible series of events hitting him as if occurring anew.

Charlotte's brow furrowed, and he wanted to smooth it out with a kiss. But once he told her, she wouldn't want him to touch her—possibly forever. "Then what?"

"I did something stupid," he continued. "A harmless flirtation."

Charlotte studied him, her mouth set in a grim line as she digested the information and no doubt grew nauseous. "Allow me to guess. With Miss Pace?"

How astute his wife was. "Yes. And Joy saw us." He wanted to defend himself to Charlotte, to remind her he flirted with every woman and it meant nothing. But the surprising lack of condemnation in her eyes kept him silent.

"Did she . . . kill herself?" Emotion choked Charlotte's voice.

He gulped for air, the horror of the memory like a powerful undertow threatening to pull him down and drown him, then grimaced at the irony of the thought. He breathed deep, trying not to panic, and forced out the answer. "It appears so. I raced after her, trying to explain, but she wouldn't speak to me. She had retreated to the dark place where I couldn't reach her. So I waited for her sunny side to return."

"But it didn't?"

He shook his head. "No. Two days later, her father arrived at our door, note in hand."

"What did it say?" Charlotte laid a calming hand on his arm.

"She bade goodbye to her parents and asked for forgiveness. And she said . . . she said . . ." Tightness clogged his throat, the words stuck and unable to break free.

Charlotte squeezed his arm, and when he met her gaze, he found the courage to continue.

"She said out of love she was setting me free. Samuel was frantic; he couldn't find Joy anywhere. We knocked on doors. Asked if she boarded a post-chaise, even though she had little money. No one had seen her, so we searched the woods. I found her floating face down in the river downstream from our favorite rendezvous place. Her body had tangled in some branches. When I turned her over, her lifeless eyes stared up at me in condemnation."

Charlotte blanched, her face eerily similar to Joy's on that horrific day. "No wonder Samuel blames you."

Not what Simon wanted to hear, but Charlotte was nothing if not truthful.

"But Simon, you didn't push Joy into the river."

"No. But my impetuosity and utter lack of regard for her feelings led her to believe life wasn't worth living without me." The undertow of his negative emotions grew stronger, pulling him under, and invisible bands tightened around his chest, constricting his lungs in sympathy with Joy. "I don't want a woman to love me. She'll either be lost in grief when I die, or I'll disappoint her if I can't love her back. Joy loved me, and that love destroyed her."

"And Miss Pace was only a harmless flirtation?" A tiny muscle in Charlotte's jaw pulsed, but she kept her gaze on the road ahead.

"At first. At least what Joy saw. But after Joy died . . ."

"I see." The very disappointment he'd mentioned colored her response.

Yet, the urge to explain himself, to restore any good opinion she may have developed for him, pressed him to continue. "I turned to Hester to seek comfort, solace in my grief. When Joy died, I thought the ground would open up and swallow me whole, trapping me in misery for the rest of my days. Hester offered an escape. And for those brief moments, I could forget. But it didn't last, and the shame of using Hester compounded my guilt over Joy. I ended it with Hester and enlisted in the military with a request to send me as far away from England as possible."

"To India, where you met Burwood."

He nodded, searching Charlotte's face for the telltale signs of disgust or loathing, but her expression remained serene, even compassionate.

Not what he expected.

"So, you had good reason to dislike me, even if you didn't realize what it was," he said.

She fussed with a fold of her pelisse, straightening it and brushing out a non-existent wrinkle. "That's not why I dislike you. In fact, it makes me dislike you less."

Lord, she was a puzzlement. "Why?"

A smile tipped her lips, not wide enough to show him the dimple that drove him mad, but one that spoke of secrets. "Which? Why do I dislike you, or why your tale makes me dislike you less?"

"Let's start with the positive. Why less now?"

"Because I believed you never experienced hardship or sorrow, and I envied that. Now I know you have, and regardless of the pain you wanted to escape, you returned to England for Burwood. You put someone else ahead of your own needs."

He'd never thought of it that way. "Drake needed me. A friend to help him navigate society."

"And to test Honoria." Her lips puckered in a little pout. "I still haven't quite forgiven him for that. He should have known Honoria loved him no matter who he was."

"I agree. And I told him that repeatedly. I believe it's the one thing you and I have always agreed upon. Remember the house party? Who would have thought we would be on the same side of things?"

She laughed. The rich throaty timbre of her alto almost as alluring as the fact she laughed at all. At that moment, he wanted nothing more than to hear her laugh more often.

To give her *reason* to laugh.

To make her happy.

His mind stuttered at the thought. When did he start caring about Lady Charlotte's happiness?

"As to why I dislike you," she continued without prodding.

He really didn't want to know.

Did he?

269

"I dislike you because you are so bloody happy all the time. That you find joy in everything around you. That people love you. It makes me bloody furious."

His head jerked back at her statement, not that she cursed—although truth be told, he hadn't expected such language from the high-and-mighty Lady Charlotte—but it was a ridiculous reason to dislike him.

"You dislike me because I'm . . . likable?" Incredulity rang in his tone. "Why?"

Smiles and laughter vanished. When she turned and met his gaze, the pain in her eyes slashed through him. "Because you are what I am not."

CHAPTER 28

G*ah!* Charlotte berated herself. Why on earth had she allowed that admission to slip out? Simon's confession must have made her soft.

He blinked. "You're . . . jealous of me?"

"Of course not." She snapped her response much too quickly. "I simply don't trust people whom everyone likes."

His upturned lips indicated he didn't believe a word of her lie. "You like Honoria, don't you?"

"Of course. But that's different."

"How? Everyone adores her." He met her gaze. "As they should. She's a marvel. Drake is one lucky bas—man."

"Because Honoria is a woman and has proven her trustworthiness."

"And Anne Weatherby? She's so much like me it's frightening." He laughed to punctuate his point.

"I tolerate Anne for Honoria's sake. But despite her silliness, she's not a bad person."

His eyes widened, and he snapped the ribbons a little more aggressively. "And I am?"

Blood *whooshed* in her ears. How could he aggravate her so easily? "Stop putting words in my mouth! What I mean is, men have ulterior motives underlying their *charms*." She held onto her bonnet. "And please slow down! My tarts will be nothing but crumbs and jam the way you drive."

"Ulterior motives such as?"

"You're a man, you should know."

"Plenty of women have ulterior motives. Leg-shackling a poor unsuspecting fellow being foremost among them."

She twisted on the seat toward him. "Are you accusing me of trapping you? Because if you are——"

"Why do you think the only reason I married you was because I *had* to?"

She huffed. "Because it's true."

"No." He shook his head as if to emphasize it. "I could have sent you back with your brother and Lord Felix, which—if I need to remind you—they wanted. And you could have refused my offer."

Reluctant to admit he had a point, she crossed her arms over her bosom.

He snapped the ribbons again. "I married you because I wanted to. Because, as strange as it sounds, it made sense. And if you would only use that sharp mind of yours, you would agree with me."

He wanted to marry her? Certain her mouth hung open, she asked, "You think I have a sharp mind?"

He darted another glance her way. "Everything I said, and *that's* what you homed in on?" He rolled his eyes. "Of course you have a sharp mind. Don't fish for compliments. It's not attractive."

"I wasn't fishing." The man was insufferable! "I'm simply surprised you have any good opinion of me."

"I don't know why you think you're unlovable, Charlotte."

If anything, Charlotte was a realist. Strong-willed, opinionated, harsh, and even abrasive, she failed to meet the submissive standard for women. But traits society saw as flaws had been her protection—her armor, such as it was, keeping people who could harm her at arm's length. Her father, and subsequently her brother Roland, had groused about the fact that she intimidated suitors, sending them scurrying for the safety of the nearest eye-fluttering miss.

They were not wrong. And she had successfully slipped from the jaws of marriage numerous times. Until Simon Beckham.

She gawked at her husband. "And you don't? You detest me."

Simon's expression softened—an odd reaction to her deliberate scowl. "I don't detest you. In fact, I'm growing to like you. If you would only stop getting in your own way."

She'd heard the expression take the wind out of the sails from naval men, but it wasn't until that moment she understood it. Perhaps Simon Beckham was the one man with whom she could not only be herself, but who was strong enough to accept her for it. Who would have imagined?

Anxious to steer the conversation away from herself, she tried to make amends. "Thank you for Trifle."

A slow smile crept across his face. "You're welcome. We'll stop by the main house to get her before we return home."

Perhaps the time had come to heed Honoria's request. Summoning her courage, Charlotte touched Simon's arm. "If you wish, you may come to my bed tonight."

◈

IF HE WISHED? IF HE WISHED?! SIMON HAD THOUGHT OF NOTHING else since they exchanged vows. Hell, truthfully, even before that, as ill-advised as it had been. Attracted to her from the moment he saw her at Drake's house party the previous summer, Simon had been devastated to learn she was the daughter and sister of the former and current Marquess of Edgerton.

Reason dictated he should immediately dislike her, and her prickly demeanor and snide comments had made the task effortless.

He didn't want to feel the pull to her, because like Icarus, if he flew too close, he would no doubt be burned—even consumed. There were so many analogies. Black widow spiders. Praying Mantises. She would entice him in and then quickly stab him in the back.

Lady Charlotte was a dangerous woman.

Or so he had thought. But over the course of the last few weeks, he'd caught tiny glimpses of the vulnerable woman she kept locked away under that harsh exterior.

The joy on her face when he'd taught her how to hold Drake's newborn daughter. Her appreciation of his family's estate. The genuine affection in her eyes as she conversed with Georgie. Softening of her features as she cuddled Trifle. The fierce determination to protect a child being mistreated.

And of course, her understanding of his own failings with Joy. She may not have realized it, but he saw compassion in her eyes, not condemnation or judgment as he expected, when he confessed all to her.

Something—or someone—made her hide that side of herself, only allowing it to slip out when she believed no one was watching, or in time of great emotion.

Lady Charlotte was a complicated woman. One who didn't mirror back his faults as Joy had, but would—perhaps, just perhaps—balance them out. As he might for her.

"Well?" She huffed, the look in her eyes more worry than annoyance belying her exasperated tone. "If you don't wish to—"

"Oh. I wish to. In fact. Hold on to your tarts." He snapped

the ribbons, sending the poor horses into a gallop, and Charlotte fell back against the seat with a squeal.

Fortuitously, they arrived back at the house in record time. Dark clouds loomed overhead as they descended from the carriage, and he scanned the sky. "Looks like we're in for a storm." He instructed the groom to leave the carriage there for their return to the cottage.

After making their apologies to his family, declining his mother's offer to stay for supper, they retrieved Trifle. Worn out, the kitten was curled up in a ball, sleeping next to Nightly.

With care Simon had begun to pay particular notice to, Charlotte scooped the kitten in her hands and was rewarded with an enormous yawn and protesting meow.

When Georgie noticed the package of tarts, she practically drooled.

His mother's gaze darted between him and Charlotte, her brow furrowed with concern. "You stopped at the bakery?"

"Yes. I've told Charlotte everything."

Although relief painted his mother's face, Georgie's brow furrowed. "Everything what?" Only five at the time, Georgie was oblivious to what happened with Joy.

"Never mind," he said, patting his sister on the head.

Charlotte gave him a censorious look. "She's not a dog, Simon, and she's too old to pat on the head."

Georgie crossed her arms over her slight chest, giving a curt nod, then stuck out her tongue, completely negating Charlotte's assessment.

And no doubt to Charlotte's disdain, Simon mimicked back the gesture to his sister. "I don't have time to explain. We need to be off before the storm hits." It was a perfect excuse, even if it was a little cowardly.

Charlotte handed Trifle to Georgie and made haste unwrapping the tarts, leaving eight for Simon's family—one for each except for Georgie, who Charlotte said could have two. "That leaves four for Simon and me."

"Two each?" Simon asked, his mouth already watering.

"No. One for you, three for me." The sparkle in Charlotte's dark eyes told him she might be persuaded to relinquish the third one if given the proper persuasion.

Quickly re-wrapping the package as Charlotte retrieved Trifle, he scooped it up and ushered Charlotte out of the house.

During the short amount of time they'd been inside, the clouds had grown darker, and the air grew thick with the building storm. In the distance, a flash of lightning slashed through the darkening sky. Simon waited for the answering *boom* of thunder, relieved when it didn't follow immediately.

"We have time. The storm's still miles away."

"How can you tell?" When the answering call of thunder finally arrived, Charlotte jumped in her seat, clutching Trifle to her bosom.

"That's how." He tipped his head toward the approaching storm. "The closer the storm, the sooner the thunder sounds after a lightning flash. But we should still hurry."

By the time they arrived at the cottage, fat raindrops plopped against the ground, slowly at first, then increasing in both rapidity and number.

They dashed into the house, with only their outer garments touched by the downpour. Trifle jumped from Charlotte's arms, eager to explore her new home.

Simon handed his hat to John, then helped Charlotte with her pelisse.

He leaned in, whispering, "You smell fresh like the rain." He allowed his fingers to linger on the soft skin at her neck, then tugged the pelisse from her shoulders.

While he gave instructions for Cook to prepare a light supper, his gaze snagged on Charlotte peering out the front window. The curtain, hooked in her hand, shook as another roar of thunder cut through the silence.

In four long strides, he traversed the floor to be by her side. About to ask if she enjoyed watching the storm, he held his tongue.

Her eyes appeared frantic, jerking back and forth as if searching the sky, her mouth set in a grim line. Lightning flashed again in the distance, and she sucked in an audible breath.

"Count, Charlotte. Slowly."

As her gaze darted toward him, her brow furrowed.

"To mark the distance and see if the storm is moving closer or farther away," he explained.

When the thunder crashed, she jumped.

The urge to wrap his arms around her, pulling her close to his chest, wrestled with his need to flee from the pain flashing in her eyes with each crack of thunder.

The least he could do was force himself to remain by her side and count the intervals between flash and *crash*.

Counts of one, two, three, four, five, and so on slipped softly from Charlotte's lips with each pairing of the storm. When the counts increased to twelve and the thunder's sound grew fainter, her shoulders relaxed, and she met his gaze, her eyes questioning.

"It's moving away. From the look of the clouds, eastward toward London. Now, will you come away from the window? We have time to refresh before supper."

He wanted to ask if her offer to come to her bed still stood, but he remained silent. She would think him a cad, only concerned about his own selfish needs. He admitted his selfishness, but he was grateful for the reprieve from the storm nonetheless.

Conversation during supper was surprisingly pleasant, with Charlotte slipping tiny bites of chicken to Trifle, who meowed at her feet.

Enraptured, Simon observed his wife. *His wife.* For the first time since they'd exchanged vows, he welcomed the words. The adoration on her face as she first admonished the kitten, then gave in to Trifle's demands, causing his heart to squeeze. If she'd see herself as he did at that moment, she would know she was lovable.

The thought brought him up sharply, and he quickly brushed it away. He *cared* about her, certainly. A husband should care about his wife's happiness and well-being. It wasn't the same as love. He would treat her well and give her affection without giving her his heart, or she give hers—surely.

"You're going to spoil her," he said after she gave Trifle the sixth piece of chicken. Purposely keeping his voice light and uncritical, he added, "Either that or make her sick. She's not used to such things."

"Did you hear that, Trifle? Your papa says no more."

The kitten's meow of protest quickly changed as he lowered a shred of chicken toward the floor, waving it to get Trifle's attention.

He chuckled to himself. *Papa indeed.* Unbidden, an image of Charlotte swollen with his child flashed before him. Warmth spread through him as he pictured Charlotte grousing over her increasing belly and complaining of the inability to see her feet.

And he found he enjoyed it—even looked forward to it. He would pamper and tease her, and she would call him ridiculous when he would insist she rest, a pillow propped under her feet and behind her back.

A grin tugged at his lips.

"What's so amusing?" Charlotte jerked his attention back, her scowl matching the image of his daydream so closely he laughed. She lifted a serviette. "Do I have food somewhere?" Even her annoyed tone made him smile.

"No. I was simply picturing you as a mother."

She arched a dark brow at him. "And you find that . . . humorous?"

He leaned in, propping his chin on his palm. "I find it delightful." And perhaps in an hour or so, they would be well on their way to creating such a child.

When she finished the last of her dessert—trifle with chocolate shavings, of course—he said, "Why don't you go up and have a nice relaxing bath? I'll have Rose let me know when you're ready."

She gave a silent nod, her expression determined, as if readying herself for battle.

And he vowed to make it the best battle she had ever lost.

Upstairs, Charlotte eased back into the tub of warm water. Rose had washed her hair and rinsed it with a solution of water and lemon juice. The lemon scent mixed with the water and coated her skin as well. Between the clean fragrance and the soothing water, Charlotte's muscles slowly relaxed.

She spoke words of encouragement to herself. How hard could it be? She sighed. If only her mother were still alive to counsel her. Everything had happened so quickly after the wedding. She'd meant to ask Honoria, but the unexpected arrival of little Kitty had made that impossible.

Charlotte had heard snippets from widows as they crowded together at balls and soirées. But the different accounts had confused her. Should she lie motionless and think of the king and England—which seemed odd and, honestly, unappealing—or should she participate? The latter seemed the more logical choice. After all, Charlotte was a woman of action. But how? What should she do?

Should she ask Simon? Would he laugh at her ineptitude—or worse, her boldness?

Gah!

No matter how nervous she was, she couldn't dally in the

water much longer. The skin of her fingers had developed tiny wrinkles. After Rose dressed her in a fresh nightrail and towel dried her hair, she prepared to braid it.

Remembering Simon's expression when her hair had hung loose, Charlotte stopped her maid. "Leave it down, Rose."

Charlotte's fingers shook as she draped a dark lock of her hair over her shoulder to lie against her bosom. When had she grown interested in garnering Simon's approval? "Wait half an hour before calling Mr. Beckham. I have a letter I wish to write."

Rose curtsied. "Very well, ma'am." The maid sent Charlotte a knowing smile, then closed the door behind her.

The supposed letter was a ruse. Charlotte simply needed to prepare herself. She breathed deeply, smoothing her palms over the soft cotton of her nightrail as she cast glances at the large bed.

A sudden *boom* jolted her from her worrying, and she raced to the window, pulling back the curtain. She squinted into the pitch-black darkness, unable to make out anything—until lightning arced across the sky, the razor-sharp strands of light outlining monstrous, menacing clouds. She counted. "One, two, three, four, five, six—" *Boom.*

Strained minutes passed while she waited at the window for another flash of lightning, counting again. She only made it to three.

Close. Much closer than it had been before nightfall, the storm had returned.

Trifle meowed at her feet, and she picked up the kitten. "Shush." Her hand trembled as she stroked the kitten's soft fur, and another flash of lightning, so close silhouettes of the trees in front of the house appeared, the answering call of thunder not even giving her time to open her mouth.

Rain pelted the window in heavy, angry drops, dripping down in streams.

She clutched Trifle so tightly to her bosom, the kitten

squirmed from her grasp, then jumped to freedom, scurrying under the bed.

Terror swept over her, the memory of that night, so long ago, clawing its way to the surface.

Alone. Afraid. A child seeking comfort and finding rejection.

Lightning flashed again, illuminating her room, and the crash of thunder reverberated through her bones. Though she tried to hold it in, a heart-wrenching sob climbed up her throat and escaped her lips.

CHAPTER 29

Not long after Simon finished bathing, thunder crashed again in the distance.

"Hurry up."

Brown's brow quirked in an irritating fashion as he held the razor at Simon's throat to scrape off the last of his night whiskers. "Do you prefer I hurry, or do you prefer to go to your bride unmarked?"

"Well. Hurry but be careful."

With a scrape against Simon's skin that—truthfully—stung a mite more than necessary, Brown lifted the razor away with a flourish. "Finished." He swished the blade off in the bowl of soapy water as Simon dabbed at his face with a warm towel. "Will there be anything else, sir?"

Simon shook his head, grateful the towel remained free of blood when he stole a peek. "And don't worry about waking me tomorrow." With luck, Simon hoped to still be naked with his similarly unclothed wife in his arms.

Stoic, Brown exited, closing the door behind him.

Another *boom* of thunder sounded, louder than the first.

Blast.

Simon pulled on the banyan over his trousers and paced impatiently, waiting for Rose to tell him Charlotte was ready.

Brief flashes of light flickered in the windows, the answering call of thunder following.

What was keeping Rose?

Simon had given Charlotte time, enjoying a small glass of brandy after supper before having a bath. He checked the time—one hour had passed since they'd finished supper.

At the window, he watched the approaching storm. Unease settled in his chest, twisting around his lungs and squeezing.

Not tonight!

He paced some more, glancing at the clock every few minutes.

Had Charlotte changed her mind? And if so, why hadn't she sent word?

Well, he would bloody well find out.

He threw open the door to his room and strode to Charlotte's room next to his. Poised inches from the heavy oak, his hand halted mid-knock at the sounds coming from within.

Unsure what he heard, he leaned in, placing his ear against the wood. Another *boom* of thunder echoed through the house. A cry followed, a hollow-aching sob. He was certain of it.

Slowly, he twisted the knob and eased the door open a crack. A ball of cream and brown fur flew past him, claws skittering against the wood floor as Trifle raced down the hall.

"Charlotte?" Another crash of thunder drowned out his whispered word, the preceding burst of lightning silhouetting her like a nimbus. Curled up on the floor, Charlotte hugged her knees to her chest, her whimpers prickling like a warning against his skin.

Every instinct in him made him itch to turn and flee. To remove himself from a situation where he would only find pain.

It would pull him under, suffocating him. Yet the sight of Charlotte so vulnerable kept him rooted in place.

Although he'd never paid much attention during Sunday sermons, one about a man facing a den of lions popped into his mind. Was it David?

No, David was the boy with the slingshot who faced a giant. Equally disturbing and frightening, but Simon also remembered the story with David and the woman he saw bathing on the roof. That story had captured his attention, and he would have surely associated David with lions if the man had faced them.

What was the chap's name?

Oh—Daniel. That was it. Simon felt very much like Daniel stepping into the lion's den.

But at the moment, he also knew he had something in common with his friend David. Because as much as he wanted to run from the sight of a weeping woman, he also wanted to comfort her. Hold her in his arms and soothe away her tears because . . . because?

Oh!

It hit him as surely as if one of Daniel's lions had pounced and hovered above him with bared teeth.

Because he cared about Charlotte.

Not just cared.

Because he loved her.

He stepped into the room, closing the door behind him with a soft *snick*. Barefoot, he padded soundlessly across the carpet toward her. "Charlotte."

Although he kept his voice gentle with the whisper of her name, her head shot up toward him, her eyes wide, her cheeks wet with tears.

Turn! Run! the cowardly voice in his head shouted.

"No." He hadn't meant to say the word aloud, only to override the overwhelming desire to protect himself when he needed to protect Charlotte.

Charlotte swiped at her tear-stained face, her brows drawn in a typical scowl. "How dare you have the audacity to tell me not to cry?"

He should have run when he had the chance. "I wasn't. I was talking to myself."

She straightened, wiping her face again, then turned away. "A likely story. Although you're daft enough to do it. I suppose you're here to claim your husbandly rights."

He crouched down next to her. "I grew worried when Rose didn't come for me. When I heard the storm, my concern grew tenfold."

"Well, as you can see, I'm fine."

"You're not fine. If there is one thing I can count on about you, it's your brutal honesty, so don't lie to me now. Not about something that matters." He softened his voice again. "Tell me why the storms upset you."

Dark curls, draping alluringly down her shoulders, brushed against her nightrail as she shook her head. "You'll laugh and think I'm ridiculous."

Seated fully on the floor beside her, he stretched out his legs. "Remember to whom you're speaking. Of all people, I'm the last to think someone is ridiculous."

A strangled burble of a laugh escaped her. "True enough." When her eyes locked with his, affection shone in their dark depths.

Taking a chance, he lifted her hand and entwined it with his. "Tell me. I promise I will remain serious. It will be a chore, I admit, but I shall prevail." He grinned at her, hoping to coax her into continuing.

"Then why are you smiling like a fool?" Her lips tipped up a fraction. Not enough to display her dimple, but enough to put forth a brave front.

He wanted to kiss her tear-stained cheeks, but that would

come later. First, he needed to listen while she unburdened herself. And to do that, he needed to be serious.

For Charlotte.

With his free hand, he wiped down his face, erasing the silly grin, replacing it with a more solemn expression. "Better?"

CHARLOTTE MARVELED AT SIMON'S FINGERS LACED TOGETHER. Larger, his hand practically engulfed hers. Warm and comforting, his touch secured her to the present.

To her own amazement, for once in her life, she felt safe. She took a deep breath. "I was always afraid of thunderstorms; the noise, the jagged flashes of lightning like daggers in the air. I turned to my mother. She would hold me, whispering soothing words, allowing me to sleep with her."

As if to taunt her, another burst of light illuminated Simon's face. She braced herself for the crack of thunder, still jumping when it arrived.

Squeezing her hand, Simon urged her on. "But something changed."

"Yes. My mother died the winter of my sixth year." She didn't have the heart to tell Simon her mother had died from complications of a difficult pregnancy—not considering how he stormed from Pendrake House in a fright during Honoria's delivery. "One night the next spring, during a particularly severe storm, Nanny chastised me, telling me to cease my foolish crying. I wanted my mother, but of course, she was gone. Roland was on a grand tour of Europe and Nash was away at school."

"Did your brothers give you comfort?" The doubt in Simon's eyes was unmistakable.

"Not Roland, of course. But if Mother wasn't available, Nash would hold my hand"—her attention drifted down to Simon's hand joined with hers—"much as you are. He'd tell me the noise was simply the angels arranging furniture."

"He sounds like a good man."

She smiled at Simon's serious expression. "Nash would laugh at that, then deny it flatly. He hides it well, but yes, he is. I miss him."

"What did you do when Nanny criticized you? And from my viewpoint, she sounds like a horrible nanny."

Another burble of strangled laughter escaped her throat. "Oh, she was. Father dismissed my previous nanny when Mother died and hired Miss Crabbypants."

Simon barked a laugh, then ran his hand down his face again, restoring his solemn expression. "Sorry. Was that really her name?"

"No. Miss Crabtree. I only called her Crabbypants behind her back."

Simon squeezed her hand again. "Ah, you developed your wit at an early age."

Even through the horrendous recounting, her heart warmed at Simon's compliment. "Anyway, I kicked Nanny in the shins and raced away in search of my father." She paused, pulling in another fortifying breath. "My father was not a kind man, but he was still my father, and as a child, I naturally sought him out for protection."

Another squeeze. "As you should."

She shook her head. "Not in this case. It was a grave error. A servant told me he was in his study and not to disturb him." She sent him a sheepish glance. "As you can imagine, I didn't mind very well."

Simon smiled but didn't apologize.

"Voices drifted from the room through the cracked door, and I peeped in. Lord Cheswick and Father were discussing something I didn't understand. Lord Cheswick said something about his daughter and how the Duke of Burwood's youngest son ruined everything by running off with a commoner."

"Burwood? As in Drake's ancestor?"

Charlotte blinked. The horrible memory so buried, she hadn't put those pieces together. "I suppose so. I could be misremembering that part. But my father's words are seared in my mind. He said, 'Females are nothing but a nuisance. Only good for two things: Rutting and making an advantageous marriage. And female offspring are even worse. I plan to marry Charlotte off the moment she comes of age.' He said he wanted to be rid of the nuisance."

With his free hand, Simon brushed away a strand of hair from her face. "Well, you showed him, didn't you? And he was wrong, of course. What happened next?"

Entranced by Simon's blue eyes, when another flash of lightning and subsequent thunder came, Charlotte barely registered it. "I raced through the door and toward my father. The look he gave me still chills me. Such anger and—loathing. I cried, telling him I wanted my mother. He grabbed me by the arm and said, 'You want your mother? I'll give you your mother.' Upstairs, he opened the door to her bedchamber—where she died." She paused, catching her breath and willing herself to relieve the awful memory.

Rather than squeezing her hand again, Simon placed his other hand on top and stroked her fingers. "It's all right, Charlotte. Take your time. I'm not going anywhere."

How could such a rake be so gentle and considerate? Her stomach knotted that she had misjudged him.

He'd promised he wouldn't laugh or think her ridiculous, and she took a leap of faith, stepping out into the uncharted territory of trust, giving him ammunition to hurt and control her.

"First, he yanked down all the curtains, leaving nothing to shield me from the flashes of lightning. Then, he locked me in her room, telling me that since I wanted my mother so badly, I should summon her ghost."

Simon's face surely mirrored her own on that night long ago. Mouth agape, he gawked. "My God, Charlotte. That's ghastly. And you were only six?"

"Yes." The word came out strangled, but she needed to finish it. "The room had been sealed since Mother's death. With no fire in the grate, the air was frigid. Wind howled, the sound seeping through a tiny crack in the window, sounding eerily like a phantom. And of course, as a child, I believed it was my mother's ghost. Huddled and shivering in a corner, my hands over my ears, I jumped at every sound, not only the thunder, but footsteps approaching the room. Any moment, I expected to see my mother's specter take shape before me. And the thought wasn't . . . comforting."

"No. Of course it wasn't." Simon stared down at their conjoined hands. "Forgive me, but your father was a bastard. If he were here, I would drink enough whisky to cast up my accounts all over him, as I did your brother."

"Thank you."

He smiled. "It would be my sincere pleasure."

She shook her head. "Not for that—well, yes, for that, but for listening and not laughing."

His blue eyes widened. "Why in the world would I laugh? Your father—I want to spit because he was no *father* to you—tortured you. That is no way to treat a child who is frightened and needs comfort."

In that moment, Charlotte realized she hadn't heard any booms of thunder. Her gaze jerked toward the window. "Is the storm passing?"

He stroked her fingers. "I believe so. Shall I stay a while longer, or should I leave? I'll do whatever you wish."

Trust. Yes. Perhaps she *could* trust this man. Her husband. "Stay, if you would, and hold me?"

"My pleasure." He wrapped his arms around her, and she settled into the warmth of his embrace.

Rumbles of thunder decreased in volume, the intervals between the diminishing bursts of light growing longer. With her head on his shoulder, Simon counted for her, softly whispering in her ear as he stroked her arm.

When his last count reached twenty, she relaxed enough to take in the sensations of him. Notes of sandalwood and spice mixed with the clean scent of shaving soap. Firm muscle met her hands under his banyan, a testament to his need to be active. Although deep, his voice remained soothing and comforting, not raised in anger or condescension. Candlelight rimmed his profile. His square jaw, free of evening whiskers, spoke of the strength under his gentleness.

"You smell nice," she said.

"I bathed. Just for you." When he grinned, she no longer found it ridiculous.

However, his comment reminded her of his reason for coming to her room. She toyed with the lapel of his banyan, keeping her gaze focused on his bare chest beneath. "Simon. About tonight."

"Charlotte, I won't hold you to that."

She licked her lips, and his gaze followed the movement. "I want you to. Will you kiss me?"

CHAPTER 30

War raged inside Simon. Every part of him wanted Charlotte, even—he reluctantly admitted—his heart. But the trauma she'd confessed, the terror she'd experienced, cautioned him.

He didn't want their first time to be associated with something she dreaded.

"Charlotte," he said, stroking her face. "Perhaps now is not the best time."

She pulled away from him, the warmth in her eyes vanishing. "Because of what I told you?" The harsh, defensive edge to her voice delivered a warning.

Rather than rushing in headfirst to defend or explain himself, he paused and considered how she might have interpreted his suggestion.

"Well?" Her eyes snapped with fire.

Oh, he had definitely offended her. What had she worried about before she recounted her tale? Oh, yes. That he would think her ridiculous and laugh.

"I'm trying to say this and not muck it up further than I have."

Her whole body stiffened before him. "How hard is it to say you don't want me? Or is it that you don't wish to be with a coward?"

"A coward?! The same woman who faced a drunken Albie to defend a child? Who resisted the pressure from an uncaring brother to marry a man who would abuse her, risking her reputation? Who has delivered setdown after setdown to me?" He shook his head. "Coward is the last word I would use to describe you, Lady Charlotte Beckham."

He took her hands in his. "Perhaps I'm the coward, because I can't bear the idea of having you think of frightening storms each time I touch you."

She blinked rapidly. "What?"

"I want you to associate our coupling with happy thoughts. And, to be clear, I've never wanted a woman more than I want you at this moment." The truth of that statement spread through his veins like warm honey—comforting and sweet. Even the desire he had for Joy, both of them in the blush of youth, paled in comparison to what he felt for Charlotte. However, the partial truth was all he was willing to share. He withheld his admission of love. She would no doubt accuse him of being insincere and manipulative.

"Nothing would make me happier than for this infernal storm to be over," she said, her head tilted, as if listening.

He held his breath and waited.

No flashes of lightning or crashes of thunder broke the connection between them.

She gifted him with a broad smile, displaying her dimple. "Which I believe it is." Giving his banyan a little tug, she said, "And I'm still waiting for that kiss."

His lips tingled just anticipating it, and he licked them as she had done earlier. "Never let it be said I kept a lady waiting."

A gentle brush at first, the kiss consumed him. He nipped at her mouth, his teeth grazing her full bottom lip. *Sweet.* Better than trifle. Better than anything.

When she ran her fingers through his hair, the spark of desire she ignited set him ablaze. Encouraged, he traced the seam of her lips with his tongue, more than pleased when she opened to him.

Tentatively at first, he darted his tongue inside, then grew bolder when she met him stroke for stroke. He groaned and broke the kiss. *Slower.* He played with a lock of her hair. "You kept it down."

She smiled, reminding him to give attention to her dimple. "I remembered you said you liked it down."

"I do, as well as this." He kissed her cheek that held her dimple, then nuzzled her neck. "You smell so good. Citrusy, like Drake's orangery." He breathed deeper. "Lemon and something else. Vanilla?"

"Yes." The richness of her alto, even more throaty and seductive than usual, rasped against his skin. Eyes glazed with desire studied him, the pupils so large as to make her already dark eyes appear black.

He cupped her cheek, cradling it in his hand like priceless crystal, then kissed her lips again, more insistently. With his other arm snaked around her waist, he pulled her closer.

But not close enough.

Lost in the kiss, he startled when she tugged on his banyan. When she broke the kiss, he chased her lips.

"Simon. Simon."

He blinked himself back to reality, dreading to hear her tell him to leave. "What?" His voice, raw with need, scraped like gravel.

"This floor is hard. Perhaps we should"—her cheeks darkened with a blush—"move to the bed?"

Simon bounded to his feet in the blink of an eye, firmly

believing he'd never moved as fast in his life—and for him, that was saying something.

When he extended a hand to assist her, those big brown eyes stared at him, her mouth opening in a little *O*. Then she laughed, genuine and hearty, and it warmed him through to his soul.

"Eager are you, Mr. Beckham?"

Unable to help himself, he grinned. "You might say that."

When she slipped her hand in his, energy crackled up his arm. If a simple touch of hands affected him that much, what would it be like to be inside her, to feel her writhing and moaning in pleasure beneath him?

He couldn't wait to find out.

⬬

CHARLOTTE'S HAND TREMBLED AS SHE SLIPPED IT INTO SIMON'S, but he didn't seem to notice. Determination tempered her apprehension. *I can do this.*

What she didn't like was not knowing what he expected of her. For the second time that evening, she wished her mother were alive to counsel her.

But it was too late for that. Simon pulled her to her feet and wrapped his arms around her waist, kissing her soundly again.

All thoughts of expectations and mothers raced from her mind.

The kiss was long and sensual. Decadent even, as if he imbued every wicked thing he intended to do with each brush of his lips.

Delicious shivers trickled up her arm and spine at the thought as he teased her with his lips and tongue. Instinctively, she palmed a path up his chest, meeting hard muscle beneath the soft silk of his banyan. She clutched his shoulders, holding on for dear life.

"That's it," he whispered, his hot breath brushing against her already sensitive lips. "Don't think. Just do. Let your body lead you." He gave her lips a light peck, then leaned his forehead against hers. "But since it's our first time together, tell me what you like. What pleases you and what doesn't."

His request gave her pause. "I don't know what I like or don't like. Aren't you supposed to know those things?"

His answering chuckle sent her stomach somersaulting. Apparently, she liked *that*.

"I can tell certain things from your responses, but that's after the fact. And there are things in general women like, but not everyone is the same." He pulled away and gazed into her eyes. "For instance, most women love being picked up and carried, but you do not."

Why did his direct gaze seem like he peered into her soul? "I might like it."

Narrowed eyes and the rakish tilt of his head told her he didn't believe her. "Then why did you protest when I assisted you across the puddle? You practically took off my head."

"Because I didn't expect it. I don't like to be surprised. It makes me feel . . . out of control."

"Ah," he said and nothing more. "In that case, may I carry you to the bed, and we can resume things there?" He winked, and even that didn't annoy her as it typically did. "It was your suggestion after all."

Her mouth had gone dry at the mention of the bed, and she could only nod.

"Arms around my neck, if you please. And try not to strangle me."

Sliding her hands around his neck, she laughed, and he rewarded her with another kiss.

"There. That's not so bad, is it?"

She shook her head.

In one smooth motion, he lifted her in his arms, then strode to the bed in four long strides, carrying her as if she weighed nothing.

After setting her down next to the bed, he stepped back, his gaze traveling over her from head to toe and back again. The lustful expression in his eyes, as if he were a starving man faced with a feast of great delicacies, heated her from within.

"Damn, but you're beautiful." With one finger, he flicked a ribbon on her nightrail. "Mind if I take this off?"

She swallowed, forcing down the lump in her throat. "Can't we leave it on?"

He arched a dark brow. "Modest? Not something I anticipated from you. You're always so sure of yourself." With movements as sleek as a jungle cat, he came closer and leaned down, whispering in her ear. "There's nothing to be ashamed of, Charlotte. Clearly, your body is as beautiful as your face."

"You haven't seen me yet."

A slow sensual smile crept across his lips, his gaze drifting down and snagging on her bodice. "I have an excellent imagination." He hooked a finger in the neckline of her nightdress. "You'll be more comfortable without all this material bunching up around you."

"We can't wait . . . just a little while?" She hated how her voice trembled. It would only support her early cowardly cowering.

Yet, his gaze softened, and he nodded. "Perhaps you'll be more comfortable if I lead the way. After all, you've already seen me au naturel." Without removing his gaze from hers, he unfastened the banyan and slipped it from his shoulders.

He turned, giving her a spectacular view of his muscled back, which angled down to a trim waist. Rather than tossing the banyan to the floor as she expected, he folded it neatly and laid it on a chair by the window. The care with which he performed the action tickled the back of her mind, as if she could trust him to be as considerate with her.

When he turned back, he merely stood before her, allowing her to fully appreciate the beauty of his masculine form. During the *incident* he spoke of, she'd averted her eyes so quickly, she'd really only caught a glimpse of him. But at that moment, she drank him in, no doubt the appreciation on her face matching his own when he gazed upon her earlier.

Well-formed, muscled shoulders, arms, chest, and stomach gave testament to a man who appreciated physical activity. A sculptor would take great joy in capturing Simon Beckham. But unlike cold marble statues, her husband was a warm, living, breathing man.

Dark lashes framed incredible blue as he studied her through hooded eyes. "Do you like what you see?"

Gooseflesh rose on her arms from his voice, low and laced with desire. Heat rose to her cheeks. Thank goodness he still had trousers on, keeping her blush to a minimum. She struggled for a retort, an insult if she could manage it, but all that sprung from her lips was, "You appear to be a fine specimen."

He blinked twice, then threw back his head in laughter. "There's a compliment buried in there somewhere." Stepping closer, he lifted her hand, holding it close to his chest, but not placing it directly on his skin. "Perhaps you would like to examine me to confirm your deduction."

Her fingers trembled as she lowered them to his stomach, but as she touched the hard planes of muscle, he sucked in a breath, and his pectorals twitched.

"Your touch inflames me," he said, his voice growing more gravelly. The blue of his eyes darkened to a dusky hue.

Power surged through her at his admission. Encouraged, she flattened her palms against him, the thrum of his heart quickening under her fingers. She continued a path up and over his chest muscles, across his shoulders and down his arms, thrilling at each tiny response she drew from him.

"You want control," he said. "You have it. Feel—and see—

what you do to me with your touch alone." His gaze drifted down to the space between them.

And when hers followed, she saw the evidence he spoke of in the arousal straining at his trousers. A knot formed in her throat, and the heat on her cheeks built to a scorching intensity.

"The question is, do I have the same effect on you?" Light as a feather, he traced a fingertip up her arm, then skimmed the neckline of her nightrail.

Tightness formed in her breasts and low in her belly. Her traitorous skin pebbled in answer.

His lips curled in a self-satisfied smile. "I believe that's a 'Yes.'"

She fought her own smile. "You don't have to be so smug about it. I can't control what my body does."

Simon arched a brow at her, his low chuckle rumbling in the quiet air. "That's typically my argument. But you do have control over what you want to do . . . want me to do." As he leaned in, his warm breath tickled the sensitive skin of her neck. "Tell me where and how I should touch you. Is there a particular place you enjoy? That feels especially good?"

How could she think when he addled her mind? Words clung to her tongue. If released, they would serve as a confession to how little joy and pleasure she'd known during her life.

Yet, a small voice broke through her foggy brain, urging her to trust him—that he was worthy of her trust. Simon wouldn't hurt her.

Would he?

She licked her lips. "I don't know."

Both of his dark brows lifted as he jerked back, his previously hooded eyes widening at first, then narrowing. "You don't know what feels good?" A beat passed. "Charlotte, have you never pleasured yourself?"

Confused, she frowned. "What?"

"When you're alone at night, do you touch yourself"—his gaze drifted down between them again—"there?"

At that moment, the storm seemed a less formidable choice.

⚜

To Simon, it was a simple question. They were married and about to become intimate. However, Charlotte glared at him as if he'd asked if she'd ever murdered anyone.

"How dare you?! I'm not a doxy."

The hellcat had returned in full measure.

"It's nothing to be ashamed of, Charlotte." He cursed the propriety forced upon women that discouraged self-pleasure.

"I assure you, I have not, sir."

Frustrated, Simon blew out a breath and drew a hand down his face. He'd never had to take such care with a woman before, but he reminded himself this was about Charlotte, not him. "Very well, then allow me to help you discover what you enjoy. We'll learn about it together. But you have the final say in how and what I do. Agreed?"

"Agreed." She held out her hand, clearly wishing to shake as gentlemen did when reaching consensus.

But instead, when he clasped her hand, he brought it to his lips. "I seem to remember a favorable response when I did this." As he placed a kiss on the pulse point at her wrist, allowing his tongue to stroke her silky skin, his gaze locked on hers.

"Oh." In answer, her eyelids fluttered as the breathy sigh escaped her parted lips.

"What about this?" He trailed his lips up her forearm to the soft flesh inside her elbow and received a similar response.

"And this," he said as he nibbled on the sweet juncture at her neck and shoulder.

She licked her lips. "Yes. That is . . . lovely."

He wanted nothing more than to continue his exploration of

her, but he stepped back. "I'm glad you approve. But to get the most satisfaction, both partners should participate. Remember, you're in complete control."

Her gaze flicked to his, and at first, she appeared unsure. But then her lips quirked in the Charlotte way he'd somehow grown to love. "I can do anything?"

Blast. His body on alert, he took a step back. "Such as? I should clarify that I abhor pain of any kind. The idea is to please your partner."

She stepped closer, her dark eyes boring into him. "Like this?" As she had before, she placed her palm against his chest, her delicate fingers raking through the sparse hair. When she rubbed a thumb across his nipple, it puckered, and he sucked in a breath.

The tease!

Desire bubbled in his veins. "You know very well that feels good. Might that be something you enjoy as well?"

"I *am* enjoying this." She delivered a wicked grin, then ran her hand downward, skimming the edge of his trousers and causing his stomach muscles to contract under her touch. She was like a drug he couldn't get enough of.

As much as he enjoyed sex—and make no mistake, he enjoyed it very, very much—this was different.

Better.

Best.

What superlative came after best?

And was it always as exciting when you loved someone?

"I meant you might enjoy me touching you like that. But first, I want another kiss." He leaned in and nipped at her lips. "Mmm," he mumbled, so enraptured with the taste of her he hardly noticed when her hand dropped to the buttons on his trousers.

Only the shaking of her fingers alerted him, and he pulled

back. "Are you sure you want to do that?" he asked as she chased his lips.

"As you said, I've seen you unclothed before." Even so, her cheeks darkened.

Would she still think the grin he delivered ridiculous? Yet, he couldn't help himself. "True. But I'm . . . different now." At her perplexed expression, he whispered, "Larger. Erect." He nuzzled the sensitive spot on her neck. "Because of you."

Before he knew it, she unfastened the rest of the buttons, and his trousers dropped around his hips. He pushed them off completely, and they fell to the floor, exposing his arousal.

Charlotte's eyes widened. "Don't you wear small clothes?"

"I decided against them after my bath. The trousers were only for your delicate sensibilities." He nipped at her neck again. "Little did I know you would be so wanton."

And nothing pleased him more.

CHAPTER 31

W anton? Power surged through Charlotte at the control Simon gave her. And strangely, that control freed her. If being wanton was being unrestrained, then she embraced being wanton.

It was almost as frightening as the storm. Because, although Simon stood before her naked, she was the vulnerable one.

Should she let her guard down? Trust him? Let him in?

The door to her heart creaked and moaned, resisting the tug to open, its hinges rusted from years of neglect. Determined, Charlotte tugged harder, the child she'd kept hidden behind it clawing her way out.

And she faced the fact that she cared about the man before her. Given time, she might even grow to love him. The idea so unexpected, a laugh bubbled up from her throat.

Simon quirked a brow. "Please tell me you're not laughing at my . . ." He cast his gaze down to his arousal.

She laughed again, the sound joyous, wonderful, and—freeing. "No. I'm laughing because I love that you called me wanton."

He pulled her toward him, his arousal pressing into her stomach. "Then I shall call you wanton more often," he said, nipping at her earlobe. "Because I love when you laugh."

Liberated, she placed both palms on his bare chest and pushed him away, quickly reassuring him as his forehead dented with a frown. "Only for a moment." When she moved to untie the ribbons of her nightrail, he stopped her.

"Allow me. Please. I've been dreaming about this since our wedding day." Seriousness replaced the sparkle of mischief and amusement usually shining in his eyes. "And if I'm honest, even before that. As much as I didn't wish to admit it, I think I wanted you from the moment we met."

"But you detested me."

His fingers played with the silky ribbon. "No. Not exactly. I hated my attraction to you because of who you were."

Ah. "Because I'm a Talbot."

"Yes." With excruciating slowness, he pulled the ribbon loose, the loop growing smaller until it fell straight against the cotton fabric. "But you're a Beckham now, and I'm eager to explore every inch of you and discover what you enjoy."

With the gown open at her neck, he tugged the material from her shoulders, then proceeded to pepper her with kisses.

She shivered with pleasure.

"You like that." The confidence in his voice normally would have encouraged her to respond with a scathing setdown.

A low moan drifted up from low in her chest and escaped, and Simon chuckled, the air from his breath tickling her skin further.

"Definitely," he said before moving down to her collarbone. "Now let me see if you respond in kind when I touch you here."

Unprepared, she pulled in a gasp when his hand found her breast and he thumbed her nipple. Her eyes shuttered as her head dropped back at the pleasurable sensations sweeping through her.

Oh, my goodness.

A sudden chill swept over her, and she opened her eyes to find her nightrail pooled to the floor at her feet and Simon staring at her as if he wished to devour her whole.

"Like a goddess. I knew it," he muttered, his voice so gravelly she barely recognized it. When he met her gaze directly, he appeared as a man possessed. "Permission to lift you onto the bed, my lady?"

How could her head be so heavy? She barely nodded her answer, then slid her arms around his neck.

Before she could blink, he picked her up and gently laid her in the center of the bed. As he climbed in next to her, his eyes filled with hunger, he reminded her of a cat stalking its prey.

Fire ignited low in her belly, and an aching need built inside her. More frightening though, tiny pangs squeezed her heart when she met Simon's eyes.

Although desire fogged her mind, she remembered his exhortation to participate. "Kiss me?" Goodness, she sounded so needy.

But he didn't laugh. "My pleasure." Holding her in his arms, he kissed her with a unique combination of passion and gentleness, as if he were trying to tell her something without words.

Lips, soft but firm, coaxed her into a state of euphoria as he nipped and drank and plundered his tongue in her mouth.

When he broke the kiss, she wanted to chase his lips, but she only moaned as he trailed hot kisses down her torso. He tongued her nipple, and she arched off the bed.

Pressure continued building inside her, wanting—needing something she couldn't name. "Simon, please."

He released her breast and returned to her lips. His hand lay on the flat of her stomach, his fingers teasing and torturing. "All right, my sweet. I'm going to move my hand down now. Remember. You are in control. Stop me if you don't like it." He delivered the last with a teasing tone, as if convinced she would not only like it, but crave it.

And as his hand inched lower, and lower, the unnamed need grew stronger, and she admitted her husband understood her body better than she did herself.

She kissed him back with equal fervor, her own tongue tangling with his and drawing sighs and moans from both of them.

Hot desire surged through her when he slipped his hand between her legs, inserting one finger, then two into her.

Breaking the kiss, he leaned his forehead against hers. "Oh, God, Charlotte. You're wet for me."

The words sent a naughty thrill through her. "Tell me I'm wanton again."

As he continued to stroke her, he whispered in her ear, "You are a very wanton woman. So wicked. And I want you to have your way with me."

Muddled, her mind searched how to accomplish his wish, but any hope of discovering it vanished as he moved to suckle at her breast again while continuing his ministrations between her legs.

And instead she sought relief—how and from what, she had no idea, only that it was as if she were reaching for something just out of grasp, but growing closer, and closer by the moment, and then—

"Oh!" The word flew from her lips as the pressure exploded inside her. Stars danced beneath her eyelids as wave after wave of pleasure crashed through her.

Simon continued his sweet torture until the last convulsion ceased.

Limp and boneless, she had never felt so relaxed.

Simon pulled her into his arms. "No need to ask if you enjoyed that."

When she opened her eyes, his ridiculous grin greeted her. "You don't have to appear so smug about it."

"About pleasing my wife? I have every right. And now that I know a little about what you enjoy, I plan to do it often."

Regardless of his boast, she had to admit she very much wished to repeat the experience. Often, if possible.

With her mind relatively cleared, she returned to her earlier thought. How could she have her way with Simon?

Oh! Surely if it felt so good for him to touch her, he would enjoy being touched, too?

Wrapped in his arms, she lay on her side, facing him, as he nuzzled her neck and fondled her breast. His arousal pressed hard against her belly. Careful not to disturb his delicious ministrations, she slipped her hand between them and nudged him to give her access.

His previously hooded eyes widened, then he grinned and moved his hips away enough to allow her to touch him. "You wicked, wanton woman." His sensual chuckle, low and seductive, encouraged her.

Curious, more than anything at first, she touched a finger to the top of his arousal, surprised to find it silky soft and a little spongy. But the long shaft was like iron, rigid and demanding as it jumped under her touch.

"Wrap your hand around me." His words came out as a growl.

When she did as he asked, his eyes fluttered shut, and he moaned. "God, Charlotte. How can your touch undo me so quickly?" His hips jerked forward, then back.

"What should I do?"

After a lingering kiss, he said, "You won't hurt me. Grip tighter and run your hand up and down." He kissed her again, and added, "My wanton wife."

Quite enjoying being called wanton, she followed his instructions, even more pleased when he moaned again and deepened the already passionate kiss.

Her heart swelled that she, whom he had called the ice queen, brought her experienced husband to abandon.

Marriage, after all, might not be so bad. Especially with Simon Beckham.

A YEAR AGO, IF SOMEONE WOULD HAVE TOLD SIMON TO ENVISION the scene that was occurring at that moment, he would have laughed in their face. And Simon had an excellent imagination.

But even more surprising was the fact that he had so much love in his heart for his wife.

Life was a wonder.

As she continued to stroke him, quite expertly, he admitted, his restraint grew thin. Not only had it been a while since he'd been with a woman—what with getting Drake's affairs in order before Honoria gave birth, his recent bout of malaria, and his unexpected marriage to Charlotte—but the love tugging at his heart as he brought his wife to release overwhelmed him.

If she continued, he wouldn't last. And that wouldn't do. He'd never needed to join with a woman more than he did his beautiful wife. To show her, even if he couldn't tell her, how much he adored her.

He stayed her hand. "Charlotte. As much as I love what you're doing, you must stop, or I will finish by your hand. And I would very"—he kissed her—"very"—he kissed her again—"very much like to consummate our marriage."

Worry reared its ugly head. With the loss of her mother so early in Charlotte's life, did she have a woman to explain things to her? And if so, were the words kind and encouraging? And what had Felix *tried* to do to her? He stroked her face, the worry mixing with love. Dread snaked up his spine at the thought of hurting her. "Sweetheart? How much do you know about the act? Our marriage was so rushed."

"A little. Honoria said it was wonderful, and she felt like she had come home. But, of course, she loves Drake."

A knife ripped through Simon with Charlotte's unspoken words. Of course, Charlotte didn't love him. He almost laughed at the irony that it was precisely what he'd asked for in a wife. One who wouldn't grieve at his death.

But at that moment, he wanted more than anything for his wife to return the new and exciting emotion filling his heart. "Did she say anything about the actual act? What happens?" He highly doubted it. Honoria was as modest as her husband.

"She said enough—about the joining of bodies." Charlotte cast her gaze down, her delicate fingers still wrapped around his arousal. "I surmised the rest."

Thank God! "Not only wanton but amazingly intelligent."

She frosted him with a glare. "Amazingly? You doubt my intelligence?"

Damn! Love had dulled his brain. How could he forget his wife's skill at delivering retorts? "Can I take that back? Not the intelligent part, the—"

She stopped his ramblings with a kiss. "I'm bamming you. I know what you meant."

"Wanton, and a tease. My favorite combination." His short-lived grin vanished. He needed to prepare her mentally as well as physically. "There may be some pain the first time. I'll do my best to be gentle but tell me if it's too uncomfortable."

"I'm not afraid of pain," she said. "But thank you for telling me."

"It's only the first time. Then it will be only pleasure, I promise." Possessed with—what he believed was—a stroke of genius, he rolled on his back. "Now, straddle me and have your way with me."

"I—what do I do?" Lines formed between her eyes, and he smoothed them with his finger.

"I'll help you. But most of it will come naturally." With a

gentle tug on her arm, he pulled her over him. "On your knees. That's it." Then he positioned his erection at her entrance. "Remember. You're in control. Lower yourself on me at your own pace."

The moment her sweet, wet flesh touched him, he fought back the urge to thrust forward and imbed himself in her softness, but he gritted his teeth and allowed her to take charge.

She frowned again. "It won't fit."

"It will. Trust me." He practically growled the words. Lord, at that pace, she would kill him.

Finally, he breeched her entrance as she lowered herself inch by maddeningly sweet inch. He grabbed her hips for purchase, gently encouraging her onward.

When he reached her maidenhead, she stopped, her gaze locking with his as if she knew the implication.

"Allow me to take over for one moment?" he asked, his voice sounding more animal than human.

She gave one quick bob of her head, her dark curls fanning over her shoulders and covering her breasts.

The glorious sight would be forever burned in his mind. His wanton goddess.

"Forgive me," he said, then thrust forward with one quick stroke.

"Oh!" Her cry was little more than a soft yelp, but still it knifed at his heart. Guilt ate at him for hurting her.

He forced himself to still inside her, and lifting his shoulders off the bed, pulled her down for a kiss. "Forgive me." Other words clung to his tongue, but he withheld them lest she think them meaningless and declared out of lust. "Let me know when the pain eases."

She blinked. "That was the pain you mentioned?" His wicked, beautiful wife grinned at him. "That was nothing."

Oh, God, how he adored her. His warrior, his wanton tease. His ice queen who melted in his arms. In his mind, he whispered,

I love you. She was perfect for him, the thought returning him to the moment—as if he could forget. Perfect was inadequate. She fit him as if she were made for him alone. So tight he could barely contain himself. And she hadn't even begun moving again.

He swallowed, preparing himself. "When you're ready, you can move. I'll help you if you don't mind." He patted his hands against her luscious hips. He'd barely managed a breath, and she moved, the pleasure shooting up his spine and down his legs—his whole body on fire for her.

Guiding her, lifting her hips and settling her back onto him, he wouldn't last long, but he'd give anything to make her climax again.

If he were only above her, he knew exactly what to do—the angle, the perfect spot. From her expression, he could see her grasping for release again. "Mind if I take over?" Mentally, he pleaded with her to say *Yes.*

When she complied—the word barely from her lips—he flipped her over, apologizing with a deep kiss, the taste of her only intensifying his desire. He had so many places he wished to taste. But they would have to wait.

He lifted her legs, wrapping them around his waist, then twisted his hips to thrust deep inside for the one spot—*ah.*

Charlotte's lips parted, her head falling back and eyelids dropping shut, telling him he'd found it.

With each thrust, he sensed her growing closer, tightening around him. "That's it, my wanton goddess. Let it wash over you again. Fall apart in my arms."

She cried out again, her fingers digging into his arms.

He didn't even mind the pain. Holding on for as long as he could while she rode the pleasure of her climax, he thrust deep and hard, hoping it wasn't too rough for her.

And then he fell apart in his wife's arms, admitting he was completely and hopelessly lost.

CHAPTER 32

L ost in the warmth of Simon's embrace, Charlotte marveled at the new sensations that had racked her body. Honoria was correct. It *was* wonderful. A bit unsettling, but wonderful nonetheless.

Simon eased off her, but continued to hold her close, tucking her into his side and stroking her hair. "Now, that wasn't so bad, was it?" he asked, his low chuckle teasing her.

She swatted his arm. "You're ridiculous. And don't be so full of yourself. You simply took me by surprise." She buried her face against his chest, hiding her smile.

He chuckled again, the sensual purr rippling across her skin like gentle waves of pure delight. "Then I look forward to surprising you on a daily basis."

Daily? Oh, my! His words thrilled her. Not only that she also anticipated experiencing such pleasure on a daily basis, but that her husband found her desirable enough to pursue her regularly.

Soft chest hair tickled her nose, and the scent of him— sandalwood and shaving soap—mingled with the lemon of her own as if affirming their union.

"So you enjoyed it?" she asked, her fingers playing with the dark hair around his navel.

No chuckle, but a full-throated laugh rumbled through his chest and vibrated against her cheek. "Immensely. And if your fingers continue their teasing, I will want to enjoy it again, but your body needs to recover."

In answer, she yawned. Sleep beckoned her, inviting her with open arms. And for once, she would go willingly. No night terrors would dare disturb her. Not while she felt so safe in Simon's care. Even the distant rumble of thunder, barely audible in the quiet room, had no hold on her that evening.

Not while Simon was with her.

Simon would protect her and soothe her.

"Will you stay with me?" she asked, trying to keep the pleading from her voice.

"Of course." Tipping up her chin with his finger, he placed a soft kiss on her lips, then grinned. "This bed is more comfortable than the one in the other room."

Gah! The cad! She should have known he couldn't be serious. The thought was sobering. Why should she expect anything else from him? Theirs was not a love match like Honoria and Drake, or Nash and Adalyn. And although she admitted her feelings for her husband had changed—softened to affection—at the moment, she was grateful she didn't love him.

To love him when he would never return that love would be unbearable. She'd endured enough rejection to last a lifetime. It was bad enough to think of the other women—Joy and Hester Pace no doubt only two among many unnamed ladies—Simon had lain with.

"How does Honoria stand it?" she whispered.

Simon pulled back, meeting her gaze. "What?"

"Thinking about the other women Drake has been with." It had to be infinitely worse when one loved the other person.

"Honoria doesn't have to worry about that." Muscles in

Simon's arm grew taut, and his gentle strokes ceased, belying the casual tone of his voice and leaving the unspoken words *like you do* dangling between them like a sword of Damocles.

A weed of jealousy sprouted in her chest, thinking about the intimacy of the act, the closeness, the sharing of each other's bodies and that Simon had given himself to other women.

He gave her side a little tug. "Thank goodness you don't love me."

Odd, even though she had said practically the same words to herself moments before, hearing him utter them cut through her.

With a heavy heart, she lifted the armor she'd just discarded and put it back in place. Where it belonged. "Quite. And thank goodness you don't love me. But perhaps we've crossed a bridge and have reached peaceful coexistence."

Something flickered in his eyes, but he cast his gaze away so quickly, she might have imagined it. "A truce," he said. "All weapons to be left outside the bedroom."

"And around the family," she added. In the short time she'd known them, she'd begun to think of Simon's family as her own. Even if she couldn't—wouldn't—love Simon, she would love his parents and sisters, and possibly be loved in return. Warmth spread through her at the thought, and she snuggled closer to Simon.

"Yes." With his unfocused gaze directed at the dark ceiling, he resumed stroking her arm. "Thank you for your kindness to them. To Georgie in particular. It means a lot to me that—if something happens to me—you will look out for them. They couldn't have a fiercer ally."

"And we must work on providing an heir and securing their future." And hers.

His grin returned. "I object to the word work, as it is no hardship at all to make love to my beautiful, wanton wife." To prove his point, he kissed her with such fervor, he made her head spin—almost enough to erase the word *love* from her mind.

But not quite. Her heart pinged. "You said make love."

He stilled, his eyes flaring slightly. "If I recall, you seem to object to the other words used to describe the act."

Of course he meant nothing by the word. It was only a way to protect her *delicate* sensibilities. How naïve of her. "Well, since I'm wanton, you are permitted to use more appropriate words to indicate your true feelings toward"—she waved her hand over their bodies and rumpled bed linens—"what we did. If nothing else, let us promise to be truthful with each other."

Heavy silence stretched between them, ominous and portentous.

What else had he been keeping from her?

The ridiculous grin vanished.

"Charlotte," he said, his tone so serious, so *grave*, her stomach knotted, and bile rose in her throat.

Light scratching at the door drew her attention away, and she sat upright. "Trifle! Where is she?"

"She raced out when I came in. Stay there. I'll let her in." He bolted from the bed, giving her a full view of his glorious backside and muddling her mind again.

As Simon opened the door, Trifle raced in, her little body shivering.

"Oh, the poor baby," Charlotte said, holding out her hands and motioning Simon to give her the kitten.

"What mischief have you been up to, little miss?" He scooped up the kitten and placed a kiss on its head before settling her in Charlotte's hands. "Although I must catch some fresh fish to reward her for not interrupting us at a crucial moment."

Climbing back into the bed next to her, Simon gave an exaggerated yawn. "Shall we all try to get some sleep?"

Occupied cuddling and calming Trifle, Charlotte gazed over to find Simon lying on his side, facing away from her. "Simon? You were going to say something."

He answered her with a soft snore.

Resigned, Charlotte stretched out next to him, snuggling Trifle between them. "Maybe I don't want to know. But you love me, don't you, Trifle?"

The cat purred and burrowed under her chin.

"Thank you," she whispered in the dark.

🙞❧🙜

GUILT SOURED SIMON'S STOMACH AS HE SQUEEZED HIS EYES SHUT and feigned sleep. Charlotte's exhortation to promise to be truthful with each other ate away at him. Of course, he wouldn't lie to her. But was it dishonest to withhold information as well?

What purpose would it serve to tell Charlotte he loved her? Would it make her uncomfortable because she didn't return his love? Would she say the words back and not mean them? And which would hurt more? Questions banged around in his skull.

No. Trifle had saved him from an egregious misstep, giving him time to remember Charlotte's earlier declaration: *And thank goodness you don't love me.*

Damn her to use my words back at me!

Charlotte didn't want his love. And what was love if not striving to make the other person happy? Hell if he knew.

Damn! Damn! Damn!

No wonder he avoided the cursed emotion for so long. The bloody thing was damn messy.

Resolved to prove his love by keeping his feelings to himself, he tried to sleep. Perhaps all would be clear in the morning.

A new day, a new start, a new adventure.

Trifle's soft fur brushed his back, the kitten purring contentedly between him and his wife.

Would there always be something between them, keeping them from a true marriage?

He pushed the painful thought from his mind, seeking and gradually finding the bliss of sleep.

Lost in pleasant dreams, Simon startled awake when something smacked him in the head. "Oooff."

Meow. Perched on his head, Trifle's little face looked down at him. Her tiny paw—claws extended—stretched out for his cheek.

"Oh, no, you don't," he whispered, snatching the kitten up and away from his face.

The delicious warmth pressed against him moaned.

Fully alert, he gazed down at the arm wrapped around his waist. Charlotte's hand draped low across him, skimming his morning erection as she snuggled closer.

Even in her sleep, she was wanton. Would she be recovered enough for a repeat performance of the previous night's activities? Before he could ponder it further, Trifle meowed again.

"We both need the necessary, eh, girl?"

Charlotte stirred again at his whispered question, and Simon put his finger to his lips as if Trifle would understand the gesture. Gently—and reluctantly—lifting Charlotte's hand from his body, he carefully scooted off the bed, kitten tucked securely in his arms.

After cracking the door to allow Trifle out, Simon strode to the water closet and relieved himself. As he pulled on his trousers, Charlotte stirred again, her arm reaching out as if searching for him.

When his stomach growled, he padded to the window and tugged back the curtain enough to peek out.

Low on the horizon, the sun poked up its bright head. The storm had cleared completely. Puddles on the wet ground bore witness to the torrent that had tormented Charlotte the night before.

Simon turned back, gazing at his sleeping wife. The bed linens had slipped down seductively, exposing her bare back yet covering her gorgeous derrière. Dark hair fanned out on the pillow and flowed down her back unfettered. Sprawled out before him like a feast, his wanton goddess made his mouth water.

How different she looked from the woman he'd first met. Prim and proper in every appearance and every action, Lady Charlotte Talbot never had a hair out of place or bow untied. She wore her icy demeanor like armor, deterring anyone from coming too close and seeing the *real* Charlotte and shielding her from harm.

Unbidden, his hand lifted to his chest, rubbing at the strange ache beneath, privileged to have been giving a peek at the vulnerable woman she hid so well. *I love you.* He mouthed the words silently, hoping it fulfilled his promise to be truthful.

His stomach growled again, and enjoying one lingering look at his wanton goddess, he strode from the room to seek out breakfast.

After confirming Trifle had been let outside to do her business, he satisfied his enormous appetite. Finished, he prepared a tray for Charlotte and returned to their bedchamber.

He smiled. *Our bedchamber.*

Would she be recovered enough for another session of lovemaking? After she had eaten, of course. Simon wasn't that selfish. Besides, she would need her strength. He chuckled to himself as he slipped back in the room.

"Charlotte," he whispered, placing the tray on a bedside table. He pressed a kiss between her shoulder blades. "Wake up, slugabed. I have breakfast for you."

"Ugh. Go away." She lifted an arm and waved it at him, then it fell bonelessly onto the mattress.

He kissed her again. Inch by glorious inch, his lips traversed down her back until he reached the bed linens. "These are in my way," he said, tugging them down. As he placed a kiss on each side of her dimpled bottom, she rolled over, giving him a full view of her voluptuous breasts and thatch of maidenhair.

"Even better," he murmured against her navel before climbing on the bed and moving southward, completely forgetting his promise to allow her to eat breakfast.

Eyes wide, she looked up. "What are you—oh!" Her head fell back against the pillow as his mouth found the sensitive area between her legs.

Although he'd satisfied his stomach, it would seem his heart would never have his fill of her.

Sweet, the taste of her like honey. How could he have ever thought her a harpy or an ice queen? His goddess was fire, a hellcat, as she grabbed tufts of his hair and held him to her, finally shuddering with her release.

"Good morning." From between her legs, he gazed up at her, thoroughly enjoying the view.

"Am I to be awoken like this every morning?" she asked, her eyes hazy but not from sleep.

He wiped his mouth on the rumpled sheets. "If you wish. Or"—he grinned—"you could wake me in a similar fashion should you wake first."

Pink colored her cheeks. "Then I shall be sure to sleep later than you."

The minx. "No doubt, as I'm an early riser." He crawled to the other side of the bed and stretched out beside her. "So you enjoyed that, did you? And if you expected to disappoint me with that vow, rest assured, I enjoy doing it as much as you enjoy receiving."

The blush deepened. "I doubt that."

He laughed. "Fair point. Although I do hope someday you may find yourself willing to reciprocate. Remember"—he winked—"you would be in complete control."

"You are in—"

"Corrigible?"

"I was going to say insatiable."

"Ah." He nodded. "That, too." Hovering above her, he placed a hand against her cheek and gazed into those dark eyes. Lord, he could fall into them if he let himself.

"How do you do that?"

"What?" He grinned—not his usual devil-may-care grin he adorned when flirting, but his I'm-so-damned-happy grin.

"Make a woman feel like she's the only one in the world?"

Ah, that was easy. "Because, for me, you are." He kissed her lips. "Now, have some breakfast before you tempt me further. You're likely too tender for anything else. I'll call Rose and have water heated for your bath."

With difficulty, he forced himself to rise from the bed and his beautiful wife. He placed the tray before her. "Now eat before the drinking chocolate grows cold. I know you like it."

When her mouth opened to a surprised little *O*, he knew he'd pleased her.

"After I wash and dress, I'm going fishing. I promised Trifle some fresh fish for being so considerate last evening."

"Considerate!? She was shut out."

"Apologize then?"

Occupied with her breakfast, Charlotte didn't answer.

Simon cast her one more glance before slipping out the door, marveling at how his luck had changed.

He whistled softly as he entered his room and tugged the bell pull for Brown. Perhaps he'd even catch Gus.

CHAPTER 33

Once Charlotte had eaten, bathed, and dressed, she sought out Simon. Her blush had finally cooled, although truth be told, each time she thought of him kissing her—there—her cheeks heated anew.

My, but the man was talented. No wonder so many women pursued him—that particular thought souring her stomach.

He promised to be faithful, but could she trust him? Did she even really know him? She had no definitive answer to the first question, but the second was a decided *no*.

"Have you seen Mr. Beckham?" she asked John, the footman.

"He went fishing, my lady."

Right. He'd said as much after he had thoroughly discombobulated her with his tongue. Her cheeks flamed again.

"He requested his curricle be readied in case you wished to spend time at the main house. I would be happy to drive you."

A deliciously wicked idea popped into her head. "That won't be necessary, John. I'll drive myself."

After donning a bonnet, pelisse, and kid leather gloves, she climbed into the curricle John had brought to the front of the house.

John cast her a dubious glance. "Have you driven one before, ma'am?"

"No. But how hard can it be?" An experienced rider, she presumed controlling the animals would be similar. She took the whip from him, reluctant to use it on the sleek animals. "Do you hit them with it?" she asked, unable to keep the horrified tone from her voice. She'd always refused to use a crop when riding.

"Oh, no, my lady. Never. Just crack it above them. The sound alone spurs them faster."

Relief flooded her. Then the rest of John's response landed as hard. *Faster.* She set the whip on the seat next to her and picked up the ribbons. The two matched chestnuts raised their heads in readiness, and Charlotte snapped the ribbons as she'd seen Simon do—careful not to strike the horses' backs.

The carriage jerked forward. "Oomph!" Charlotte refrained from reaching for her bonnet and instead held tight to the reins.

"Be careful, my lady!" John's voice drifted off behind her.

Charlotte's confidence grew as she guided the horses forward, following close to the path she'd walked the day before. Moving at a trot at first, the horses seemed to yearn to break free into a gallop.

Or was that her imagination? Perhaps she'd been around Simon too long. She laughed at the notion, then picked up the whip. "Please don't let me hit them," she mumbled, then cracked it in the air above them.

The horses broke into a gallop, throwing Charlotte back against the small bench-like seat's back. "Oomph!" she said again, a little more loudly.

Wind rushed against her face, the smell of the previous night's rain, fresh and clean, tempting her nose. A rabbit scurried from the path ahead of her, and her heart rose to her throat, hoping the horses didn't trample the little thing. She imagined it shaking its little fist in the air and cursing her for her reckless driving.

By the time she reached the main house and pulled back on the ribbons, she was windblown and completely exhilarated. A footman opened the door and raced forward to hold the horses. Mrs. Beckham hurried forward. "Charlotte! Oh, my dear! Is something amiss?"

As the footman assisted her down from the curricle—which she no longer considered a death trap—she laughed. "Not at all. Simon is off fishing again, and I've come to call."

Mrs. Beckham held a handkerchief to her bosom. "Oh, thank goodness." She wrapped an arm around Charlotte's waist and led her inside the house. "Although I should definitely have a talk with my son about leaving his lovely wife alone so frequently this early in your marriage."

How quickly Charlotte had grown to like Simon's family. "It truly is fine, Mrs. Beckham. Simon grows so fidgety if he isn't doing something, he would drive me mad if I insisted he stay in the house with me."

Mrs. Beckham's smile widened. "My son chose wisely when he married you. You understand him well. Call me Judith, Charlotte. Remember?" The warmth in Judith's eyes pinged Charlotte's heart but not as much as Judith's next words. "Or Mother."

As Judith instructed a servant to bring tea, Charlotte marveled at her good fortune. Who would have imagined being caught in a scandalous situation would have such a positive outcome? Not only had Simon made good on his promise not to force her in the marriage bed, he'd actually proven to be a gentle and giving husband.

That alone would have satisfied Charlotte, but she'd also gained a loving family and a beautiful home. The Beckhams had welcomed her with open arms, and although Judith would never completely fill the void left by Charlotte's mother, acceptance into their family overwhelmed her. Never one prone to tears, a strange sensation pricked Charlotte's eyes.

But would the Beckhams be so accepting if they knew the real reason Simon had married her?

As she settled onto the sofa next to her mother-in-law, the truth burdened Charlotte. "Judith, there is something you must know about my marriage to Simon."

"If you're talking about what the scandal sheets reported, I don't put much credence in gossip." Judith's cheeks darkened. "Although I will admit I enjoy reading it."

Charlotte blinked. "You knew?" Charlotte's appreciation of the woman's kindness increased tenfold. "Well, in my case, it's true. Part of it anyway. Simon married me to save my reputation. Ours is not a love match."

With her lips pressed together, Judith delivered a look perfected by all mothers when chastising their children. "Charlotte. I have eyes. You may not love my son—yet—but Simon's heart is yours. It's written all over his face every time he looks at you."

In the past, such a statement would have resulted in Charlotte suggesting the individual consider acquiring spectacles, but she held her tongue. She was enjoying the newfound relationship with Simon's family too much to jeopardize it.

Luckily, Judith continued, patting Charlotte's hand. "And I have no doubt in time Simon will win you over. He has a way about him."

Indeed. A way he used on all women. Perhaps Judith's active imagination was selective, and the affection she witnessed on Simon's face was no different from when he gazed at any other woman.

A maid deposited a tray with tea and scones, and Judith poured them both a cup. She handed one to Charlotte. "In fact, I would venture to say you're on your way to loving him," Judith continued, apparently not able to drop the subject. "You have a certain glow about you this morning."

Charlotte choked on her tea.

Judith's eyes crinkled at the corners as she gazed at Charlotte over the rim of her cup.

Salvation rushed to her aid in the form of Georgie. "Charlotte!" She plopped next to Charlotte on the sofa, her dark curls bouncing against her slender shoulders. "You came back!"

"Of course she did," Judith said. "She's family."

Oh. That strange pricking occurred in her eyes again.

"Where's Simon?" Georgie asked.

"Fishing," Charlotte said, happy to have Georgie change the subject. "How is Sir Night of the Meow Table faring? Was he frightened of the storm last night?"

Georgie's blue eyes widened. "He was! How did you know? Was Trifle scared, too?"

"Not as frightened as I was." Goodness, did she just admit that? She blamed it on the Beckhams and their unfailing acceptance.

"Oh, you're being silly," Georgie said, giving Charlotte a gracious out.

A footman entered, then lowered a silver salver toward Judith.

Charlotte recognized the cream-colored parchment Judith lifted from the tray.

A copy of *The Muckraker* had made its way to Wiltshire.

SIMON WHISTLED AS A FAT BROWN TROUT FLOPPED IN HIS NET. "Ah. You will make a fine reward for Trifle." Not even the fact Gus had evaded his lures yet again could sour Simon's mood.

Sunlight dappled the ground and streaked the river's surface. Fish had descended deeper, reducing his chances of any further catches. Simon packed up his tackle and headed back to the house, eager to see Charlotte again.

Had he really missed her after only being apart for a few hours?

Perhaps loving someone, being in love, wasn't so bad after all. At least Charlotte didn't love him in return. When he finally succumbed to the accursed malaria, she wouldn't grieve. And if things continued as they had the previous night, she would have a child to dote upon and occupy her mind. Perhaps many children.

He quickened his pace at the idea of making said children.

When he arrived at the cottage, John told him Charlotte had taken the curricle.

"You didn't offer to drive her?" Simon asked, unsure if he was more surprised or angry.

"I did, sir, but she insisted." John leaned forward, his gaze casting around him before whispering, "She can be rather frightening, sir."

Simon laughed. "Indeed. And her bite is even worse than her bark. She punched Albert Mooney in the nose."

John's eyes widened. "She didn't?!"

"She did. It was glorious to see. Bloodied him good." Just remembering the fire in Charlotte's eyes spurred him to find her. "Have Joseph ready a horse for me, and here"—he handed John the basket with his catch—"have Madge clean this and prepare it for Trifle."

John peeked in the basket, his brow lifting. "The whole fish for the kitten, sir?"

Simon scrunched his lips together and huffed. "Perhaps not the whole fish. But as much as Trifle wants, then Madge can do what she wants with the rest."

John nodded and raced off, no doubt imaging a good fish pie for his supper.

Charlotte driving his curricle. Simon shook his head. He'd love to have seen it. Perhaps he'd leave the horse at the main house and have Charlotte drive them both back. Back and forth, he paced in front of the cottage. *What is keeping Joseph?* Simon could have been halfway to the main house already.

Finally, the groom approached with Simon's favorite horse, Max. Not waiting, Simon rushed forward and mounted, taking off like a shot and leaving a trail of windblown cherry blossoms in his wake.

Upon arriving at the main house, he tossed the reins to a groom and his hat to a footman. "Where is my wife?" *My wife.* Damn, but he'd grown to like the sound of that. *My wanton wife.* Even better.

"In the drawing room with your mother, sir."

At the doorway to the room, he paused.

With her back to him, Charlotte had her head bowed. Trepidation tickled up his spine. What was wrong? However, when Georgie looked up from her place beside Charlotte and grinned at him, he relaxed.

He held a finger to his lips and sent his sister a conspiratorial wink, catching his mother's attention as well. Then, silently, he tiptoed up behind Charlotte and placed his hands over her eyes.

"Guess who?" He placed a soft kiss on the nape of her neck.

"Someone who has been catching fish. Ugh, Simon, your hands reek of it."

Blast. Right. The woman had him so befuddled he didn't even think to wash his hands before rushing off to see her. "At least you acknowledge I caught some. One, to be exact. Trifle shall feast upon it."

Georgie stuck out her bottom lip. "You didn't bring any for Nightly? You are my least favorite brother."

Simon tousled Georgie's curls. "I'm your only brother." The statement reminded him of his duty to his family and, more pleasantly, the prospect of producing an heir.

But as he gazed down, he saw the reason for Charlotte's bowed head. He plucked *The Muckraker* from her hand.

"What the devil is this doing here?" His gaze darted toward his mother. "Are you still sending for this tripe?" He waved the detestable paper before him.

Chagrin painted his mother's face. As well it should! "I meant to cancel my subscription. Truly I did."

"Hmm. A likely story." He scanned the contents, his gaze snagging on the name Felix Davies.

Reports have indicated Simon Beckham has whisked his new wife, Lady Charlotte Talbot Beckham, off to Wiltshire away from the prying eyes of society. One can only guess at the reason, but this reporter speculates that the new Mrs. Beckham is increasing. No doubt the couple will welcome a birth before the decent period of nine months has passed.

Felix Davies, who had courted Lady Charlotte, and in fact had proposed marriage, is heartbroken. Witnesses state Lord Felix is appalled at Lady Charlotte's scandalous behavior, wondering—if he had in fact married her—would the first child of their union even be his?

Simon tossed the gossip rag aside. "I should call him out."

His mother gasped, and Georgie let out a whoop of excitement.

The more sensible of the three, Charlotte arched a brow. "Who? The Worm or the perpetrator of *The Muckraker?*"

"Both." Anger bubbled in his veins like molten lava.

"The Worm?" Georgie asked Charlotte.

"Lord Felix," Charlotte answered. "Although he doesn't deserve the honorific. He's lower than a worm, but it's the best I can do." Charlotte turned her attention to him. "There is something about the article that is bothering me."

Simon huffed. "Well, that's obvious."

She waved it away. "Not what you're thinking. There's a clue in there somewhere. I can feel it."

Simon moved around, nudged Georgie away, and sat next to

his wife. "About the identity of the instigator of *this?*" He lifted the wadded-up gossip sheet.

Her eyes full of questions, his mother's gaze bounced between him and Charlotte.

"May we tell Mother?" he asked. When Charlotte nodded, he proceeded. "Charlotte and her friends are on a mission to unmask the perpetrator."

"Oooh. How exciting." His mother straightened, and he could envision the wheels turning in her mind, no doubt hoping to become part of the quest. "And you think the article provides a clue?"

"Yes. It's there, tickling my brain"—she motioned at her head —"but it's eluding me. Why is there so much attention on us in the last few issues? It's the height of the Season, and the other bits of gossip in that rag are benign reports. Who cares about Lord Middlebury's gout?"

"Do you think the cad has a vendetta against us in particular?" Simon asked.

"I don't know." To her knowledge, the scandal sheet had not reported Simon's impromptu visit to the gaming hell on their wedding night. Not that she wanted to mention that in front of Judith. "Judith, when did you receive the issue prior to this?"

Judith darted a chagrined glance toward Simon. "Right before we received word from Simon about your betrothal, the one we were discussing earlier."

"And you receive every issue?"

"I will cancel, I promise."

"It's fine, Judith. No one is blaming you for the havoc this blackguard wreaks with his pen." Charlotte pressed her lips together, frustrated the answer danced just beyond her reach.

"Perhaps you need a distraction. To clear your mind," Simon said, waggling his brows.

Pink darkened Charlotte's cheeks, and his mother lifted a hand to cover her mouth.

"What?" Georgie asked, her blue eyes narrowed.

"Never you mind." Simon waved a finger at his sister before returning his attention to Charlotte. "What say you, Lady Wife? Would you care for a ride?"

Georgie's body straightened to attention. "Can I come?"

"No," both he and his mother said in unison.

"You are incorrigible," Charlotte muttered.

Leaning in, he whispered, "And don't forget. Insatiable."

Eager to return to the cottage, Simon rose and offered his hand, pleased when Charlotte slipped hers into it willingly and—dare he hope—as anxious as he to be alone?

"Before you go," his mother said, rising to bid them goodbye. "The town's May Day celebration is two weeks from now. Everyone will expect you both, to wish you joy upon your marriage."

"Not everyone," Simon muttered, thinking of Samuel.

Charlotte glanced toward him. Then his goddess came to his rescue. "Is there anything I can do to help?"

The beam of joy on his mother's face warmed his heart. "I hoped you would offer. I'm on the committee for food and decorations, and with old Mrs. Bailey's rheumatism acting up, we're short a person. Your experience among the *ton* will surely give our yearly gathering a touch of elegance."

"Mother is very proud of her part in things, but I think she's right."

"Well, I would be happy to assist. Besides"—she graced Simon with a mischievous grin that displayed her dimple—"I'll need something to occupy myself while Simon is fishing."

Lord, he needed to get her back to the cottage as fast as possible. After a quick goodbye, he escorted Charlotte from the room, calling to a footman to bring his curricle around.

As they waited at the front door, he pulled her close. "I can't believe you drove over here yourself."

Charlotte squared her shoulders, and he kicked himself for possibly offending her. He needed to be in her good graces.

"And why not? I'm just as capable as any man."

"Well, if you drive like you pack a punch, I would say not only as capable, but more capable. I only meant you seemed to dislike fast vehicles."

"Only because I'm not in control. Once I got used to it, I found it most exhilarating."

With the carriage awaiting, he handed her up. "Did you drive fast?"

When she nodded, he climbed in beside her and handed her the ribbons. "Then, by all means, take us back to the cottage posthaste."

A quick snap of the ribbons, and Charlotte had the horses taking off so quickly, Simon had to hold on to his hat.

He liked this marriage business, and he liked his wife.

No. Scratch that. He loved his wife.

CHAPTER 34

The two weeks before the May Day celebration passed in a blur. Charlotte's days were filled with committee meetings, creating the decorations—she did more overseeing than creating them herself—and planning the food items. Everyone on the committee listened to her opinion with rapt attention, eager to have their modest celebration rival that of *ton* gatherings.

As for her nights—and sometimes her afternoons and mornings—she spent them in Simon's arms. He continued to be a generous and giving husband, providing her time alone or giving her his undivided attention as she needed it. Their lovemaking continued to surprise her—often gentle, with whispered words and tender caresses, but at times more vigorous —as Simon described it. Once he didn't even wait to get her to the bed, but braced her against the door of their bedroom, lifting her body and rucking up skirts so she could wrap her legs around his waist.

Surprised to discover she rather liked such spontaneity, Charlotte concluded her perspective had changed because she trusted her husband. When she rewarded his impromptu expressions of affection, he vowed to surprise her often.

And with each passing day, she grew to care for him more.

Instead of seeing Simon as a rake who used his smile and easy manner to manipulate and control others, she acknowledged his genuine joie de vivre. Simon simply loved life and lived it to the fullest. Rather than constantly annoy her, his sunny disposition became contagious, and she found herself laughing frequently. Being married to Simon Beckham had changed her.

For good.

The day before the May Day celebration, Charlotte sat at the escritoire in the parlor of their cottage, poring over the last-minute food changes she had suggested. Lost in her task, she startled when hands pressed over her eyes and warm breath brushed against her neck.

"Guess who?" Simon whispered in her ear.

"John. I thought you'd never arrive. Quick, undress! We must hurry before my husband returns!"

Simon's hands dropped from her face, and she held her breath. When she turned to face him, he stared wide-eyed, his mouth gaping open like one of the fish he would catch. Had he misinterpreted her joke and taken offense?

Then he threw back his head and laughed. "Minx!" He pulled her from the chair and enveloped her in his arms, kissing her soundly. "As if I don't keep you busy enough." He kissed her again, his lips traveling down her neck to skim the bodice of her gown. "But if you ever decide to take me off guard like that again, please give me fair warning. My heart nearly stopped."

"Where would be the fun in warning you?"

He laughed, the sound vibrating against her skin in sensual ripples. "Who are you and what have you done with my prim and proper wife?"

"You don't like this side of me?" She sent him a saucy grin.

"I love every side of you. Which speaking of"—he hooked a

finger in her bodice and pulled it down. "Since you were expecting a rendezvous with our footman who, I should mention, is old enough to be your father, let it not be said I don't aim to please my wife." He turned toward the open door. "John! My wife wants—"

She slapped a hand over his mouth and tugged up her bodice. "You wouldn't dare!" Her face flamed as John appeared in the doorway.

"Yes, sir?"

Simon only grinned at her before saying, "My wife wants a bit of privacy. If you would ensure we're not disturbed."

She breathed a sigh of relief when John left, closing the door behind him.

"Now"—her husband pulled her into his arms again— "where were we?"

After a quick peck on his nose, she placed a hand on his chest and pushed. "None of that. Mother is coming over to review everything for tomorrow."

He hitched a dark brow. "You're calling her Mother?"

She blinked. Had she? The word had flowed effortlessly off her tongue. "She asked me to." And frankly, Charlotte wanted to. Certainty settled deep within her that the Beckhams had burrowed their way past her defenses and taken root in her heart.

Little by little, they had won her over. Like Elizabeth Bennet when she first saw Pemberley, Charlotte had fallen in love with their home, but it was a superficial love based on appearance.

Yet, as she witnessed the kindness, the warmth, and the affection dwelling within the house, Charlotte had come to understand what made it a home. The gentle teasing, the hugs of comfort, words of encouragement and praise filled the space until it overflowed to all who inhabited it.

An aching tenderness bloomed in her chest, and she pressed a hand to her bosom at the unfamiliar sensation, accepting the reason with surprise. She loved the Beckhams, and as she gazed at her husband's quizzical expression, she admitted she loved him, too. However, she refused to speak the words. Not when he had adamantly stated he didn't want a woman to love him. After all, they had made a pact, and she would abide by his wish.

It certainly had nothing to do with protecting herself.

"Now go!" She gave him a little push toward the door. "You'll be in the way."

At the entrance, he peered over his shoulder and graced her with his ridiculous grin. "We'll continue later."

And as he exited the room whistling, she hoped to conclude her business with Judith quickly.

Because she could hardly wait for *later*.

The next day, clouds gathered in the blue sky, fluffy and white like little puffs of cotton. Simon breathed a sigh as he looked out the window, relieved the view held no threat of storms.

He wanted the day to be perfect for Charlotte. She had worked so hard organizing the May Day celebration, he didn't want anything to spoil it. And although stormy weather dampened anyone's spirits, it paralyzed Charlotte.

"Are you going to stare out that window all morning, or are you going to finish dressing? The festivities begin in less than an hour," his bossy and adorable wife called.

Simon allowed the curtain to fall back into place. He'd lain in bed too long that morning, boneless and completely relaxed from their long sessions of lovemaking.

Lovemaking. He chuckled to himself, remembering the conversation he'd had with Charlotte when he proposed their arrangement and she had taken offense at the word sex.

Because making love was exactly what it had become to him.

Even in heated, frantic moments, he found it difficult to think of what they shared in the marriage bed as anything less.

He slipped his trousers on over his smalls and winked. "I was waiting in the event you wanted a repeat performance."

Charlotte's lips pressed together in a straight line, but the sparkle in her brown eyes gave her away. "You are . . ." She shook her head, then released the laugh she'd been withholding.

Yes, he wanted the day to be perfect for her. Not only because of her part in the town's celebration, but he had decided to confess his feelings for her.

He didn't expect her to reciprocate, but he wanted her to know she was loveable. That he loved her. Unconditionally.

Confident the perfect moment would reveal itself, Simon slipped the shirt over his head, then tucked it inside his trousers. "Promise me one thing."

"What?" Charlotte asked as she checked her appearance in the looking glass, which, in his opinion, was perfect.

"That when you dance with me this evening, you won't step on my feet."

Although she faced away from him, her smile rang in her voice. "What would be the fun of that?" She rose and strode toward him. "Plus, it will bring back fond memories."

"Fond for whom? Certainly not me. My toes hurt for days." Still, he pulled her into his arms. "But if it pleases you, stamp away. It will give me an excuse to refuse all the other ladies vying for my attention."

She slapped his chest. "You overestimate your charm, sir."

He hitched a brow. "Do I?" he asked, lacing as much seduction in his words as he possibly could, then lowered his head and captured her lips in a searing kiss.

Ten minutes later, he finally finished dressing, wishing to God they didn't have to leave so soon.

When they arrived in Swindon, the festivities were in full swing. Brightly colored streams of ribbons dangled from a tall pole in the middle of the town's main street. People had dressed in their finest for the occasion, waving as Simon pulled his curricle up and handed Charlotte down. It only took a moment for him to realize they were greeting Charlotte rather than him.

"You've attracted a crowd, Wife."

A girl about four-years-old approached, holding out a bunch of flowers. "For you."

Simon flung a hand to his heart. "For me? How thoughtful."

The child's dark curls bobbed as she shook her head and giggled. "No! For her." She pointed at Charlotte.

Simon couldn't help but imagine his own daughter with Charlotte's dark hair and eyes and feisty spirit. True, he needed a son, but he wanted a daughter just as much, especially if she looked like Charlotte.

Charlotte crouched before the child, smiling warmly. "Don't mind him. He's a bit of a nodcock. What's your name?"

The girl cast her gaze to the ground, then peeped up under her lashes, giving Charlotte a shy smile. "Lizzie."

"These are lovely, Lizzie. Thank you."

Flowers delivered in Charlotte's hands, Lizzie grinned up at Simon, then raced back to her family, burying her face in her mother's skirts and sneaking peeks at Charlotte and then Simon amid her giggles.

Simon sighed. "Charmed by a fair lady, only to have my heart broken once again."

"She's a little young for you, don't you think?" Charlotte's lips curved up slightly, making him want to kiss her right there in public.

"I want all ladies to feel special and beautiful. It's my mission in life. Besides, she might wind up with our son someday, and I want her to like me."

Charlotte's dark brow arched. "Our son, who isn't even possibly conceived?" She scoffed a laugh. "You have extraordinary faith in your abilities, husband. And she would be at least several years older."

"There's something to be said for older women. Speaking of"—he winked—"I never asked your age."

"Because it's rude to do so."

He waved it aside. "I should know how old my wife is, don't you think?"

"You first."

"Twenty-nine."

Her lips twitched as if holding in a secret.

Interesting. He most definitely needed to find a secluded spot and whisk her away for a kiss. "Your turn," he said.

"Also twenty-nine."

"Ah, but when is the date of your birth?"

She hesitated, then sighed. "Tomorrow, actually."

"And you didn't tell me?! We'll celebrate today." Keeping his voice casual, he added, "Mine isn't until December, Christmas Day, to be exact." He leaned in and whispered in her ear, "I rest my case about older women."

Before she could answer with a scathing retort, his gaze snagged on his family descending from their carriage, and he waved to catch their attention. "Our family has arrived."

Her lips opened in that enticing little *o*. Her eyes shimmered with a thin line of moisture forming at the rim. She blinked it away. "*Our* family?"

"Well, yes. You're a Beckham now whether you like it or not." Did she like it? He hoped so, but she averted her gaze so quickly, he worried he may have offended her. "Charlotte, I know you didn't choose me but—"

"Simon!" Georgie raced forward, throwing herself in his arms. At least his sisters liked him. Well, most of them, at least. Frannie and Beth were questionable.

"Georgie!" his mother said, rushing up and out of breath.

"How many times have I told you? It is not appropriate for a young lady to run."

"Oh, I don't know," Simon said. "Charlotte runs when I chase her around the bedroom. But then again, I just discovered she's older than I am, so—*oof*"

Charlotte elbowed him in the ribs, then completely ignoring her malicious action, smiled sweetly. "Your mother is correct, Georgie. It's not seemly." She gazed askance at Simon. "At least in public."

"Minx," he whispered for Charlotte's ears only.

His mother linked an arm into Charlotte's. "Ignore him, my dear. Let's inspect your handiwork. Simon, were you aware our Charlotte managed most of the details herself? Even Mrs. Bailey admitted to me she was impressed and has decided to bow out completely. Your wife is a marvel."

She was indeed. The evening couldn't come soon enough. Perhaps while they slipped outside the crowded assembly room and strolled in the moonlight, he would tell her he loved her more than the moon itself.

⚜

SATISFACTION OF A JOB WELL DONE SWELLED IN CHARLOTTE'S chest as she took in her surroundings. Garlands of flowers draped over shop doors, and windows displayed wreaths in vibrant colors. She couldn't wait to taste the food on the menu for the dance at the assembly that evening.

Simon pulled a white anemone from the bouquet Lizzie had given her.

Charlotte slapped his hand. "You're ruining it."

His lips curved upward, not as wide as his usual grin, but more thoughtful and . . . affectionate? "This particular flower belongs elsewhere." He tucked the flower into her hair above her

338

ear, then stood back to assess the effect. "Perfect. You make it even more beautiful."

Her stomach tumbled at the light in his blue eyes. If she didn't know better, she would think he—loved her. She dismissed the impossible notion. "Don't think your flattery will have me swooning at your feet. You forget who you're flirting with."

His laugh rolled over her skin, a wave of sensuous pleasure. "I could never forget that."

Georgie made a gagging sound, and Rebecca, Beth, and Frannie sighed.

Kate said, "I agree with Georgie. You two lovebirds are becoming sickening."

Charlotte dismissed Kate's comments as well as the others' reactions. Surely, they must be imagining things.

"Oh, dear," Judith said. "Samuel appears positively livid."

Sure enough, the baker glared at them from the doorway of his shop.

Simon grasped her by the elbow and whispered, "Let's steer clear of him as much as possible today."

And as the day progressed, they did exactly that. Samuel's accusatory glare faded into the background amid laughter and sunny smiles from the other townspeople.

During the maypole celebration, as dancers wove their colored ribbons around in intricate patterns. Georgie said, "I can't wait until I can join in the maypole dance."

Simon groaned. "Perhaps when you're eighty. You're already too devious for words. I shudder to think what mischief you will machinate when you're older."

Charlotte laughed. "Look who's speaking."

The dance ended and as children unwound the ribbons, the mischievousness Simon accused Georgie of glinted in his eyes. He tugged on Charlotte's hand. "Come, let's do the next one!"

"Isn't that more for couples courting?"

He only grinned, and her heart fluttered at the implication.

CHAPTER 35

Simon used every opportunity to flirt with Charlotte during their dance around the maypole. He purposely brushed his fingers against hers as they passed each other under loops of the vibrant ribbons. He winked, smiled, and delivered sultry gazes, promising every carnal delight he could imagine—and make no mistake, he imagined quite a few.

However, when the dance ended, he noticed more than Charlotte's darkened cheeks and lust-filled eyes. Hester speared a glare at Charlotte as if she wanted to wrap her hands around his wife's neck as tightly as the ribbons around said maypole.

Make that two people for them to avoid the remainder of the day.

They'd done a jolly good job of it, enjoying the festivities and each other. He couldn't remember when Charlotte had smiled and laughed as much as she had that day. He couldn't wait to hold her in his arms again, to see that smile—that dimple— forming for him alone.

When the dancing commenced in the assembly room, he bowed before her. "May I have the honor of this dance?"

"Men don't usually dance with their wives." She gave her fan a little snap, spreading the pleats apart and displaying a pastoral scene, and her brown eyes teasing above it.

"I think we've established I'm not one to follow the rules. Remember Drake's house party?"

Her laugh, low and throaty, heated his blood. "How could I forget?"

"Besides, this isn't a formal London ball of the *ton*. This is a country dance, with simple country folk who couldn't care less about rules of etiquette."

With another snap of her wrist, the fan closed. "Very well. They're your toes."

God, he loved her. "It's a small price to pay for holding you in my arms." He meant every word. If loving Charlotte meant enduring moments of pain to experience monumental joy, he would do so willingly.

"It's a country dance. There will be no *holding*."

"Then you must promise me the waltz as recompense for my sacrifice."

As she slipped her gloved fingers into his offered hand, she said, "You drive a hard bargain, sir."

And although touching her was limited to brief brushes of fingers, his toes remained surprisingly unscathed during the dance. Only at the final moment, when they faced each other to bow and curtsy, did she extend her slipper and press lightly on his foot.

When he led her from the dancefloor, she whispered, "Lest it be said I don't fulfill *my* promises."

Although the musicians weren't as skilled as those at London balls, nor the dancers as graceful, Simon wouldn't exchange his time with Charlotte at the simple country gathering for a thousand *ton* balls. His heart swelled with pride as man after man approached and practically begged for a chance to dance with her.

At first, he worried she would insult them with her sharp tongue, but she accepted each offer gracefully, smiling prettily even when she winced at her own stomped toes.

"You've done well, Son," his mother said, slipping beside him. "Charlotte has won over the whole town."

"Not the whole town." Simon tipped his head toward Hester. "I don't trust her, Mother. She has something up her sleeve."

His mother's eyes widened. "Charlotte or Hester?"

"Hester. I trust Charlotte with my life." Not mere words, the truth of them filled his whole body with light. He *did* trust her.

"Have you told her?"

Reluctantly, he pulled his gaze from Charlotte and turned toward his mother. "What? That I trust her?" He shook his head.

"No. That you love her. You forget I read that gossip rag. I know you married Charlotte out of a sense of duty. When did you discover you love her?"

He wouldn't break Charlotte's trust and tell his mother about Charlotte's fear of thunderstorms, but it was a valid question. "I would say it hit me like a lightning bolt, but I don't think that's precisely right. I think I fell little by little until I couldn't escape the truth. It's a sneaky bugger thing this love bit. I'd almost say insidious."

His mother slapped her fan on his arm. "Surely not! Love isn't harmful."

"Isn't it?" His gaze drifted to Samuel. Tucked in a dark corner, the baker stared holes into Simon. "Do you forget Joy?"

"Joy was a child. You both were."

"She loved me and ended up dead."

Compassion shone in his mother's eyes. "Joy was a troubled girl."

The room became stifling at the memory of Joy's lifeless face, and he struggled to breathe. "I'm going outside." He squeezed his mother's hand. "Don't worry. I'll be fine." He winked. "And I do plan to tell Charlotte this evening."

Carefully weaving his way from the crowded assembly hall, Simon finally reached the door, only to bump into Albie Mooney as the man stumbled against him.

"Watch where yer goin'," Mooney grumbled, his words slurred.

"You reek of whisky, Mooney. Go home and sleep it off before you get locked up again."

Mooney delivered an obscene gesture, then proceeded inside on shaking legs.

Simon shook his head in disgust. Three people to avoid. The list continued to grow, but he refused to have it spoil the evening.

Once outside, he pulled in great lungfuls of the crisp May air, reviving his spirits and clearing his mind.

To say Charlotte wasn't Joy was a gross understatement. And besides, he was the one in love, not Charlotte. If anyone would suffer harm, it would be him. And although that prospect was less than appealing, it wasn't as horrific as he would have thought mere weeks ago. Oh, certainly it would pain him for Charlotte not to return his love. Not something he would either look forward to or relish.

But Charlotte was his wife, bound to him by law, and if Simon was anything, he was optimistic. Charlotte may not love him yet, but he would wear down her resistance until she had no other choice but to succumb.

Drake was right about one thing. Simon loved a challenge.

With renewed hope bubbling inside, he gazed up at the moon. Soft beams of light drew long shadows. Footsteps crunched against the pebble walk, and a woman's shadow loomed from behind him. Hands pressed against his eyes.

A smile stretched across his lips as he remembered performing the same action on his beautiful wife the day before. *The minx.* But before he could turn and pull her into his arms, he tensed.

The fragrance was all wrong.

Breathless from the lively country dance, Charlotte hurried back to find Simon.

Where is he?

She scanned the room, searching the couples pairing for the next set. Her brows drew down.

"He stepped outside."

Charlotte spun around toward Judith's voice, a smile replacing the frown. Of course he did. "Restless again?"

Judith laughed. "You know him well. But I think perhaps it was another reason this time. Hurry, and you should catch him." She gave Charlotte a little push toward the exit.

Stepping outside, Charlotte rubbed her hands on her arms. The night air cooled her skin, overheated from the crowded assembly room. Stars sparkled in the sky, and the moon, not yet full, shed the perfect amount of light and shadows for clandestine lovers.

A thrill trickled up her spine at the thought of surprising Simon and stealing a kiss or two—or more.

Movement ahead caught her attention, but something seemed off. She narrowed her eyes as they adjusted in the moonlight.

"Someone will see us," a man's voice said.

Charlotte froze. Not any man. Simon. A chill having nothing to do with the night air raced through her veins. The shadowy figures took shape, the unmistakable flow of a skirt outlining someone much shorter than the one of Charlotte's husband.

"Let them," the woman's voice answered.

Careful to tread lightly, Charlotte crept forward, catching the movement of the woman's hand caressing the man's arm.

"Sorry to interrupt," Charlotte said, tamping down the ache in her heart and keeping her voice nonchalant. She refused to give Simon the satisfaction of knowing his actions upset her.

Simon practically threw the woman off of him.

Hester Pace.

Charlotte should have known.

"Charlotte! This is not what it appears to be."

"Oh?" Charlotte said, the ache in her chest near unbearable. If loving someone meant enduring such pain, she'd been wise to avoid it so long. No wonder Simon wanted no part of it. Was it too late for her, or was she doomed to live in misery because she allowed him to sneak into her heart? "What might that be then, *Husband?*" She laced as much vitriol in the address as she could muster.

Hands extended in supplication, Simon stepped forward. "Charlotte."

She held a palm up to stop him. "Stay back." She couldn't think straight if he was near her, and if any situation called for a clear head, it was the current one. Unable to keep the hurt from her voice any longer, the next words leaked out of her like a cry. "You *promised*."

"Nothing happened. I'm innocent," Simon's voice pleaded.

"Ha!" Hester gave a malicious laugh. "Your wife seems an intelligent woman. Sometimes things are exactly as they appear. Might as well confess, Simon, love."

Simon spun on Hester. "Don't call me love. And don't touch me again." He brushed aside the arm Hester extended toward him, then turned back to Charlotte. "She's lying."

"Am I?" Hester's answer sing-songed on the night air, and Charlotte caught the smirk playing on her lips. "Face it, dearie. Simon can't resist a skirt, and he'll whisper those sweet words of love to get what he wants. No doubt you believed he meant it when he said he loved you."

Simon straightened, his eyes meeting Charlotte's. "Charlotte?"

Hester's words sank beneath Charlotte's anger, cooling it.

"You are correct, Miss Pace," Charlotte answered, the truth clear in her mind.

Simon's face crumpled. "Charlotte, no."

She held up a quelling hand. "Allow me to finish. True, Simon is far from innocent in most things, and he does love women. I appreciate that you've managed to cobble together enough sense to recognize my intelligence. However, I'm intelligent enough to know there are different types of love. I've seen the love Simon has for his mother and sisters, for our dear friend, the Duchess of Burwood, and even the compassionate love he has for women like you."

Charlotte waited for Hester to digest her words, but the troublemaker continued to smirk. Clearly, the woman wasn't as bright as Charlotte generously presumed.

Oh, but Simon! A different matter entirely. A broad grin—no longer ridiculous—broke across his face.

"Now. If you would kindly allow me a word in private with my husband." Charlotte stretched out her arm, motioning for Hester to leave.

As Hester passed, the cloying scent of rosewater assaulting Charlotte's nostrils, Charlotte leaned in and whispered. "Dig your claws into another man, Miss Pace. Leave my husband alone or you will answer to me. And please, save yourself some money on perfume. Dousing yourself with an entire bottle is both unnecessary and sickening."

The troublemaking hussy stomped off in a huff.

Silence stretched between Charlotte and Simon like the night itself.

"Well?" Simon took one step toward her, and she didn't try to stop him. "How did you know she was lying?"

Charlotte waved his question away as she would a pesky insect. "Simple. Although as I told her, there was some truth to her words. But you have never said you loved me, and I sincerely doubt you would say it just to get your way."

He took another step closer. "No, I wouldn't. Especially with you. With you, I would mean it."

Moonlight shimmered in his seductive eyes, mixed with something else. "May I?" He held his arms out by her waist, beckoning her in.

"Yes." She slipped into his embrace, threading her hands through his hair. "Now, I would like a stolen kiss like the one Hester professed to have received."

"Please don't mention her name again, or I will have to do this." He lowered his mouth to hers, capturing it with a kiss that sent bubbles through her from her head to the toes in her slippers.

When he pulled back to allow them both a breath, she whispered, "Hes—"

His chuckle vibrated against her lips as he silenced her again, the kiss growing desperate.

"We should go back inside," she said when they finally broke apart. But as she turned, he tugged her hand.

"Wait. I have something to tell you. It's about what Hester said—sort of."

The confidence he'd worn so easily moments ago seemed to melt away, leaving an unsure lad before her. Worry tightened like bands around her chest, squeezing the air out of her lungs. Had she believed him too readily?

"What is it?" She wasn't certain she wanted to know.

"But first, promise you'll believe me."

Oh, that wasn't good. "I can't promise you something before I know what it is."

He ran a hand across the back of his neck and spun away from her. "Christ. Why is this so hard to say?" He nodded once, then turned around to face her.

"For goodness' sake, Simon. Say it!"

Before Simon could force out whatever had him so upset, a carriage pulled up.

Charlotte squinted at the crest adorning the door of the fine vehicle, both announcing the occupant's importance. She sucked in a breath, and her hand reached out for Simon's, squeezing his fingers in a vise-like grip.

A liveried servant jumped down from his post behind the carriage, opened the door, and lowered the step.

And Edgerton descended.

⚜

SIMON STARTLED AT CHARLOTTE'S STRICKEN EXPRESSION, THE death grip of her fingers crushing his. He turned to see what had captured her attention and cursed. "What the deuce is he doing here?"

"Whatever it is, it can't be good." Charlotte released his hand and strode forward.

"Wait!" Simon called. "Make him come to us."

When she returned next to him, Simon wrapped a possessive arm around her waist and tugged her close. "A united front."

She nodded, but her muscles were like granite against his palm.

Edgerton gazed around, his nose high in the air as if he were sniffing them out, the moment clear when his eyes finally locked on them.

Simon's grip tightened around Charlotte's waist. Ice crystalized in his veins at what she must have endured as that miserable wretch's sister. He didn't want to imagine. But he would protect her if it killed him.

Lord, but the thought of dying was even more distasteful now that he was in love. And he hadn't even had the chance to tell her.

Damnation, Edgerton. The man's timing was abominable.

Edgerton stood still, no doubt expecting them to come bowing and scraping in front of him. When it became clear in his repugnant mind that Charlotte would stand her ground, Edgerton slithered forward.

Moonlight at his back cast him in shadows like a specter, his expression indiscernible.

More the better.

Simon had no desire to experience his brother-in-law's sinister gaze more than necessary. Yet that same moonlight illuminated both him and Charlotte.

"Smile," he whispered from the corner of his mouth. "It will confuse him."

Although Charlotte's effort fell short of the easy smiles she'd graced him with most of the day, Simon was proud of her attempt.

It proved effective as Edgerton jerked to a halt.

"Edgerton!" Simon threw his free arm out in greeting. "So glad you could join us. Hasn't Charlotte done a magnificent job organizing our celebration?"

Edgerton's dark eyes bored into Simon, then, without further acknowledgement, turned his attention to Charlotte. "I've come to take you home. Surely, you've come to your senses and are finished with this *nonsense*." He punctuated the last word with a glance toward Simon. "I'll have your sham of a marriage annulled, and you can marry Lord Felix as planned."

Simon's warrior wife's spine stiffened under his palm. "Under no circumstances will I marry Felix. I would rather die than be forced into such a marriage."

Perhaps the darkness played tricks on Simon's eyes, but he swore Edgerton's shoulders slumped. More importantly, Charlotte's words bounced off Edgerton and landed squarely in Simon's chest, knocking the air from his lungs.

Did she really prefer death to being trapped into marriage?

"And yet, you were." Delivered cooly, the icy truth of Edgerton's statement drew Simon back, driving the painful words home.

He wanted to shout, *That was different!* But was it really? Oh, he would never strike Charlotte, but hadn't he harmed her by taking away her choice—her control? If anyone would protest Edgerton's accusation, it must come from Charlotte.

Thick, foul bile rose in his throat, the fear rising as seconds ticked by without Charlotte's rebuttal when she stiffened before him.

She did feel trapped, helpless, like a trout caught on a lure and scooped unwillingly into a net. And if he loved her, he should release her to swim free.

CHAPTER 36

Stunned, Charlotte glared at her brother, ready to tell him she loved her husband. But when she gazed askance at Simon, she withheld her words. He appeared as ghastly as the day they'd been forced into the untenable situation.

Oh, for her it was no longer untenable. But for Simon, her brother's words had struck home. Simon didn't want to be married to her, and he certainly didn't want her love. He'd made that perfectly clear. Only his optimistic nature had allowed him to make the best of the situation.

No, if she professed her feelings in front of Roland, Simon would either brush her words off as lies to dissuade her brother or, worse, consider them an abomination he wanted no part of.

And she couldn't abide being rejected—again.

For once in her life, she held her tongue.

And it was torture.

"Sister," Roland continued, his sugary sweet voice no doubt taking aim at a chink in her armor. "Come home and let us quell the gossiping tongues and put an end to this unfortunate incident.

I vow to you, I will not force your hand into a marriage you do not freely choose."

Well, that was a surprise. She narrowed her eyes, doing her damnedest to discern his motive, which was most likely self-serving and vile.

"I'm already married."

"And as I said, I have the power to see it annulled."

"Charlotte." Simon's gentle voice caressed her skin, and, unlike Roland's, rang with sincerity. "May I have a word?"

When she nodded, he grasped her elbow, his touch as gentle as his words, and pulled her aside. Pain radiated across his face.

"Are you becoming ill again?" Her voice edged upward in the register as fear gripped her.

"What? No." He flicked his gaze away, took a breath, then met hers directly. "I release you from our marriage. Accept your brother's offer of an annulment, and free yourself from something you never wanted."

But she didn't wish to be free. Not now. She swallowed her pride. "What do you want?"

"I want you to be happy."

She wished the same for him. Perhaps releasing him was for the best. "Then we are of like minds." Hope, a tenuous thing at best, glimmered in the distance, and she grasped at it like a lifeline. "What if I'm . . ."

"Pregnant?" Closing his eyes, he pressed his lips together, and sucked in an audible breath. "Have you missed your courses?"

"Not yet."

"Then hopefully we'll know soon. But if you are, an annulment is out of the question. Not only would it prove we consummated the marriage, but I will not allow even a whiff of illegitimacy to taint our child's life. However, you can either return to your brother or remain here at the cottage without me. I only ask to be part of my child's life." A wan smile crossed his lips but didn't sparkle in his eyes. "And if it's a son, you will have fulfilled your promise to me, more than I have to you."

Other than a sharp tingling in her fingertips, Charlotte's entire body felt numb. How had things changed so quickly? Her cold heart, asleep for so long, had finally been resurrected, and—with a few words—it retreated to safety in its deathly slumber. She should have known better; should have trusted her instincts.

Normally able to make quick decisions, Charlotte needed time to sort through the quagmire of thoughts meandering around in her skull. She strode back to her brother with Simon on her heels.

"Give me time to consider your proposition—alone, if you please." That last word stuck in her throat like an overcooked piece of mutton. But she uttered it more for Simon than Roland.

"Of course," her husband answered. "My *lord*." He gestured toward the assembly hall. "After you."

"I expect an answer before the evening is out." With his nose in the air, Roland pushed past Simon and tromped toward the building.

"Take as long as you need," Simon whispered, then followed her brother inside.

Sweet birdsong from a nightingale drifted on the hyacinth-scented breeze, more beautiful than the strands of music from the simple country orchestra. Should she free Simon from their marriage? Could she trust Roland to keep his promise?

She rested a hand on her abdomen. What if she was already with child? She had no doubt Simon would love the child, regardless of its sex. What would entail him being part of the child's life? Would that include her, or would he insist she make herself scarce during his visits? Worse, would he insist the child live with him?

An odd ache filled the void in her chest at the thought. She'd never wanted children, or so she'd thought. Not like Honoria. But with the real possibility before her, she questioned her belief.

Because a child would be part of Simon—and her. Their child. Goodness, what would that combination be? A smile tugged at her lips.

And like the sun breaking through thunderclouds, scattering a threatening storm, and saying, *Not today*, the answer came to her.

She would march back inside and tell Simon that she loved him. Let him rail and complain all he wished about not wanting a woman to love him. He would have to accept it and live with it. And Roland could go back home—or better yet, to the devil.

Neither her brother nor her husband would bully her out of the one good thing in her life. And if Simon couldn't love her back, so be it. She wasn't a greedy woman. He would love their child, and that would be enough for her.

Shoulders squared, head held high, she prepared for battle. But before she could turn to go back inside the assembly hall, footsteps sounded behind her, and a hand clamped over her mouth. The cold tip of a blade pricked against her neck, and hot breath brushed against her cheek.

"Scream and I'll cut your pretty throat. It's not you I want. It's your husband."

Simon's stomach roiled as the heat from the assembly room pressed in on him. *Damn!* Surely, it was too soon for another malaria attack? He bit back a laugh at the absurdity of it all.

Leave it to him to refuse to do anything by halves. Much like his wife.

The bleak truth surrounded him, phantom hands clutching and dragging him under. Was he to lose everything in one cruel twist?

Perhaps this whole mess had a bright side. He couldn't ache for Charlotte if he was dead. The harsh laugh burst from his lips.

"What amuses you, son?" Rather than curiosity from her

question, concern shone on his mother's face. "And where is Charlotte? Didn't she find you?"

"She did."

"Well?" The impatience in his mother's voice reminded him of when he was a boy and she stood, hands on hips, waiting for an explanation for his latest mischief. "Did you tell her?"

Ah. "Not yet. If you haven't noticed, we've received a visitor who's put a pall over things." He jerked his chin in the direction of the pompous arse Edgerton.

The man stood off by himself, a handkerchief pressed to his nose and his dark eyes drilling holes into Simon.

"I presumed Charlotte invited him. She had your father post a letter for her the other day."

She did?

"Why didn't she ask me?" And why did it bother him that Charlotte wouldn't come to him for such a minor task? Oh, right. Trust. "You didn't see the recipient's name?" From Charlotte's reaction to Edgerton's arrival, the letter did not contain an invitation to her brother, but Simon was in no rush to tell his mother that his marriage was about to fall apart.

"No. Shall we ask your father?"

Simon shook his head. "I'll ask Charlotte later."

Regardless of who Charlotte wrote to or the reason, why was he allowing Edgerton to slither his way between him and Charlotte? Wasn't their marriage worth fighting for? Oh, he would still give her a choice, but she needed all the facts before deciding.

Hadn't he badgered Drake to do the same thing the year before? And the longer Drake waited, the more obstacles rose in their path.

Time to take his own advice. He needed to tell his wife he loved her.

Even if Charlotte rejected his love and chose to live without him, at least he would have tried.

What was taking Charlotte so long?

Unable to wait any longer, Simon made his excuses to his mother and threaded his way through the crowded assembly room. People stopped him, offering their felicitations on his marriage and expressing their admiration of Charlotte. As Simon nodded his thanks, the hair on the back of his neck rose to attention, remembering not everyone wished him and Charlotte well. *Where is Albie Mooney?* And for that matter, where were Samuel and Hester?

Icy panic trickled up Simon's spine.

Standing near the door, Edgerton eyed him suspiciously. "Where are you off to?"

Ignoring him, Simon had almost made a clean escape when Hester rushed toward him from the entrance. "Simon. Come quickly."

As if she had burned him, Simon jerked away from where her hand clutched his arm. "No. I'm going to find my wife and tell her what I should have told her weeks ago."

The sinister smile creeping across Hester's lips chilled him through. "Then you best hurry while she's still alive to tell her whatever's so important."

What?! No longer caring about what Hester might think, he grabbed her by the upper arms and shook her. "What are you talking about?"

"The longer you wait here, the less time you'll have with your precious bride."

"What's going on here?" Edgerton demanded.

"I don't know." Simon's voice sounded frantic to his own ears. "But I think Charlotte is in danger."

Edgerton's eyes flared. Perhaps the man did care, or perhaps he only wanted to avoid another mention in *The Muckraker*. "Then why are you wasting time with this trollop?"

Simon rushed out the door as Hester's voice boomed behind him. "Watch who you're calling a trollop!"

Footsteps pounded behind him as Simon raced outside, searching wildly for any sign of Charlotte.

"Where is she?" Edgerton panted behind him.

"Over there!"

Simon turned at Hester's words, his gaze straining in the direction she pointed.

Bile rose in his throat as his earlier nausea returned.

"Samuel. For God's sake, release my wife!" Simon's gaze locked on the knife point against Charlotte's throat.

"Don't come closer, or I'll slit her throat right now."

Simon skidded to a halt, Edgerton right behind him. Hester sauntered up to Samuel and Charlotte as if she had nothing better to do.

"You're party to this?" Simon croaked out the question, struggling to believe the tableau before him. "Why?"

"Because I don't believe you'll do what Samuel wants," Hester said.

None of it made any sense. "What *do* you want, Samuel?"

"I want you to feel the pain I did when you killed my daughter."

"What's this?" Edgerton said, taking a step closer.

"You stay back, too!" Samuel pressed the knife into Charlotte's flesh.

Simon's eyes locked with hers, registering the flinch of pain as a dark spot bloomed on her skin. "Please don't hurt her."

"Did you kill his daughter, Beckham? Perhaps an annulment is too good for you. I'll see you hang instead." Edgerton's threat bounced off Simon.

"Annulment?" Hester said, looking hopeful. The woman was daft. As if he'd ever consider taking up with her again. No other woman could take Charlotte's place.

Like being trapped in a tunnel, everything other than Charlotte faded from Simon's mind.

Fire blazed in Charlotte's eyes. "Samuel, you, sir, are a nodcock!"

Oh, God, he loved her spirit, but she would get herself killed if she antagonized Samuel any further.

However, Charlotte's declaration startled Samuel, and he lowered the knife a fraction.

Simon didn't know how Charlotte kept her voice passionless and calm. "Although you make the most delicious plum tarts, and I truly hope to enjoy them again if I'm not dead, you are wasting your time. Kill me and you cause my husband no pain. Goodness, he more than likely will be relieved to have been freed from the burden of my presence. He might even thank you— before you swing from a rope, that is. My brother is the Marquess of Edgerton"—she gave an infinitesimal nod toward Edgerton— "and he enjoys watching people hanged. And Miss Pace will no doubt *worm* her way back into Simon's arms as she did after your dear daughter died."

The knifepoint pricked Charlotte's throat again, and Simon drew in a breath. He wanted nothing more than to be able to communicate with his wife the silent way Drake and Honoria did. *Too far, Charlotte.* But there was something buried in her message directed only to him. If his mind weren't in such a tangle, with time, he'd puzzle it out.

His face contorted like a mad man, Samuel sneered and pressed the knife into Charlotte's skin again. A drop of blood trickled down her throat. "You know nothing about my daughter's death. The bastard killed her as sure as if he pushed her into the river himself."

Charlotte flinched but continued her attempt to dissuade the man. "And my husband loved Joy and grieves her death just as greatly as you. Don't you think he's punished himself enough all these years? It's why he vows never to love or be loved again. He told me himself. My husband doesn't love me, and in fact has released me from our marriage to return to my brother. You would gain nothing by killing me, Samuel."

Simon felt all eyes on him. From the smug look on Edgerton's face, he no doubt believed he'd won the battle to take Charlotte away. *Bastard.* Why wasn't he more concerned about his sister's life? Hester appeared even more hopeful than when Edgerton had mentioned the annulment. But Samuel—Samuel seemed unsure.

With his arm still wrapped around Charlotte's waist, Samuel lowered the blade. "Is that true, Beckham? You don't love her and are planning on ending your marriage?"

For once, Simon weighed each word, examining every argument and possibility in order to speak as truthfully as possible but appease Samuel and end his misguided vendetta. Simon recalled Charlotte's carefully crafted reply to the vicar during their meeting to obtain a special license. Clever, truthful, but with hidden meaning directed only toward him.

He took a breath, preparing himself for the most important argument in his life. "My marriage to Lady Charlotte was not a love match. An ill-timed and unfortunate discovery of impropriety forced us into the union."

Edgerton snorted.

Simon ignored him. "Neither of us loved one another. In fact, it's fair to say we barely tolerated each other. It's also true the marquess has offered to arrange an annulment, and I have offered to release Lady Charlotte from her promise to me— should *she* wish it." At the last, Simon locked his gaze with Charlotte's, willing that magical connection of his friends to make her see the truth.

"My wife is not one to be controlled by anyone. She makes her own decisions. You will derive more satisfaction by allowing her to live, because I suspect she will decide to stay married and vex me for the remainder of my days." And although it pained him to do so, he forced the grin his wanton wife had deemed ridiculous.

A strange glimmer appeared in Charlotte's eyes, perhaps a trick of the moonlight, for her voice remained steady. "The only one to lose in this situation is you, Samuel." She sighed, the exasperated one she exhaled when bored. "And me, for I shall sorely miss your plum tarts."

"Drop the knife, Samuel." Palms out, Simon held up his hands and took one tentative step forward, pleased when Samuel didn't raise the blade again. "Let's walk away and end this."

Relief flooded him when Samuel dropped the knife to the ground. Simon raced up and kicked it aside. He wanted nothing more than to pull Charlotte into his arms and cover her with kisses. But at the moment, they needed to continue the farce. "Go home, Samuel. Promise to leave my wife alone, and we'll speak no more about this incident." As much as he wanted to call for the town constable, Simon had pity on the man who, had circumstances been different, might have been his father by marriage.

"You're not going to allow him to walk free!" Edgerton boomed.

As Simon turned, prepared to tell Edgerton to take his pompous arse elsewhere, a rush of footsteps sounded behind him.

And his heart rose to his throat again as Albie Mooney appeared from nowhere, snatched up the knife, and lunged toward Charlotte.

CHAPTER 37

M uch like the events that led to her marriage to the man
she had grown to love, Charlotte would never be certain
of the sequence that followed. She had barely pulled in a relieved
breath after Samuel dropped that bloody knife when Simon
turned toward her, his face a mask of horror, his voice booming.

"Charlotte! Get out of the way!"

Knife clutched in his hand, Albie Mooney lunged toward her,
his gait unsteady. "I'll teach you to interfere where you
shouldn't."

Before she could do as her husband commanded—and if she
survived, she would have words with him later about his demands
—Simon threw himself between her and Albie.

Albie slashed at Simon, his arm swinging in a wild arc.

Quick on his feet, Simon leaped away.

"Lemme at 'er!" Albie's slurred words matched his stumbling
steps as he charged forward, this time at Simon. He slashed the
blade in a wide arc.

Unbidden, Charlotte's hand rose to her throat as the knife
sliced the air toward Simon.

Blocking her view of Albie, Simon jumped back, then darted a glance over his shoulder. "One of you fetch Mr. Cooper!"

Albie took advantage of Simon's distracted attention and slashed again, and Simon stumbled.

Gah! What was happening?!

Damned if she'd leave her husband alone in such a dire situation, Charlotte didn't hesitate to delegate the task. "Go, Roland! Your command as a marquess should light a fire under the man's arse."

Although Roland hitched a brow, he nodded once.

She yanked Roland's abominable cane from his hand. "For defense, should I need it. Now, hurry."

Captured by the ongoing melee, Samuel watched with interest, and Hester stood, frozen in horror.

Useless nodcocks!

Simon managed to grasp Albie's hand holding the knife, then pulled his arm back and planted a facer.

Albie stumbled backward, releasing the knife.

Charlotte raced behind Albie and, wielding the cane like a cricket bat, whacked him on the back of the head.

The man staggered, then crumpled to the ground.

For a moment, with only Albie lying at their feet between them, Charlotte and Simon stared at each other.

Even Hester's whispered question couldn't break their connection. "Did you kill him?"

In answer, Albie groaned.

The ridiculous grin broke across Simon's face. "Well done, Wife. Although, I had matters in hand."

Charlotte dropped the cane and thrust herself into Simon's arms. "Shut up and kiss me, you buffoon."

"Bossy. Is that the thanks I get for saving your life?"

"Saving *my* life? I saved *your* life."

As she slid her hands around Simon's arms and shoulders, a sticky wetness coated her fingers, and she pulled back.

"Tease! Where's my kiss?" Simon reached for her, but when she lifted her hand to show him the dark substance, his eyes widened, and he grabbed at her hand. "You're hurt."

"It's not my blood." Other than a tiny knife prick on her throat and being manhandled by Samuel, Charlotte survived the ordeal unscathed. She touched Simon's left arm again. "Your coat is torn here."

With trembling fingers, she unbuttoned his coat and shoved it off his shoulders. Blood oozed beneath the slash in the white linen shirt.

"No wonder my arm hurts like bloody hell."

Voices and footsteps grew louder as the constable and other men raced forward.

Mr. Cooper's gaze bounced between Simon, Samuel, Charlotte, and Hester. "What happened here?"

Albie groaned again and pushed against the ground in an effort to rise.

Roland stepped forward, as if he'd had control over the whole situation from the beginning. "These men"—he pointed at Samuel and Albie—"attacked Lady Charlotte."

Simon leaned in and whispered, "Do you want Samuel punished?"

Did she? "I do enjoy his plum tarts."

Simon laughed then, grabbing his injured arm, winced.

Charlotte faced the constable. "Samuel seemed to be under the misguided notion that my husband was responsible for his daughter's death. But I believe we've resolved that misunderstanding"—she turned toward Samuel—"haven't we, Mr. Waters?"

Samuel's gaze darted to Simon, who wrapped his hand around his throat and mimicked choking. "Yes?" the baker answered.

"And Samuel has agreed not only to drop this vendetta

against my husband, but in retribution, he will make me a dozen plum tarts every week. Free of charge."

Simon chortled.

"What about him?" Mr. Cooper pointed at Albie, who sat cross-legged on the ground and rubbed his head.

She hoped the vile man's head hurt like the devil. "Oh, definitely lock him up. The man not only came after me, but he hurt my husband. And I will not tolerate that."

As two men hauled Albie to his feet, Mr. Cooper turned toward Roland. "My lord, is all this agreeable with you?"

Before Roland opened his mouth, Charlotte stepped between her brother and the constable. "Why are you asking him? He has no say in this. He wasn't the one threatened or injured."

Roland's dark brow hitched again. Apparently, she had surprised him twice in one day. "Leave us." Roland waved a hand at Mr. Cooper and the men restraining Albie. "I require a word with my sister."

As Charlotte expected, Simon strode to her side, tugging her close and glaring at her brother. "I'm staying."

Charlotte stopped Samuel as he attempted to slink off. "Samuel, please stay. You too, Miss Pace. I have something to say I want you all to hear."

Both of Roland's brows hitched. "The only thing you have to say to *these people*," Roland said, as if spitting out a disgusting taste, "is goodbye. Pity I didn't receive word of your involvement in this ridiculous peasant event sooner. You are returning with me to my estate in Chippenham and then to London two days hence."

Simon's hand tightened around her waist.

Metaphorically, Charlotte dug in her heels. "No."

Next to her, Simon exhaled.

"I made my decision before all this"—mimicking her brother, she waved her hand around—"happened. I choose to stay with my husband and vex him for the remainder of his days. Samuel, you may not believe it, but Joy's death has wounded Simon, too, shuttering his heart."

She turned toward Hester. "And Miss Pace, you would be advised never to risk my wrath with your machinations toward my husband. You have witnessed what I'm capable of." Charlotte retrieved Roland's cane and gave it a *swoosh*, pleased when Hester paled in the moonlight.

She handed Roland's cane back. "And brother, did you not hear the bargain I struck with Samuel? Why would I leave when I can have free plum tarts every week?" Glancing up at Simon, she smiled, hoping the dimple he liked so much was on full display. "And besides. I love my husband."

৩১৯ৎ

SIMON FROZE AT CHARLOTTE'S WORDS, UNCERTAIN HE HAD HEARD her correctly. "I'm sorry. Would you mind repeating that?"

Charlotte tugged his coat back into place by the lapels. "I love you, you buffoon. I know you don't want me to love you but consider it the way I will vex you for the rest of your life."

Simon let out a *whoop* of joy, sweeping Charlotte off the ground and spinning her around. Then the pain hit him. "Damn, my arm hurts."

As everyone around them gaped, Charlotte took charge, rolling over them like a boulder on a downhill trajectory. "Samuel, make yourself useful. We need a physician—and not someone who uses leeches. My husband is losing blood; he doesn't need those slimy creatures removing more. Hester, find someone to bring our carriage around and inform Simon's family I'm taking him home. Roland, leave. We have no need for you."

Charlotte's barked orders had Samuel and Hester slinking off, each peering over their shoulders, no doubt worried Charlotte would pounce on them if they disobeyed. Simon wanted to laugh.

Edgerton, on the other hand, remained rooted in place.

As if Simon needed her support, Charlotte wrapped an arm around his waist.

He rather liked it. But it was time he took care of his wife as well. "Lord Edgerton, before you leave, thank you for your assistance and for your concern about my wife. Rest assured I will do everything in my power to give her the best possible life." He paused, locking eyes with Charlotte. "Because I love her."

Charlotte's lips parted, a tiny gasp escaping, and he hoped she saw the sincerity in his eyes.

Tearing his attention away from Charlotte—and it truly was a feat of great strength as he wanted nothing more than to plunder those rosebud lips—he continued addressing Edgerton. "And it's much too late for an annulment, if you understand my meaning, my lord."

Edgerton huffed. "Lady Charlotte, are you with this . . . this *man's* child?"

Simon prepared to answer, but Charlotte gave his waist a squeeze.

"If I'm not yet, I expect to remedy that as soon as my husband has recovered from his wound."

Oh, definitely. Simon gave her the most ridiculous grin he could muster.

Edgerton stomped off, muttering about regrets and the idiocy of love.

"Roland didn't deserve your kindness," Charlotte said, her gaze traveling to his bloodied sleeve.

"No, but I was feeling particularly magnanimous because my wife *loves* me."

"Don't let it go to your head, you buffoon. It's already the size of France."

Simon threw his head back and bellowed a laugh. "Not China or Russia?"

"No. Because *I'm* feeling magnanimous."

He tugged her closer to his side, which, to be honest, made his arm hurt more. "Well, then I should get you home and take advantage before you return to your normal self. We need to make good on that promise for a child." He lowered his head and savored her lips.

"Simon! Simon!" Voices pulled him from the haze of love enveloping him. It couldn't be Charlotte; not while his tongue tangled with hers.

His wife gave him a gentle push, and he broke the kiss. "Your family is coming."

For once, Simon wasn't thrilled to see his boisterous, gregarious family.

Georgie barreled into him first.

"Oomph!" Simon staggered back, exaggerating the force of Georgie's impact. He grabbed his arm. "Careful, I'm an injured man."

The rest of his sisters followed, each fawning over him in their own way until his mother pushed them all aside and smothered him with kisses. "What's this about Samuel and Albie Mooney?" She pulled back. "And what happened to your arm?"

Before he answered, his carriage pulled around. "All in good time, Mother. At the moment, I need to take my wife home and then collapse myself. Tomorrow, I promise to have a lengthy and enthralling account of the events. If Dr. Rutledge comes looking for me, tell him I'll be at the cottage."

He kissed his mother on the forehead. "Don't worry."

Amid shouts from his family, Simon ushered Charlotte into the carriage.

His wanton, adorable wife—who *loved* him—scowled. "That was rather rude."

He waggled his brows. "I take my cues from the best."

Rather than bristle, Charlotte laughed. "Touché. Georgie said you were skilled at fencing."

"You're not offended?"

Charlotte shook her head, a few strands of dark hair tumbling loose from the intricate arrangement. "Not in the least. I know you meant it in the best possible way—because you *love* me." She narrowed her eyes. "You *do* love me? You weren't bamming me?"

"I've never been more serious. I was going to tell you before everything went to hell around us. But when your brother arrived, I wondered if I could make you happier by letting you go."

She gently tugged his coat free from his shoulders. "And I made my decision to stay before Samuel restrained me, to tell you I love you."

The wonder of her words washed over him. "You're incredibly brave."

"I detest bullies."

"Not that, although you put the fear of God into Hester. However, you don't have anything to worry about, even if you didn't threaten her."

She canted her head, exposing that long neck he wanted to kiss. "Then what?"

"It took great courage to confess your love and make yourself vulnerable."

Speechless, she blinked, her lips gaping seductively.

God, he wanted nothing more than to make love to her on the spot. If only his arm didn't hurt like bloody hell. "And to show Samuel compassion." He shook his head, still in disbelief. There was so much about his wife he didn't know and couldn't wait to discover.

"Both Samuel and my brother will receive punishment—by

368

seeing how happy we are." After tugging the coat from his arms and placing it aside, she kissed him.

Catching his breath, he rested his forehead against hers. "Not that I'm complaining, but are you planning on undressing me in the carriage? I'm loath to admit it, but I'm not in the best form for ravishing at the moment."

Her laugh, full-throated and seductive, heated his blood. "I want to examine your injury. How trustworthy is this Dr. Rutledge? Should we send to London for Ashton?"

"It's a flesh wound. I'll be fine, especially with you hovering over Rutledge and glowering. He wouldn't dare make a misstep. But I do need something to keep my mind occupied away from the pain until we arrive home."

As she tenderly peeled back the blood-soaked sleeve from his body, she said, "Shall we stop the carriage so you can run about?"

"No." He pulled her close. "Tell me you love me and kiss me again."

A sly smile broke across her lips—lips she would soon press to his. "I love you, you buffoon."

❧

FIVE DAYS PASSED AND SIMON HAD PRACTICALLY GONE MAD FROM the inactivity Charlotte demanded for his recovery. Constantly hovering over him, Charlotte monitored the time his family spent with him when they came to check on his recovery. Like clockwork, she would shoo them all out after thirty minutes. His wife would have made an excellent commanding officer in the military.

She'd insisted Simon provide some financial support to Albie Mooney's family while he remained incarcerated—anonymously, of course. "We can't have Albie's family suffer for his heinous acts. Especially the children. Perhaps Mrs. Mooney will take the children and move far away from that monster's reach."

The fierce determination in his wife's eyes told Simon she would be an even stauncher defender of their own children. Which, speaking of, he was more than eager to start making.

He rang the little bell on the side table, then stretched his legs out on the sofa. The stitches in his arm itched like the devil.

Charlotte rushed into the drawing room, her usual alto voice rising in pitch with concern. "What is it?"

"I need my medicine." He placed a hand over his wounded arm and adopted— what Charlotte had taken to calling—his sad puppy expression. Curled by his side, Trifle gave a pathetic little *meow* of camaraderie.

"More willow bark tea?"

The day after the *incident*, Charlotte had insisted on sending a message to Ashton by express post, requesting his opinion on Dr. Rutledge's course of treatment. Ashton had written back posthaste, commending Charlotte for cleaning the area thoroughly before Rutledge had sutured the wound. In addition, he sent packets of willow bark with instructions to keep the wound as clean and dry as possible and to send for him if the area became red, swollen, or oozed pus.

"No more of that abominable tea, please." Simon's stomach revolted at the mere thought.

His wife laughed. "Such a baby."

"I need something stronger."

Like the slash of a blade, the words cut off her laugh, and she raced forward, placing a gentle hand on his forehead. "Are you feverish? Another episode of malaria? Do you need your quinine?"

Guilt squeezed his chest that he had frightened her. "No. Something sweeter. Your lips."

She scowled and drew her hand back. "You are incorrigible!"

Grasping her fingers, he kissed them. "But you love me."

"And those are *your* lips, not mine."

"Care to remedy that?" He laughed at his own pun.

The lips he desired twitched at the corners. "Buffoon."

"Minx."

Careful to avoid jostling his injured arm, she settled next to him on the sofa, displacing Trifle, who meowed in protest.

"I believe little doses at a time are called for—to ensure your tolerance. It is, as you say, strong medicine." Pressure no more than a light brush, she kissed the corner of his mouth, then moved to his cheek, his eyes, and his nose.

He grinned up at her. "This is supposed to be making me feel better, not torturing me."

She rolled her eyes, the hint of the dimple on her cheek belying her annoyance. "Impatient man."

"You know me well." No longer waiting, he pulled her down to him, capturing her lips in a glorious kiss. "Mmm. Much better. I'm feeling stronger already. In fact . . . go lock the door."

Her dark brows arched, informing him she gleaned his meaning. "But your arm?"

"If I go one more day without being inside you, I'll have a relapse. I'll simply lie here, and you can have your way with me —exactly as you like." He wiggled his own brows.

She shook her head, rolling her eyes once more, but she rose and did as he asked.

Twenty minutes later, she curled next to him on the sofa. He wasn't certain who was purring the loudest—Charlotte, Trifle, or him.

Fingertips stroking the length of Charlotte's arm, he exhaled a deep sigh of contentment.

Ah, the purring came from his wanton wife, and she nuzzled her face against his chest.

"Charlotte?"

"Hmm?" she replied dreamily.

"Marry me."

She gaped at him, her dark eyes still hazy from their coupling. "We're already married, you dolt."

"I know. I just wanted to ask you again. To let you know I want to marry you for all the right reasons." He kissed her again. "Because I love you."

She laughed. "Of course you do." And his heart swelled at the whispered addendum. "And I love you, too."

Perhaps this love thing had a silver lining after all.

EPILOGUE

ONE MONTH LATER . . .

Charlotte peeled back the curtain from the front window, searching the path leading to the house, eager for Simon's return. Although overcast, which Simon explained was perfect weather for fishing, no lightning or thunder lit the sky or boomed in the distance. And if such portents had appeared, she had no doubt Simon would return posthaste to hold and reassure her all would be well.

However, the gloomy skies were not what made her anxious to see her husband, but rather the latest copy of *The Muckraker*.

Regardless of the idyllic month they'd spent at Rosehaven Park after the incident, most of the time in each other's arms, they had planned to return to London later in the week. Drake had written, emphasizing all was well with Honoria and little Kitty, but from Simon's furrowed brow as he read the letter, something hidden in Drake's words concerned her husband. And as Charlotte clutched *The Muckraker* in her other hand, waiting for her husband's return, she wondered if the two things were connected.

Trifle meowed at her feet, as if commiserating Simon's absence. Charlotte glanced down, wondering if they could take the kitten with them. No doubt the scamp would require frequent stops much like her husband.

At last, Simon appeared around the curve in the path, his worn fishing hat tilted at a jaunty angle. My, but he was dashing! From his expression, he'd had a productive morning. Charlotte hated the fact she would put a damper on his positive spirit.

He stepped inside, tossing his hat aside and handing tackle and basket to John. "Tell Madge to save a large piece for Trifle." When his gaze snagged on Charlotte, his grin widened, and he opened his arms. "Where's my greeting?"

Not hesitating, Charlotte flung herself into Simon's embrace. "I'm so glad you're home." After one quick sniff, she pulled back. "You smell like fish."

He laughed. "As much as I love the greeting, you haven't given me time to wash."

"Because there isn't time." She waved the gossip rag in front of him. "We must leave for London at once."

Ignoring her complaint about the fish smell, he pulled her close. "First, a kiss to shore me up for what I suspect is going to be bad news."

Long seconds passed, and Simon's lips made Charlotte forget the pungent odor of trout. Who would have ever imagined she'd be so in love she could ignore such a thing? Or that a man like Simon could turn her brain to mush with a kiss?

When he finally broke the kiss, she stared at him in a daze.

"Well?" he asked. "What's so important?"

"Hmm?" Her murmured answer elicited a chuckle from her husband.

"You were waving that gossip sheet in my face and telling me we needed to return to London immediately."

"Oh, right." Grasping his hand, she led him into the drawing room and pulled him next to her on the sofa. "Here. Read."

Handing him the scandal sheet, she waited.

※

SIMON BRACED HIMSELF. CHARLOTTE WASN'T ONE TO BECOME riled over most gossip, so the news must be particularly troublesome. Either that or she had grown soft. He chuffed a laugh at the unlikely notion, then read the first paragraph of the detestable paper.

Rumor has it that Lady Charlotte Beckham and her commoner husband created quite a stir during the May Day festivities in Swindon. This reporter normally does not cover such banal events occurring in the country, but the Marquess of Edgerton heroically intervened on his sister's behalf, possibly saving her life.

He glanced up at Charlotte. "Is this hack serious?"

Charlotte ignored him, urging him on. "Did you get to the part about our behavior?"

"Edgerton a hero, my arse," Simon mumbled, then returned to the rag.

One wonders why the marquess would make such an effort. His sister seems to have forgone all decorum, practically copulating with her husband in public. It's no wonder they had to marry so quickly. Shall we expect a child to arrive several months sooner than the usual nine after their wedding? And will the child look like her husband, or some other fellow?

Simon crumpled the paper in his fist. "When you discover who this culprit is, I want first crack at him."

"Although it grieves me to consider the possibility, what if it's a woman?"

"Then I shall take great pleasure watching you land one of your magnificent punches on the harpy's face." He shook his head. "You should have whacked your brother over the head with his own cane. Surely, he had a hand in spreading this *news* to whomever writes this rag. Who else could it be?"

"It is strange that what happened here would appear in a London scandal sheet," Charlotte said. "However, there's more. Read on."

"Worse than hinting that you've been unfaithful to me?" Simon cared less that the culprit had subtly called him a cuckold and more that the miscreant maligned Charlotte's reputation.

"You and I will survive that nonsense. Read," Charlotte commanded.

Using his thigh as a table, Simon did his best to flatten out the crumpled parchment, then dropped his gaze to the section under the lies about him and Charlotte.

In addition to the scandalous behavior of Mr. Beckham and Lady Charlotte, not only in Swindon but prior to their marriage as well, which this reporter notes occurred in the Duke of Burwood's London home, news has reached our ears that the duke's sister, Miss Juliana Merrick, posed for a portrait painted by Mr. Victor Pratt, heir to Viscount Cartwright. The news would seem unremarkable, as Mr. Pratt is known to be an aspiring artist. However, the reports state that Miss Merrick did so in a state of undress. It would appear that the new duke's home has become a hotbed of scandal.

Simon peered up from the calumnious article. "This is beyond the pale. Juliana is too sensible to pose so scandalously." *Isn't she?*

"Something in Drake's recent letter concerned you. Could it be related to this?"

"I—perhaps. Drake mentioned being anxious to leave London and get back to his seat in Dorset, but I thought perhaps it had something to do with little Kitty. Do you think he wants to get Juliana away from Victor Pratt? He seemed like a fine fellow to me. Would he take advantage of a young innocent?" Simon's head pounded at the thought.

"I don't know him well enough, although scandal follows his family. But regardless, Drake and Honoria will need our support. They're not as tough as we are."

He pulled her into his arms. "God, I love you."

She grinned at him. "I love you, too, even if you're——"

"Incorrigible?"

She gave him a sly, secretive look, then shook her head. "Even if you're going to forget all about me when your son or daughter is born."

He laughed. "I couldn't forget about you in a million years. You're a force of nature. Why——" He stopped, her words finally registering in his racing mind. He held her in front of him at arm's length. "Charlotte Beckham. Are you saying what I think you're saying?"

"It took you long enough. Now, kiss me, you buffoon."

And he kissed his wanton wife as if his life depended on it.

Which, in truth, it did.

❧

Would you like a peek into Simon and Charlotte's future (if nothing else, to see if Charlotte hasn't killed him 😉)? Scan the QR code on the next page and sign up to my mailing list for fun contests, book news, and subscriber only extras and get a bonus scene as a thank you. You may unsubscribe at any time—no obligation.

If you enjoyed the book, why not let other readers know by leaving an honest review?

AUTHOR NOTES

Where do I begin? This book was a delight to write. I certainly hope it is a delight to read as well. There have been a handful of times when writing my books where I felt I "knew" the characters so well I allowed them to completely direct the story. Simon and Charlotte are both among those select few.

I knew I was taking a gamble with Lady Charlotte Talbot, especially pairing her with Simon Beckham. Talk about oil and water. Yet, together they make a lovely, tasty dressing, and I can't imagine them with anyone else, can you?

People loved their verbal sparring in *A Duke In The Rough*. Charlotte has been in the periphery popping up occasionally in the *Hope Clinic* series, but it wasn't until *A Duke In The Rough* that I got to know her better. She's very much a female version of Nash, her brother, which is quite understandable.

If you subscribe to my newsletter, you've heard me wax poetic about the Enneagram (probably ad nauseam) and both Nash and Charlotte are Eights—The Challenger. It makes sense that being reared by the same tyrannical father would leave them fearful of being controlled. But Charlotte brings a new dynamic to this assertive, no-nonsense personality type. She's female. While we admire men for their strength and forthrightness, people often call women who are assertive by a certain name, and it's not a flattering term.

I hope I've done Charlotte justice in showing the "whys" of her personality and the soft, kind heart she protects so well. Good thing Simon was up for the challenge of winning her love.

Simon was just plain fun, a real cinnamon roll rake. As Charlotte muses early in the book when she considered her options, marriage to Simon would never be boring. I also enjoyed giving Simon a large, fun-loving family who accepts Charlotte into their fold and gives her what she lacked throughout most of her life.

As for research, which always has me looking up odd things, I learned a lot about thunderstorms, especially those occurring in colder weather. The scene where Charlotte recounts her traumatic experience to Simon—warning spoiler ahead if you haven't read it yet—was loosely based on *Jane Eyre*, one of my favorite books, when Jane is locked in the red room where her uncle died.

I also did some research about the early treatments of malaria and its outcome. People did indeed survive, but, like Simon, they were the lucky ones.

My editor was intrigued by the new character, The Captain, the owner of the gaming hell *The Knave of Hearts*. Expect to see him featured in the rest of the series. I dropped some hints as to his true identity. Did you catch them?

As for *The Muckraker*, some clues were dropped but they were pretty vague and subtle. My critique partners have admitted to me they have yet to figure out who is responsible.

ALSO BY TRISHA MESSMER

☙❧

The Hope Clinic Series
No Ordinary Love (Prequel Novella)
The Reluctant Duke's Dilemma
A Doctor For Lady Denby
Healing The Viscount's Heart
Saving Miss Pratt
Redeeming Lord Nash

☙❧

The London Ladies' League
A Duke In The Rough
Every Rake Has A Silver Lining

☙❧

Contemporary Romance
Different World Series
The Bottom Line
The Eyre Liszt
Look With Your Heart

ABOUT THE AUTHOR

※

Trisha Messmer had a million stories rattling around in her brain. (Well, maybe a million is an exaggeration but there were a lot). Always loving the written word, she enjoyed any chance she had to compose something, whether it be for a college paper or just a plain old email. One day as she was speaking with her daughter about the latest adventure going on in her mind, her daughter said, "Mom, why don't you write them down." And so it began. Several stories later, she finally allowed someone, other than her daughter, to read them.

After that brave (and very scary) step, she decided not to keep them to herself any longer, so here we are.

She hopes you enjoy her musings as much as she enjoyed writing them. If they make you smile, sigh, hope, and chuckle or even cry at times, it was worth it.

Born in St. Louis, Missouri, Trisha graduated from the University of Missouri – St. Louis with a degree in Psychology. Trisha's day job as a product instructor for a software company allowed her to travel all over the country meeting interesting people and seeing interesting places, some of which inspired ideas for her stories. A hopeless (or hopeful) romantic, Trisha currently resides in the great Northwest.

f

Printed in Great Britain
by Amazon